Can love exist
in a world
that is truly
hell on earth?

It was like setting a match to dynamite.

He electrified every soaking wet nerve until she thrummed to life in his hands. Ached under his angry, desperate, demanding assault. She caught fistfuls of his thin tee-shirt, twisted the fabric tighter against the hard expanse of his chest. Dragged the sodden material up to reveal hot, wet skin and that amazingly defined muscle.

He fed on her incoherent moan, slid his tongue between her lips. He didn't seduce; he took, claimed. Every inch of her body clamored for more. She cried out in mingled pleasure and shock.

Silas wrenched his mouth away, cursing.

She blinked. Jerked her hands away as if they burned. As her heartbeat hammered in her ears, Jessie fought to even her breathing.

What was she thinking?

Sex in an alley, with a man who frightened her. Who tempted her. Who'd kill her if he ever found out about her gifts.

Stupid.

By Karina Cooper

BLOOD OF THE WICKED

Coming July 2011
LURE OF THE WICKED

KARINA COOPER

BLOOD
OF THE
WICKED

A DARK MISSION NOVEL

AVON
An Imprint of HarperCollinsPublishers

AVON BOOKS
An Imprint of HarperCollins*Publishers*
10 East 53rd Street
New York, New York 10022-5299

Copyright © 2011 by Karina Cooper
Excerpt from *Lure of the Wicked* copyright © 2011 by Karina Cooper
ISBN 978-0-06-204685-7
www.avonromance.com

First Avon Books mass market printing: June 2011

Avon Trademark Reg. U.S. Pat. Off. and in Other Countries, Marca Registrada, Hecho en U.S.A.
HarperCollins® is a registered trademark of HarperCollins Publishers.

Printed in the U.S.A.

10 9 8 7 6 5 4 3 2 1

*For Aron,
who put my butt in that chair
and told me I could do anything I really wanted,
and the family who stood behind us both.
I love you all.*

BLOOD OF THE WICKED

CHAPTER ONE

Operation Echo Location reeked.

Silas Smith knew bullshit when he smelled it. Sure, it smelled a lot like sweat and cigarette smoke and desperation, but it was pure bullshit. Shoved into a manila envelope and jammed down his throat.

Fuck, his head hurt. The overloud electronic crap they called music at the Pussycat Perch began its skull-wrecking vendetta the instant he stepped through the door. The pain fed off the industrial bass rocking the foundations of the converted warehouse, played counter to the painful throb of his left knee. Between light, sound, pain, and the shitty mood he'd been nursing since he'd returned to the damned city, it was all he could do to figure out where the hell anything was around him.

Silas blinked in the scattered flash of multicolored beams of light. Every breath burned, smoke and humid energy sliding over his tongue. Dancers filled the floor to capacity, writhing in a sea of light and limbs and gleaming, sweaty skin. Gyrating, mostly naked women wrapped around bolted poles at three stages, and the cacophony skewered through his brain, pissing him off even more than when he'd walked in.

Finding anyone in this mess was going to be a complete pain in the ass. As with every joint like it, the Perch had built its success on too-loud music, too many people, too much skin.

Sex, drugs, and debts too deep to ever climb out of. He'd see it here in the too-bright eyes of the avid voyeurs and the dead, doll-like stares of the women who danced for them.

So he'd find Jessica Leigh and get the hell out again. Where the fuck was the bar?

It took him several minutes to find it, scarred wood countertops hidden behind a sea of demanding customers. It took longer to force his way through the oversexed crowd. Dancers thrashed around him, drunks staggered by, and he'd made it halfway through the mess before white-hot static shorted his brain on a crackled snap of pain.

Instinctively he caught the woman who'd slammed into him, elbow to gut and knee to knee, barely cognizant of her slurred apology. He pushed past her, cursing, forging through the masses as he fumbled in his pocket for the aspirin he kept close.

The chaos around the bar was an ocean of calm compared to the death trap of a dance floor. He grabbed the edge of the wooden bar to stake his claim to a foot-wide piece of real estate, even as he popped the painkillers into his mouth dry.

"What'll it be?"

Silas turned at the husky half shout near his ear, caught an eyeful of red velvet and smooth, bare skin. He swallowed the bitter pills on pure reflex.

She was sex wrapped up in gold ribbon.

Tight, trim curves smoothed out a wine-dark corset strapped with gold. The overhead lights cast radiant colors over her bare arms and shoulders, gleamed over her wavy tousle of black hair. Her wide mouth curved up at one corner, painted bloody crimson and guaranteed to make a man like him take notice.

He did. So did his dick. Contrary to every vicious reminder of how much he hated strip joints, he was suddenly, viscerally aware of the rhythmic bass thudding inside his chest. And his jeans.

"I said," she repeated, throaty amusement coloring the half-shouted words, "what'll it be?"

Sweat and sex and your mouth on my—

Jesus Christ, that wasn't right. He hadn't come out here to troll for ass. Silas reached into his inner coat pocket. "Looking for someone."

"Sorry, they're not here." Bright. Smooth.

Silas studied her light brown eyes. Whiskey eyes,

he thought, and frowned. "How do you know who I'm looking for?"

"Doesn't matter." She braced slim arms on the bar top, giving him a tantalizing view of the cinched-up swell of her small breasts. Notched, grimy bills peeked out from beneath her bodice, startlingly dirty against the clean shine of her skin.

He jerked his gaze back up to her face. "I need—"

"They aren't here," she repeated, firmer this time. Velvet and steel. "So what do you drink?"

Lust warred with annoyance. Pure frustration. So the Perch was one of those places. Hell, and why not? Silas settled for a nod. "Beer."

He peeled a few small bills from the clip in his inner jacket pocket. It gave him plenty of time to admire the taut curve of her ass under barely-there gold shorts as she bent over the back counter, retrieved an unlabeled brown bottle. Glass hit the bar with a thump, and her fingers closed over the money.

He held on just a second too long. Just long enough to make his own point.

Her gaze dropped to his hand, to the money and the wooden beads strung on a leather cord around his wrist. The black tattoo half concealed under the hem of his sleeve. "Nice ink." She plucked the bills from his loosened grasp. "Holler if you want another."

With a whirl of gold ribbon and practiced rhythm, she turned and strode back down the bar. Silas watched her go, unable to help himself as his gaze raked over her long bare legs.

Tempting. And because it was, she was interesting. He didn't do strippers. And, he reminded himself, shifting on the stool, he had work to do. His fingers itched to pull out the photo from his inner pocket, to refocus. From the moment he'd laid eyes on the picture, Jessica Leigh's laughing, youthful face had captured him. Branded itself on his brain. She was radiant, caught in a moment of complete candid delight. Wholesome. Fragile.

Nothing like the cunning, son of a bitch witch in the picture with her.

So here he was, because he'd gotten a call from a ghost he'd thought he'd long since left behind with this damned city and didn't know how to say no.

Find her. Land her. Easy, right?

He waited with a raw impatience that ate at his already fraying control. By the time an hour crawled by, he'd finished his beer and the pain in his knee had mellowed to a dull ache. He was four aspirin down and seven come-ons up, and annoyed as hell when the latest in a string of stage-light strippers turned out to be bleached blond and *not* Jessica Leigh.

He set the empty bottle on the counter, turned to wave the bartender over, and found her tucked back by the employee hatch. One hand curved around the hinged slat of wood, holding it up while she withdrew a small wad of bills from her cleavage.

The short blond in front of her took it, nodded, and Silas's pulse spiked hard as adrenaline surged through his system. The riot of noise in the club amplified through his skull as he half stood, ready to move. Get her, get the hell out. She turned, and Silas blew out a disappointed breath.

Damn it. Just another blond in a fake leather halter, and one hell of a rack to frame in it.

He was getting tired of this undercover shit. He sat back down, reached for his drink. Remembered it was empty and jammed his elbows on top of the counter instead. Fuck. This. Job. He wasn't a subtle investigation kind of guy. More got done at the business end of the revolver tucked beneath his jacket, but he'd let himself get suckered into this one.

Damn Naomi West for finding him.

He glanced over when the hatch slammed closed. The long-legged bartender locked it in place and sauntered across the floor. Silas watched her because, hell, her hips swayed like she knew what five inches of gold spiked heel did to a man.

Sharply sweet floral perfume speared through his nose as the new blond with the impressive boob job snagged his empty bottle and tossed it into a bin behind her. Glass shattered. "Another one, sugar?"

"No, thanks."

She followed his gaze, grinning a full-lipped, cat-like grin. "Your favorite? She's hot enough, I guess. I told her she'd make better tips if she stayed blond, men love it. Does she listen to me? Hell, no. I've only been in this business for three years, you know? I make damn good money."

Only half listening, Silas grimaced, shifting his leg to ease the pain. Yeah, the brunette was hot, but she wasn't what he needed. Jessica wasn't here. He'd come back tomorrow, and the next night. See if she showed up, or if the intel had been wrong after all.

He paused. Frowned. *She'd make better tips if she stayed blond.*

Light brown eyes. Full mouth. Wide cheekbones— *Hell*. Jessica.

Silas shot to his feet in time to watch the employee door swing closed. Damn it.

He reached over and grabbed a fistful of synth-leather beside him. The tattooed man jerked out of his grasp, rounded on him. "Fifty bucks," Silas said flatly, cutting him off mid-snarl. "Can you take a punch?"

As soon as the employee door closed behind her, Jessica Leigh hit the hall running. *Shit. Shit. Shit!*

Her hands shook with fear and adrenaline as she pushed into the changing room. A missionary. A *witch hunter*, right in front of her. She'd known who he was, *what* he was the second she'd seen that damn tattoo. It had taken everything she had to bluff it out. Wait out her shift. No sudden moves.

No sudden screaming.

She'd never seen a hunter up close before, never smiled into flinty eyes like he wasn't anything special. Tonight she'd done both. For a solid hour, she'd worked under the steel green edge of his blatant scrutiny.

Now she had to go.

"Damn," she hissed as she swung open her locker. The only three women in the back room weren't paying any attention. Mickey was flying high again, and Ramona and the new girl she didn't know yet were too wiped to do more than wave halfheartedly at her.

Jessie smiled brilliantly back, slinging her heavy black backpack over her shoulder. "Night, girls," she called. She forced herself to head casually toward the bathroom. Shift over, time to go home, no big deal.

She wasn't new at this. Just short-term stupid, apparently.

Slipping inside, she locked the stall behind her and kicked into overdrive. She stripped off the black wig and shoved it into her pack with shaking hands. Slow down, she told herself. Fear and adrenaline could lead to mistakes. She couldn't afford to screw up now. Breathe. *Think.*

She had to get out of here.

Regret clutched at her throat as she peeled off her corset and shimmied out of the matching gold shorts. She should have left two weeks ago, and she knew it. She'd gotten lazy. Complacent.

She'd made friends.

Jessie blinked back a sudden sting of tears as she shook out a pair of faded jeans and stepped into them. "Don't be stupid," she said aloud, striving for steady. She'd known better. Decent pay and a few friendly people wouldn't keep her alive.

Running would. It'd keep her one step ahead of the damned witch hunters and three steps ahead of the rest of the world. It was the only way to survive. Off the radar, out of the system.

Exhausted, run ragged. Downright paranoid. And for what? Certainly nothing even resembling peace and quiet.

She pulled on a gray tank top, wriggled into a matte black neoprene jacket and zipped it up to her throat. In the lower edges of New Seattle's civilized levels, she'd fit right in. It was the work of moments to shake out a short, choppy red wig and pull it on.

She scrubbed off every trace of makeup, flushed the damp wipes down the yellowed toilet, and tucked her sky-high shoes into the backpack. Shoving her feet into plain, thick-soled black boots, she checked the plastic watch on her wrist and frowned.

The whole process had taken less than five minutes. She was too damn good at this.

Jessie creaked open the door, checked the hall. When she didn't see anyone there, she stepped out and made short work of disabling the alarm on the emergency exit. Two seconds later, she was in the home stretch.

The alley flickered dimly under the purple and pink neon light flashing overhead. Girls, girls, girls. "Minus one," Jessie murmured, and shut the door quietly behind her. It clicked with a finality that made her chest squeeze.

It really wasn't fair.

But then, she understood that life hadn't been fair since Mother Nature had flipped a gasket and unleashed rampant destruction on most of the planet. Jessie hadn't even been born when the San Andreas Fault had split so far that Seattle had slid right into the crevasse, but that didn't matter to a world full of terrified, struggling people.

Pre-quake, witches had lived on the fringes of a world that didn't care. They didn't have to hide.

They weren't always welcomed everywhere, but they weren't stoned to death in the streets, either. Then the world had gone to hell and the Holy Order of St. Dominic had stepped in to lay down order. Spread some so-called morality.

Five decades should have been enough for the worst of the witch hunts to die down. It wasn't; a fact that Jessie acknowledged every damn time she packed up what few belongings she owned. Instead the Church had slipped into bed with the federal government, and suddenly they were best friends over the barbecue of innocent people.

Worse, the radical Mission—once considered a brand of extremist terrorism—had turned into the Order's right hand. Sanctioned killers at the end of a very deadly leash.

These days, life for a witch was injustice and persecution in a very real sense. It was survival in a society desperate to blame something—hell, anything—for the devastation of fifty years ago.

Hadn't Jessie spent her whole life running? Seen her own mother murdered? Didn't she learn anything from the streets that had tried so hard to chew her up and spit her out?

Hadn't she taught her baby brother the very same thing?

Which was why, she reflected grimly as she raised her collar against the rain, she knew better than to stay in one place for as long as she'd wallowed in the Perch. Stupid.

Jessie could have been the next notch on the Mission's docket tonight. When the hunter had looked her in the eye, she'd have sworn she saw her own death there. It had been damned hard to play at calm, not to panic then and there, take off running right over the bar.

She took a deep breath, barely noticing the familiar stink of rotting garbage and the faint tang of the cold rain. So she couldn't work at this particular club anymore. So what? She'd find another. These lower city levels were chock-full of dives like the Perch.

If Lydia Leigh had taught her children anything, it was how to rebuild.

She stepped off the broken stoop as lurid purple light flickered through the dismal drizzle. Each do-over just got harder and harder, but hell, she didn't have much choice. Witch hunters killed witches.

Exclamation point.

Her boots splashed in stagnant puddles, stirred up loose grit and gravel. She barely noticed when a wide shadow detached itself from the mouth of the alley, then hesitated when it stepped into her path. She didn't have time for this.

Pink neon outlined his heavy build, the blaring smear of tattoo ink and the light-catching saturation of beaten synth-leather spiked with metal. Big. Grabby, probably. He seemed the type.

She'd dealt with it before. A casual smile, a flirty wink, a breezy reminder of the bouncers right around the corner, and he'd be back inside eyeballing someone else.

"Nice." The burly man spread his arms to block her way. "Way nice. Easiest score I ever made."

Vapors washed over her; alcohol and the spicy

afterburn of something less than legal, even in the Perch.

Just her luck.

She shaped her mouth into a sassy smile and made damn sure it reached her eyes. "You're in the wrong spot, honey. All the best girls are—"

"Right here," he drawled, bending until he was all but nose to nose with her. The scent of sweat and beer wafted over her face in a nauseating combination.

She stepped backward before she could stop herself, giving ground she knew was going to cost her.

Never show weakness.

"I'm on a break," she lied smoothly, praying he was too far gone to notice the heavy backpack slung over her shoulders. "You want to see me dance, you'll want to be inside in five minutes."

"Maybe I'll just see you wiggle right here." He took another step forward. Jessie's body tensed, mouth dry.

Shit. She didn't have *time* for this. Any minute, that hunter was going to come sniffing. The back of her neck itched with the certainty.

Neon popped overhead, highlighting the alley around them in vivid purple. It bled through his full brown beard, glittered off his array of facial piercings and toothy smile. It picked out a lot of sweaty, veined muscle.

And the leering jester inked into one thick arm.

I see death and a laughing joker.

Her heartbeat leaped into her throat. "Fuck," she whispered, and jumped when he laughed.

"Not yet, baby," he said, reaching for her. Her vision tunneled in on the biker's stained, shit-eating smile, and without warning, Jessie's patience guttered out.

She felt herself go. Almost like when she tapped into the power that simmered beneath her conscious mind, but this was sharper. Angrier. Focused.

He was every man who'd ever leered at her. Every man who'd ever groped her in the dark confines of every bar she'd worked at. The ones who'd laughed at her and her baby brother on these goddamned merciless streets.

Jessie's body surged into motion before her brain made the call. She stepped into him, into the wild clasp of his arms, and pure satisfaction rippled through her as his smile cracked into surprise. Her fist collided with his smirk and sent him reeling.

His flat features contorted into shock. Rage. "Bitch!"

Adrenaline pushed her forward; she tried to dart past him, choked on her own collar as a meaty hand snagged the back of her jacket and hauled her back into the alley. Slammed her back against the broken, pitted brick, hard enough to force the air from her lungs. Jessie's vision dimmed as she swung again, connected with something metal on his coat, and yelped as her arm went numb from fingers to elbow.

If the joker gets his hands on you, Jessie, that's it. That's the beginning of it all. Don't stop for him.

Her brother's voice, the memory of it, rang sharply in her head. Too damn late.

She tried to jerk away, cried out again as his fist tagged her mouth. Pain exploded inside her skull, lights flashing violet and pink and red as she dropped to her knees.

Blood pooled on her tongue, coppery and warm. Jessie choked on tears of pain, of humiliation and fury, even as she struggled to get off her hands and knees, and hit him again.

And again. And—

"What the *fuck*," she heard, and a riot of energy roiled around her. For a dazed moment it looked as though her attacker split into two, dancing awkwardly away from her like two halves of a broken mirage. One staggered upright, thick and meaty, the other long and lean as they wrenched apart. With a bellow, the biker swung at the second man who was nothing more than a trim, fast-moving shadow dancing just out of his reach.

Jessie shook her head hard, forced herself to her feet. She stumbled hastily for the alley mouth. *Get out, run like hell*. She couldn't get caught up here, not as long as that hunter was— *Oh, God*.

Her knees buckled violently. She whirled to plaster her back against the wall, grabbed rough brick for support as she stared at the fighters. *Him*. Shocked, she jammed her fingers against her bleeding mouth.

Neon flickered, seared, and she saw tanned skin, black ink, and rough denim as the witch hunter blocked with his left forearm, snarled something, and curved out a wicked right hook.

His body moved like an oiled machine, brutally efficient as he followed up with two jabs to the drunk's nose and an elbow that crunched loudly on impact.

Blood spurted, near black in the neon light.

"Run!" The witch hunter threw it over his shoulder, only to twist awkwardly when the biker stomped hard on his knee. Jessie saw his face go shock-white, heard his agonized grunt of pain.

Fury and fear forced her to move. She caught her backpack in one hand, swung it with all her might. The black canvas bag sailed through the violent neon air, graceful as a brick, and slammed into the side of the biker's head with a dull crack.

He toppled, slowly.

Jessie stared in horror. He didn't move. God. Had she killed him? She had enough problems without adding murder and cops to the list. She panted for breath, unable to suck in enough air to keep spots from mottling the corners of her vision. Was he dead? She didn't know if a thirty-pound bag could kill someone of that size, and she desperately didn't want to check.

She reeled.

Strong fingers curled over her upper arms. "Hey!"

She blinked. Stared into a face carved from something even more unyielding than the brick surrounding them. "Can you walk?" he asked. Demanded.

Jessie's brain flailed. "Is he—?"

"Try," he ordered, and hauled her bodily out of the alley.

He was limping. It was the only rational thought she managed to form, and wordlessly she ducked under his arm and slipped it over her shoulders. He hesitated, resisting her, but she dug her fingers in to his side and held on. She felt the flex and slide of hard muscle as she fisted her hand in his shirt.

As much as Jessie wanted to slip away from him, use his injury to put as much space between them as she could, she couldn't just leave him there. He'd helped her. She had to help him.

And the truth was, she needed something to hang on to, just for a moment.

She followed his lead as he pointed to a rusty orange pickup truck. He wrenched open the door, half lifted, half shoved her inside the driver's side, and pushed her farther over as he swung up painfully behind her. He wasted no words, and she had plenty of time to study the implacable set of his features as he gunned the engine and slammed it into drive.

Talk about a rock and a hard place.

A witch hunter. And a hero, at least for the five seconds it was taking her brain to process and reboot. He'd saved her.

She'd saved him, too. She wondered if he'd have been so heroic if he knew who and what she was. She'd bet her tip money that he'd have left her there to die if he'd had any real clue she was a witch.

As the truck pulled a U-turn, tires squealing, Jessie twisted to see if the drunk had moved. She glimpsed him facedown, dead still, exactly where they'd left him. And her bag. Shit!

The hunter took a left, swerved around a trailer. "He'll live."

"Lucky him," seemed harmless enough. Vacuous enough. Jessie glanced at the witch hunter as he adjusted the rearview mirror with one rough hand. Despite his terrifying vocation, he appealed on some deep level. A rough shadow darkened his angled jaw.

It framed a mouth that bowed at the top, which she'd noticed the instant he'd sat down at her bar.

She'd briefly toyed with the idea of leaning over the counter and tasting it. Now she was glad she hadn't. Not even for the extra tip money that flirty act would have netted her.

His hair curled in short waves, dark brown and shaggy, and Jessie couldn't help but admire his easy strength as he'd hauled her down half a city block, even despite his limp.

It was the same strength he'd probably developed strangling innocent people in the night.

She set her jaw.

Anger rolled off him in palpable waves, an aura of fury that she didn't need preternatural senses to recognize. Long, all-too-capable fingers gripped the steering wheel with white-knuckled intensity as he drove with purpose.

Drove where?

Death and the laughing joker. Two different people? Shit. Caleb's prophecies never made *sense*.

Jessie scraped back the fringe of fake red hair with one shaking hand. "Thanks for the help and all." His mouth twisted. "But," she continued lightly, "you can drop me off here."

He didn't reply, didn't slow down. Didn't acknowledge her. She bit her lip, winced when it throbbed in protest.

It had to be a coincidence. She'd never heard of a witch hunter saving a witch just to kill her himself. Unless he was a real freak of nature.

Or didn't recognize her in her disguise.

Short red hair, no makeup, street clothes designed to blend; it was a far cry from the vamped-up brunette bartender he'd met. The alley had been dark. He'd seen a woman in trouble.

Could she stake her life on a witch hunter's good intentions?

Would she be heading to her own death if she did?

No. It was still a risk, and the laughing joker hadn't killed her. That didn't mean she was safe. She'd just toppled the first domino of her baby brother's worst prophecy. Christ. Shit.

She wasn't going to die, damn it.

Jessie casually draped her hand on the armrest, her thumb resting on the door release. The second he slowed down, the moment she saw her chance, she'd be gone.

"Don't even try it."

"Try what?"

"We're going sixty. In half a minute, we'll be on the carousel. You'll be a smear if you jump, and I'm not slowing down."

What was he, psychic? Her temper spiked. "I'll take my chan— Let go of me!" His hard, cold fingers were implacable as he gripped her forearm.

"I didn't haul you out of that bastard's rape fantasy to lose you to asphalt," he said flatly.

Jessie's teeth clicked. "I don't need a hero," she gritted out. "Let me go."

He did, but only so he could put both hands back on the wheel. "Stay fucking put."

Her heartbeat roared in her ears. Her lip throbbed, but the small pain was going to be the least of her problems if the jump out of a moving vehicle didn't kill her first.

Steeling herself, she reached again for the latch on the door.

"Your friend was right," he said. "You're a better blond."

CHAPTER TWO

H er hand froze near the handle. Silas kept his gaze on the road, but his peripheral vision was perfect. He saw her eyes swing to him. Jesus, *felt* her eyes on him.

Fury snapped over his skin like a live wire; it barely salved the sheer agony lancing from his toes to his hip. He'd have to sweat it out, even as every angry fiber of his being wanted to turn the truck around and slam it into the overeager son of a bitch who'd laid his damn hands on her.

Who Silas had *paid* to lay his damn hands on her.

His fingers tightened on the wheel. "I almost didn't recognize you, Jessica. Even after seeing you with the black hair."

She hesitated, a fraction of a second, before she

eased back from the door. "Yeah, well." She smiled
ruefully. Tightly. "We like to change it up. Sometimes
the men in there get . . . grabby."

Fuck. His back teeth clenched. It did nothing for
his headache, either.

Headlights of oncoming cars cut through the dark
cab like a searchlight, and he saw her wince as she
touched her bloody lip with the back of her hand. He
fished out a handkerchief from the same pocket he
kept her photo in. "Here," he said tightly, at least a
semblance of civility.

She chewed over her options as she stared at his
hand, her mind clearly working. Hell, he could practically smell the smoke. She was probably planning
another escape.

He let her, eyes steady on the road. The traffic
speed on the carousel didn't leave any room to jump,
not if she valued her life. He could drive all damn
night, if he had to.

God knew there was enough road for it. Fourteen
years had passed since he'd last taken the New Seattle carousel, but looking at it now made him feel
like he'd never left.

The winding highway wrapped around the towering city, ramps connected to each level like the legs
of some kind of strangling centipede. Only the na-
tives knew how to navigate the damned thing, and
it annoyed him that he still remembered what ramps
circled where. Little enough had changed.

A drive through the littered streets of the lower
city levels had been enough to make that clear. The
desperately poor survived in the deeper levels while

the sickeningly rich lived smug and happy topside. The only real place to see honest-to-God sunlight.

Anyone lucky enough to be caught halfway spent his life grazing in those middle civilized edges. Like apathetic sheep, cataloged and separated by profit; industrial, migrant, the middle class with its few twisted trees and shades of sunlight.

The permanent neon lights of the seedier districts barely qualified as civilized. Just this side of acceptable, like the Perch's less than classy clientele.

Or like the dark streets of a Church orphanage.

Yeah. Fourteen years hadn't changed much. He still hated this soul-sucking city every bit as much as he'd missed it.

"I'm fine." Her cool declaration dragged his attention back to the now. Where it damn well needed to be, he reminded himself. The mission, not the past. And not on the unpainted line of her mouth.

Or the mile-long legs he knew she hid beneath those jeans.

Damn it. He thrust the handkerchief at her. "Just take the damn thing already," he growled. "You're bleeding."

Glaring, she grabbed the white fabric. Tore it from his hand, one part temper and mostly impatience. "Who the hell are you?" she demanded. "How do you know me?"

For another long moment, Silas concentrated on driving. It bought him the time he needed. The answers that leaped to his tongue wouldn't ensure the kind of cooperation he had to get from her.

The sooner he did, the sooner he could leave.

Not a bad start, really. Bloody the woman he had to con into helping the Mission. Don't let her know that her brother was top of the Witches to Be Executed for Crimes Against Humanity list, and lie through his teeth about what they intended to do when they caught the kid. No problem.

And . . . *go*.

"My name is Silas Smith." She watched him silently, his handkerchief a white stain at her chin. "I'm a government agent, and we need your help."

Goddamn, that sounded lame. Even to him.

"Ah." A noncommittal sound. She might as well have called bullshit, but to his surprise, she asked mildly, "And what do you want from me?"

"We've been looking for you for weeks." She stiffened, so subtly he would have missed it if he wasn't hyperaware of her every move.

Which pissed him off. Telling himself he was only watching her for signs of escape just pissed him off more.

He hoped the missionaries choked on this shit later. "Fuck me," he muttered, and scowled at her sudden snort. "Look, the short story is that your brother's gotten himself mixed in with a bad crowd." Silas glanced at her across the semidark cab. "The kind of crowd that gets attention from agencies like mine. We need you to help us find him."

Her mouth pursed. "Firstly, even if I had a brother—"

"You do."

"Even if I *had* a brother," she repeated stubbornly, "I have no reason to trust you. Where's your badge?

Your official— I don't know." She gestured at him, her long fingers devoid of jewelry or polish. "Your uniform or whatever?"

Silas caught himself eyeing her bare hands and wondering if she lived with anyone. Was she sleeping with anyone? The file he'd been given had been sparse.

If she was, the guy had to have the patience of a saint to date a stripper.

He shook his head. "Not that kind of agency."

"Great," she muttered. "Of course not." She folded her arms, creasing the snug neoprene beneath her breasts. "And if you find this person, what do you intend to do?"

"*When* we find your *brother*," Silas corrected tersely, "our intent is to use him to gain access to the rest of the group and dismantle it."

"Why him specifically?" Jesus, she was quick.

But he had this much thought out. "Caleb Leigh's been flagged by our security forces. According to his file—and yeah, he's got a file," he added, cutting off the question he heard forming in her sharply indrawn breath. "He's just a dumb kid in over his head." He glanced at her just in time to see her lashes narrow. A fraction. "We're not in the habit of nailing dumb kids to crosses for kicks, but we know an in when we see one."

Lies upon lies upon lies. He jerked his eyes back to the road before her honey brown eyes saw more than he damn well wanted to show. He wasn't sure he could explain the anger. Or the too-sharp awareness of her body heat, inches away.

And she was nobody's fool. "Why should I believe you?"

"You shouldn't." At least that much was true. Silas drove across three lanes of traffic, ignored the horn blaring behind him as he cut off a sleek silver racer. "But what are your choices, Jessica?"

"Jessie."

His gut kicked. "Jessie," he repeated quietly. Her eyes flickered. Silence stretched, all but vibrated as the gears in her head turned over and over.

Hell, he could practically see the sparks.

Finally her wide, bare lips twisted in bitter resignation. "You're the man with the badge, so I guess I don't have any choices, do I?" She kicked one black-booted foot up on the dashboard. He winced. She didn't notice. "Fine. What do you need from me?"

"Answers." Silas didn't smile.

She'd been too damn easy.

Sister to a witch. As soon as the Mission got their hands on her, she was as good as screwed.

She shrugged. "Ask away."

"Not tonight, it's late. Where should I take you?" He glanced at her. "I can pick you up in the morning." Like hell. He'd camp outside her place all night and ransack it later, if he had to.

Her lashes dropped, shadowing her cheeks as she studied the blood-spotted handkerchief stretched between her fingers. "I don't have a place."

"Where do you sleep?"

"Where I can," she said, and raised her chin.

That stubborn, silent spark of pride found an answering twist of memory, of corded sympathy, in Silas's chest. *Shit*. No place to sleep? He at least owed her that much.

Quickly, before he could change his mind, he curled his fingers around the steering wheel and sliced across two more lanes of traffic. The carefully maintained engine thrummed. "I know somewhere."

"I don't—"

"I'm not going to hurt you, Jessie." The shadows in the cab hid his face as he checked the GPS unit wired to the topside of the dash. "You have my word."

And in between the waves of pain radiating from forehead and knee, all Silas could smell was bullshit.

Relief that he hadn't asked her about her supposed lack of living quarters warred with righteous fury. The bastard was trying to use her to get to her baby brother.

Just hearing *Agent* Smith say Caleb's name brought bile to the back of her throat.

The guy had nerve. Serious nerve.

To think she'd saved his life. Or at least saved him a beating. She should have let them beat the snot out of each other in that filthy alley.

And yet, despite the fact that he was her enemy— *Caleb's* enemy—she couldn't keep her eyes from sliding sideways. The man had a presence, she'd give him that. He filled up space in ways that made her feel like she wasn't getting enough air.

Every breath she took smelled like old leather, rusting metal, and something warmer. Decidedly masculine. His fingers were scarred, his face edged, even his clothing was worn. She had more than a suspicion about the definition of his muscled body beneath that jacket.

A hard man with a hard body, in clothes easy to move in. And, she reminded herself harshly, easy to kill in. She probably sat in the trace remains of some poor dead witch even as she thought it.

But his hands looked strong and capable. Protective. She watched him guide the steering wheel with easy, sure movements. Studied the leather cord around his wrist and the polished wooden beads tucked against his tanned skin.

White letters gleamed in the dark. *Nina*. His wife? His daughter?

It didn't matter, she thought, and gave herself a mental shake. Silas Smith, agent of the Holy Order of St. Dominic, was the enemy. She had to remember that. And if the Church was after Caleb, then it meant they knew he was a witch.

If they knew he practiced, what did they have on her?

What in God's name had Caleb gotten mixed up in that would put him on the Mission's radar?

The questions tumbled end over end inside her head until she thought she'd scream. Or punch something. Not that she'd managed to get anywhere by punching anything so far.

Jessie shifted, propping her other foot up on the seat. She rested her chin on her knee. "So," she said slowly, letting the word fill the silence in the cab for a long moment. He glanced at her, eyes shadowed. "Tell me about this bad crowd Caleb's involved with."

More silence. And then, "How long has it been since you've seen him?"

Annoyance gathered sharp on her tongue. She swallowed it back, hard enough to mildly offer, "About a year." That was true, at least. A whole year since he'd vanished in the night, leaving everything behind. Including her.

"Long time," he said.

No kidding seemed unhelpful. She shrugged, smiled flatly. "Siblings argue. We fought with the best of them. About a year ago, Caleb decided he'd gotten tired of listening to me and split."

She'd never had problems lying. Her lies had saved their butts more often than not. They had been fed, clothed, occasionally hired on a bank of lies.

Hell, it helped that these lies sounded plausible, arguing siblings and hotheaded tantrums. She wasn't going to tell a missionary that her brother had foreseen something that had scared him so badly, he'd taken off with only a few cryptic metaphors and a warning.

Don't find me, Jessie. Don't even try.

She'd been jumping at shadows since. For good reason, apparently. The laughing joker didn't kill her, but God knew the future came in riddles.

Shit, shit, shit.

Jessie watched him as he watched the road, telling herself it was only so she could catch it if even a hint of dishonesty flickered in his too-rugged features. The fact that she had an itch to rub her cheek against the black shadow of his planed jaw was something she'd do her best to ignore.

He glanced at her again. Even in the dark, she felt the weight of his gaze.

She had an insane urge to cover her chest with her arms. Not that the jacket she wore was even remotely indecent—and she had to get a grip. She was *not* fantasizing about the enemy.

Or his tousled dark hair, or the shape of his mouth as he spoke, or—

"What do you know of the Coven of the Unbinding?" he asked suddenly, and Jessie shook her head, relieved for the distraction.

"The what with the who?"

He frowned. "It's a terrorist cell," he said, and shifted the truck up to speed. Jessie grabbed the bar over the window as the cab shook ominously. "Terrorists who do a hell of a lot of scary shit, all in the name of an ideal that doesn't care who or what they hurt."

Jessie straightened. *Shit!* A coven. "And you think Caleb's in with them?" It took effort to keep her voice steady. Curious, not panicked.

Covens meant groups of witches. Groups of witches meant Mission intervention. Slaughter. Hunts.

She shook her head again, the very picture of loyal certainty. "No way. There's no way my brother would be in a terrorist group, not ever."

He didn't look at her again. "Maybe."

"No," she repeated loudly. "Not *maybe*." She shifted, braced against the seat as a massive transport rumbled past them on the New Seattle byway. "Look, when Caleb was thirteen, he accidentally ran over a cat on his motorbike. He cried for days, Agent Smith. Days. And you think he'd be in some sort of terrorist group?"

Jessie still remembered holding him as he sobbed, knowing there wasn't a damn thing she could do to help. He'd told her he should have seen it coming. His gift was the future.

She'd told him it didn't work like that, but she'd never been able to tell him why.

"A man can change a lot over a year," Silas pointed out, as implacable as granite. And as sympathetic.

"He's not a man." She gestured, wishing she could shove him out of his own damn moving truck. "He's my brother, and he wouldn't change that much. I'm telling you, even if he's where you think he is, he's not one of *them*. Whoever they are."

"If you say so." He still didn't look at her as he changed gears again, shifting down, and Jessie wanted to scream. Instead she sat back, gritting her teeth.

"Like I said, we want to use his ties to infiltrate the group and tear it down. There's a lot of flexibility for a kid who helps that happen."

Pretty talk. Jessie recognized the curt evasion for what it was: just shy of a promise. If the Church was after Caleb, and if he'd turned stupid and joined an honest-to-God coven, they'd never offer leniency. No matter how useful he tried to be. Not, she reminded herself as she kicked both feet on the dash and deliberately ignored his frown, that she bought any of this.

She tucked her hands under her arms, staring sightlessly out the window as the truck turned onto one of the many mid-level off-ramps.

For a whole year, Caleb had managed to dodge

her. It was as if he'd dropped off the face of the planet, swallowed by the Old Sea-Trench that cracked wide beneath the city's foundation. Even her powers were useless to her.

Her gift was the present. She should have been able to find him, but wherever Caleb was, whatever he was doing, either he'd figured out how to block her . . .

Or he was dead.

And she knew, just *knew*, that he wasn't dead.

Which meant that he was blocking her. That worried her more than anything else. He needed her help.

I see death and a laughing joker.

Six feet and some inches of smoky-eyed, rangy witch hunter qualified as death. But was it her death that Caleb had really seen, she wondered, or his own? Someone else's?

Damn, she wished she had a future decoder ring.

Jessie had heard of other covens over the years. There'd even been a few when her mother had been alive, but they'd never joined. Lydia Leigh had called them poison, neon lights just begging for the Church's attention. The ones that gathered in the big cities tended to last longer, but only just.

Populations all over the world had come too damned close to Armageddon to tolerate a second go.

Whether it was in the heart of New Seattle or deep in the isolated wastelands of middle America, Jessie's mother had never given them the time of day. Bands of witches garnered interest.

Interest eventually led to hunters.

Witch hunts never ended well.

Now, a Church-funded killer was telling her that Caleb, the baby brother who had inherited their mother's magic, was wrapped up in a coven. And not telling her what Jessie knew; Caleb was as good as dead as soon as they finished with him.

Except Caleb had said that he'd seen *her* in the flames. She rubbed her eyes with both hands as frustration clawed at her brain. She hated fortune-telling. With a passion.

It hadn't done her mother any good.

"We're here."

Jessie pulled her attention back to the present, back to the uneven parking lot that spread out from her window. She blinked. "Where?"

"It's a safe place."

"Descriptive," Jessie muttered as she swung open the truck door and leaped lightly to the ground. The hinges squealed angrily, echoing across the near-empty lot. Only the occasional car took up space in the gritty asphalt, most of them run-down and battered. He circled the fender, his stride severely hampered by the limp that twisted his left knee.

Jessie flinched under an unwanted wash of sympathy.

But his eyes gleamed at her as he approached, deadly, even. Dangerous. Compassion? She doubted he knew the word, and she'd have to keep reminding herself that. Especially as warmth gathered in places she had no business thinking about anywhere near him.

She ducked out from under his arm as he palmed the passenger door over her head. "We'll stay for the night," he said. If he noticed her jumping around like a scared rabbit, he didn't show it. He shut the door, shoving hard against the recalcitrant hinges, and took the lead without a backward glance.

He probably earned that limp killing someone.

The cold thought helped Jessie regain her mental balance as she hurried after him. "Is this your place?"

"Belongs to a friend." He pulled open a metal faceplate screwed into the wall by the plain side door and punched in a code. There was a click, a hiss of air, and the door popped open.

She raised an eyebrow. "Fancy." And expensive. She'd seen her share of mid-level security, and this blew most of it out of the water.

So the Church wasn't stingy when it came to its own. Great.

The elevator had another code, and she noted he carefully angled his body so she couldn't see it. Smart. Annoying, but smart.

"This is going to be the safest place, so do me a favor," Silas said once they were inside. The elevator groaned, dipped once, and then jerked upward.

Jessie grabbed the railing. "What?"

"Stay here, at least long enough to get some rest. Tomorrow we'll meet up with the others and find your brother."

Others? Alarm bells clanged in her head. "Wait a sec—"

He caught her arm. Her stomach somersaulted all the way up into her throat, smothering every mental alarm with it.

"One night, Jessie," he said quietly. "Give me that much."

It sounded like a promise. An offer. One night of gasping, twisting, sweaty carnal pleasure. She knew, just knew without a shadow of a doubt, that he could give it to her.

She stared into his eyes, suddenly very, very glad that he wasn't capable of reading her mind.

Agent Silas Smith raised one callused finger and gently touched the fresh scab at the side of her mouth. "At least let me make up for this."

Her blood, sluggish in her tired body, warmed. His voice rasped over her skin like whiskey and velvet. Inches. Mere inches were all that separated her mouth from his.

What would a witch hunter's kiss taste like?

The fact she was even asking herself forced her to muffle a yawn she didn't feel. One night alone with him? And then meet up with *more* witch hunters?

He was out of his goddamned mind.

"All right," she lied. "One night."

CHAPTER THREE

Just one night, and then his role in this charade would be done. The witch's sister would be delivered to people better equipped to play nice, and he could wait for the kill orders to come down the line.

Or, better yet, get the hell out of this wreck of a city and away from anything to do with mile-long legs and dark honey eyes. He wasn't equipped to deal with civilians. He never had been.

Silas shut the door behind them, touched his thumb to the electronic sensor, and waited for its distinctive click.

"Just out of curiosity, why are we meeting more of your people?"

He turned to find her studying the apartment,

hands splayed around the denim stretched over her trim hips. There wasn't much in the place to study. The carpet was threadbare and patchy, and its grainy noncolor didn't match the shabby red couch taking up most of one small wall. To her left, a change of flooring from carpet to cracked and scarred linoleum led to a kitchen barely wide enough to fit two people beside the old appliances tucked into the single counter.

A few end tables devoid of anything and two doors took up the rest of the space between narrow, curtained windows. He watched her take it all in with a dubious raised eyebrow, then slanted him a skeptical look from under her fringe of fake red hair.

"This is it," he confirmed to her silent inquiry, but his lips twitched. Picky stripper. He shrugged out of his jacket and draped it over the back of the couch as he limped to the tiny kitchen. "At the heart of it, the Coven of the Unbinding is your standard terrorist organization. It's worldwide, but it breaks into splinter cells to achieve whatever small goals they've got for the area."

"Mm-hmm."

He cracked open the freezer, grimaced when all he saw were bags of flash-frozen instant meals. "Cardboard for dinner, if you're hungry."

"I'm not." A grimace twisted her delicate features. "I ate at work."

Silas took out one plastic bag and turned back for the couch. The bones of his knee ground together with every step. Grunting with the effort, he sank into the thin cushions and set the frozen bag squarely over his left knee. "Damn," he muttered, half in protest and half in relief as the icy burn spread swiftly over the swelling pain. He closed his eyes. "We're meeting with more agents because there's more of the bad guys. Trust me when I say that taking on an entire group of tangos isn't a good way to live through the day."

"How many of them?"

"The Coven? We're not sure."

"No, I mean how many of you?"

Usually at least four. A leader, a technical agent, two field agents. Silas didn't think it had changed in fourteen years. Didn't know for sure.

He didn't need to see them to feel the beads at his wrist. Dead weight.

He cracked open an eyelid to find her staring at him. Patient. Calculating, unless he misread the gears grinding away inside that red-capped head of hers. "Probably about four, maybe five."

She pressed her lips together, watched him closely for a long moment. Stared at his knee. Asking her to dance for him, Silas reflected in grim humor, probably wouldn't be the right thing to do.

She studied him the same way she'd taken in the apartment, and he wasn't sure she came away impressed now, either. Pride rankled about a split second behind resignation.

"Why don't you get some sleep," he said. He didn't bother making it sound like a suggestion. Her eyebrows furrowed, so he added, "You can have the bed."

This time, her lips curved in a way that reached her eyes. "That couch is pretty small."

It was. And by the feel of it, stuffed with rocks.

But Silas closed his eyes again and shrugged. "I can sleep anywhere. You shouldn't have to. I'll wake you in the morning."

If silence had words, Silas figured he'd have been stuck with a monologue of annoyance. He kept his eyes closed, forced himself to look relaxed despite the weight of her gaze. His knee hurt like a bitch, the couch poked broken springs into his back with every breath, and that goddamned neoprene jacket would come off like gift wrap in his hands.

Finally, when the quiet stretched too long, too taut, he sucked in a breath to—

Something. Say something. Warn her. Demand her cooperation. Seduce her right the hell out of her clothes and onto this ugly, uncomfortable couch.

What came out instead growled. "Jessie, I'm not in the mood to talk, so if you want company, you better be naked."

Her silence changed quality, shifted into something pointed. Barbed.

He heard her feet shuffle over the carpet, heard hinges creak. The bedroom door clicked closed, not the slam he imagined any other woman would have chosen, and Silas breathed out on a long, frustrated exhale.

Nice. Real nice. At this rate, it wasn't the witches who would cost him the operation, it was his own damned impatience. He had to get a grip on himself, on this whole laughable joke of an operation, or the Mission would lose their only link to Caleb Leigh.

And then Naomi would have his ass for target practice.

Silas opened his eyes to study the pattern of water stains on the ceiling. Not a day in her company, and he'd already hurt a civilian. Maybe not directly, but it was his fault the scumbag had even been there to look at Jessie, much less put a hand on her. A fist to her lush mouth.

She shouldn't be a part of this.

Just like another girl, another time. Another mission.

Silas stretched out on the couch, wincing as his knee throbbed. Pain didn't go nearly as deep as the memories he read in rust-brown water stains on the ceiling, but it was enough to remind him.

His knee wasn't healing right. Part of it, Silas suspected, was the fact he didn't rest long enough to let the tendons knit back together. The other part, which he didn't need to suspect, was that he was getting too damn old for this job. Too many years in the Mission took its toll, physically and mentally.

Spending too much time with missionaries and witches definitely dulled the polite side of his brain.

Then again, Jessie's trimly feminine silhouette turned his brain to nerve soup anyway.

"Fuck me running," he muttered, and tossed the thawing bag of rations onto the cushion beside him. He clambered to his feet, already feeling like a jackass, and limped across the shabby carpet.

He knocked quietly on her door.

No answer. He winced. "Jessie?" He felt stupid, hanging outside her door like an awkward kid with a crush. "Are you asleep?"

Relief warred with guilt when he didn't hear her

husky voice on the other side of the door. She'd probably worked herself into some kind of feminine snit.

He didn't think that cleared him of any wrongdoing, though. In fact, it probably just made it worse. Silas rolled his eyes to the ceiling as he said gruffly, "I just wanted to say sorry for my"—suggestion? offer? *fantasy?*—"inappropriate comment." He dragged his hand over his face. "You've been through a lot."

Still nothing. Only the occasional drum of rain against the window behind him. He turned away, shaking his head.

Then he paused.

Slowly he turned back, studied the door. Tiny seeds of doubt germinated in his Mission-trained brain.

Jessica Leigh was a stripper. She made a habit, a fucking *art*, out of living off the grid. He'd found her only by pure luck, and he'd told her that he worked for the government. Which was about as on-grid as she could get.

He threw the flimsy door open, already knowing what he'd find. Wind and rain blew in through the open window, pushed aside the cheap curtains, and let the mid-city lights stream through. It lit up the small bed. Highlighted the stripped sheets and the knot tied tightly around the furnace beneath the windowsill. The metal creaked.

Unbelievable. Surprise, resignation, pure annoyance all tangled together as he took four long strides to the window. He followed the visual beacon of white sheet against stained rock, picked out her soaked silhouette plastered against the wall.

Her makeshift ladder shorted her one whole floor. She dangled too damned far above the paved ground.

"Jessie!"

She looked up. He watched her jaw set, the pale oval of her face gleaming in the golden light. She tucked her head back down against the rain splattering the wall around her as her feet kicked out, searched along the moldy siding.

Idiot woman. He fisted the sheet in both hands. "Hold on!" The fabric stretched taut as he braced himself against the sill.

He didn't have to guess what happened when the sheet went slack and he staggered backward, a whiplash of his own strength. The sheet zipped through the window, slapped into his chest in a sopping coil. He let it fall to the carpet, grimacing through the pop and twang of his knee as he stuck his head out the window again.

She clung to the gutter pipe bolted to the wall. Damn it, what the hell was she trying to prove?

"Don't fucking *move*," he shouted.

Her hair caught the light in shades of copper as she tipped her head back to look up at him again. Her eyes narrowed.

And then she let go.

Silas's chest clutched as she dropped like a stone. He was already running for the door before she hit the ground.

This would hurt, but she'd known that going down.

Knowing it, ready for the impact, Jessie deliberately forced her muscles to relax. The ground rushed to meet her, hard and fast, and pain shot through her legs as she hit the ground rolling.

She finally came to a stop with her back against asphalt, the world spinning around her. Her feet throbbed, shocked into numbness, but Jessie didn't have time to think about how much it hurt. She rolled over and pushed herself upright.

She needed to get to the city carousel. Each progressively lower tier of the city expanded, got darker and darker, like some kind of twisted metal layer cake, and she knew how to hide in the depths of those streets just above the walled-in ruins of the old city.

The carousel didn't allow foot traffic, but the stairs near it bored through cement and structured metal to connect the mess of city levels. Even better, they'd been enclosed. All the commuters using the maze of roads comprising the upper-level streets would never have to see the poor peasants who had no choice but to take the stairs to get around. Like her.

If she was lucky, the missionary and his friends would assume she'd go back to her job as the one safe place she had. Maybe she would have, under any other circumstances. Not this time. She'd have to start all over.

It took her a few tries, but Jessie's legs remembered how to move before she kissed the ground again.

The rain pounded the city into submission, making visibility difficult at best. She lowered her head as she ran for the nearest street, hoping she hadn't misjudged the distance from the block of low-income housing to the highway that wrapped around New Seattle like a coiled serpent.

The kind of fly-by-night motel she'd need to hide out in hunkered two levels below the Perch, sleazy enough to pay by the hour and destitute enough not to haggle for the amount of cash she had on her. Going up was out of the question; too far, and she'd end up in front of security checks, sec-comps with tasers set to *strongly dissuade*, and a distinct lack of survivability.

With all of her belongings left at the Perch, Jessie was at a serious disadvantage. It was going to take a lot of effort to build up her resources again, but she could do it. She'd done it before.

She ducked into an alley, lungs squeezing as she tried to catch her breath, and scraped her wet hair back from her eyes. When tangles pulled at her scalp, she realized the red wig had come off her head at some point—probably in the fall—and hissed out a curse.

She might as well have been naked. It had been a long time since she'd hit the streets with her natural hair. Still, she could barely see ten feet in front of her. There was no way anyone else could see her easily enough to get on her tail. Could they?

The thought made her nervous.

Ducking her head, she pulled up the collar of her jacket. There wasn't anything else to do but run.

She was good at running.

Limping slightly, Jessie ignored the angry beat from her abused ankles and hurried down the alley, stepping over sodden refuse and discarded plastic crates. She squinted against the sharp rain, at the lights of New Seattle that flashed through it.

Layers upon layers upon layers of humanity. Cement and metal foundations, glass skyscrapers at the top like something out of a twisted fairy tale. She could barely make out the glittering upper spires through the sudden storm, but she didn't need to see them to know they were there. This was the edge of civilization, the City of Glass.

A new hope for a struggling humanity.

Jessie's mouth twisted. She'd never intended to come to her mother's birth city, but it was easier to hide in a metropolis. Especially a metropolis as divided as this one. Years buried in the chaos of New Seattle, and she still hadn't exhausted the city's cushion of anonymity.

Caleb hadn't liked it much. Maybe that was why he'd left, in the end.

Maybe he just wasn't as ready to live hand-to-mouth, to travel from rat-infested apartment to apartment, to work and steal and run. It stung when she thought it, but maybe she'd done everything wrong, right from the moment she'd found their mother murdered, crammed into her own bakery oven like so much useless baggage.

Headlights jarred her out of her introspection an instant before she tripped over the curb. A cargo truck bore down with breakneck speed, its angry horn screeching through her head and vibrating like drums in her chest.

Instinct exploded into movement. Unable to bite back her breathy scream, she lurched back out of the thoroughfare and away from the vehicles that whipped by her with careless indifference. She hit the corner of a cobbled building, an old brownstone, and clung to it. Water splashed over her legs as cars drove through the runoff pooling along the side of the tilted carousel road.

"Maniac!" she shouted, knowing it wouldn't help.

Shivering, she straightened from her half crouch. Here and now. She had to focus. She couldn't afford to be anywhere else but the present.

What she needed was to hit the stairs across the eight-lane highway, climb six levels down, head east to the tenements, and keep to the shadows. If she could lose herself in the squalor of the lower edges, it'd be a done deal.

And now she had a lead on Caleb, if what Silas had told her was true. She didn't need anybody else's help to find her brother. How hard would it be to find a coven? "Because that's the dumbest move ever," she sighed, blowing her soggy hair away from her mouth. She eyed the steady rush of traffic, gauged her moment, and darted across the first lane when the vehicles thinned out enough to let her through.

She heard him call her name two lanes in.

Arms windmilling, she spared a look over her shoulder to see Silas leaving the alley behind her, murder in his scowl. "What the hell are you doing?" he roared.

Jessie gritted her teeth and leaped through a gap between cars. Before she could get her balance, another gap opened, and she chanced it.

An angry horn blared as the side mirror of a rusted old boxcar tagged her shoulder, spun her wildly. She flailed, staggered into the lights of an oncoming speeder, and swore her life turned into a sudden cliché as it flashed in front of her eyes.

There should have been more to it, she thought, and braced for pain.

Solid arms banded around her chest, jerked her backward. Jessie's legs spun out. She yelped as she caught tread off the gold trim of the speeding sports car. Silas's voice growled something in her ear as he wrenched her back with monumental effort, muscles taut against her back, wrapped like iron around her ribs. Somehow, the world whirling in a blur of limbs, metal, and asphalt, he launched them both into the same alley she'd just vacated. Headlights twisted into shadow, the wind slammed out of her lungs, and then there was only broken cement at her back.

Shock filtered through her muscles, turned them to icy liquid as she stared into Silas's taut, furious face. Dimly she realized that headlights of passing cars grazed over them at too-fast intervals. That the smell of rain-stirred muck and exhaust turned the air to something hard to breathe. Somewhere in the back of her head, a dire warning urged her to get up. Get away.

But her senses were full of his hands anchored on either side of her head, of her heart pounding a staccato rhythm inside the cage of her ribs.

"What," Silas gritted out, his eyes burning into hers, "the *hell*?"

She licked her lips, tasted salt and the faint traces of acid from the rain. "I thought—"

"Don't," he said roughly, and hauled her up by the

front of her jacket. He wasn't gentle as he set her jarringly back on her feet.

Jessie sucked in a breath. "Don't what?" Anger and adrenaline-scored fear fueled her, made her reckless as she shoved at his rock-solid chest. "Don't think? Don't try to escape from some crazy guy who— Damn it, let me go!" Jessie tipped her face up to his and glared.

Soaked to the bone, he should have looked comical. Or at least less threatening. His dark hair lay plastered to his head, tendrils dripping into his eyes as his gaze bored into hers. Lightning and headlights illuminated the alley, painted him in demonic orange and gold. Every line of his body radiated tension. Tension wrapped in rangy, chiseled muscle.

"Don't," he said again, the one syllable vibrating with something bottomless and raw.

Jessie's fingers curled into fists. "Go to—"

"*Christ*," he gritted out, and caught her face between his palms. Before she could think, react, *breathe*, he seized her mouth in a kiss that left no room for anything else but stark, raw heat.

It was awkward. It was almost painful, with her head half tilted on her neck, her shoulders suddenly flattened against the cold wall. It was forceful and angry and it should have frightened her.

It was like setting a match to dynamite.

Arousal simmered from her lips to a pulsing warmth between her legs so fast, so intensely that she gasped. He swept in to claim that sound, to taste the damp heat of her mouth with a groan every bit as angry as his tense fingers twisted into her tangled hair.

He electrified every soaking wet nerve until she thrummed to life in his hands. Ached under his angry, desperate, demanding assault.

She caught fistfuls of his thin T-shirt, twisted the fabric tighter against the hard expanse of his chest. Dragged the sodden fabric up to reveal hot, wet skin and that amazingly defined muscle.

He fed on her incoherent moan, slid his tongue between her lips. There wasn't anything refined or gentle about it. He didn't seduce; he took, claimed, forced his way inside her mouth as if he'd absorb every last iota of heat she had to give. He let go of her head to grab her hips, to seize her close and pull her hard against the undeniable ridge of his erection.

Every inch of her body clamored for more, ached for more of that pressure just where she needed it. She cried out in mingled pleasure and shock.

Silas wrenched his mouth away, cursing. It was a strangled sound, even as his fingers flexed at her waist.

She blinked. Jerked her hands away from his shirt as if they burned. As her heartbeat hammered in her ears, Jessie fought to even her breathing.

What was she thinking?

Obviously sex in an alley, with a man who frightened her. Who tempted her. Who'd kill her if he ever found out about her gifts. *Stupid*.

Jessie tried to straighten, tried to reclaim what ground she'd lost as she lifted her chin, but he didn't let her move. He caught her arm before any words coalesced in her spinning brain.

A conflagration of arousal and pure confusion gave way to icy shock as cold metal banded around her wrist.

She half turned under his shove, gasped when her other wrist joined the first behind her back. "What are you doing?" she demanded, struggling against the same hands she'd been struggling to put herself into not sixty seconds before.

"Taking you back," he replied, his voice edged with ice. "Move."

Fury ignited, a sudden rage of heat that made her shake with it. "You have some nerve." She wrenched at his grasp. Didn't care that her shrill voice rebounded off the alley walls around them. "Who do you—"

"You can yell at me later," he cut in. She stumbled under a hard push to her lower back. "Move it."

Common sense barely managed to keep her from doing something stupid, like kicking him squarely where it counted. Instead Jessie dug her feet in. "I'm not moving," she began, and cursed as blue as she knew how when he caught her upper arm and yanked her down the road instead.

Silas didn't even look at her as he half dragged her beside him. "You are. Now shut up, Jessie."

Her lip curled. "Fuck you, *Agent* Smith."

Mouth thinned, he didn't say another word as he marched her all the way back to the run-down complex. Wet, furious, *handcuffed* for God's sake, Jessie tried to ignore the way her lips felt swollen in the stinging rain. How they tingled as if she'd pressed them to a live conduit crackling with electricity.

She held her tongue in mutinous silence as he pushed her into the elevator. Didn't look at him once as she shivered and dripped all over the scuffed floor. She hoped he felt guilty, the miserable son of a bitch.

She hoped he dreamed about the way her body had curved into his.

A flush of embarrassment, of stubborn arousal, clashed with the bitter cold of processed air wafting over her soaked clothing.

"For what it's worth," he finally said as he thumbed the lock open, "I'm sorry about this."

"Yeah, I'm s-sure you are," she muttered, teeth gritted tightly to keep them from chattering.

In her peripheral vision, she saw his jaw shift. It worked silently as if he had something to say, but instead he just splayed a hand across her lower back and guided her to the bedroom.

He didn't push. She was grateful for small favors.

Her body hurt like hell.

Shaking back her hair, she stepped again into the plain, cramped bedroom she'd just vacated and tried not to look at the open window. The sheet lay in a sodden pile, and Silas kicked it aside.

She could climb right back out it again.

"Sit," Silas ordered. He caught her shoulder, forced her to the floor.

The first vestiges of trepidation fluttered in her stomach. "You aren't—"

"Shut up."

She did, because she was all too aware of how much man had been packed into the lean frame looming over her. She was all too familiar with the muscle and the speed and the sheer animal grace of him, mere feet from where she stared up at him from the floor.

He wouldn't kiss her again. He wouldn't try to hurt her.

Would he?

Jessie bit her lip. Bit it harder when his hands moved to his belt and undid it with a snap of metal and nylon. It hissed free of the denim loops holding it in place. Her gaze leaped to his implacable face, the hard, angry pinch at his eyes.

Fear skittered through her mind. Was he—?

Was this her punishment? Oh, God, was he going to—

"I know you'll run," he said. He knelt behind her. She tensed, flinched when his fingers grazed her arms. Metal clicked as he unhooked the cuffs, but he caught her wrists before she could do more than flex in surprise. "I'm doing my damnedest not to treat you like a fugitive, here. Do us both a favor and just stay put."

"Yeah, well your hospitality sucks." Jessie held her breath as the callused edge of his fingers rasped against her skin as he knotted the belt around her hands. Then he hooked the other end to the heater behind her. "And this isn't the warmest— Ouch!" The lead snapped taut behind her as she twisted.

Silas stood again, feature implacable. "You've got enough lead to lay down and the belt won't dig in as much as the cuffs will." His mouth twisted. "Believe me, I know. So just get some sleep."

Relief that all he'd done was tie her up suddenly shattered into simmering fury. She pressed her fingers together tightly, twisted them hard. God, she hated witch hunters.

Jessie didn't dare move. Her heart pounded so loudly that she was sure he heard it as he turned and left the room. The door shut hard behind him.

She counted to ten, taking a slow breath between each number. The metal heater behind her pinged twice, groaned, and spit out air only a little warmer than room temperature. Still, she was grateful as it seeped into her wet clothes. Slowly, so slowly that she was sure she'd go crazy from the effort, she tugged at her wrists.

They snagged on nylon. Twisted tautly. The bastard knew knots. She pulled, writhed, until her skin burned with effort.

"Goddamn it," she whispered, and sank back against the warmed metal. Her vision blurred behind a press of hot, angry tears, but Jessie blinked them roughly away.

She couldn't afford to cry, not right now. Once she got free, once she found Caleb and pulled him out of whatever mess he'd landed in, she'd give in and have a good long wailing session.

She exhaled loudly.

Closing her eyes, she tried to imagine what kind of people she'd be meeting with come daylight, and whether she'd survive the encounter. It was going to require every last bit of nerve she had, but she was going to have to lie to a room full of witch hunters and live to laugh about it.

Even if her laughter bordered on hysteria.

God. What had she done to deserve this? What had Caleb done? Was it really just about their gifts?

Was something else going on?

Exhaustion rolled over her in a violent, vision-blurring wave. She shifted, tried to get comfortable, and simply gave in when she couldn't keep her head up anymore.

It would be morning soon. With the help of these unwilling missionaries, Jessie was going to save her baby brother.

Period.

CHAPTER FOUR

Sunlight seeped through the open window. It sliced through her eyelids in a muted shade of blue, an insistent slant that split gentle dreams of maternal laughter and candlelight into waking blindness.

Jessie bolted upright, banged her head against the protruding heater knob, and swore as pain shredded the last vestiges of sleepy comfort. She tried to grab her head and grunted as her shoulders twisted, wrists catching on the belt and her skull ringing.

Shaking her head hard, she leaned back on her still-bound hands and blinked until the stars cleared from her eyes.

A faded blue blanket pooled at her waist, warm from her body heat. "What?" she muttered thickly, staring uncomprehendingly at the faded edge. "With the where?" When had the blanket showed up? Who had put it there?

Silas? It seemed the likeliest explanation—he probably hadn't wanted his star informant to catch pneumonia and die, after all—but why hadn't she woken up when he'd entered her space?

Christ, just thinking about him in the same room while she'd slept like the dead was enough to raise the fine hairs on her arms to prickling unease. She shifted, struggling to get her legs under her without her hands to help for balance, and froze as she shifted farther than she expected.

What the hell?

Twisting, she frowned fiercely at the bubbled edges of Silas's belt trailing on the floor behind her. Bits of seared nylon clung to the inside of the metal bars, evidence of the heat trapped behind the slatted bars.

Some freaking luck. Quickly, Jessie worked her bound hands around her legs. Once in front of her, it was the work of moments to pick the nylon apart with her teeth.

What time was it? This apartment was mid-level, higher than her usual haunts, which meant enough sun to paint the air in muted shades of blue. Judging by the brightness, it was morning. Where were the other missionaries?

What about the damned *meeting*?

She clambered to her feet, alarmed, and barely kept from pitching back to the thin carpet when her body snapped back on agonizingly stiff muscles. "Jesus," she groaned. She didn't bother trying to figure out what part of her night she could blame for this one.

Assaulted by a tattooed meathead, jumping two stories, playing tag with cars, sleeping on the floor; she would have laughed, if it didn't hurt just to suck in a breath. She wanted a bath. Desperately.

None of this, she thought as she gritted her teeth and forced herself upright, could ever be classified as a brilliant plan. God, she hurt.

It took effort, but every step toward the bedroom door allowed her muscles to give a little more. With the grating rasp of synthetic wood on wood, the door opened under her careful, questing tug.

He hadn't locked it. Was he stupid?

Clouded daylight filtered into the stark living room, left no room for a mote of dust to move undetected, much less a missionary hovering somewhere over six feet.

Jessie frowned deeply. If he'd left her, she was going to—

What? Climb out the window again? Shit. "Agent Smith?" she called, moving stiffly through the empty apartment. She tapped on the bathroom door. "Silas? Are you here?"

The answer clicked into her brain, sudden enough to make her growl a wordless sound of aggravation. Yeah, he'd left her. The son of a bitch had left her.

Now what? As she stood in the middle of the empty room and stared down at the worn, spotted carpet, the same questions clattered around in her head. *Why* had he left her? Wasn't she part of his hunt? His method to capture Caleb?

Wasn't she necessary to them?

Or had he lied?

The first inklings of suggestion slipped like oil through her thoughts. Beckoned. She could check on him. See where he was.

See where he was.

Her fingers flexed in nervous anticipation. Jessie hadn't used her magic in a long time. Not since her last futile attempt to find Caleb had backlashed on her in a wash of power that had left her nursing a headache for a week.

But Silas was something else. Something less protected.

It could be worth it. Beyond worth it to know what Silas Smith, witch hunter and total bastard, was up to when Jessie wasn't looking. What the rest of his witch-killing team had planned.

Lie to her, would he?

Disappointment simmered just under her surge of anger. Hypocritical, she knew. She'd done nothing but lie to him from the start, so it wasn't as if she had any right to complain. Still, she had to admit to a flicker of disappointment. He'd seemed so . . . earnest.

"Oh, come on, Jessie," she sighed, rubbing at the already fading knot decorating her skull. Of *course* he sounded earnest. He killed witches, the scum of the earth according to his Church keepers. He was pretty damn sincere about that one, wasn't he?

How many times did she have to remind herself? He'd kill her, if she let him. Determined, she retraced her steps to the bedroom and shut the door. She didn't bother removing her shoes.

Stretching out full length on the stripped bed, Jessie draped one arm over her eyes, laid the other hand over her heart. It thudded against her palm, strong and sure.

There was a trick, a knack, to unlocking the magic she kept leashed so tightly inside. Once upon a time, she'd sat at her mother's side when she did this. Both of them had used focus items. Amulets. Candles. Stones. Lydia had guided her, with gentle hands and gentle voice.

But all that changed in a wash of blood. Now Jessie used nothing that would draw suspicion. No inks, no charms. Just herself.

It made her weaker. It also kept her alive. People got jumpy when a girl started pulling out rocks and knives.

Squeezing her eyes shut, she took in a slow, deep breath and counted her heartbeats. Center. She had to find her balance, that quiet place deep inside herself.

The magic flowed through the core of her body. It shimmered, gurgled like a hot spring of power and warmth, and it had taken Jessie years to get used to the slide of it under her skin. Now it thrummed. Eager to be free. Eager to be used.

She pictured Silas in her mind's eye, shivered when he rose so clearly, so effortlessly stark against the backs of her eyelids. His smile, fleeting and hard, and the way his eyes went foggy when he was angry. When he watched her.

When he kissed her.

Slowly the smooth, cool texture of the mattress faded away beneath her. The shabby room, painted shades of blue and gray in clouded sunshine, became nothing more than a vague suggestion.

She hovered, coalesced, a slip of consciousness that carried her gently, resolutely away from the here and now to simply the *now*.

Silas Smith. Where was he? What was his location?

A single thread pulsed amid the tangle. Shimmered silver. *Silas*. The magic reached out before she thought herself into it. It was easy to follow, a flare in the dark, and she mentally skated over the strange place where all the threads combined.

Reeled when the dark crumbled to burning gold.

He paced the length of a bright room. His long legs ate up the floor, a caged rhythm between each turn, heedless of the sunlight outlining his broad shoulders in fire and light. Skylights yawned overhead, the source of the blinding sunlight that burned into her mind now. Jessie squinted, there and not there, and focused herself. Focused on the room.

Wide, luxurious windows and a room big enough to fit every apartment she'd ever slept in, side by side. In the center, a thick, dark wood table dominated the palatial floor. The damn thing could seat over fifty comfortably, but Silas didn't sit in any of the ornate chairs around it.

He paced like a snarling animal, as out of place as granite among delicate crystal.

Jessie's mind raced. They were somewhere topside. Closer to the spiraled heights that opened up to the sky.

That meant wealthy. Beyond wealthy, and if this was Church ground, it was no wonder.

Jessie was as formless as a thought, unable to feel the sun coursing through the ceiling glass or taste the clean air that wafted across the heavy wall hangings. She knew it had to be sweet.

Nothing like garbage and mold, acid and bone-deep hunger.

Silas ignored it all. Of course he did, he'd be used to it, wouldn't he? His face was a mask of repressed impatience, a chiseled line of annoyance as he rounded on the group of people arrayed around the end of the table.

"I won't do it," he said flatly, and the surge of awareness Jessie felt for him sent her pulse knocking in places she didn't dare acknowledge. Not when she rode the magic; not this close. She gritted her teeth and focused on the room. The people.

On Silas.

"I don't think you're being given a choice." The only woman in the room sounded more than a little amused. She sat on the corner of the table, swinging one heavily booted foot. Back and forth, back and forth.

She was beautiful in ways every dancer Jessie had ever known craved to be. Her hair was black and pulled up into a spiky knot, streaks of violet popping like firelit wine in the sunlight. Metal studs and bars decorated her ears and one eyebrow, thick metal spirals shone at her earlobes. A ring glinted in the center of her overly lush lower lip.

Exotically mixed features combined to give her tilted almond eyes and ridiculously full mouth an edgy appeal. At least some part Asian, maybe Japanese, the rest of her was all attitude.

Recognizable a mile away. Jessie committed her to memory as the woman licked at that thin silver ring. "Besides," she added, her tone thick with something that felt like baggage to Jessie's sensitive awareness, "you got more to prove than we do."

"You called me," Silas snapped, every line of his powerful body tense.

Another man grimaced. "Naomi's right, Smith. Despite your past—"

"Come on!" Silas threw up his hands. "You pulled this one, Nai, remember? Don't lay that bullshit card on me."

Jessie's fingers curled into her palms as the urge to reach out seized her.

Stop it. Get a grip.

The power of the present wasn't just a viewing screen, not just a video feed. She didn't know what the Mission could do if she messed up now. If she let the power interfere.

The other man who had spoken had no hair to speak of, older and grizzled. The chair made him look smaller than he was, but there was no mistaking the shrewd intelligence behind his hazel eyes. He tapped his fingers on the polished table. "Can you use the sister to hunt down the boy or not?"

Silas's fists clenched. "That wasn't my job. You needed an unknown missionary to bring her in, so I brought her in. You needed someone to ensure her cooperation, I damn well ensured her cooperation."

"Then where is she?" Naomi's uniquely blue-violet gaze glinted in the brilliant light. "You do have her, right?"

"She's sleeping," he snapped. "Treating her like a prisoner wouldn't get that cooperation, would it?"

Jessie's vision crackled. Shimmered like a heat wave under the pressure of her own annoyance. Tying her up was definitely *not* the way to ensure her cooperation, which meant he was lying. Why?

"He can't do it," Naomi said, shrugging her shoulders. The vibrant red top she wore revealed gaps of pale skin where it had been artfully shredded. "I should have known—"

"The coven cell in this city has killed thirty-seven people." The timbre of this man's voice tore through their collective voices like a foghorn. All three hunters turned, gazes swiveling to the man who sat at the head of the long table. The skin around Silas's eyes tightened.

Jessie studied the man whose face registered only a quiet, palpable determination. His hair was iron gray and cut close to his scalp, his sideburns shaped along his square jaw to perfection. He was much older than any of them, but the lines around his blue eyes didn't detract from the sheer force of will that surrounded him like a net. To Jessie's magical eyes, it was as real as a shroud.

Or a shield. Any witch worth her salt thought twice before messing with a human with this kind of willpower.

She let out a slow, steady breath as the older man continued. "Thirty-seven people," he repeated. "In

one year alone. Caleb Leigh has been personally responsible for five of them."

Jessie's body tensed on the cool mattress. Her
focus sharpened, taut as a bowstring. More lies.
They had to be.

"I'm aware of the facts," Silas began, but the man
who had to be his director raised a weathered hand.
Cut him off as neatly as if he'd sliced Silas's words out
of the air with a knife.

"It's reasonable to assume that the coven has
marked every member of the Mission here in the city.
You are not a member of this Mission."

"I don't think—"

"You are not called to think, Silas Smith." The
way the older man used Silas's full name set Jessie's
teeth on edge. It dripped with condescension. With
pointed arrogance. "If the sister is in league with the
boy, then she will know us on sight as well."

Well, she would *now*. Lying, murderous son of a
bitch. All of them. The scene jerked, faded as Jessie's
focus caught on the edge of anger. She scrambled to
smooth out the corners, to shut down the adrenaline
and fury scoring through her control.

God, she was rusty at this. Her fingers twisted
over her chest.

Then every hair on the back of Jessie's neck rose as
the man's words took on an icy edge. "Therefore, it
requires someone alien to this city's battlefield. You,
Mr. Smith. You must use her to retrieve the boy, to
bring him to this Mission, and if possible, undermine
the stability of this coven."

Silas's hands clenched and unclenched as he faced

the table. Naomi watched him, a lazy half smile curving her mouth. The bald man worried at a thumbnail, brow furrowed. Only the deep-voiced missionary sat in poker-faced patience.

Jessie watched in taut silence. Would he say no? Would he give her, give Caleb, to them?

Silas looked away first. "Fine," he said. "I'll use her to infiltrate the coven."

"You will remain in contact with your team"— Jessie watched a muscle leap in Silas's jaw—"at all times," the leader finished simply.

"No—"

Naomi shifted. "Wait a fucking second," she broke in sharply. "What about the rest of us, Peterson? Are you telling us to sit on our asses this whole time?"

Silas shut his mouth.

"On this matter, yes." The woman's lips compressed as Peterson shifted his attention steadily to her. "The less momentum, the less risk of being discovered. The rest of you are double-assigned to a second situation. Report back to me in one hour."

The bald man whistled a three-note tune. "Just out of curiosity," he said, caution practically radiating from his earnest stare. "Smith isn't leading this merry band of thieves, is he?"

Silas's shoulders squared. "Oh, hell, no."

There was a beat. Then Peterson's baritone. "I am in charge, always. You are dismissed. Mr. Smith, remain."

"No way, what other situ—"

"I said *dismissed*, Miss West."

Jessie leaned forward, half aware of the smell of

old carpet and dust, but focused on the bright room with the ancient furnishings. Both men stood silently until the room emptied, Silas's posture as uncompromising as the set of his angled jaw.

"Silas Smith," Peterson said slowly, mulling over the name as if working out a particularly offensive problem. Slowly he set a digital readout on the table between them. "Orphan. Lone missionary. Wounded soldier."

Silas jerked back. "Not interes—"

"Sit *down*."

He didn't. But he didn't move, either. He wrapped white-knuckled fingers around the back of a chair and waited.

Jessie itched to pick up that readout and throw it in the smug bastard's face as the man said in low, menacing tones, "I am watching you. I have been watching you since Miss West threw your name into the ring. I do not tolerate lone wolves, and I will not tolerate you for any longer than I must. Do you understand?"

Silas stared at the folder, a tic leaping at the side of his jaw. "Yes, sir."

"When your mission is complete, I *will* be requesting a full physical. I expect that it will prove what you and I already know."

"What's that?" But Jessie thought that Silas didn't sound curious, as if he already knew. Had expected it.

What the hell kind of politics was this?

"That you," Peterson explained slowly and with great relish, "are well beyond your prime years. That you're a liability in the field, and a tragedy anywhere else." Silas's eyes burned holes into the innocuous digital panel. "I am well aware of your history, and rest assured, you will not be given a chance to repeat your mistakes. Once this mission is completed, you'll never again work in any Mission in this country. Am I clear?"

Silas didn't stop to mince words. "Crystal," he bit out, and turned away. Jessie's sympathy welled up, thick and unwanted. Choked her anger.

"I have not dismissed you, yet." Peterson's tone hadn't changed, but suddenly Jessie could taste the menace in the air. Feel it sting her skin.

No, not hers. *Silas's.*

Back ramrod-straight, he roiled underneath a thin veneer of control. Jessie gasped, knew she did, but she only heard Silas's teeth grinding.

Felt it as if it were her own.

She struggled against the pull. The magic resisted her. It *wanted.*

"See that you are in touch frequently, Mr. Smith. Your team will be watching you. Carefully."

Red speared through her mind, through her vision, as Silas stalked from the room. She cried out, spread her arms as if she could catch herself on something, anything else.

Her control failed. Resentment, a bone-deep fury so great that it drew her in like a sparkling net. A vortex of emotions too damned complex for her to work them out now, but all Silas.

His need called out and the magic answered, roiling on its own. It all but pulsed in her blood. The scene dipped, darkened, all in the space of a second.

She tried to apply the mental brakes, to cut the flow of power and withdraw, but the magic unfurled like a banner and snapped into place with an audible, soul-wrenching *click*. Power to passion; emotion was a hell of a focus.

Suddenly she was inside Silas. Inside his head, his skin. Jessie gasped with the force of his anger.

Crimson rage mottled her vision, closed her throat until it ached.

Bitter memories filled her mind, her chest, too fast to catch anything more than blood and fire, vicious words and a splatter of blood on white plaster.

Too close. Too fast.

More than she ever wanted to see of the witch hunter who'd rather see her kind dead.

Jessie struggled to free herself from the tangled skeins of his fury. Mentally she pulled away, thrashed free of the threads of magic. Pain flashed along her wrist. No, damn it, *his* wrist. A bright seam of blue light seared flesh both hers and not hers, burned through the magic so fast that Jessie's awareness lurched back from the room. It ripped away from the man that jerked his angry gaze up to the bright sunshine. His lips moved; it was soundless in the vacuum her consciousness left behind.

The view tilted. Upended. Golden sunlight faded to hazy blue. Opulent wallpaper withered to mottled paint, and Jessie lurched back into herself with pain, fear, and pure rage beating at her skull.

Only half of it was her own.

They were going to *kill* Caleb. They knew he was a witch, thought he'd been killing people . . .

No.

Nausea slammed into her body, her stomach twisting. She had only a second's reprieve before it splashed into the back of her throat.

Jessie staggered toward the bathroom.

She retched into the toilet until her stomach wrung itself dry. When she could move again without feeling as if the ground rolled out from under her, she stood, shaking, and staggered to the cracked sink. She gripped the edges for balance, stared her pale, dripping reflection in the eye.

"Pull it together," she told herself. She breathed in, counted to three. Her wayward, roiling stomach refused to settle.

The nausea wasn't new. Snapping back like a rubber band always left her feeling like she'd left half of her necessary organs behind, but it had been years since she'd connected so completely. So effortlessly. And even then, only with Caleb.

What did it mean?

And what had she seen?

Missionaries, they called themselves. Killers, every one of them, and she'd seen four. Silas, the exotic woman they called Naomi West, the leader named Peterson, and the bald one.

Four, Silas had said. *Maybe five*.

A fully fledged mission. To kill her brother.

Jessie twisted the tap, splashed cold water on her face until she could breathe without the acidic burn of bile on her tongue. She patted her face dry, checked her reflection again.

She was still pale. Tired. The corner of her mouth,

noticeably purple around the rough scab, looked as if she'd gotten caught chewing on a leaky pen. But her chin was high and her eyes seemed steady, bright in the weak bathroom light. Jessie smiled tightly.

If they thought she was going to gift wrap her brother for them, they had something else coming.

CHAPTER FIVE

Three hours and thirty-six minutes.

It was an eternity to spend trapped in the tiny, ruined apartment. The sharp, lingering scent of smoky incense and fouled carpet made it almost impossible to breathe.

She still tried.

Each gasping breath battled against time, a struggle to pull oxygen into her lungs and expel the fluid that gathered there instead. Minute by minute, drip by bloody, agonizing drip.

Down in the ruins of the old city, where even the sun couldn't push through cracks in cement and every day was a fight for survival, no one would miss her. She'd probably rot here, alone and forgotten. Her body would decay, flesh sloughing off from her fragile bones to melt into a viscous puddle useless to everyone but the hungry, vengeful city she putrefied in.

The City of Glass.

The city of magicians and fools.

She moved. A shudder. It rippled across her naked body, sucked at the breath gurgling deep inside her chest. She had been beautiful once. Even before her pale skin had been carved with ritual symbols, before the incisions had hobbled every joint and seared bloody and black into every bone.

She had smiled once.

Now she lay splayed on the floor, bound by silk and iron. Her long, long legs pointed to the east and south, held open by a length of carved wood that pierced her thighs. The concave dip of her belly twitched, strained to suck in the air her body so desperately craved, and fresh scabs split again to drool bloody tears over her thin hips.

She was naked. Of course she was naked. It wasn't sexual. It had never been sexual, this ritual. Far from it; it was the worst ritual he'd ever witnessed.

And so necessary.

Blood dribbled from the corner of her mouth, sprayed over her chin and chest with every shallow exhale. The only possession she had been allowed to retain winked now in the sickly green light of the glow rod beside him, but she couldn't see it. Her eyes had been the first to go.

But she *had* been beautiful, and the charming gold promise ring at her right hand said someone else had once thought so, too.

He checked his watch. It was nearly noon, not that

the lack of light down here would ever have told him that.

"I—" The word gurgled deep in her chest.

He knelt in the small circle of light. What little carpet remained after the degradation of time squelched. Blood oozed into the fabric over his knees, sticky and cold.

Silk whispered, butterfly soft. Even its infinitesimal weight was too much for her shattered arms to move. "I wish—" She choked, coughed. Droplets sprayed from her cracked lips, and he turned his head as they splattered like warm rain against his cheek.

"Shhh," he whispered gently, and touched her cheek with his bare fingers. They came away wet, tingling. "Easy, Delia. It's almost over."

The ruined shape of her face twisted, and as she wheezed, he realized she was trying to laugh. He caught her cheeks between both hands and held her still.

Blood gathered like a well inside her open mouth, a pool of bloody words. She hacked out a foaming cough, sucked in a breath, and choked again instead.

He leaned over, released her wrists from the restraints that held her, and brought her hands to his chest. Her fingers splayed, seeking. He didn't cringe beneath the patterns of blood she left behind on his gray shirt.

"Promise me," she whispered, so faint that he had to concentrate to make out her words. "Promise me."

His grip tightened. He knew what she asked. He knew what he'd already promised. Because it cost him nothing, because it had cost him nothing to promise a dying prostitute even before she'd undergone the ritual, he said it again. "I promise."

For a brief, silent moment, as the tortured holes where her eyes had been turned upward to the ruined ceiling, she rested peacefully.

Then her body spasmed. Her fingers curved like talons into his chest. He seized her wrists, but it wasn't to push her away. He held her, hung on to the delicate bones of each hand, kept her close, as he said he would.

Kept her close, and squeezed every last drop of latent power from the dying shell of her body.

Another spasm seized her muscles, another searching, desperate grasp. Pain burned a line into his neck. One cord snapped, the beads of one of a handful of his charms clattered to the thinned carpet in a singing rain of metal, but it was she he watched as the last breath rattled thickly in her lungs.

He whispered in her ear, even as the life seeped from her skin like water from a ragged sack.

Latent magic. Unfulfilled potential. It would never be as sweet, as strong, as true power, but heart's blood was something else entirely. He claimed it. Gathered it. Pulled it from her body with a last, whisper-soft brush of his lips against her ruined mouth.

When she was truly dead, he tipped his bloody face to gauge his watch once more. Three hours fifty-three minutes. He was late. Not enough to send out a search party, but enough to garner curiosity. He was never late.

Now he'd skewed the pattern.

Slowly, painfully, he got to his feet. He stretched

the joints that ached from staying still for so long, rolled the kinks from his neck and shoulders.

She lay in the center of a dark, gelatinous stain. In his visual memory, it was red, but the hours had aged it to brown and black. He turned, snapped closed the glow rod case, and pocketed the rechargeable device.

"Rest in peace, Delia," he murmured. "Finally."

Each step squelched, gummy and clinging. The wreckage of the shattered apartment was the only tomb she'd get. But each breath of foul, stale air thrummed through his charged body, a crackling whip of stolen energy.

He pulled the door shut behind him, wedged it tightly. Let no one seek shelter in this damned, cursed place. Let no one find her, twisted and rotting. Especially the sister who wouldn't ever understand.

Cordelia was dead. Her problems no longer mattered to her, or to him.

And death had never been Caleb Leigh's particular problem.

CHAPTER SIX

The coven was on the offensive.

Silas waited with barely leashed impatience as the elevator creaked its slow, rickety way to the fourth floor. His wrist no longer ached, but the memory of its backlash burn lingered as he rubbed the ink.

Magic. The protective seal of St. Andrew had done its job, warned him and blocked the power, but he didn't know what the witches had hoped to do. Attack him? Watch him? Lay a curse of some kind?

Fuck. The choices were endless.

The elevator pinged feebly. He hurried to the safe house door, mind working. They'd targeted him. Why? As far as anyone else knew, he was the new guy in town. The faceless missionary brought in specifically because the coven supposedly knew every other face.

How had they known about him? Was there a leak in the Mission?

And why the fuck hadn't he told anyone else?

Except that one was easy. He hadn't raised the alarm when the magical warning had lanced up his arm because David Peterson had pissed him the hell off.

They all had, but a special reserve of piss and vinegar simmered for him. A hell of a lot had changed in fourteen years. The director these days had a control problem.

So did Silas. He didn't like being controlled.

He jammed his thumb against the sensor.

Now he had to use Jessie to get to Caleb Leigh. Use her to get close to the kid, and without telling her that no matter what, he was as good as dead.

And . . . go.

The door banged open, slammed into the wall under one angry push.

Filtered sunlight painted the room in shades of reflected blue. It shimmered through the glass, unfettered by the curtains and giving the room a cozy, almost homey feel. He half expected to smell bread baking, or dinner cooking, or whatever it was real people with real families were supposed to do.

Silas's fingers clenched on the manila envelope. "Jessie!" he barked.

No response.

She couldn't still be sleeping, not at noon. While he'd intended to be back sooner, the Mission briefing had taken much longer, which meant his clever little captive had been allowed way too much time alone. If a two-story jump didn't faze her, he doubted a few knots would.

Tying her to the heater had seemed a great idea at the time. When Silas had crept in later and found her asleep and shivering, he'd tucked a blanket around her and tried not to think about the trim curves beneath her damp clothes. Or the smudges of exhaustion that deepened the shadows beneath her eyes.

Letting her sleep this morning had seemed kind. And a salve to his already frayed patience. Now, it seemed stupid.

Grimly Silas shut the door behind him and threw the envelope onto the tiny kitchen's single counter. Damn it, he didn't have time for this shit.

He stalked to the bedroom door, shoved it open. Swore when all he saw were folded sheets and the end of a broken belt. "Motherfu—"

"Hi, honey," she drawled from behind him. "How was work?"

Her voice burned every nerve he had. Anger throbbed a heartbeat behind as he whirled. "How the hell did you get free?"

Her eyes gleamed. "That bad?"

"How did you work through my knots?"

Her lips twitched, but her tawny eyes faded to a wary edge. And annoyed. Or maybe still annoyed, given her hard bed last night.

Yeah, he'd been a bastard. Now he was going to top it.

She turned, claimed a seat on the shabby couch

and crossed one ankle over her knee. "Your belt melted," she said, and propped her head up in classic fuck-off pose. "Your knots were fine, thank you so much."

His fingers twitched. Hell, his dick twitched, and that just pissed him off more. *Go, go, go.*

Silas swiped the folder off the counter and stalked the three steps to the sofa. Threw it into her lap. She caught the spinning projectile.

"Cheerful, aren't you?" she said cautiously, spreading both hands on either side of the folder. "What's this?"

"Open it."

Her eyes flicked to him. "Come on."

"Jessie, shut up and open it."

Maybe it was the raw aggression he didn't bother to filter out from his voice, or the way he didn't sit. Didn't stop pacing. Didn't want to stop and watch her face as she opened the folder and a handful of glossy photographs spilled out on her lap.

He knew what she'd see. How her mind would latch to the color red and stay there, mired in it. Rotting in it, like the bodies captured in each picture. Black, brown, red, saturated. Detailed.

High-resolution carnage.

Her gasp slapped him across the conscience. He steeled himself and turned around, knowing he was an ass and ignoring it anyway.

White-faced, mouth open, she stared at him, accusation written over her pixie-fine features. One photo bent in her hand. "Why?" she whispered.

Why. Silas almost laughed. Instead, because he

had to, he pushed. "Melissa Calhoun. Bobby Jenkins. Katie Angela Morris." Each name stuck in his throat. He forced them out on a verbal acid burn.

She blanched.

"Two don't have names," he continued, brutally ignoring the tension snapping over her rigid body. "They don't exist, and this city could give a rat's ass." Her gaze dropped to the glossy paper again. Her mouth worked, but no sound came out. Silas crossed the tiny living room, sank to his haunches in front of her.

Eye to eye with the witch's fragile, innocent sister.

Do it, he thought, and cruelly twisted the emotional knife. "Your brother, Jessie, made them scream."

The photos fluttered into the air as she jerked back. She slid halfway up the back of the couch, feet scrabbling to escape the glossy paper that Silas knew burned. Seared the mind and heart and soul.

"No," she denied, shaking her head. Her hair slid over her cheek like silk, and Silas cursed, seized her arm and yanked her back to the couch. A photo crinkled under her hip.

"Look at them," he ordered. He slid his fingers under her leg, freed the photo of Melissa Calhoun and the shattered remains of her mutilated pelvis. "Caleb Leigh and his coven tortured these people to death. Don't think it was easy. It was a long, slow, painful way to go."

Jessie, white and shaking under his grip, turned her face away.

It wasn't enough. He spread the photos, one by

one, across her lap. "Maybe they liked your brother, Jessie, until he started to cut them up. Until he dug a red-hot knife into their bodies and bones and turned them into a sacrifice for whatever demons he's following now."

She jerked, but he was stronger. Her skin burned hot under his palm. Edges of green slid in around her nose and mouth, and it still wasn't fucking enough. "Stop it," she whispered.

"No." Silas selected another, one of the nameless two, and held it up to her face. "Look at him, Jessie. *Look at him.*" Naked without clothes, naked without skin. "They flayed this kid alive. Do you know what that feels like?"

The photo tore from his grasp as she swiped it away, scattering the pictures. "Stop it!"

He seized her wrists. Yanked her arms down and found himself practically nose to nose with her. Eye to eye.

Staring into her tears.

Jesus, don't cry. "Maybe it wasn't Caleb," he said roughly. "Maybe they forced him to be there. Maybe he's some kind of hostage. Help me find him, Jessie. Help me find out."

"It's not—"

"It is," he interrupted, ignoring her efforts to free herself. "Look at me, Jessie—"

"No!" With monumental effort, she ripped free of his grasp, thrashed back at him with fists and feet. Silas clenched his teeth when she grazed his knee with her foot, swore as her knuckles slammed into his chest.

Twisting, he forced her to the thin couch cushions. Pinned her legs down with one of his own, swore again when she arched back like a spitting cat and shoved against him.

His patience snapped; a thin line between righteous fury and bitter frustration. "It will happen again, don't you get it?" he snarled, so close to her face he could see the flecks of gold bleeding through her brown eyes.

They shimmered in shadowed grief and fear. She froze underneath his weight, gasping for breath, face flushed. Rigid with strain.

She was so warm, so soft in a world where he'd forgotten what soft felt like. And so angry. It wasn't enough. She needed to understand.

"Because it *will* happen again," he repeated, quieter. Deliberately gentler. "Whoever's calling the shots, Caleb will know. If it isn't him, then he can lead me to the leader. Do you understand?"

Her eyes narrowed, chest heaving with every breath. He could feel every line of her body against his own. Every furious breath pushed her breasts firmly into his chest, small and erotic and so real. Her pulse pounded in the delicate wrists he held pinned above her head, echoed in a flutter at the warm skin at the base of her throat.

Silas was suddenly, achingly aware that she was helpless beneath him, and his body responded with a tidal wave of sudden arousal. It swamped him. Raw instinct and sexual need.

The timing sucked. "Christ," he grated out, and rolled off her. Landed hard on the carpet, on the photos scattered over the floor. Pain jarred through his back, his knee. His head.

No less than he deserved.

Throwing an arm over his eyes, he did his best to block out the haunted uncertainty of her so damn fragile face. To block out the angry, determined mask of her faith in what he knew was the only family she had left.

Goddamned son of a bitch witch and his goddamned son of a bitch coven.

His mouth twisted. And the goddamned son of a bitch witch's sister was *his* responsibility. *His* civilian to protect, to use and to keep safe and to lie to, and he couldn't keep his eyes and mind off her *goddamned* mouth.

Fuck. This. Job.

Jessie didn't move. Didn't sit up. He imagined her stretched full-length on the couch cushions, her dark golden hair thrown over the edge in a wave of tangled wheat, staring at him.

She made him think of sunshine and honey, shades of warmed gold and sweetness.

He didn't deserve it. Any of it.

"How do you know he's a witch?" Her voice shook, every bit as strained as he felt. It bothered him that he wanted to find her hand and hold it.

He wasn't fucking *built* for hand holding.

"Research shows that every witch shares a common allele in the pattern of their DNA." Brutally Silas yanked his thoughts back to blood and bone and hollow sockets. "Your brother's blood showed up at five locations."

A beat. She shifted, old springs squeaking. "Bullshit."

But it lacked heat. Conviction. He had her. Damn him to hell, he had her. "I can show you the workup," he said wearily. "Don't know if there's a correlation between the DNA and the evil shit they do or if humans just can't keep their goddamned hands off the magic once it's theirs."

"So, what? All witches are evil?"

Silas squeezed his eyes shut beneath the hard ridge of his forearm. "Yeah." Blood painted the back of his eyelids. Blood and a young girl's terrified smile. "Yeah. They always go that way."

She took in another deep, audible breath. Let it go slowly, and even as it trembled, all Silas could think of was honey.

How the hell could she stay so . . . so untarnished? How could she sit there with the corpses of the dead at her feet and make him want to tell her that everything would be all right? Want to protect her?

He didn't know what to do with honey.

So he poisoned it.

"Blood tells, sunshine. It *always* tells. Mine, yours, a goddamned baby's, it doesn't matter. The allele is there. Caleb's was *there*. We don't catch him, or the people who are forcing him," he added, knowing it for the bullshit that was, "then they'll find and kill more innocent people. Torture *them*. The bodies will add up."

"You're lying," she said quietly. "You're making this up, trying to get me to—"

"One way or another," he cut in, "he has to be

found. You can be part of it, or I can lock your sweet ass up topside and we're just going to have to kill him. Your call."

"But I—"

"No." He cut her off again, smiled grimly at her sharp, indignant sound of frustration. "No buts, Jessie, it's a decision. Are you in the game or out of commission?"

Jessie stared up at the stained plaster ceiling and knew she didn't have any choice. She had to be in.

She had to find Caleb, get him out. Get him safe, or they'd kill him.

They'd kill him anyway.

Shit.

Caleb would never kill anyone. Never hurt anyone, not like that. That was evil. Pure evil, and Silas was wrong. Not every witch was evil. That was Church bullshit.

She'd *know*, damn it.

And how the hell had they gotten their hands on Caleb's blood? How did they know it was his?

She'd find out. She'd use the lying sack of a witch hunter she knew for a fact wanted to kill him, the man who had lied to her in order to get to him, and she'd use the gun she'd felt tucked up into a holster under his arm as he'd pinned her with his body.

That hard, powerful body. Oh, she was in so much trouble. Jessie drew in a slow breath. "In," she whispered. The word stuck in her throat, so she tried again. Stronger. Caleb needed her to be stronger. "I'm in. I'll help you."

He stirred, but Jessie didn't dare look over. Not now, when she wasn't sure if her practiced mask of lies was still in place. Closing her eyes, she counted to ten and didn't say what rose to her lips and burned.

Silas would help *her* find Caleb. Help *her* get close, and *she'd* rescue him from whatever terrible people claimed him now. Maybe Silas could kill the evil ones, get inside and destroy this coven, but she and Caleb would be long gone before he knew what hit him.

Oh, Caleb, she thought, an ache knotted angry and tight in her throat. What had he gotten into? Why was his blood—

She choked as the first fleck of magic blossomed inside her skull.

"Jessie?"

Silas's voice dimmed under a wash of red and foggy white. Shaking, she jammed her palms into her eyes.

"Jessie."

The power stirred. By itself, it warmed inside her skin. Beat inside her head. She gritted her teeth. "Give me a damn second." She managed to sound normal. Tense, angry, but normal.

Not as if she struggled to keep the sudden wash of recognition locked behind her teeth. *Caleb*. He was alive. Like a light switched on somewhere deep in her head, in that vault of power, she knew. Sensed it. Something had changed. Something had been . . . broken, a shield cracked, a ward shattered. His power called to hers; it was faint, but she seized it with all her strength.

Caleb was out there. He was alive, and he was out there. She could feel it. Follow it.

But she couldn't *see*. Why couldn't she see?

Was he in trouble? Did he need her?

Jessie dropped her hands. Sat up sharply enough to send the couch springs creaking. Energy, manic and sharp, snapped through her like overwound springs.

Think. She had to play this one carefully.

"Okay," she said. She ignored the speculative way he studied her. Part uncertainty, part wariness, he watched her as if waiting for her to fall apart.

Maybe she would, but not in front of him.

"Okay," she repeated, harder now. She forced herself to meet his eyes, to dim the pulsing beacon tugging hard on her thoughts. "You want him? Let's get him. There's one place we can check."

He rose to his feet, raw power in a wall of muscle. She tried to disregard how her mouth went dry and her vision snagged on the play of rock-hard flesh beneath his T-shirt, but it took her several tries.

Several taut, vibrant moments. *Focus.*

He ran both hands over his head, leaving the shaggy ends of his hair tousled. "Why didn't you—"

"Really?" Her short exhale of derisive laughter snapped. "You expected me to roll over on my brother because you said so?"

Silas frowned. "No."

"Great." The couch springs twanged as Jessie got to her feet. The sun-dappled carpet warmed the sole of one foot, but her other met cold, glossy photo and she recoiled. Jessie's stomach pitched.

He moved like a cat. Before she could even gasp, he caught her shoulders, steadied her with that easy, powerful strength.

Suddenly her vision was nothing but green and gray, fog and forest. Piercingly aware, his eyes met hers from only a breath away. Too close to avoid. "I, uh . . ." His fingers flexed as she ran her tongue over her dry lips. She tried again. "I didn't trust you."

Silas stared at her mouth. One beat, another. Jessie swallowed, didn't dare move. Breathe. Was he thinking of kissing her? Of peeling off the jacket she wore like armor and exploring her body?

The way she itched to run her fingers over his biceps and trace every muscled edge of his chest?

Enemy, she reminded herself, and deliberately stepped back. She disentangled herself from his grasp and knew he let her.

"Smart of you," he said, both rough and practical. More rough than practical, but she gave him points for trying. Jessie wanted to smile. Couldn't.

Silas was going to kill her brother. Which meant she just might have to kill the missionary first.

"It's a safe place, I think." She moved around him, avoided the photographs and made sure her own voice was light. Breezy. Sure.

None of the things she felt now.

But she lied easily. Too easily, and he bought it. Survival was a weak salve against the unsettling sting of guilt.

The man brought it on himself.

Silas swept up the photos, stacked them neatly back into the folder, and gestured her out the door. She followed, mind working through what fragile plans she could make with what vague information she had. A coven, dead people, rituals she didn't recognize.

God, she needed more information.

I'm coming, Caleb.

He unlocked his side of the truck and waved her in. She slid into the cab, glancing at him sidelong as he pulled himself in after her. She studied the hard line of his profile. His high cheekbones and the whiskered shadow of his jaw.

What the hell took a man into a profession based on murder?

Silas's keys jangled as he jammed them into the ignition. "Where to?"

"Um." Jessie clasped her hands tightly. "Old Seattle."

"Are you serious?" When she nodded, he shrugged. "What are we driving into?"

"I don't know," she said, honest at least with that. "I think it's been his . . . getaway, I guess."

"Safe house?"

She nodded. "Something like that."

"In the catacombs? Is he suicidal?" The derisive look she slanted him made his mouth tighten. "How close to the edge of the trench?"

Shit. Details. She didn't have those details. "Not that close," she hedged, and hoped it was true. The southernmost edge of the old city ruins wasn't just dangerous, it was a literal death trap.

If Caleb was hanging out there, things were going to get far more interesting.

Silas tucked one hand into his coat. She knew he was checking to make sure his gun was safely holstered.

He might need it to shoot her brother, after all.

She shifted. "Just drive. I'll have to remember the landmarks as we go." And hopefully make it seem organic enough that she wasn't obviously following a thread of power in a tangled, twisted place.

Neither spoke as the truck began the winding, circular drive toward the half-forgotten streets of Old Seattle. Jessie rested her temple against the window and watched the familiar stone and metal buildings pass by.

The cars thinned out, turned off the carousel one by one until theirs was the only vehicle left. Nobody went this far down. She traced a finger on the glass, idly following the rusted, twisted curve of the byway guardrail.

"Do you live in Seattle, Agent Smith?"

He didn't look at her. "No." He hooked his fingers loosely around the steering wheel. "I haven't lived here for a long time. And you can call me Silas," he added.

She wasn't sure she could. Still, she tapped the glass. "You know the history, don't you? Of the old city?"

This time, he glanced at her, weighing her question as if she'd laid a trap in it. After a long moment, he shrugged. "Who doesn't? The West Coast tore itself apart. Earthquakes, floods, volcanoes. Same general story as everywhere else, give or take a few years."

So simply put. So quickly said. Jessie could only imagine the destruction, the fear. "My mother didn't talk about it much," she said. "She was born and raised here. I read that people woke up to an ash cloud that covered the sky."

"Have you ever spoken to anyone who survived it?"

She shook her head. "It's not really something that comes up," she said with a wan smile. "But sometimes, you look into the eyes of an old drunk in the corner of the bar and you just . . . know what he saw."

Silas watched the road for a long time. Finally he said, "Seattle wasn't the only city to go down."

"It's the only city who answered Mother Nature by building higher," she retorted dryly. "A few religious words, some high-energy zealotry, and they built right on top of the old city, bridged the trench like it was just a pothole." She rolled her eyes to the buildings that thrust into the sky like spears. "Better, stronger, with even more glass."

Other cities had fallen, drowned, burned down or been blown away in those terrifying years. Without rhyme or reason, everything had spiraled out of control.

Zealotry wasn't strong enough a word.

She closed her eyes. Fifty years wasn't so very long ago. Her mother had spoken of one old witch who had lived to tell of the storm that had all but swept Paris off the map. Could she survive as many years by herself?

Did she want to?

He grunted. "That fault's, what, a mile across at the widest?"

Jessie snapped her eyes open. "I don't know. Maybe. It's deep, though." Deep enough to swallow half the old city. One giant, blackened tomb. "I've never really thought to explore it."

"Damn straight. They sealed the whole ruin off

for a reason." He frowned into the rearview mirror. "Even fourteen years ago, the place was a kill zone. Unsteady pockets of road near the fault, unexplained seismic activity. Hell, they lost half the drones they sent out to recon the fault line."

Jessie dropped her gaze to her hands. Damn it. He sounded *smart*. She bit her lip. "The city's built like a giant layer cake of metal and glass. Don't you think they'd have made sure it was safe enough before they started building?"

"You'd think so, huh?" His rueful grin, crooked at one corner, launched her heart into a sudden, loud staccato. Her fingers curled into fists. "Way I heard it, they dropped a couple thousand support beams, paved over the whole damned thing, and called it good."

Silas's deep voice slipped beneath her guard too quickly, curled in somewhere soft and trusting. Jessie pursed her mouth and tried to figure out why. Why was her first instinct to trust him? Especially since she knew he would only kill her, kill Caleb, in the end?

Maybe, she decided, she was just so tired of running.

"I guess it worked." She opened her eyes and watched the ruined brown walls of a tunnel slide past the window. "I thought I'd get to really see it when Caleb and I came through the import lanes. That was a disappointment."

"Why?"

She flicked him a glance, but he watched the road. The truck slowed, and she followed his gaze to the rubble that scattered over the rapidly deteriorating asphalt. Nobody cared for the lower streets, not anymore.

She shook her head, didn't bother lying. "Well, first, the transport didn't have windows," she said on a long exhale. "Caleb and I were hidden in crates shipped to some business uptown."

He frowned. "Crates? You were crammed into airlocked crates?"

"Yeah." She didn't try to paint the picture. She didn't want to. It had been the longest four hours of her life, dark, cramped, and stifling. "The driver dropped us off in these lower levels and that was that. Not to mention," she added with a wry shake of her head, "they'd built the lanes to skip the catacombs. Probably smart."

He didn't smile. "How old were you?"

"Fifteen."

"Jesus, you were just a kid."

Never. She flicked him a hard glance. "We'd been on our own for a long time, thank you. We did fine."

The look he slanted her burned. "So fine, one of you is in a cult of killers and the other's stuck cleaning his mess."

Heat climbed into her cheeks. Struck mute by a whiplash of anger, she turned her face back to the window and said nothing.

She knew he was right. Jessie could talk and lie and posture all she wanted, but the witch hunter was right. Maybe it was her fault Caleb had ended up in trouble. Maybe she should have stayed somewhere quiet, a real community out in the vast, empty country where it was easier to live. To have a normal life. Friends. Girlfriends. School.

But the coolly rational part of her brain said she'd done the right thing. Their mother had been murdered. Maybe Caleb hadn't seen it happen, maybe he'd hidden away before the killer had found Lydia alone and unprotected in their cozy, rustic home, but Jessie wondered. Every day, she wondered if the twelve-year-old Caleb had watched her die, had known why their mother's power of future sight had suddenly shot itself into him and bloomed.

Maybe that was why he'd been such a grim little kid.

Or maybe just seeing the future had made him that way.

Outside the window, the light had darkened as they moved deeper into the low streets. Now, the only illumination came from the truck's headlights and the occasional barrel of burning refuse. Though she stared hard out the window, she didn't see any evidence of people. No bodies hunkered by those barrels, no shadows of motion or children running. As the truck slowed to navigate through strewn rubble, Jessie realized that the people who inhabited these broken streets lived an inch from hell.

Her chest ached just thinking about it.

The city had tried to seal off the twisted skeleton of the old byways and ramps, but time and neglect had taken its toll. The cement roadblocks once charged with keeping out vehicles like theirs had long since fractured, been moved by the desperate or the curious. In the twin circles of Silas's headlights, the road vanished into a darkness so thick, it practically breathed on its own.

"Are you ready?"

Jessie rubbed at her breastbone, her voice thick as she said, "I don't understand how this place is just left open for anyone to walk in."

"Not really open," Silas said, and tipped his head to the windshield. She leaned forward, blinking up at the mass of black pressing down on them from overhead. The faintest glow signaled the very limits of the electric lights illuminating the lower edges of the civilized levels. Mid-low, they called it. Higher than the dregs of the streets they navigated now, but too low to matter.

"I feel like we're the only people alive down here," she murmured.

"May as well be. We're on the bottom level of New Seattle. Only the morons with a death wish go this far. The import lanes come through this tier, but not on these roads."

"Great." Taking a deep breath, she sat back and gripped her fingers tightly. She could do this. The insistent tug of Caleb's beacon remained steady, if faint. "Let's go be morons, then."

Some said the ruins held the only way out of New Seattle that didn't involve sec-comps and passports.

Then again, Jessie had worked for enough strip clubs and die-hard bars to know a desperate wish when she heard one. She'd never heard of anyone coming back from deep inside Old Seattle with a map and a ready deal to make. If she knew anything, it was that information about an escape route would sell.

Silas was right. Too far in to the ruins, and even a determined refugee needed God's own luck to survive. As they passed the broken husk of a faded billboard, she studied the graffiti and wondered how many destitute travelers had tried anyway. Enough that someone had painted a message in the vibrant orange of construction paint.

Abandon all hope.

Someone had a sense of humor.

Silas navigated around the roadblocks and piles of rubble. The tunnel walls closed in on them, an inky field of echoes and stone. "Where to?"

Jessie closed her eyes briefly. The memory of Caleb's signal and her own magic coalesced into a single, faded thread. She didn't know why she saw everything as strings connecting together. Symbolism wasn't her strength.

But it worked, and that's what she liked.

She opened her eyes again and stared intently through the windshield. "Keep straight, I guess. This tunnel has to end sometime." The cab bounced and swayed. "It's hard to imagine that this was once a thriving city. We're not even a minute in, and it feels like driving into a tomb."

"May as well be. Two million people died in the quake, and that's just in Seattle. Effectively a tomb, isn't it?" Silas held the steering wheel tightly, bent over it to keep a close eye on the dark pressing in on all sides.

"That's horrible."

"That's life," Silas countered.

Jessie bit her lip before she said more. Before she took his figured casualties and included the numbers of people tried, executed, murdered, and burned to death. Two million? It wasn't nearly high enough.

The tunnel opened up in front of the headlights, swept over a broken expanse of cracked asphalt. The dark didn't ease. It was as if they were still in that tunnel, Jessie thought. A broken, haunted maze.

"And we're in. Recognize anything?"

"No," she said, frowning. "I can't see jack." The truck navigated around fallen, twisted metal and potholes the size of the windshield. "Silas, I don't get it. How does the city stay upright? I mean, there's millions of tons of metal and glass on top of us."

"Architecture isn't my field," Silas replied dryly, and slowed almost to a crawl as the battered pickup forged through a standing valley of stagnant water. "By all accounts, Seattle was built on an older version of itself even before the earthquake. I guess they're just carrying on the tradition."

"Dumb tradition," Jessie said, and blinked as he flicked a switch. The headlights brightened, unfurled like a beacon to illuminate a brilliant swath through the dark. It bounced over a canvas of pitted metal, reflected back at them in a sea of pipes and rust.

Her eyes widened. "Holy—"

"Fuck me," Silas breathed. "How close is that ceiling?"

Close enough to reach out and touch, if she felt like it. Jessie stared at the artificial sky above them. The road dipped down, eased into a slant that pushed the ceiling higher and higher. The twisted beams faded into the darkness that Jessie imagined had once been a beautiful sky.

Sadness clutched at her. People had died here by the tens of thousands. She felt like an intruder.

"What landmarks are you looking for, exactly?"

Jessie jerked her thoughts out of what-if and once-was to frown at him. Frowning was a safe option, and so much better than forgetting herself and reaching out to touch him.

God, she wished he wasn't so . . . so *there*.

"What?" she asked. "With the who?"

"Landmarks," he repeated, taking a moment to turn his cool gray-green eyes to her. "You're looking for landmarks, right?"

Oh. *Right.* Jessie nodded to the widening road in front of them. "This will lead to a square." She didn't explain how she knew that. She just did. "I think there was a statue there once, but the pedestal is still there. I hope," she added, because it sounded more like honesty if she allowed doubt to creep into her voice.

He nodded, as if in agreement. "I don't know how much things change down here."

"I don't, either. But either way, barring a total cave-in"—the thought made her spine go cold—"it should be familiar enough." She jumped when the first splatter fanned over the windshield.

"The hell?"

"What was that?" Jessie asked at the same time, bracing both hands on the dashboard. Water slid across the glass in a current. Another fat drop splashed over the driver's side, and Silas turned on the windshield wipers. "Oh! Do you have a flashlight?"

"Glove box."

She fumbled with the catch, found the heavy plastic light, and spent an extra few moments searching for the switch. With a rough sound of amusement, Silas reached over and depressed the button embedded into the tail end.

The powerful beam sheared through her window. It speared through the dark, stripped away a path of light that found the ceiling and outlined the maze of metal. "Oh," she gasped, and touched Silas's leg beside her to get his attention. "Look!"

The artificial sky rained. As the truck eased into the rubble-strewn square, water poured from the pipes twisting out of the structured asphalt overhead. It was the only rain the old city streets could ever know again, and the water poured wild and cold from the tangled weave of piping.

Silas eased the truck to a stop. For a long moment, neither spoke. Instead the oddly musical tone of water dripping onto metal, glass, and cement filled the tomblike serenity of the courtyard.

Muscle shifted. Jessie was abruptly yanked back to the realization that she still wrapped her fingers around his thigh. That Silas hadn't drawn away. Neither had she.

She stared at her hand, palm to denim.

Jessie snatched her hand back, fumbled for the door latch. "Come on," she said quickly, feeling like an idiot. She hoped it was too dark in the cab to see the embarrassment she knew turned her face red. "We can walk from here."

"Keep the flashlight, you'll need it."

"Don't you need one?"

She didn't stop to check his expression as he followed her lead. "I always have one on me. I wonder," he said thoughtfully. "This must be the drainage from the upper city when it rains. Another storm must have rolled in."

"Don't like the weather? Wait ten minutes," she said wryly. An odd, unnerving glow of satisfaction warmed her at his amused grunt.

She bit down on her lip, winced. *Behave.* "Come on. I'm pretty sure we aren't far, now. And the road's worse up ahead."

Jessie mentally kicked herself as the words fell out of her jumbled brain. Her overeager mouth. He studied the other end of the broken cobbled square, shrouded completely in inky shadow. "How can you tell?"

"I'm guessing," she lied quickly. Smoothly. She tucked the flashlight between her knees while she gathered her hair up into her hands, hiding behind the efficiency of the motion.

"The place looks like hell," Silas observed, but he watched her.

Her, not the surroundings. His hands moved, checked the gun in its holster, zipped his faded jacket halfway, locked the truck doors behind them, but it was her he studied.

Did he sense the lie? Jessie rolled her shoulders. It didn't ease any tension. "Let's just go." Without waiting, she grabbed the heavy flashlight and set across the rain-splattered square. She tried hard to keep her attention on the uneven cobbles underfoot. She knew without looking that he fell into step beside her.

The man radiated presence. She'd have to get used to it. At least for now.

Within moments, both were soaked to the skin and Jessie had unzipped her jacket to let the cold water steal away some of the inane heat curling in her belly. The air smelled coppery, and when she licked her lips, she tasted a tang to the water that reminded her of metal.

Where did all this water go? A sudden image of rampant flooding made her grit her teeth. Letting her imagination run away wouldn't help her now. It had rained regularly for fifty years, the water had to go somewhere.

The thought was cold comfort as she walked beside Silas. She peered at every crumbling wall, every empty, skeletal frame as they navigated the twisted maze of roads.

As she followed the magic.

Jessie pointed down what had once been a side street, at least before the whole underground had become just that. "I think it's this one."

Wordlessly Silas reached into his coat and withdrew a small penlight. The high-powered beam cut through the artificial night like a knife. "Stay close."

He led the way this time, cutting her off before she could do more than raise her foot for the first step. She glared at his back. "Expecting trouble?"

"Always."

The single, flat word took some of the wind out of her irked sails. Always? How . . . sad.

How familiar.

Jessie aimed her flashlight at the treacherous street at her feet and followed, blinking water from her eyes. She didn't say anything at all as he picked his way across rippled, broken pavement. He stepped over a mound of twisted earth and asphalt, said, "Careful," as he continued past it.

Jessie blinked at it. Frowned. Without warning, it coalesced into a full picture in her mind. "Oh," she breathed, crouching down to touch the massive hump. Something soft and green ticked her palm around the angled edges of old cement.

The earth was reclaiming this forgotten city. Jessie didn't need to *see* to know there were roots jammed through the mound. Roots and moss and broken stone. "Wow," she whispered, because she didn't have the words to explain the joy, the sheer amazement that slipped underneath her wariness, her anger, and bloomed.

There was hope, primal and alive.

"What did you find?" Silas called from the shadows ahead. His voice bounced from wet stone to rotting siding, eerily surreal.

Jessie raised her head, blinked quickly. Yanked her brain firmly into focus. "Nothing!" she lied. He wouldn't understand, anyway. She gently patted the mound of life and ruined city, stepped over it, and hurried to catch up.

This time, the magic seized her by the throat. Her awareness fragmented outward like shrapnel, too many images assailing her at once to see any of it. Then her power flared, wrapped around her consciousness, and forced it all together into that single thread, faded even further and harder to pick out from the real world that battered at her from all sides.

Rain, metal, silence.

There.

She shook her head, hard, and touched the door beside her. "Caleb," she whispered. Without waiting, without daring to breathe, she pushed against the half-rotted door.

Splinters came off in her hands. Water poured into the hole left behind. Jessie slanted her shoulder against the ruined frame and, gritting her teeth, pushed harder.

CHAPTER SEVEN

The rotted door slammed open, tumbled Jessie into a tiny, cramped space. Dust and decay clouded the air, coalesced like a fine mist around her, and she coughed as she stumbled through the forgotten room. The smell was awful, sealed rot and mold.

She breathed through her mouth, sneezed anyway, and clapped both hands over her nose. Her eyes watered.

Outside, Silas called her name, his voice muted behind the uneven rhythm of the rain. She ignored it, knew she'd get hell for it later. It didn't matter. Not if Caleb was here. She bypassed old wooden crates piled with things, junk, some long since disintegrated in the damp air, and stepped over heaps of garbage and forgotten treasures. Old tools, their wood rotted away. Plastic toys, filthy beyond recognition. A metal wheelbarrow rusted into the ground.

Jessie wound a careful path between them all. Across the room, picked out by the powerful sweep of her borrowed light, the remnants of wooden stairs decayed beneath a door set a foot up into the wall. She climbed over piles of ruined garbage toward it.

One part eerie, one part awe-inspiring, Jessie realized she trespassed through time. That she stepped over the sad remains of someone's life, someone's home or business.

Broken, abandoned, destroyed. Like so many since the earthquake and after.

Old wood crunched under her boots. She bent, rifled through the disintegrating remains of something long past recognition, and couldn't help her low, regretful sigh. "Whoever you were," she murmured, "I hope you lived."

The odds were slim at best. By all accounts, fire and flooding took care of whatever survivors could have held on long enough to be rescued.

She stood, unable to do more than hope, and dusted off her hands. The door the steps had once led to was solid, protected from the elements and mottled by mold. She braced her hands against it and pushed.

Nothing. It creaked, but it stayed put.

Behind her, a second, thinner beam of light caused her shadow to dance wildly across the moldy panels. "Stay close," Silas said, anger edging every word, "means letting me know when you wander off."

"Sorry," Jessie said, and didn't mean it. "We need to get through here."

"Have you tried the doorknob?"

Jessie shot him a scathing look over her shoulder, eyes narrowed. Her gaze caught on his wet, disheveled hair. His face was set in hard, angry lines, sheened with water. His own smoky eyes raked over the door in front of her, and that little surge of heat licked through her blood again. "Y-yeah," she said, and had to stop to clear her throat. Damn. She needed to stop that. "It's stuck or something."

"Move." Silas put the penlight between his teeth and pushed her away from the frame. He set his shoulder to the door, one hand on the panel for balance, and shoved.

Wood groaned.

"Damn," he grunted, and shifted his weight onto his back foot. He withdrew the metal flashlight from his mouth and ordered, "Protect your face."

"What?"

Jessie rolled her eyes and covered her face with one arm when he only glowered at her. She heard him move, feet hard on the floor, and then wood splintered beneath a heavy thud. Another one, and the door cracked, slammed inward.

"*Fuck*," he said suddenly. "Jessie, don't—"

She ignored him, dodged his warning grasp with ease. "I'm sure we're almost—"

The words, her thoughts, shriveled on her tongue. Black and brown. Blood and bone. The smell rolled over her like a physical push, putrid and sharp. She gagged. "Oh, God." She staggered back toward the wall, her flashlight clattering to the ground at her feet. "Oh, God. *Silas*."

She felt his hands clamp on her shoulders, knew she'd been turned around, but all she could see was the corpse in the center of the tiny room. Half gone. Half liquefied. Half—Oh, God, was she standing in it?

Was she standing in *Caleb*?

Every hair on her body prickled in a wave of cold sweat as her stomach lurched. "I have to—Let me go!"

He didn't. Silas caught her against him, pulled her close and tucked her face against his shoulder. His arms wrapped tightly around her, pulled her back out of the room. Back into the dusty storage space, into the gloom that didn't have the same colors.

The same corpse.

She struggled, he only held her tighter. "Jessie," he said, as unyielding as the arms he wrapped solidly around her, as the hard muscle of his chest beneath her seeking hands. She caught fistfuls of his jacket and didn't know whether to push him away or hang on for dear life.

The smell was terrible. Now she knew why.

"Oh, God," she whispered again. "Who is it? Why?"

Silas slid one large hand around the back of her head, cradled her head. The small of her back. "Breathe," he demanded. "Come on, Jessie, breathe. In. Out. Through your nose—goddamn it." He hauled her around as her body spasmed, jerked her into the dim light of her fallen flashlight and caught her face between his hands.

He glowered down at her. His eyebrows furrowed, mouth set into a hard line. "Breathe through your nose," he said again, resolutely maintaining eye contact. "It'll kill off your sense of smell. Focus on me." She did. In. Out. Just like he said. "Keep doing it. You'll get used to it, just breathe."

Get used to it?

Didn't it bother him at all?

She clenched her teeth. Inhaled. Slowly, inch by inch, the world righted itself around her.

Jessie's jaw ached, her throat ached. God, her soul ached. "I can't tell," she whispered, her eyes burning. "I can't tell. Who is it?"

"I don't know." He smoothed back her hair. "If you can stay here, I'll—"

"No." Jessie sucked in a breath, held it until her lungs screamed for air. She let it out angrily. "I can do this."

"Damn it, Jessie, you don't have to."

"Yes, I do." She wrapped her fingers around his wrists, pulled his hands from her face. "I have to."

His eyes hardened. More stone than ice. She met them, stared into them, and mentally clung. But she had to let go. She stepped back.

"Okay." His agreement was reluctant at best. Angry and unsure. "Stay close to me, and if you have to get out, you say so."

"I will." This time, she wasn't sure it was the lie she wanted it to be. God, if that was Caleb in there. If that was her baby brother, she had to know.

Tears gathered in her eyes as she picked up the flashlight and followed Silas back into the tiny room. Everything blurred, but she didn't have to see it to feel the gooey, gelatinous squelch of the carpet beneath her boots. She circled around the edge, wiped her face as surreptitiously as she could.

"Jessie?"

"What?"

Silas crouched by the body, the thing bloated and splayed. He stared at it, studied it, so calmly, so impassively, that Jessie's heart went out to a man whose life had become so hard that he could look at something like this without screaming. Calm, unflinching.

She scraped shaking hands through her hair. Tightened the knot of it in place because, damn it, she didn't know what else to do. "I don't see anything . . ." *Out of place* sounded horribly wrong. She shook her head. "I guess it just—"

"It's not your brother," he said flatly. "It's a woman."

Relief warred with pure terror. Utter guilt. "How long?"

"Don't know." He grimaced. "Can you collect samples?"

Her mind balked. Jessie stiffened, raised her chin. "Of what?"

"Blood." Silas reached into his coat pocket and withdrew a small plastic cylinder. "One from each end of a circle around the body. I'll cover it."

He tossed her the cylinder. It rattled as she caught it in her free hand. That. It. Not a her, not a name, just an it.

She stared at the cylinder, more than a little dazed.

"Pop the top," he explained. His voice was calm. Patient. "There should be four swabs capped by sealable plastic. Collect a gob of blood, cap it."

"Right." Sure. She could do that. She could pretend to be efficient and composed. Jessie turned and picked her way across the floor, trying not to think about how much blood she walked through. The body—the *woman* had to have died from blood loss.

She couldn't imagine anyone losing this much blood and surviving for very long.

Jessie knelt, dug out the first swab.

Where are you, Caleb?

Why did the magic direct her here? The corpse wasn't her brother, and she was relieved beyond all reason to know that, but why here?

She swirled the swab in the crusted, terrifying ooze and sealed it before a spine-deep shudder could cause her to fling the bloody thing away in a fit of hysteria. "One down," she said, proud when her voice trembled only a little.

"Good," Silas praised, but he wasn't watching her. He moved the corpse, using the handkerchief he'd given her earlier to keep his hands clean. "This ritual probably used blood as a focus."

You think? just sounded snotty. Instead Jessie smiled weakly and stepped around him to collect a sample from the other edge of the room. She crouched, swabbed. Frowned. Gold glinted in the muted light.

A clue? Jessie reached for it, hesitated, and glanced at Silas.

He ignored her, too focused on the ruined shell in front of him.

Gold. Mired in blood.

Damn it. She plunged her fingers into the cold,

clinging layer of bloody mucus, ignored the full-body shiver rippling from head to toe. She swallowed back nausea and disgust with every ounce of willpower she possessed.

She needed to know.

Metal, streaked red beneath the dried upper layer it hid under. Real gold? She doubted it, not in this shape. Fake gold.

Plated gold, one of six, three on each side. A good number, a solid number for magical means. A bond. A seal. *Oh, Caleb.*

Her heart in her throat, Jessie raked her fingers over the crusted carpet, rolled them through the sodden layer around her feet. Three more beads spun into the light, and she struggled not to make a sound as her fingers caught on something sharp and cold.

Horrified at what she knew she'd found, Jessie shot a look back at Silas and clenched her fingers hard around a leaf-shaped pendant. It was silver, real silver, and its delicately folded edges cut into her palm as she sucked in a shaking breath.

She'd given the pendant to Caleb for his twenty-third birthday. It was the last thing she'd ever given him before he left.

The perfect focus for a spell of concealment. From her.

Why was he hiding?

Why was it *here*?

"What'd you find?"

Jessie's eyes jerked to Silas. He watched her. Measured her.

What had he seen?

She swallowed back the bile in her throat. "Nothing," she lied, and raised her grimy, blood-streaked hand. "I slipped."

"Shit!" Silas shot to his feet, crossed the slippery floor in seconds. He seized her wrist, held her hand out from the rest of her body. "Get outside, wash that off," he ordered grimly.

"It's blood," Jessie replied, marveling at how calm her voice seemed. So different from the inside of her head, which screamed and screamed. She mustered a wan, humorless smile. "And I think she's a little past caring."

"Diseases, Jessie." Silas pulled toward the stairs hanging from thick, rusted cables. "Bacteria, anything could be in blood this contaminated. Christ, don't touch anything."

Jessie thought of the bloody pendant now nestled into her boot and said nothing.

She was the bravest civilian he'd ever seen. Silas pulled Jessie up the stairs and knew he was going to regret her involvement in this. Already did.

So much blood, and now she'd fallen in it.

He shoved open the door, its lock long since rotted away, and hauled her out into the false rain still shimmering from the pipes. It caught on the roofs and arches that crumbled around them, but the air was fresher.

He inhaled gratefully, knew she did the same when he turned to point out a running wash of water pouring from a gutter pipe beside them. His hand with the light was steady, but in his grip, Jessie felt like a major earthquake was desperately trying to erupt from her skin. He shouldn't have let her inside, damn it.

"There, wash your ha— *Fuck*."

It struck without warning, a seam of fire and power that curled around his wrist. The flashlight jerked. A blue glow crackled, arced over his skin, and Jessie's eyes snapped to something behind him, widened to white-rimmed saucers of shock. Warning. "Silas—"

Silas seized her collar, jerked her down to the pavement moments before gunfire cracked across the water-spattered silence. Stone chipped just where he'd been, shards slicing through the wet air.

"Hands up, hunter!"

The command rang from the street behind them. Masculine, jeering, it was the voice of every witch who'd ever thought he had him dead to rights. Jessie's teeth sank into her lower lip.

He touched her cheek, just by the corner of her bruised mouth. "Run," he said.

Her eyes narrowed. "No, I'm not—"

"Hey, hunter!" Another bullet chipped the wall above them, showered moldy plaster over them both.

As the echoes died away, Silas calculated the odds. There'd been five shots, with a report that sounded like a standard clip handgun. Five shots, five misses. One to go.

Hastily he yanked open the zipper of his coat and pushed his gun into her hands. "Aim," he said harshly, "pull the trigger. No questions, no tricks. Just kill them, or they will kill you. Got it?"

She nodded jerkily, her skin shock-white beneath the wild tendrils of her damp hair. Silas touched her cheek again. Stood. "All right," he said, hands out by his sides. He saw Jessie scoot away in his peripheral vision. "Now what?"

A man stood ten feet away, gun held loosely in a sideways grip that told Silas everything he needed to know about the man's lack of skill. His shock of red hair was plastered to his face, and the lazy smile shaping his mouth made clear what he thought of Silas. Not a threat.

Idiot.

"If she takes one more step," the witch said cheerfully, "I'm going to shoot you."

Jessie froze in the dim light outlined by Silas's dropped flashlight.

Damn it.

"Didn't anyone ever tell you magic doesn't work on me?" Silas pitched his voice loudly, as mocking as he could. *Watch me, not her.* "Seems to me you're a lousy shot and a bad listener."

The witch's lips twitched. "Big bad killer like you can't tell the difference between a greeting and a threat, huh?"

"You're one to talk," Silas replied calmly. He stepped along a semicircle, put himself between Jessie and the gun-toting man.

"Tsk tsk." The man jerked his head. "I wouldn't do that."

Behind him, Jessie screamed. No small sound of fear, it ripped out of her on an endless, throat-tearing note of panic, of pain. His stomach clenched as he whipped around.

What he saw didn't match the bone white pallor

of her skin, or the way she panted for breath as her screams faded into echoes. Another man stood behind her, one arm wrapped around her chest, the other hand encircling the wrist with the gun. An older witch, he met Silas's gaze over the top of Jessie's rain-darkened hair and waited.

Real pain etched deeply into the taut lines of her face as she stared at Silas. Real fury.

Her mouth curved up in a tight, reassuring smile.

His heart constricted. *Shit.*

"Fine," he said. He turned back to the red-haired witch and took three steps forward. *Don't turn around.* One witch at a time. "What do you want from me?"

"You? You, I want dead. She's no hunter, though, am I right?"

Silas lowered his hands, smiling in slow, deliberate provocation. He showed a whole lot of teeth. "You want me? Come on, then."

"Oh, man." The witch cocked back the hammer on his gun, sighted down the barrel. "They're gonna love this."

Silas dropped to the ground, hit the pavement with a grunt of pain. The gun fired a split second later, capped on Jessie's ragged scream.

Six!

He rolled, caught the barest glimpse of the other man struggling with an armful of Jessie, and pushed back to his feet as the gun-toting witch stormed forward.

"I hate hunters," the man snarled, and threw the gun at him.

Silas flung up an arm, swore when it collided with the makeshift projectile. Searing pain numbed his arm from the elbow down.

Silas grunted, launched himself at the now defenseless witch and hoped to God he could drop this one and get to Jessie.

The witch raised both arms, ducked Silas's fist to bring his shoulder up into Silas's gut. All the breath whooshed out from his lungs. He hit the ground gasping.

The air crackled around him.

Fuck. He rolled moments before a blue-white line of electricity lanced across the street where he'd been. A black path of seared ozone and glittering asphalt curled into an acrid stench.

He got to his feet, and it took too much effort this time.

"Funny thing about this kind of magic," the witch said cheerfully. "Once I pull it out of thin air, it's as real as a bullet." He shot out a hand. "Wanna see if your little tattoo can suck it up?"

Another sizzle of sudden electricity in the air, another rift of reality and power. Silas jumped to the side. He felt the small hairs of his body curl as lightning jolted too close. Too hot.

Where was Jessie?

As if on cue, more gunshots rang out. One, two. Three. Sheer adrenaline propelled Silas forward, slammed him hard against the surprised witch. Power unleashed like a storm around them, backlashed against the seal of protection caught between both bodies as Silas bore him to the ground.

Goddamn, it hurt. Electrical energy and heat scored across his skin, raked deep and arced between them both. The witch screamed, lashed out like a cat, nails bared.

The pain of blood drawn didn't even register next to the voltage that rocked them both. Silas gritted his teeth against it, fought back the white-hot lance of agony trying to fry every synapse he had. He rolled to pin the witch down, seized his head. Strained.

The witch screamed once as Silas pounded his head into the street. Again as his skull bounced off the broken pavement. Still, over and over, until bone cracked and oozed under Silas's strength and his fingers sank into mush. The power around him crackled. Curled in and bled away to nothing but burned ozone.

The witch shook in his grasp, thrashed, until he also went still.

Deathly still.

Skin still sizzling, Silas toppled over, caught himself before his forehead bounced off the same pavement. No time. No time to hurt. He shoved himself to his feet. Enough adrenaline cured everything.

"Jessie!" he roared, and ran like hell.

CHAPTER EIGHT

Run, run, run, run.

The refrain pounded in her head, keeping time with the slap of her wet boots against shattered streets. Jessie dodged creeping wires and the tangled vines of some forgotten garden plant, pushed through dark alleys in what she hoped was an unpredictable path guaranteed to lose her pursuer.

Who was she kidding? As her breath hitched into a cramping knot at her side, she just hoped Silas was still alive and she wouldn't get killed before he found her.

Terror fueled every step. She stumbled over the scattered remains of a broken wall, caught herself against the opposite corner and tried not to panic as she looked right and left. Her shaking light swept over the back street, picked out hardy moss poking up from the crevices and cracks underfoot before it was swallowed by shadow. Pipe rain poured in a waterfall around her, shearing away blood and mud from her skin and—please, God—muffling her panting breaths.

She dragged her free hand back through her hair and trusted her gut. Her gut said left.

Her brain demanded to know why.

No time. She turned left. The street, no more than a one-lane path, didn't lend itself well to running. Every other step clattered, shifted, twisted on roots and stones that seemed to get thicker with every minute. She battered away clinging strands of wet cobwebs as she ran into them, the light weaving wildly in front of her, and bit back a scream as a fat-bodied brown spider smacked into her cheek and rebounded away on a tensile thread.

Shuddering, she clenched her fists, ducked low, and tried not to think about eight grasping legs tangled in her hair.

She couldn't stop to check, couldn't give in to panic.

The man who'd tried to kill her didn't seem to feel the kicks she'd aimed at him. He didn't stop when she'd stomped on his foot, or when she'd jammed her stiff fingers into his neck.

But, oh, she'd felt every brush of his fingers. Like pins and needles, like fire ants marching over her flesh, he'd hurt her. Made her feel it. Made her fear it, all in the space of a second.

A hell of a power to claim.

She jammed Silas's gun into the waistband of her jeans and wondered how many bullets she had left, if the pain witch had even cared when she'd shot wildly behind her as she ran. Wondered if she'd be able to pull the trigger when he caught up to her, looked him dead in the eyes.

She ran across the bisecting road without stopping to check the area. Her skin crawled, and she tried not to visualize the big man with a thatch of graying hair behind her. Stalking her.

Smiling at her.

Rocks clattered somewhere nearby. Footsteps splashed, or at least she thought it was footsteps in the pounding rain. Maybe it was just water cascading from the ceiling, so far ahead. Maybe it was him.

Maybe he was right behind her.

Her breath sobbed in her lungs as she jumped over the low, rusted fence separating the ruined road from whatever lay behind it. Twisted metal snagged her flesh, tearing through her palm like so much shredded paper. She yelped, landed on the other side in awkward pain as the ground dipped much lower than she expected.

Cradling her injured hand to her chest, she staggered upright and limped for the stark stone building thrust toward the asphalt sky. If this were any sort of ghost story, she realized as she froze in place, lightning would spear through the ambient dark like a warning.

The artificial ceiling didn't allow for lightning. And, damn it, this wasn't a ghost story. This was real.

Jessie stared in horror at the giant, old-fashioned clock mounted to the small stone cathedral.

Its glass had been shattered, leaving jagged remnants of white to grin ominously through the dark and rain. The heavy iron hands had rusted in place, and whatever mechanism had kept it grinding before the earthquake had long since died. The light began to waver as her hands shook violently.

"Beware the tomb that time forgot," she whispered. Her skin went clammy, colder than even the rain. She tightened her grip on the gun and didn't know if she should scream or laugh.

Beware the tomb that time forgot. I don't know what happens there, but if you find it, you can't stay. Don't stay, Jessie.

A shattered clock over a ruined church. Caleb's prophecies had never been wrong. She turned, her heart hammering.

"Where are you?" The masculine voice slipped through the eerie silence of the Old Seattle streets. Fighting back a scream of terror, of violent frustration and fear, Jessie turned back toward the church and ran for her life.

The steps she jumped were crumbling, time and erosion wearing away the edges. They led down to a shallow moat of standing water, green and brown with algae and slime, and she slipped and splashed through it. Taking the stairs two at a time, she climbed toward the ruined shell of the abandoned church and pulled the gun from her waistband. Her grip was clammy.

Time had eaten any defenses the church once had. She pushed past the entry arch, staggered into what had maybe been a lobby before. Maybe a meeting room. Now it echoed and glimmered in faded, absentminded glory. Shadows filled it end to end, caught on broken remnants of statuary and fallen icons. Littered remains of rotted red carpet curled like forgotten paper in the rain.

She crossed the ground, searching wildly for another way out. Another exit, a window that didn't have protective bars wrapped around them to save stained glass that no longer existed. A door that didn't rot in the shadows of crumbled walls and fallen ceilings.

There was only the one.

She wasn't safe here.

Don't stay, Jessie.

Torn between pain and prophecy, she wavered.

"Jessie."

She screamed, the flashlight clattered to the floor and sent echoes skittering from wall to wall. Whirling, she pointed Silas's gun at the menacing silhouette in the doorway. Her arms shook beneath the weight of the cold metal, her eyes stung, but she couldn't waver. She couldn't let him see her flag.

Beware the tomb that time forgot.

Her tomb?

No. *His.* She braced herself, cupped her gun hand with her wounded palm.

"Jessie," he said again. He moved, detached from the shadows that clung to him. "Jessie, don't shoot."

She trembled. "Don't move," she warned. The wet stone ate at her too-high voice; bounced it back in a million echoes. "Don't move. Don't fucking touch me again."

Silas spread his hands, slowly at his sides. "Easy,"

he said, so gently she wasn't sure she heard it over the hammering of her heart. "Easy, sunshine. Don't shoot."

"Stay back!"

"It's me, Jessie." His voice reached out across the small divide. Cut through the cold and sweat and the fear. He took another step, hands in plain sight.

She bit hard on her lower lip as tears began to blind her. Her finger tightened on the trigger.

"Jessie," he said sharply. Harshly. Another step. "It's me, it's Silas. Everything is okay, you're safe. You're okay."

"N-no," she whispered, shuddering.

Silas closed the distance, step by infinitesimally slow step. "He's dead, Jess. You got him. He's dead, do you hear me?" He reached out, cautious. "Give me the gun. Let it go."

Her arms shook. Her shoulders screamed at the deceptive weight of the gun. She took in a deep, shuddering breath as his hand closed over the barrel.

Shockingly fast, he pulled the pistol from her hands and tossed it to the side. It hit the wet floor, skidded. She sobbed in relief, sheer nerves, as she curled her fingers into his jacket and yanked his mouth to hers.

Maybe it wasn't what he'd expected, or what she'd intended. He grunted in surprise, but she gave him no time to rationalize. To think.

She didn't want to rationalize. She didn't want to think of anything but the hot, hard, strong maleness of his body, the taste of his lips against hers. She pushed into him, against him, as if she could crawl inside his coat with him. She tried to climb him as she devoured his mouth and his warmth.

Surprise turned into a wildfire of wanting. Silas gripped her hips in both hands and dragged her closer, shoved them both back as he took over the kiss. Deepened it. His tongue plunged into her mouth, danced with hers as she tried desperately to reclaim possession of the moment.

He didn't let her. He curled his fingers against the soft curves of her ass, lifted her hard against him. She gasped in surprise, in shock as cold stone hit her back, whimpered with absolute pleasure as she wrapped her legs around his hips and ground herself against the erection clearly fighting the prison of his jeans.

He didn't waste any time. Fiercely, almost angrily, he shoved at her jacket until it slid off her shoulders. Yanked at the hem of her camisole until one fragile strap snapped and her breasts spilled into his hands. The barely controlled aggression simmering under every movement only drove her higher, burned hotter.

Silas tore his mouth away from hers with a muttered curse and dropped his lips to one nipple, a damp circle that had her crying out in wicked encouragement. He laved at the sensitive point, pinched the other with clever, callused fingers until she writhed beyond all thought or reason.

Their gasps and low sounds of pleasure reverberated back from the damp walls, whipped her up even higher as she heard raw, aching need in every sound he made. That she made.

Jessie dropped her fingers to her jeans, struggled to unbutton the wet denim and laughed when he forced her hands away to work on it himself.

His eyes burned into hers, wildly green in the shadows and glittering with impatient desire. Desire for her. For her body spread beneath him, for her cries against his skin. She knew it as clearly as she knew her own wants.

And she wanted this. Him. *Now.*

Power shimmered. She ruthlessly stomped it down.

This was her time. Hers.

He seized her legs, uncurled them from around his waist and lowered her to the floor. Wordless, even rough, he spun her around, pushed her against the wall with one warm hand centered squarely over the tattoo inked across the middle of her back. She gasped as cold stone pressed into her sensitized flesh, groaned as her nipples scraped against it in a white-hot point of pleasure-pain. Cool air ghosted over her thighs as he peeled her rain-stubborn jeans down to her knees.

Jessie cried out in shock and torturous need as he found her wet and swollen beneath his questing fingers. His own encouraging murmur answered back, praise and curses both. She splayed her palms against the wall, pressed her fiery cheek to the cold stone. Reveled.

Wanted.

Silas was everything she had to have. Fire and hard demand, tumultuous need. Her body strained against him, her hips lifted in desperate, silent encouragement, and she gasped against the wall as his erection nudged at her swollen flesh. She whimpered, a gasping "Yes!" as he plunged deep, hard and thick and perfect.

Overloaded, oversensitized, it was all she could do to hang on to the wall and feel him fill her. Warm, solid, *real*. Hers.

For now.

He locked his arms against the wall, braced himself against her, every muscle in his body shaking as he tried to hold back. To wait. "Jessie," he began, tortured control and, oh, God, concern.

She didn't want concern.

She shoved back, rocked against the rough denim still covering his hips. He threw back his head, grabbing her waist in both hands. So controlled. She rocked again, harder. He swore.

She smiled through the flush of her building orgasm. Rode a wave of spiraling heat. He pushed inside her, withdrew, filled her again and again. He stroked her body with every thrust, took her higher, tighter, until she arched back with a wild cry and fragmented on the waves of a climax that rocked her down to her curling toes.

He was a breath, a guttural shout behind her, pulled into the same vortex of uncurling sensation by the shuddering clench of her own muscles around him.

She collapsed against the wall and gasped for breath to fill her aching, winded lungs. He fell over her, his hair dripping across her shoulder, his clothing wet and rough against her back.

It took her a moment to realize that his hand covered her own, their fingers entangled against the wet, cold wall. Polished wood gleamed. *Nina.*

Her heart slowed its frenetic beat.

"Jessie," he murmured against her shoulder. "Jesus, sunshine. Are you hurt?"

She wasn't sure she had an answer for that one.

Cursing, Silas withdrew, made her gasp as he spun her around. His eyes searched hers. "Jessie? Did I hurt you?"

Only since they'd met.

She shook her head. "No," she said. She pulled up her jeans as an excuse to break his hold. "Quite the contrary," she added, letting her lips curve into the smile that hovered over her confusion. Let him see the lazy, deeply spent satisfaction he'd left her with.

And none of the fear.

His brow cleared, but only marginally. Her poor missionary.

I don't know what happens there, Caleb had said, but Jessie knew. She shouldn't have stayed.

Beware the tomb that time forgot. It would change everything.

And nothing at all.

"Fuck me."

Jessie looked up from retrieving her jacket, languidly amused. "What, again?"

Silas didn't laugh. Instead he reached for her, spread his palm over the ruins of her tank top. Her heart sped up again in her chest. Greedy heart.

"You're bleeding."

She looked down in mild confusion. "What? Oh,"

she added as she held up her palm. The tear bisecting her lifeline oozed sluggishly. "I forgot. It's just a scratch."

Anger crackled around him as he encircled her wrist. "It needs a bandage."

She frowned. "It needs a washing and it'll be fine."

Silas looked down at her in silence, waiting. Patient as all hell *now*. She rolled her eyes, defeated annoyance. "Okay, fine. Take me back to your safe house and out of this—" Blood. Rot. Golden beads in a room drowning in death. "This godforsaken place." She blinked hard. "Please."

He touched her cheek. It was the worst thing he could have done.

It was exactly what she needed.

She turned her face into his warm, callused palm and resigned herself to heartbreak for it when he dropped his hand as if she'd burned him. He stepped back. Wordlessly he collected the gun he'd thrown away.

If she survived this mess, she knew it wouldn't be unscarred.

Jessie fisted her fingers around the ache in her palm. "Let's get out of here."

CHAPTER NINE

"One down for sure."

Caleb Leigh stared at the pedestal thrusting up from the mossy brick circle. Behind him, the pretty black-haired witch he only knew as Alicia watched him.

"Nick was the first one they found," she added. Prodded.

He knew all this already. He'd known when he woke up this morning after a fitful few hours' sleep, and her faintly mocking tone only dragged claws down his patience now.

He grunted a nonanswer.

She took that as invitation and circled around to stand beside him. Like him, her eyes settled on the pedestal. There was something remarkably . . . empty about its hollow slant. "All signs point to one hunter for sure, maybe two. There were a few signs Nick tried to zap whatever hit him, but no other bodies around." A beat. "Except the one in the circle."

Caleb glanced at her. "Too dead to be much help," he said dryly.

She shrugged. "If Kojo—"

"Alicia, she was obviously dead *before* the hunter came," he explained impatiently, cutting into her what-if. "She only knows what she saw when alive. Kojo's powers of the dead won't help here." Or rather, it would, but not in a way that'd help *him*. He needed the zombie witch's raising magic well away from the corpse of Delia Carpenter.

After all, she'd died with his secrets fresh in her mind, and his face was the last thing she had ever seen.

Caleb should have cut out her tongue when he had the chance.

Alicia's bright blue gaze would have scalpeled the skin from his body, if it could. In his peripheral vision, she smiled tightly. "As you say, soothsayer."

He knew a problem when he saw it. Alicia was the coven master's pet witch, and she knew it, but it wasn't enough. She desperately wanted power. She relished the coven master's attentions, and she bided her time like a cat, waiting for the moment when Caleb would slip up and end up with his ass in the fire. She'd want ringside seats, and he was determined to make sure she never got the chance.

At least for the moment, he was safer than she could ever be. He knew the future; his prophecies were as invaluable to the coven master as gold. That was something Alicia of the sky blue eyes would never harness. Not unless she tore it from his still-breathing body, which wasn't something she knew how to do.

Few of his fellow coven witches knew how to forcefully transfer power the way he did.

He smiled back at his reluctant ally, knew it for the grim slant it was and didn't care to mitigate his even tone. "John is dead."

"How do you know?" He said nothing. He didn't have to. After a beat, a dull, red flush crept up under her pale skin and she fisted her delicate hands. "Where?"

"Pattern out. You'll probably find him out in the open."

She nodded tersely and spun around without another word. He heard her footsteps stalk away, crunching over moss and brick and shattered stone.

Caleb closed his eyes, his chin drooping. John Cunningham had been the closest thing he'd had to a friend. A hard man to get close to. He'd taught Caleb how to play poker, real poker. They played for laughs.

Now he was dead.

And he wasn't going to be the last.

"Fools," he muttered. *Morons*. Magical puppets dancing on the end of a very tangled string. He had to make sure they stayed the fuck out of the tiny room with its bloody decoration, and he had to redirect them away from further inquiries while he could.

Delia's wasn't the only corpse in Old Seattle, but

he wasn't responsible for them all. Another dead body wouldn't necessarily lead right to him; it was just another gruesome scene in a tomb that fed on them.

But the Mission's presence changed everything.

He withdrew a small metal penlight from his pocket and studied the plain black cylinder. How had they found the scene of his crime?

Caleb was not a man who believed in coincidences.

If he could bring the hunter's name and description to the coven, it'd be another achievement for him. Another fuck-you for Alicia. It'd buy him more time, more freedom, and earn him greater trust from the coven master who guided them all.

It would take a ritual to focus on the greater picture, but as he curled both hands around the metal cylinder, he was unable to help himself from taking a peek now. From tracing the pattern that wove itself around the item, as clear as a mark of ownership to his magical sight.

Caleb had an ace up his sleeve sharp enough to kill. He knew about the Mission tattoos, the holy protection that was just another version of magic—not that the Church would ever admit it.

What they didn't know was that the seals didn't matter to his brand of magic. As long as he focused on time, as long as he didn't touch the hunters themselves with his searching power, the tattoos failed to activate.

Loopholes. They always missed the loopholes, and the future, past, and present of a man was a damned big loophole.

Swallowing hard, Caleb seized the magic.

He expected to see death, to see the determined glare of a witch hunter's bigoted stare. He wanted a look at the man or woman who killed without remorse or mercy, who beat a man's head in with raw strength and bare hands.

What filled every sense he possessed sent his heart pounding into his throat.

Jessie.

Her smile, her laugh. Her skin smeared with blood as she fought fiercely for her life. The sky rained fire down upon her. The water turned bloody at her feet. She screamed.

She screamed his name.

Caleb tore himself free of the vision to find himself on his knees, huddled around the tiny metal cylinder as if it could protect the sister he'd long ago abandoned. Standing water seeped into his pants, soaked into his legs, and reminded him that members of his coven fanned out around him.

They searched for the corpse of their brother.

They couldn't see Caleb like this. Weakness would beget questions, and questions would cause suspicion to undermine everything he worked for. Shaking, heart hammering, he sucked in a harsh, gasping breath and straightened.

The witch hunter who owned this little tool was going to kill her. One day, someday soon maybe, he'd stumble on her trail and hunt her down, a fragile fox tormented by bloodthirsty hounds.

He knew the scene of her death as if it were carved onto the backs of his eyelids. It was his own prophecy, dreamed a year ago as he slept on the anniversary of his mother's death. But now he had the face, the name to go with the warning. Now he knew *how* her death would arrive.

Caleb had to make sure she was alive. Time ticked by, too fast, damn it.

He needed to know more. To see more. Could he risk it?

He set his jaw, knowing he had no choice. All the preparations for the Coven of the Unbinding, all the plans and careful maneuverings weren't going to mean anything if Jessie was just going to be executed anyway.

Caleb had already sold his soul to the coven. He'd murdered. He'd tortured and schemed and made deals with the demons that rode his back, but a man had his limits. His sister was off-fucking-limits.

She had to be.

He turned and strode across the square, leaving the others to sanitize the area.

By the end of his spell, he'd know everything he needed to know about Silas Smith, missionary and murderer.

Dead man walking.

CHAPTER TEN

Once they'd cleared the old city tunnel, Silas pushed the engine for all it was worth. There weren't any cops this low in the city, and he wanted the hell away from the ruins.

No, he wanted *Jessie* away.

She shifted beside him, her scored hand curled against her chest. "It's okay," she began. He shot her a look that telegraphed every icy calm, murderous fantasy he was feeling at the moment. She shut up.

She also looked away, which made him feel even more like an ass than he already was.

That was twice he'd put her in danger. Twice she'd been hurt because of him, because of her goddamned brother and because Silas himself was incapable of keeping her out of trouble.

He wasn't going to be responsible for her funeral, too.

The truck lumbered through the barren streets and it was all he could do to keep the wheel from coming off in his rigid grip.

As if it weren't bad enough, as if he hadn't screwed up enough already, he'd gone and shoved her against a wall in the fucking ruins of a fucking dead city and watched her come apart against him. Around him.

Silas clenched his teeth. Her body had been slick and tight, her voice breathy and fragmented as he filled her. Bent against a goddamned wall.

Gentle, Smith. Really tender.

But he didn't goddamned do tender.

"Oh, stop." Her voice cut through his thoughts like a sharpened knife.

He glanced over, met her eyes. They remained shadowed, dark smudges of exhaustion like bruises at her cheeks, but her mouth curved up. "If you're scowling because you're trying to come up with a way to apologize for what we did, save your breath. I'm a big girl."

"I should." Silas shifted his gaze back to the road. "It wasn't exactly—"

"Yes," she cut in with entirely too much gratification. "Yes, it was."

"Damn it, Jessie." He scowled. "You're bleeding, exhausted." And he could have gone his whole life without knowing how warm her skin was around the odd bar code tattoo imprinted into her spine.

Or how tight her body was around him.

And how she breathed his name when she orgasmed.

His jaw clenched hard enough to audibly pop.

Her eyes narrowed. She shifted in her seat to face him, old springs creaking. "Wait a minute. Is that your problem? That I was hurt?"

He guided the rattling pickup onto the main carousel and breathed deeply through his nose. It didn't help. He smelled old leather and rain-drenched woman. Her warm, welcoming scent. His cock stirred; damn it, he wanted her again. Still.

"No," she decided, shaking her head. "You're mad you weren't in control."

"You're covered in blood." It whipped out of him like a fist. "You wouldn't have even been down there if I hadn't taken you—"

"Whoa!" Jessie leaned across the cab to shove her face directly into his line of sight. A thunderstorm frothed wildly behind her summer eyes. "Hold it right there, Agent High-and-Mighty. You didn't *take* me anywhere, I went because I knew where to go and you didn't. *I* took *you*."

Silas didn't like that any more than he liked seeing traces of blood cling to her neck from the hand she cradled against her chest. Didn't like knowing she was right.

He glanced over his shoulder once, cut across three lanes of traffic, and firmed his grip on the wheel. "This is how it plays out," he said, low and tight. "We're going back to the safe house. You are going to stay there—"

"Fat chance."

"You are going to *stay there*," he repeated louder, overriding her hot challenge by volume and single-minded authority. His head pounded. "Where it's safe and where the bastards that peeled apart that woman can't find you."

"No." She straightened her shoulders. Daring, determined.

Jesus. She was going to haunt him forever.

Especially if she died, which was a sure possibility as long as she stayed with him.

"You don't have a choice," he said. "If you won't stay put, I'll handcuff you to the goddamned bed."

Her eyes gleamed. "Dare you."

"*No.*"

She didn't laugh. Challenge practically screamed from every line of her body as she settled back into her corner of the cab. Watched him. "You need me. I know things you don't. We're partners."

"Bullshit, we're not partners," Silas growled, so low that it ripped out of his throat. She flinched, as if he'd reached out and slapped her. She turned away.

That's right, sunshine. I'm a total bastard.

He forced his attention to the road. "I'm the agent here, I'm the goddamned one trained to hunt and retrieve and kill." Her face jerked back toward him, her eyes narrowed to catlike slits. "You're a stripper, Jessie, you're trained to sucker men. Don't ever think there's more to this than what it is."

Icy realization crystallized behind her drawn, exhausted features. "You son of a bitch," she said. Only part was hurt. The rest was pure feminine insult.

Hell, she was spectacular.

"That's right," he said tightly.

"Yeah." She turned in her seat, faced the front

again with her arms folded stiffly over her chest. "Well, fuck you, too, Agent Smith."

Silas swallowed back an angry kick of his own conscience as he set his sights on the windshield and drove them back to safety. The rain had eased to a light drizzle, barely even enough for the windshield wipers he clicked off.

He'd call in someone else to watch her.

As he guided the truck onto the off-ramp, he wondered if he could trust anyone else to do it.

Jessie lasted all of five minutes in boiling, seething silence before she lost the battle with herself. "For the record," she said tersely, shattering the uneasy silence like a gunshot, "I've never stripped in my life."

His knuckles went white against the steering wheel. "I don't care."

"I do," she shot back. "I worked at the Pussycat Perch as a bartender."

"You say tomato—"

"*Tomato* doesn't even *sound* like bartender, you asshole." Jessie struggled to rein in her temper. Staring at the stacked blocks of tenement housing passing out the window didn't do anything to make it easier. Images of knocking him on his ass danced across her vision. "I sling beer, but I've never slung my body." *So there* seemed juvenile. She settled for a scathing "Unless you're planning to leave some money on the table . . ."

The safe house complex eased into view, its dim lights a steady blue-tinged beacon in the lower city gloom. Silas's teeth clicked together. "Leave it, Jessie," he said through them, downshifting so fast that the truck dipped.

"*You* leave it," she shot back, reaching for the dash before the lurching momentum made her kiss it. A car blitzed past them, horn blaring loudly. She ignored it. "You're the one who—"

A shudder rippled up her spine.

Magic.

Jessie's eyes abruptly unfocused, left her blind as the murky lights of the street shimmered.

Power coalesced, tangling like a net spun too fast. She felt it, prickling like needles over her skin, *saw* it with senses that she couldn't name. She sucked in a breath.

"Jessie?" Silas's voice, muted as if through a layer of cotton.

Magic spun, invisible but *there*. Tighter, faster, sparking. *A trap.* Right now. *Right, now.* "Go right," she said hoarsely. "Silas, turn right."

"What?"

"Now!" Jessie grabbed the steering wheel in both hands. She jerked it, hard enough to fall back into the passenger side of the cab as Silas swore and struggled to guide the careening truck around the other cars around them. The tires squealed with the effort, caught air and listed to the side.

The air scorched white-hot around them. A nanosecond later, Silas stomped on the gas pedal as a ball of fire exploded through the Mission safe house.

Jessie whirled in place, seized the back of the seat. Framed in the rear window, she watched as flames ate at the old brownstone. Glass and wood rained to the street below, sparks and cinders smoldering to smoke on the wet pavement. Debris peppered the surrounding tenements and shattered windows as tires screeched, car horns shrieking in futile warning as fenders collided. Silas deftly guided the shaking truck through sudden chaos.

Lights blazed from nearby windows, doors slammed open as wild-eyed people staggered out to watch the sudden show. There would be casualties. A death toll.

A magical trap. Just for . . . Who? Her?

Silas?

How had she known to *look*?

It took her a long moment to realize she was shaking.

"What the hell was that?"

Jessie stared out the back window as the flames licked higher. Hotter. Hungry. Just fire and heat. The sense of magic was gone. "I—" She what? She *saw* it?

"Jessie."

She licked her lips, slanted him a sidelong smile. "You won't believe me." Truth.

"Try me."

And the lie. "I've lived on my own for a very long time. You learn what to look for, or you end up dead."

He watched the rearview mirror closely as he navigated through the flickering orange streets. Cars stalled, slowed to watch the carnage, but he didn't use the truck's horn. "What did you see?"

Jessie turned around when she heard the sirens blaring in the distance. New Seattle took fire seriously.

God forbid anything happen to the foundation that kept the sparkling glass towers high.

She sighed. "I don't even know for sure. I just saw the building and something seemed off. Kind of out of place."

He grunted.

Was it enough? Jessie cradled her wounded palm in her lap. "I figured your security's tight enough, if something was out of place there had to be a big reason."

When he only scowled at the windshield, she gloated. Just a little. "I guess that puts a kink in your plan, doesn't it, Agent Smith?"

That telltale muscle leaped in his jaw.

Gotcha, she thought. She pulled the ancient seat belt over her chest. "Where to, then?" A beat. "Partner."

"Fuck." Silas glanced at the GPS on his dash. "The upper city is the only option left to keep you safe."

Jessie stiffened. "Topside? With your agents?"

He glanced at her. "We've got a suite of offices on the executive levels. It's considered part of topside, yes, but I can get us both through the security checks without a problem."

Hell, no. "How do you know it'll be any safer there?"

He opened his mouth to retort something guaranteed to annoy her, or at least make her life even more complicated than it already was. But then he closed it, surprising her, and said nothing.

Jessie seized the opportunity. "You're thinking the same thing I am," she said. "How did they know where the safe house was? Will I actually be any safer topside with all that security?" Where she'd stick out like a sore thumb, watched every moment by cameras and witch hunters and rich people.

No way.

"What do you suggest, then?" he said, clearly aggravated as he rolled his shoulders. "We can't drive forever, damn it."

"No, but we don't have to." She cast a short, mental prayer that what she remembered was as accurate now as it was then. "Stay off the carousel and head east."

He frowned at her, clearly unhappy with her direction. "What's east?"

Witch hunters had their safe houses. Witches had theirs.

At least, Jessie desperately hoped so. "A few years back, I worked for a place called the Pink Beaver." She shot him a glance, but his eyes remained on the road.

Smart hunter.

"It operated on lower streets than the Perch, a real dive. I met a girl there who slummed it for kicks or something." Jessie silently apologized to the witch who'd taught her how to blend into the lower city flesh markets. "She set up an apartment for some of the more trouble-prone girls. Said anyone who needed it was welcome to stay until the trouble passed."

"Nice of her."

"She was a nice stripper," Jessie replied mildly, and glanced to the streetlights flicking on along the street. More lights shattered the darkening city around them, red and blue speeding toward the orange glow framed by Silas's window.

His profile cut a hard silhouette against the lit glass. "Which way?"

Jessie ran the odds. What were her options? Topside, levels above everything she knew and surrounded by witch hunters? Or the safe house possibly occupied by witches.

No contest. She gave him the address.

CHAPTER ELEVEN

The back roads were a bitch to navigate, but the satellite system guided him unerringly through the maze of the mid-level streets. The carousel would have been the easier route. Shorter, quicker.

Instead he called himself a fool as he drove through the darkening city streets and watched her sleep beside him.

Exhaustion had finally taken its toll. One minute she'd been watching the light dim toward night, and the next she'd tilted toward the dashboard and would have fallen to the grimy floor if he hadn't been ready to catch her.

Now she slept curled on the seat. Her boots were

tucked against his hip, her cheek nestled in the crook of her arm beneath the passenger side window.

Silas knew that kind of fatigue. She'd been on the go for nearly twenty-four hours, never mind the piss-poor sleep she might have managed tied to that heater. That she lasted this long made something in him warm.

Pride. Approval.

Annoyance.

He turned his eyes back to the road. Deliberately ignored the silken strands of gold clinging to her mouth.

By now, the local Mission chapter knew he wasn't checking in. Peterson was probably popping a gasket and demanding his team perform a miracle to provide him with answers.

He needed them to leave him alone. Especially if there *was* a leak in the Mission offices.

A hunter working with witches? Some sort of electronic espionage? God only knew. If he shared his suspicions with just anyone, he could tip off the mole.

If there was one. *Fuck.* He hated politics, but she was right. Since that first magical attack at the Church hall, the seed of doubt had been germinating.

Silas held the wheel steady with one hand, reached below the seat with the other. It took some fumbling but he managed to haul the dark green duffel bag from its place with minimum noise. One eye on the road, he found the comm unit tucked into its customary side pocket and flipped it open.

A whole mess of calls. Each angrier than the last, he'd bet.

Ignoring the alerts, he punched in the number from memory and clipped the earpiece to the shell of his ear. The tiny microphone tucked against his temple vibrated, a near-silent signal that the call connected.

"How long has it been since your last confession?"

Silas curled a lip. "Smith, checking in."

"Hot damn, Smith! Where the hell have you been?"

Beside him, Jessie murmured something husky and low as she shifted on the narrow seat. "Around," he said quietly. "Who is this?"

"Alan Eckhart," replied the man that Silas could now place as the bald hunter with the three-note tune. "I'm on the tubes tonight."

Silas nodded. Good. "Here's what I've got, are you ready?"

"Fire away, chief."

Quietly, careful to keep his voice at an even level, Silas told him about the body below the streets, the witches outside the grisly scene. The Mission house up in flames.

Silas left out the details no one else needed to know. Like Jessie's surprising tattoo. The sound she made in her throat as she'd climaxed around him, and the way she'd turned her face into his hand as if she trusted him. God damn it, she shouldn't trust him.

"That it?" Eckhart asked. At Silas's affirmative sound, the older man whistled his odd tune again. "Hell on toast, Smith, you get around."

"Tell me about it."

"You said one of the witches pulled lightning out of thin air, right? Red hair? Smile like a jack-o'-lantern?"

"You know him?"

"Like recurring herpes," Eckhart replied dryly. "We know his name is Nick Wallace, but that's all we've got on him. He's one of the more ballsy witches in this city. His blood's linked to at least fourteen ritual killings in the past year alone."

"Fuck me running," Silas muttered. "Well, he's dead now."

"And the Leigh witch?"

Silas hesitated. He glanced at Jessie beside him, grimaced. "Nothing yet. Your lab ready to receive some blood?"

There was another, longer pause. "Whose blood?"

"The dead woman's, and some random samples from the scene."

"Oh, sure. Where?"

Silas found his gaze sliding back around to Jessie's sleep-furrowed forehead, the downward curve to her mouth. "Got a street number. Take it down." At the missionary's confirmation, Silas rattled off the address pulsing on the navigation screen.

"We'll hit the burning wreck you left us first. Peterson's got us on double duty, so we'll see you by oh-six," Eckhart said, so cheerfully Silas almost believed he wasn't talking about six in the morning. "You safe there tonight?"

"I think we lost anyone tailing us," Silas said, slowing the truck as the satellite system flickered a notice. "The seal's been quiet and she's out cold."

Eckhart grunted, something that sounded more curious than sympathetic. "Hurt?"

"Her or me?"

"Yes," he replied without missing a beat.

Silas turned the engine off, and withdrew the keys, annoyed with himself to realize he did it all while trying to make as little noise as possible. He sighed. "Minor," he replied shortly. "Peterson talk to you?"

The line was quiet. Eckhart's voice was a carefully modulated verbal shrug as he said, "About what, exactly?"

"Fuck, Eckhart."

The man whistled. "No, not really. But he didn't need to. Your reputation precedes you, man. Just remember you don't have to work alone."

Right. Just like he didn't have to wrap himself in Jessica Leigh or kill her homicidal brother. Pain spiked through his hands, sudden and sharp, and he blinked to find his fingers curled so tightly around the steering wheel that they'd gone bloodless with strain.

He peeled them off, one by one. "Sure. I'll see you guys in the morning. Smith, out." He disconnected the line before Eckhart could say anything else.

Annoyed with himself for the knot in his chest, angry at the pictures that slid jumbled and colorful through his mind, Silas took a deep breath and held it.

His eyes scanned the street.

Were they safe? Here? Compared to a dark alley in the middle of a witch-infested city block, sure. By any other standards, he'd seen better.

A lot better.

The lights flickered weakly in the dark, a faint crackle of energy overwhelmed by the rush of traffic barreling past. They hadn't spared the space for this run-down complex. The carousel shoved right up against the shabby buildings.

If the middle levels of the city counted as extreme working class, then this was the wrong side of the shithole tracks.

Lights glowed in a few of the windows. Silhouettes passed, punctuated by the occasional raised voice and the constant hum of passing cars. He didn't see anyone loitering outside, but that didn't mean they weren't there.

Still, it seemed harmless enough. He'd take an ordinary idiot over a witch with a grudge any day.

Silas glanced at Jessie's sleeping figure. Weighed his options. Mentally kicked himself. He was an adult, and more than capable of reining in his sexual drive. Despite what his dick telegraphed to his brain.

Briskly, deliberately, he splayed one hand over her hip—Christ, she was warm—and shook her gently. "Wake up, Jess."

She shifted. Her lashes fluttered once as she inhaled deeply, stretching her long, long legs over his lap. Everything in his body stood to attention, from his pulse to his crotch to the part of his brain that demanded her body beneath him. Writhing against him. Preferably naked.

He'd take mostly naked. There was room in the cab.

Damn. He had to get a grip. Ignoring her fluid stretch, he reached over the dash and turned off the nav system. It gave him something else to handle, something that wasn't the smooth curve of her calves, or the warm inside of her thigh.

"Hey," she murmured sleepily.

"You awake?"

Jessie pushed at the tangled fall of her hair, blinking. "Maybe." She elbowed herself upright on the seat, withdrew her legs to set both feet on the dirty floor. "Define awake."

"Get your brain working." Silas cracked open the door. "I'm going to check it out, so stay put."

"We here?"

"Yeah."

"Key's in the knocker." She rubbed at her eyes, the gesture too fucking delicate for his peace of mind. Silas got the hell out of the truck before he gave in to the temptation to haul her across the seat and onto his lap.

Before he tasted her sleep-softened mouth, her skin. Her goddamned sweet skin.

The chilly air did little to cool him down as Silas strode through the arch that was all that passed for a welcome. It was long past dark, but three children watched him stride by with wide, curious eyes. They rolled a ball listlessly between them.

Sporadic bursts of Spanish filtered out from the door behind them, melded with rapid gunfire from a television blaring too loud. To his right, a wall of mailboxes had been mostly torn apart. Only the occasional white envelope peeked from a crooked panel bolted in place.

Secure, it was not.

He looked up, briefly studied the wall hemming the courtyard, and let his gaze climb the towering silhouette of the city proper.

What was it that she'd called it? A layer cake. Fitting enough. A myriad of electrical stars twinkled far above, muted by distance and the sheer volume of lights between these poverty-stricken streets and the glassy gleam of the upper city.

The skyscrapers were almost indistinguishable from the rest of it, nothing more than a muted haze. Maybe topside would be safer, but not at the Holy Order's facility. He was fourteen years out of this city's game; who else could he trust?

No one.

The key was in the knocker?

Silas found the apartment number in the corner of the littered courtyard. The door had once been painted some sort of brown-red color to match the brick half missing underfoot. Now it was a peeling mess of gouged paint, mud, and footprints.

It was solid, at least. That was something.

He studied the plain brass knocker. Nothing seemed out of place. Two wide bolts drilled into the door on either side, nailing the metal knocker to the door so securely that it didn't so much as wiggle when he tested it.

Footsteps crunched behind him. He didn't have to look to know she'd defied him. Again.

"It's not hard." Jessie stepped up to the cement block that pretended to be a front stoop. "You just have to— Oh, what?"

"Didn't I say wait in the car?" Silas took her arm, tugged her between his body and the door. It placed her between him and the rest of the world.

She rolled her eyes. "Sorry. I thought you might need help." Sleep-tousled, dewy-eyed, she looked about as dangerous as a newborn kitten.

He grimaced. "So where's the key?"

"Plain sight magic." Jessie slid her finger along the wide, flat back of the knocker. She pressed, twisted, and something clicked inside the metal support.

Silas stared. "I'll be damned."

"Genius, isn't it?" The segment of the brass unhinged, slid out in a long length of filed metal. With a twist, a jimmy, the whole damn thing came off in her hand. She inserted it into the doorknob and grinned over her shoulder at him when the tumblers clicked open.

He was still shaking his head as he followed her inside.

The apartment boasted more clutter than the mission house, but it had a lived-in feel that Silas noted. It smelled neater, somehow, more homey, with lingering traces of something smoky. Cigarettes? No, not sharp enough.

Jessie paused as his fingers encircled her arm. "Hang on," he whispered. She shut the door with a nudge, but to his relief, she nodded.

Silas quickly checked each room.

The bathroom was small, plain, with a cracked tile tub and a mirror framed in old metal hanging from the wall. The bedroom surprised him as he shoved open the door. Woven blankets hung from every available hook and corner, a riot of color and patterns. He pulled a few down as he passed, ensuring nobody hid beneath the heavy folds, but only shrugged when the same smell of spice and—

And what? Cigars? Incense?

He rubbed his face. Did it matter? No, it damn well didn't. Proof positive he needed sleep. At least a few hours would do it. He'd lived on less.

Silas dropped the blankets on the single bed and turned away.

This time, much to his surprise, she'd waited in the living room. Three out of four deadbolts had been slid into place, and she sent him an inquisitive look as she locked the last one in. "Shower?" she asked.

The blood fled his brain to pulse thickly in his jeans. He swallowed. "Flip you for it."

"Literally?"

Silas opened his mouth, saw visions of himself hauling her to that colorful bed, tearing off her clothes, sliding deeply into her warm, wet body until her eyes went blind and that teasing, sexy mouth called his name.

Damn it.

Her smile faded. "Silas?"

"Take it," he said gruffly, even as she said, "You can have it." They stared at each other for a long moment. Awkward. Uncertain.

Stupid.

When she laughed, it crept out from between the fingers she raised to her lips, skimmed over his skin like something hot and spicy on a winter day. Her eyes gleamed. "No, you go ahead," she offered firmly. Lightly. "I'll see if there's anything to eat."

Silas shook his head, hard enough to pop the bones in his neck, and muttered, "Fine." He escaped into the small bathroom before he turned himself into a fucking idiot.

Wasting no time in stripping down, he paused to lean over the stained sink and study the scratches that marred his right cheek. Scabbed, somewhat ragged, they curved over his cheekbone and had already crusted over.

His smile lacked anything resembling humor. Between the new scratches, the bruises darkening over his ribs from the fight, his busted knee, and one seriously intractable dick trying to steal the blood from his brain, he was in great shape.

For an old-timer.

He turned away from the mottled mirror, pushed aside the faded curtain. It took some work to wrestle the faucet on. It sputtered like a car engine before spitting out an orange torrent at high velocity. He turned it on full cold, waited for it to run clear of the rust buildup.

When he stepped into the tub, the first icy shock of it had him swearing through gritted teeth. Silas ducked his head under it, let bitterly cold rivulets glide over his sore back and thread over the stubborn hard-on he desperately wanted to kill.

Bad for business. Bad for his own peace of mind. Hell, he was bad for Jessie, and his head knew it. Screamed it at him. His body didn't care. His body still remembered what she'd felt like as he shoved her hard against that damned wall and slid deeply inside her willing body.

Warm, wet. Willing. All his favorite adjectives.

"Fuck," he hissed. The cold water treatment did exactly jack for him while his thoughts wandered over her naked curves. He cursed again, once more for the sheer aggravation of it, and changed the water back to hot.

Steam soon billowed as he braced himself beneath the spray and closed his eyes.

It'd been a long time since he'd contended with an eternal erection. It wasn't something he particularly wanted to take care of now, not with Jessie in the next room, and he'd be damned if he resorted to his own hands when she actually *was* in the next damn room. He'd cope, deal. Overcome.

He always did.

When the mission was over, he'd—

Right. He'd what?

Silas heaved out a hard breath, repositioned himself under the water. It slid down his back, hot rivulets working a warm, soothing trail across his aching shoulders. If he was going to be honest with himself, he knew there wasn't going to be an *after this*. For anyone else, *after this* meant civilian life.

Work. Home. Family. Normal, everyday life.

The kind of shit he'd never figured out.

He braced his forearms against the broken tile and let himself sag, let the wall take some of the weight his knee throbbed under. Muscles rippled across his chest and shoulder, stiff with tension and the abuse he'd let the red-haired witch heap on him.

He felt like he'd been kicked down a fucking flight of stairs, and this after only one fight. Jesus, it was no wonder hunters over thirty became desk jockeys and team leaders. He wasn't just pushing it at thirty-four, he was painting a solid gold bull's-eye on his back.

Jaw clenching, he rested his forehead against his crossed forearms. He didn't have to see the leather cord around his wrist to know it was there.

There'd be no desk in his future. No leading. And since Peterson had a thorn up his ass, no more Mission, either. Not after this operation ended.

As the water beat down on his tired body, washed over his tired thoughts, Silas couldn't hear the door ease open. Didn't see the silhouette as it moved across the tiny bathroom, and only too late realized what was happening as the curtain slid open. Before he could say anything, do anything, Jessie stepped into the tub with him.

Her eyes gleamed, quiet and dark, filled to the brim with a sympathy he didn't know how to acknowledge. As if sensing it, as if she knew what warred in his mind, she waited. Her naked body glistened like marble in the poor light, her skin dappled by the water spraying off him. It rolled in wet rivulets, traced slim curves and the mouthwatering valleys of her body.

He stared at her. Swallowed hard. No words made it through the haze of primal lust and hot-blooded arousal, of deeply rooted alarm.

What the hell did a man say to a goddess?

Absently, even self-consciously, Jessie raised her long, slim arms and gathered her shoulder-length hair into a knot, scraped it back from her face. The motion drew his gaze to the bare curve of her breasts, pink-tipped and already hardened to puckered points. Because of the cooler air?

Because of him?

His gut clenched. "Jessie—"

"I think—"

She stopped, bit her lip. Her white teeth left an indent that Silas desperately wanted to taste, to tongue away.

She'd let him. He knew she would, and she'd like it.

It took monumental effort, but he didn't reach for her. Muscles locked tightly against every instinct screaming in the back of his mind, he forcefully fisted his hands behind him. Very carefully shifted away from the inhuman temptation of her soft, wet, naked body.

Humor, challenge lit her eyes to gold. "You're one of those men that think sex is something else, aren't you?"

Shit. Jesus. "Exactly the opposite," he said flatly. "Sex is sex. Two people, two orgasms."

"Only two?"

Oh, fuck. Silas laughed hoarsely, surprise and amusement and, damn it, appreciation sliding through him. And need. God, the need. "At least two."

Jessie slid forward, bare feet gliding effortlessly across the slick tub. He sucked in a breath, smelled her scent on the steam. Something sweet, something soft. Jesus, even her skin smelled like sex.

Dangerous, debilitating, mind-bending sex.

His chest muscles jerked as she laid both palms on him. The sudden flex mimicked the sudden velocity of his heart, the thunderous rush of blood pounding in his ears. "Don't," he warned through gritted teeth.

She paused. Didn't move. "You've said that before," she said lightly. "Do you mean it?"

Yes, fuck, yes, hell, yes.

Silas searched her eyes, fought with himself. With his own pulse and his own craving. She was a witch's sister. She was going to loathe him for killing her brother.

She was going to get hurt. Maybe even killed.

No, he didn't mean it. *Idiot*. Hell, no.

Silas closed his eyes against the searching uncertainty buried deeply behind her smile, nearly groaned under the sheer torture of it as her fingers slid over his wet skin. Edged into the aching muscle and skimmed across his left nipple. "Jess, I'm not—"

Her fingers curved, nails dragged over his skin. He shuddered. Uncoiled like a spring wound too tight.

"Damn it." Silas pulled her into the hot water. She tripped on her own feet, gasped and laughed as he whirled her around and plastered her back to the tile. She hooked a limber, damp leg around his hip, met his eyes in fierce appreciation. His body hummed—hell—*roared* approval as she arched into the water, into him nestled between her legs.

As if she'd been made for him. To fit him.

So wrong. Silas's thoughts fractured into a thousand shards at the sleek, wet warmth of her body stroking his straining cock. Beckoning. His hips jerked, slid against her flesh, and he swore viciously as her heat scorched him to the bone.

So, so hot.

Jessie wrapped her hands around the back of his

neck, cheeks flushed, and bit out a cry as he stroked himself against her, coated himself with her. Breath hitched, her lashes swept down to shadow her cheeks. Silas thought she was the most beautiful thing he'd ever seen in this godforsaken world.

He couldn't do this to her. He knew he'd walk away, and she'd have only a corpse to remember him by.

"Jess," he groaned, unable to help himself. Unable to stop, damn it. "This isn't—"

"Don't." Her eyes sparkled, snapped, as she opened them to meet his gaze. "Don't think. Stop thinking." Her hips rolled, twisted, and he snapped his teeth on a groan as every nerve from crotch to brain sparked.

Detonated.

"Not here," he managed, incoherent with need. He palmed her breasts in both hands, rolled her nipples between his fingers until she cried out. "Not here. Damn it—"

Half laughing, half whimpering under his assault, Jessie uncurled her leg from his hip and kicked the faucet. Once, twice. The water trickled off. Silas pulled her close, crushed his mouth to hers as he yanked her off her feet and guided her legs around his waist.

She hooked her ankles in the small of his back, devoured his kiss with as much desperation as the wild need clawing inside his skin. She bit his lip, licked it when he grunted in mingled pleasure and pain. Laughed against the wet curve of his neck when it took him three tries to get the goddamned door open.

Wet, shivering, he wrapped his arms tight under

her amazing ass, found the bedroom by luck. She speared her fingers through his hair, sank her teeth delicately into the sensitive shell of his ear.

Cursing, Silas tumbled them into the double bed, into the nest of colorful blankets, and covered her body with his own. She was all long limbs and soft skin, damp heat and, God, her laughter. Like sex in the sunshine.

"Now," she demanded, breathy and wanton. She grabbed his hair, spread her legs for him. "Now!"

Silas obliged. His arms braced against the mattress, he pushed himself up, met her eyes, and buried himself to the hilt inside her. For a second, a single split second, his vision went black. Pleasure ripped through him, tore bloody furrows across the chains of his control, and he moved before he was ready. Before she was ready.

She moaned, locked her legs tighter around him as she reached blindly for something, anything to hold on to. He thrust into her, pulled out, angled his hips and slid himself against a spot that made her seize the blankets in both hands and cry out his name.

Heat spiraled into blatant greed, but Silas wrestled with his own control. Struggled to tame the angry edge of his desire. He watched Jessie writhe beneath him. Her eyes tightly closed, her skin flushed, he stroked long and hard and deep inside her.

He watched her mouth twist, watched her clamp down on her lower lip. Fight herself.

"Come on," he whispered hoarsely. God damn it, he'd barely survived the first time. "Come on. Don't wait—"

Jessie arched, breasts thrust so close he couldn't stop himself from tasting them. Lowering his head and drawing one nipple into his mouth even as he thrust again and again. Bit down hard enough to feel her shudder and clench around him.

"More," he demanded against her heated, damp skin. Sweat blossomed across his back, gathered over his shoulders as he fought to reclaim himself. To watch her come apart beneath him, hands buried in the blankets.

She did. Holy God, she did.

Her eyes snapped open, ethereal gold against the tangled waves of her burnished hair. Bottomless, half blind with pleasure and lust, he read her climax there first, felt it follow as her muscles clenched hard around him. He lost it.

Lost the battle, lost himself.

Jessie's hips bucked as he thrust hard and deep, rose to meet him as he shuddered. Smooth, tight, she clamped around him so powerfully he gritted out something wordless, something guttural as his own orgasm left him without thought or reason.

He didn't collapse on her. It was a near thing, but he caught himself before he crushed her to the mattress. Braced on his elbows, balls-deep inside her pulsing flesh, he gasped for breath against her shoulder and tried to remember what it was like to think. To breathe.

Her heart pounded wildly against his ear. Around his body.

In his head.

Fuck.

Jessie stirred, stretched languidly beneath him. "Silas?"

He raised his head, met her muted, steady gaze, and everything inside him braced for impact. *Shit*, here it'd come. The declarations, the recriminations.

But she only raised one hand to his, skimmed his left wrist. The tattoo. "Who's Nina?" she asked.

CHAPTER TWELVE

She'd made a mistake. As soon as the question slid out of her mouth, she'd sensed him flinch, felt him withdraw mentally as much as he did physically, sliding out of her and rolling away.

Now he hunted for something to cover up with, and she wasn't sure how to ask again. If she should.

If she wanted to know the answer.

Jessie propped her chin on her palm and studied his profile as he wrapped a blanket around his waist. She didn't bother. Naked, shivering a little as the sweat cooled on her skin, she watched light play across his broad shoulders and edgily defined muscle.

He had an amazing body.

That probably belonged to someone else.

That would never, ever belong to her even if it

didn't. Jessie slid out of bed, pulling a blanket with her. "I'm not going to go all clingy and demanding on you," she said, struggling to keep her voice light. Easy. "If you have a wife somewhere, I underst—"

He turned so fast, she barely registered the motion. He was simply there, a sudden frenetic beat of energy that overwhelmed her senses, made her flinch as he thrust his face in too close to hers. His eyes blazed. "No," he cut in, a single syllable of serrated fury. "Don't push. Not on this."

She blinked, barely cognizant of his fingers like iron bands at her upper arms. Half-raised on her toes, she stared into his gray-green eyes and saw the same anger, the same pain that she'd *seen* when he'd stood in front of his Mission team.

Felt it like shards of glass, brittle and sharp.

Her throat ached around a sudden lump of grief. "Oh, Silas." The tears rose from nowhere, sympathy, bitter compassion.

Understanding.

The sharp edges of his fury softened, rearranged to something repentant, fiercely uncomfortable. "Don't," he said again. Silas let go of her arms to cup her face. Swiped at her tears with callused thumbs. "Jesus Christ, don't do that."

Jessie couldn't stop her watery laugh. "Don't sympathize?"

"Don't cry." He gathered her close, wrapped strong, bare arms around her back. Tucked her head against his chest. "Not for me, Jess. There are better things."

Were there? Really? She inhaled deeply, took in

the scent of his skin. Strong, musky. Masculine. Her shoulders twisted. "It's just—"

What?

Just that he seemed so alone? So unhappy? That she knew what it was to feel both? To feel for him? Her brother's hunter?

She squeezed her eyes shut. Battled back her tears, her idiocy. Sympathy wouldn't help her. It'd only get her killed.

He stroked his hands over her hair, over her back, and rested his chin on top of her head. "You really want to know?" he asked quietly.

Jessie drew back. Studied his face. Did she?

Her mouth shaped the word before her brain could argue. "Yes."

Silas's eyes closed. "Nina Arbor was fourteen when a coven of witches kidnapped her from school. She was the third in as many weeks, and I was fresh out of training."

Witches. Of course. Jessie slid her hands over his hips, hooked her thumbs into the rolled blanket.

"It was supposed to be in and out," he continued as his fingers skimmed over the bare skin of her back, traced over the patch of ink stamped crookedly over her spine. She shivered. "As easy as it gets. A lead, two field agents, a tech."

"Except?" she prompted when he fell silent. "Something went wrong?" Beneath her cheek, his heart thudded steadily. She flattened her palm against his muscles, felt him suck in a deep breath.

"Yeah," he replied on a hard exhale. "I wanted to take them down. So I made the call. The two field agents went in, started taking out the guards, and I went in around them."

Jessie's chest squeezed. His voice was flat, as cool as if he read it all from a report. She pressed her lips to his shoulder, barely even a whisper of a kiss.

"The tech covered my six best as he could, but I was on my own. I found Nina by her screams." His voice roughened, snarling somewhere in his chest. "The bastards had cut her. For the ritual, they—they took her blood, cut her open."

Oh, God. Acid sizzled in her stomach. Blood was a damn good focus. Her hands tightened at his waist.

"With a black knife," Silas said hoarsely. "And she looked up at me with these— Fuck." He cleared his throat. "She looked at me with these big blue eyes and smiled. Terrified, but she smiled like she knew I was going to make it all right."

His fingers tangled into her hair, and Jessie could only close her eyes at his pain that festered so deep, to the bone.

"I didn't wait. I killed the bastard with the knife, but there were three others. One came at me, and one just . . ." Rigid with strain, Silas dropped his forehead to her temple and let out a tight, angry breath. "One just pulled out a gun and shot her. Right in the head. That little girl's brains splattered over the altar before he turned the gun on the other witches and shot them, too. I killed him before he could do it himself."

Jessie closed her eyes. "Oh, Silas."

"The worst part," he said, his breath hot at her cheek, shaking. "The worst part was the communication. They were ready. Knew what to do if they were interrupted. Had a contingency. I found Molly's body on my way out, and when I heard the explosion, I got there in time to see Paul's corpse hit the dirt by the truck."

She shuddered, cringed when his arms tightened around her. He shouldn't do it, she shouldn't let him, but she couldn't stop it. Didn't want to. She eased closer, tucked herself so close that she fed on his body heat. Tried desperately to give her own.

He met her searching gaze, his own raw and fogged with pain, with the memories that slid under his skin like broken glass. His smile drew blood, it was so sharp. "Hardly a complete waste," he said in gritty, mocking optimism. "Jonas killed two before the blast shattered every goddamned bone in his body and left him maimed for life."

Oh, God. Tears slid over her cheeks. She framed Silas's face in her hands. "Oh, no. No, don't do that," she whispered unhappily. "Don't make it so . . . so soulless."

He curled his hands around her wrists. Held on as much as holding her away. "It is soulless," he said flatly. "We go in, we kill, we leave. Everything dies, in the end. Every one of them. Do you understand that?"

Her breath sobbed out on mingled anger and grief. She knew it. She knew it too well, and all she could do was shake her head.

"Don't you get it? Witches kill, Jessie, and they— Son of a *bitch*." Silas yanked her hands from his face, violently wrenched her away from his body. She teetered, but he held her steady, one long-fingered hand viselike around both wrists. Kept her from falling, from fleeing. His eyes burned into hers. "Witches kill and maim and destroy. Your brother kills, maims, and destroys. You wanted to know. Now you know. Don't think it'll change anything."

It changed everything. And it changed nothing at all. She'd known it already.

She raised her chin, met his eyes. He'd just given her one less lie, that was all this meant. It changed nothing.

God damn it. It changed nothing.

Silas's jaw set. "Say you understand, Jessie."

She did. More than he knew. So she twisted, just enough, and the blanket unwound, pooled to the floor in a stream of color. Naked, trapped by his grip on her wrists, she stepped into him. Naked skin to half-naked skin.

Curve to hard muscle.

His eyes darkened. "Say it." But his muscles strained, as if he desperately wanted to push her away. Desperately needed to pull her closer.

Heart pounding, Jessie licked her lips. "I un-derst—"

He bent his head, swallowed her words with a kiss that set the world on fire. Angry, aggressive, he stripped the blanket from his waist and backed her toward the bed. He found her damp core with hot, searching fingers and worked her body until she twisted, needing.

She sobbed his name as she came, forgot everything but torturous pleasure and liquid heat when he thrust inside her and began all over again.

When they were both exhausted, tangled in the blankets and each other, Jessie listened to the steady thrum of his heartbeat under her ear and knew, understood, that Silas Smith was going to be the death of her.

If he didn't kill her, Caleb's prophecies would.

CHAPTER THIRTEEN

Sometime in the early hours of the morning, storm clouds rolled over the city. Lightning barely made it this deep into the mid-lows, but thunder jarred Silas out of the thoughts circling around and around inside his aching skull.

Mechanically he checked the time, saw he had an hour before the others showed up.

But he didn't move.

He stared at the window over his steepled fingers and told himself he was just being watchful. Prepared. Protective. That his knee hurt like a bitch and he was just taking it easy, making sure he didn't stress it any more than he already had.

Not that he was scared shitless to walk back into

that room and feel the gut-wrenching need to curl in to that warm bed again. To wrap himself around Jessie's sleepy, pliant body and fill his hands, his arms, his soul with her.

He grunted, scraped his hands over his face. Anger simmered low in his belly, right under the goddamned lust kicking his ass from here to Sunday Mass.

Operation Echo Location should have been called Operation Clusterfuck.

The Mission wouldn't have agreed.

Then again, they weren't screwing a witch's sister. And didn't know he was. And wouldn't have approved if they did. And wouldn't approve when they—

Hell, who was he kidding? He'd gotten her to help. If all it took was a little deep dicking to ensure they landed Caleb Leigh and his coven, they'd line up to do it and smile while they did.

Thunder rattled the glass, rain splattered in thick rivulets. Silas stared at the current of water and thought of a rain-slick wall deep beneath the city proper.

Terrified blue eyes were rapidly turning whiskey brown in his mind's eye. Clutching at his head. His chest. Shit.

Shit.

He needed to do something. Anything.

Make the rounds.

He surged to his feet in a sudden flurry of energy, ignored the angry twang of his knee. He rubbed at his wrist, unaware of it until he found wooden beads jammed under his thumb. The letter N, warm to the touch, gleamed in the pale light.

He'd be damned if he added another name to this cross.

Pacing the confines of the living room, it was barely four steps across in either direction. Window to wall to door to kitchen linoleum, and back again. He didn't know how long he kept it up, working out the kinks in his thigh muscles, swearing silently.

He only stopped when he heard the pipes groan in the wall behind him. Silas glanced down the short hall, saw a corner of light spill from the bathroom door. Heard the rushing water from the shower.

She was awake.

And he had things to do.

He headed for that half-open door, ruthlessly throttling back the urge to join her in the water. To touch her skin. Arouse her, feel her come apart in his hands. To take the damned bottle of feminine lavender soap he'd found earlier and rub it over her body, into her hair.

Because he was *stupid*. And greedy.

Silas rapped on the fake wood, propped it wider. "Hey."

Steam wafted around her as she stuck her head out of the battered curtain. Her hair dripped into her sleepy, sexy eyes. "Hey. Are we heading out?"

"Shortly." He leaned against the doorjamb because it was safer than crossing the threshold. "There's dry cereal on the counter. Only thing worth eating. You can take it with."

"Mmm." Jessie vanished back behind the curtain, and Silas found himself wishing the damn thing wasn't opaque. "I'll be done soon. God, this feels like heaven."

Despite himself, his mouth quirked in amusement. After the day she'd had, he wouldn't deny her the luxury of hot water. "Take your time, sunshine. Soon as you—"

The back of his neck prickled.

He jerked to the side, jammed an elbow backward, and collided with the man who'd sneaked too close behind. Both staggered, and Silas caught himself on the hallway wall before the man did.

The dark-haired man threw out a hand, grated out a word Silas didn't understand.

Torture didn't need a translator.

Silas dropped to his knees, croaked out something lost under a wave of excruciating pain. It burned, ate at him from the inside out. Maybe he screamed. Maybe he just tried to. Agony. Nerve-exposing, skin-peeling agony overloaded his mind until all he could see, all he could taste, was his own torment.

Light blazed blue, ice and fire, and the seal's warning clawed up his arm. Too slow, it wrapped around him like latex. Silas's muscles bunched, rigid with strain as he forced himself to breathe. To think through it.

Ride it.

"This is the one," he heard as the pain dulled beneath the seal's holy protection. "Went down like a— Well, damn."

Silas surged to his feet. The walls rattled as he braced himself between them. Sweat clammy on his skin, he locked his eyes on both figures staring at him.

The dark-haired witch eyed him in surprise, maybe even wincing respect. The other, a woman, in speculative interest.

"Well, well." The woman lifted a tattooed palm. "My turn." Magic slammed into him again. Tight. Angry. Sharp as hell, and much more focused.

The skin under his right eye stung, but it was nothing compared to her partner's attack. Nothing to the seal that burned diamond blue. Silas pushed forward. Step by step. "Come on," he gritted out from between his clenched teeth.

"Silas!"

The magic faltered at Jessie's scream, weakened enough so he could leap, collide with them both. The man staggered free but the woman hit the floor under his weight. Silas punched her twice, savagely snapped her head around with each impact. He caught a glimmer of movement in the corner of his eye and looked up just in time to catch a boot squarely in the face.

Reeling, he pitched off her. Grunted, swore, as the man took the advantage to kick him hard in the ribs. Silas's world flashed red and white.

"Leave him alone!" Jessie leaped out of the bathroom, cleared Silas's spot-ridden vision in one bare-legged stride. Wrapped in a towel, hair tangled and dripping, she clung like a monkey to the man's back, clawed at his face.

Silas picked himself off the floor and returned the goddamned, bloody favor. The man's eyes bulged as Silas's boot caught him squarely in the balls, crunched. It took the big man a moment to find the breath. When he did, he let it out in a ragged scream.

Silas yanked Jessie away, both hands fisted in the towel at her waist. "Run!" he ordered, pushing her toward the front room. She made it three steps before she froze. Silas plowed into her back. "Keep—"

She clutched at him. "Get down!"

The first bullet shattered the plaster by his head. The second whined by his ear as Silas grabbed Jessie by the damp towel and threw her to the side. She hit the couch, yelped as she went over it in a tangle of bare limbs. She'd hurt for it later.

But the bullet that tagged him didn't get her, and that's what mattered. Pain seared white-hot through his shoulder as he lowered his head and charged the dark-skinned witch in the living room.

Behind him, one of the attackers spilled out of the hallway. Threw out that goddamned hand again. Pain skewered him squarely in the back as his shoulder rammed into the black-skinned witch's stomach. Silas buckled.

"Get the bitch," he heard behind him. "Bethany—"

"I'm on it."

On Jessie? *Hell, no.* Over his dead, bloodless corpse.

Rage gave him strength. Muted his own injuries as he wrestled the gun out of the witch's hand and turned it on him.

Dark, almost black eyes met his. Flickered. "Go to hell," the witch spat.

Silas squeezed the trigger. Blood sprayed, an explosion of red and gray and pink that cut short the witch's short, sharp scream.

The man went limp. Silas swung the gun around and squeezed off two more shots in quick succession. The other man yelped, vanished around the hallway corner in a puff of plaster.

"Drop it, cowboy."

Silas snapped his head around, sighted down the barrel of the gun. Automatically his finger tightened on the trigger.

Honey brown eyes stared wildly back at him.

His heart stopped. He jerked the gun to the side. "Jessie."

"Sorry," she said lightly, but her voice came high and tight with fear. Pain. Her eyes were too-wide, skin too pale. Her throat convulsed behind the long, thin red line at her neck. Ear to ear. Shallow, and bloody.

The witch called Bethany stood behind her, one hand twisted in Jessie's dripping hair. The other hovered, angular tattoo bared over her throat.

Bethany's eyes glittered with barely leashed rage. Wild, malicious magic.

Silas lowered the gun to his side. Watched blood slide in a fine sheen along Jessie's neck. It crept toward the edge of the towel she clutched over her chest.

And his own blood boiled.

"You with me?" he asked quietly.

Jessie's mouth curved, a sickly sort of smile. Thin, petrified reassurance. "Too early to die. Get the bitch— Agh!"

Every muscle in Silas's body went rigid as the witch's hand splayed. As an inch of Jessie's skin parted, just *split* along that thin red seam. Blood welled from the shocked wound, blossomed, and Silas's vision narrowed. Tunneled.

Helplessness. Fury.

Fear.

"What do you want?" he heard himself ask, and dropped the gun.

"That's what I like," Bethany said slowly, pleasantly. "Cooperation. The world needs more cooperation, don't you think?"

Jessie's fingers clenched tighter over the towel. Her mind flipped through images, thoughts, plans. None of them felt like success.

All of them would hurt.

She swallowed, cringed as her throat burned.

"Cooperation requires trust," Silas said, his eyes blank and steady on her. Studying her. Telling her something?

What?

The witch laughed, her breath hot on Jessie's cheek. "You're a nice Church boy. Don't you believe in faith?"

"No."

"Oh, that's too bad." Jessie stumbled when the woman tugged on her hair. "Because me and this sweet girl, here, are going for a ride. You're just going to have to take it on faith that I won't kill her. Isn't that right, Jessica?"

Silas's eyes narrowed to slits.

Jessie stiffened. "How—?"

The witch's fingers tightened in her hair, painfully sharp. "How do I know your name?" the witch asked brightly. Almost cheerfully. As if she hadn't just watched two of her friends get shot.

Hadn't just flexed her fingers and made Jessie bleed.

"I don't know you," Jessie said uncertainly. "Do I?" She couldn't see past the woman's arm, couldn't make out anything more than the angular shape of one high cheekbone and a pointed chin.

"No, you don't," Bethany agreed. "But we all know you, Jessica Leigh. We've been looking for you for a long time. So, let's go."

"No." Silas stood between them and the door. Immobile. Unmoving, save for a muscle that leaped near his temple. Jessie's gaze flicked to him. Studied him.

Memorized his face, his steely gray-green eyes. The rigid line of his body. Would he let this woman carry her off? Carry her to Caleb?

Why the hell not? It was an opportunity. A way in. She frowned at him, rolled her eyes in the direction of the door. Tried to telegraph what she thought.

Come on, you idiot.

He ignored her.

She set her jaw. "Fine," she said. "I'll go with you."

"No," Silas growled. Suddenly he wasn't so stern anymore. So unyielding. Fury twisted his rugged features as he shifted stance, and Jessie had a split second to imagine him charging at them like a bull.

And the blood that would spray out of her magically sliced throat when he did.

"Silas, don't," she said quickly. It hurt to shake her head, but she did it anyway. Short, quick. "I'll be fine."

"Good girl," Bethany praised. She tightened her grip in Jessie's hair, wrapped it like a rope around her fist and pulled her sideways. Circling Silas.

Circling the corpse.

Jessie frantically tried to stay on her feet.

"If it's any consolation," Bethany said in her ear as they backed toward the door, "I don't plan on killing you unless the hunter does something stupid." The wattage on Bethany's smile could have melted plastic. "So, you tell him to stay put."

"Silas?"

He shifted his weight. Watched them. "Why her?" he demanded.

Bethany hesitated. She cocked a hip in a stance that kept Jessie squarely in front of her. Neatly between her and Silas. "You don't know?" she asked thoughtfully. "Really?"

Jessie's spine filled with ice. "I don't—"

"Really," Silas said flatly.

Bethany nodded. "All right. Since she looks an awful lot like her brother, she was easy to ID." She patted Jessie's cheek with her free hand. "Spitting image, really. And the reward on her delivery is pretty sweet. So—"

Silas moved. "Why?"

"Uh-uh." The witch dug her thumb into Jessie's wounded neck, and Jessie gasped. Swallowed back a scream as her mind detonated in pain.

Silas froze, mid-stride. Mid-fury. Through her watery, clouded vision, his jaw shifted as he stared at her, at the witch behind her.

"You want to know, you'll have to find Caleb."

Bethany removed her thumb, and Jessie sobbed in a breath. "In fact, I kind of hope you do."

"Is that why you're leaving me alive?" Silas fisted his hands at his sides, all but vibrating with rage.

"Yeah, actually. I like the idea of you finding her body later."

"Bitch."

Bethany laughed. "Oh, I'm hurt. You remember that word when I use this pretty girl's corpse as a stepping-stone to coven leadership, okay?" She yanked Jessie back, closer to the door. Jessie grabbed her arm with one hand, the grimy towel with the other, stumbled as the petite woman maneuvered her by her own hair.

Silas's fists clenched. "Politics? You want her for heretic politics?"

"Shut the *fuck* up," Bethany growled, so sudden and thick by Jessie's ear that she felt the bitter blast of it straight through to her bones. Bethany pointed at him, a line of bloody accusation beside Jessie's face. "You have no idea what it's like down there. What it means to fight for food, to be hunted, scared." Every word sprayed Jessie's cheek with spittle.

Every word reeked of grief and bitterness.

God, she knew. Knew exactly what Bethany felt. How she lived.

"No more," Bethany raged. "Now I've got leverage, I've got the girl we've been hunting, and they'll have no choice but to see me now. No choice but to let me stand at that altar with Caleb and rip her mag—"

Instinct launched Jessie into action. She threw herself backward, deliberately tangled the witch up in her flailing limbs. It jerked Bethany off balance, shut her up on a curse as she struggled to maintain her own equilibrium without losing her shield.

Jessie cried out as the witch's grip tore at her scalp. "Don't move!" Bethany shrieked at the same time, and the door slammed open behind them.

Jessie didn't know what hit her. One moment, the witch had manhandled her upright, the next she staggered under the woman's weight. She sprawled, tasted carpet and dirt and pain.

Cold, wet air rushed over her back. Gunshots shattered the air over her head. Something warm and wet splattered over her shoulders. Over her back.

Jessie rolled to the side, her skin crawling, pushed herself to her feet. Wavered.

"No." Bethany's eyes gleamed brilliantly green in her shock-white face. They pinned on Jessie, stared at her, as the witch raised a trembling hand to the gaping, lurid hole at her chest.

Jessie's stomach clenched. Turned over. Bile boiled into her throat and burned. Bethany pitched forward, sprawled gracelessly in the pool of blood and brain matter coating the carpet, and Jessie's mouth worked soundlessly. A scream built somewhere in her chest, her throat, but nothing came. Crimson covered the living room, flecks and drops and streaks and smears.

The blood drained from her head. Her knees buckled.

"No, you don't." Silas moved. Hands like vises around her shoulders, rugged features pulled into a mask of fury and grim control, he shook her hard enough to rattle her teeth. "Jessie, don't you dare faint."

Her mental tether pulled taut. Twanged. Jessie snapped back into herself, back into the painful crawl of her own body, back into the smell of blood and death and fear.

Jessie smiled. Thin, wan. "I don't faint."

He yanked her into his arms. Pulled her hard against his chest and held her. Tight. Safe. "Jesus," he said gruffly into her hair. "Shit. *Shit.*"

For a long moment, Jessie let herself soak him in. Let herself smell the musky scent of him, feel the warmth of his body against her.

She could forget that she wore someone else's blood. That her throat ached, and that somewhere in that private back hole of her mind, she was screaming.

"Go get the kit," Silas said over her head. His voice thrummed through his chest, reassuring and real.

Talking to someone else.

Jessie stiffened. She forced herself to stand alone, to push away from Silas's warm, solid arms. "I'm fine."

"Sit down." He tugged her to the couch. Though she fought it, her rubbery knees collapsed out from under her. Silas knelt at her feet, tilted her head back with careful hands. "Jesus, Jessie."

She laughed. It hurt. "It probably looks worse than it is."

"Great." She heard the familiar voice, recognized it moments before a memorable part-Asian beauty with blue-violet eyes stepped into her circle of vision. "Since you look like hell."

Jessie's smile faded.

"Easy," Silas said, slanting the woman a hard, impatient glance. "Naomi's safe."

Safe. *Right*. More hunters.

Naomi's full, lush mouth curved in edged, sardonic civility. "Oh-kay. So you found her." She patted Silas on the head. His hands jerked, a leap of cracked control, and grimly he pressed rough gauze to Jessie's neck. Mopped up the blood. "Congratulations. And the rest?"

"Samples are in the truck," Silas said, his tone even. "Let me take care of Jessie, I'll get it for you."

"Take your time," Naomi said lightly. She leaned against the couch and peered down at Jessie. Weighed her with eyes that didn't reflect any lightness at all. "I'd rather be here babysitting you than topside kissing ass. So which one of you fucked up this time?"

Jessie sucked in a breath, hissed out a long, violent curse as the first spray of disinfectant burned it out of her.

"Easy," Silas said again, as calmly as if he hadn't heard Naomi's barbed anger. "Almost done. I didn't come back here to fight with you, Naomi."

"Yeah? Too bad." Naomi hooked her thumbs into the pockets of her snug jeans. "You should have checked in way before this. Peterson's on *my* ass because *you're* the one with the hero complex, so now you get to deal."

Jessie closed her eyes, feeling battered from all directions. Pushed.

She snapped them open again when Silas stood. "Keep pushing, Naomi, and plans can change."

Black humor darkened her eyes as Naomi continued to watch Jessie. "Yeah. I know. You're good at changing plans. We count on it. You done with this poor girl?"

"I have a name," Jessie said wearily.

Naomi patted her on the head, too, the same way she might have patted a small, annoying puppy. "Of course you do."

Jessie flinched.

"That's enough," Silas growled.

"Oh, that's cute."

Jessie's patience snapped. "Shut up."

Naomi blinked at her, all lush eyelashes and tolerant smile. "Really?"

Jessie shoved herself to her feet. Met that razored edge of Naomi's smile with raw temper. "I'm not going to sit here and eat your attitude because you woke up bitchy," she said flatly. "Don't treat me like I'm some kind of leashed dog."

Naomi raised a double-pierced eyebrow, her arms folded over her cropped, shiny purple jacket. "And what'll you do, princess?"

"You need me." It was more than a guess. It was flat fact, and Jessie watched it register. Watched Naomi's stance shift, in the same way Silas tensed when he sensed trouble.

Maybe it was a killer thing.

"You both need me, and you need each other," Jessie said. "So shut *up*, sit *down*, and quit pushing each other's buttons, or so help me, I'll let the coven burn the city to the ground."

So it was a bluff. A big one. But right at the

moment, as she all but vibrated in place, she silently dared either one of them to call her on it.

The woman's almond eyes narrowed. "Look who's got balls."

"Yeah." Jessie's fists clenched hard at her side as raw violence swept through her. "I'm hoping we can get something done while we're waiting for yours to drop."

Naomi's bee-stung mouth quirked. "Jesus, Smith, maybe she'll kill you yet."

"Fuck you, Naomi."

Jessie took a step forward. She didn't know what she could do, not about the undercurrents of tension between the two hunters that crackled and sparked. She didn't know what was wrong with her, only that she shook with rage, white-knuckled and tunneled in it.

Hitting one of them seemed like a start. Preferably both.

"Jessie." Silas stepped in front of her. Caught her chin in one hand and forced her to look at him, at the warm glow of his gaze, and damn her to hell, her heart stuttered. Eased. "It's okay," he said.

"But she—"

"Forget it." He touched her cheek. "Go finish your shower. I'll deal with her."

She frowned. "I'm not a child."

"Sunshine." The word, the goddamned name, made her tongue knot up. Silas grabbed her shoulders, turned her physically around. He pushed her firmly toward the hall. "You're covered in blood. Go get clean."

Because she didn't know what else to do, Jessie obeyed. Step by step, she circled around the bodies. The blood. Stepped back into the bathroom, turned on the faucet.

She kicked aside the bloody towel and climbed into the tub. Very carefully she arranged the curtain until all she saw was its mottled color. The water spiraled red and brown into the drain at her feet, and she tried very hard not to look at it.

Not to smell it, thick and nauseatingly familiar.

Jessie lasted all of a minute beneath the hot, stinging spray before she broke down. The roar of the water drowned out her bitter sobs.

CHAPTER FOURTEEN

Silas turned his back on Naomi's appraising stare and picked up his gun. He didn't holster it, instead palming it neatly in both hands as he mapped a trail of blood back to the bedroom.

He didn't expect to find anything but an open window. Still, annoyance bit deeply when he found exactly that.

Movement in the hall told him Naomi had followed. "Lose one?"

"Yeah." He holstered the gun, pushed past her again.

She caught his arm. "What's with the kid?"

Silas stared at her hand, mutely aware that it was the same look he'd seen Jessie give his hands when he forced them on her. Christ, she was rubbing off on him.

Or she liked to imagine breaking his wrists, the way he was picturing now with Naomi. His shoulder burned like a mother, his knee ached in tune with the drills boring through his temples, and Jessie and *kid* weren't compatible in the same thought.

So he grunted wordlessly and shook her off.

Naomi had never been big on picking up cues. "Well?" She followed him into the bloody living room. Without any direction from him, she bent over the woman's corpse and shouldered it up. Blood slid over her figure-hugging jacket, but she didn't bat an eyelash.

She was one hell of a missionary. Shitty at just about everything else.

Reminded him of himself. "What do you want, Naomi?"

"She's got something." Naomi jerked a thumb back at the bathroom door. "Some sort of hold on you. I figure . . ." She paused, barely stooped under the dead woman's weight across her shoulders, and slanted him a look that cut. "Fuck, Silas. Did you get stupid and bang her?"

A muscle in his cheek twitched. He hauled the other body into his arms, wrenched it up onto his shoulders in a mirrored fireman's carry. "I'm here to kill a witch and make sure she doesn't die," he said when he was sure he had it under control. The body, his voice.

The angry, guilty kick in his chest.

She snorted, led the way out the door. "You still can't lie worth shit."

Silas glowered. Rather than answering, his gaze swept over the flooded courtyard. No one had wandered out to see what the gunshots were about.

He hadn't expected the neighbors to risk it. Bonus for him.

And no one had gotten caught in a crossfire. Bonus for them.

"I don't have to lie," he finally said, sloshing through the ankle-deep water rippling under the rain. "It's called honesty, Naomi, you should try it sometime."

"Hey, I enjoy the hell out of honesty." Naomi wiped the rain from her eyes with an impatient forearm. "You're the one practically salivating after her."

"Give it a rest."

"No." She tossed the body to the ground without any regard for care and keyed open the back of the Mission jeep. With the same cavalier sense of duty, she hauled Bethany's corpse up by the collar and slammed her onto the seat. Limbs bounced against the taut upholstery, an awkward thud of dead weight.

Silas left the larger corpse on the ground beside her. He circled around the jeep to his own truck as she wrestled with the man's dead weight. The hinges squealed as he yanked open the passenger door.

"Silas?"

"What do you *want*, Naomi?"

Naomi wiped at her forehead, her almond eyes intent over the hood of the jeep. "Seriously? Find out why they want her."

Silas pulled out the old duffel, unzipped the pockets. Took his time answering. "Use her as bait, you mean."

"Give the man a medal."

He shook his head. "Not going to happen."

Silence, filled only by the patter of the rain and the frenetic hum of electricity, city life. After she wrestled the corpse into place, she circled around, leaned against the truck. The old metal fender creaked faintly. "Look, they want her, you should find out why. What does she mean to them?"

"Her brother—"

"Bullshit easy answer, and you know it," Naomi said. "Think with the brain you men pass around like a football and go deeper than that."

"Jesus, Naomi." Silas jerked the sealed plastic bag of bloody swabs from the duffel. Practically threw it at her.

She caught it easily. "You trust her, obviously."

"The only family she's got is going to get killed as soon as she leads the way to him." Silas slammed the truck closed, locked it with stiff, sharp movements. "She knows that."

"She what?" Shock twisted her features. "Are you serious?"

"Yeah."

"Shit." Light glittered at her studded ears as she scraped back sodden tendrils of purple-streaked hair. "I'm stranded topside, gearing up for some kind of surveillance operation—with Peterson for fucking company, let's not forget—and you're down here *telling* her how you're going to ice her brother? And you think she's just fine with that?"

Silas stared at her. She'd always been exotic, even as a kid. He had vague memories of her, lost and alone, too fucking serious at six years old. Too proud. But the fascination with piercings, or maybe with pain, wasn't something he remembered.

He swallowed back a nasty surge of guilt. Pocketed his keys. "She's not stupid, whatever you think. It amazes me how much of a bitch you are sometimes."

She said nothing, worrying her lip ring as she followed him back to the apartment. Her stride splashed in the swampy water of the courtyard. Then, her voice sharp with the tone that said she wasn't laying off, she said, "Silas, maybe—"

He rounded on her, one finger raised under her silver-ringed nose. "Look, no matter what, no matter where we go, they've been finding her. That makes her useful, right?" Naomi's blue-violet eyes flickered. "It means that they want her bad. I get it. It also means that they'll keep coming. That's an in."

The crease in her lower lip deepened as she twisted her mouth. Her eyes flicked to the door. Back again. "You're going hunting."

"Yeah." Silas reached back, palmed the doorknob. "But not without more information, and I sure as hell am not going to drag her into the nest. So either you can ride my ass and point out everything I'm doing wrong, or you can call Jonas right now and put him to work."

A flicker. Maybe worry? Maybe irritation. Naomi wiped the rain from her face with both hands. "Shit, Silas, you should do that."

He couldn't. Wouldn't. Jonas had enough to cope with without Silas's input. "I'm out of here the instant that kid is dead," he said, forcing down the guilt, the crushing press of responsibility. "You do what you need to, keep Peterson happy and off my ass. I'll let you know where to be and when. That should be a nice promotion for you, right?"

Naomi's eyes narrowed. "Typical. In alone and out alone." She flicked her fingers through the air, a vicious slice through the hot swell of words in his throat. "What do you need?"

Silas gritted his teeth. What didn't he need? "Painkillers," he said, and didn't smile when she snorted. "Test the blood, ID the bodies, and let me know what the hell we're dealing with. Figure out what those tattoos are on the woman's hands, and whether or not we can duplicate it."

Naomi's eyebrows shot up, winking more silver. "Duplicate it? The tattoo?"

"Yeah." Silas pushed open the door. Grunted at the visual punch, the olfactory miasma, of crimson.

Red was a color that didn't match anything.

The shower had stopped, which meant Jessie would be out any second, so he spoke fast. "If they can use tattoos as a focus, maybe you can crack it. Use it like, hell, some sort of signature or something. Isn't my thing, so pull Vaughn out of wherever he is and get him on it."

"Vaughn's dead."

He winced. "Shit. How?"

"Heart attack, four years ago. Silo's our new librarian."

"Well, then, get whomever that is on it," he said grimly. "We're ass-deep in alligators."

"Oh-kay," Naomi said, in that long, drawn out way of hers. It meant she didn't agree. Or didn't like it.

And he didn't care.

He shot her a glance, found her picking up the stained cloth he'd used to mop the blood from Jessie's neck. A curl of anger spiraled deep in his chest. Burned white-hot. "I'm not going to let her get killed," he said tightly.

She shook her head, just once. A curt gesture. "I don't want her dead, either."

"*Her* appreciates it."

Naomi's eyes flicked beyond him. Banked. She folded the cloth neatly into a square. "Hello, Jessica," she said, her voice an even slide of silk. "Feel better?"

Silas turned, had to keep himself from reaching out as Jessie walked out of the hall. She was pale, her hair freshly brushed back in its mass of dark gold. Her eyes were red-rimmed, but her gaze was steady and clear.

She'd been crying.

"Jessie," Silas corrected, and when it earned him a faint smile, he mentally kicked his own ass. He had no business responding to that smile.

Basking in it.

"No time for arguing, so here's how this will go," he said crisply. "That witch hauled ass. If he survives, it's a sure bet he's going to report Jessie's existence. Naomi, take the blood, get it labeled. Will you be able to be where you need to when I give the word?"

Naomi shrugged, pocketing the square cloth as

she surveyed the remnants of carnage that stained the living room. "One way or another."

Jessie frowned between them. "What?"

"Chin up, prin—" Naomi corrected herself. "Jessie. He's going to dress you pretty and dangle you like a carrot. If he's good, which he might be after all these years, you'll survive. Any issue with that?"

"Jesus, Naomi!" Silas rounded on her fiercely, but Jessie didn't rise to the bait. Didn't argue. She simply shrugged her shoulders in that beat-up neoprene jacket that hugged every curve she had.

If he didn't know better, he would have pegged her for a veteran hunter in that flinty, effortless movement.

And that wasn't *right*.

"No problem," Jessie said as she brushed by them both. "Let's go."

The fist of edgy worry in Silas's chest flattened to annoyance as Naomi caught Jessie by the shoulder. She towered over Jessie's shorter frame, but to Jessie's credit, she stared back without flinching.

"Why do they want you?" the missionary asked. "What are you hiding?"

Jessie's smile tightened. "One, your subtlety sucks. Two, my brother probably knows I'm in your hands and wants me out of them. Three, the witch mentioned some sort of ritual, but as I don't have a black book of magic or a death wish, I can't help you there. You tell me."

Silas pushed between them, forced them apart with a hand on each shoulder. "Naomi, Christ, lay off already."

"No," Jessie said. "It's fine. She's just doing her job." As if to prove she had nothing to hide, she leaned forward, rose up on her tiptoes until she was eye to eye with the woman.

Honey to violets.

"I don't know why they want me, Miss West," Jessica assured her. "I don't know what they plan. As far as I know, I have nothing they want. Okay?"

For a long moment, Naomi stared at her. Then, a short, tight smile. "I'll go see about those errands, then, shall I?"

She left without another word, sauntering out the door and into the rain. Silas closed his eyes before he did something rash.

Like punch something.

Or grab one hell of a stubborn blond in both hands and kiss her stupid. "Jessie."

Her shoulders stiff, she whirled in a sudden fit of hot temper. "Don't even. I don't care." Her eyes flashed at him, warned him off.

And he wanted her anyway.

Silas ignored every signal his brain sent him, every warning, and closed the distance between them. He grabbed her by the front of that damned jacket and hauled her mouth to his.

She resisted at first. Tried to move away. To disentangle her lips, his hands. Then she moaned fiercely, raggedly, and seized his hair in her fingers. Met his kiss, returned it.

Feeling her melt in his hands warmed him down to his goddamned rain-soaked toes.

As abruptly as he'd captured her, he let her go.

"Okay," he said on a hard breath, unable to disentangle his fingers from her jacket. His forehead bumped hers, rested there. "That was one for the road." One for the rest of this operation, and to sustain him when he left her somewhere safer.

It wasn't enough.

Jessie licked her lips, color high in her cheeks. Her eyes gleamed, but with none of the anger they'd spat moments before. "Didn't your mother ever teach you not to kiss an angry woman?"

His lips twitched. "I never knew my mother, and no, in my experience, angry women kiss like the world's on fire."

"You're an ass," she accused. It lacked any sting.

Silas nodded, tucked tendrils of her drying hair behind her ear. "Yeah. And I'm going to protect you."

Her eyes widened. Darkened. "Don't say that."

"Save it, sunshine." He touched her bottom lip with an index finger. "That's the way it is."

Whatever fear made her eyes cloud in nerves or trepidation, it faded under a smile that cocked one corner of her mouth into a teasing challenge. "We'll see who's protecting whom. So let's get on with it before that guy comes back with help."

He scraped back his hair as she strode out the door, rubbed both hands tiredly down his face. Tried not to think about how fucked he really was.

Jessie wasn't going to like being left behind. He wasn't going to give her a choice.

Hell. At least Naomi left the first-aid kit. He grabbed the dented metal box and his jacket, bit off a curse when denim hit the bullet graze carved shallowly into his shoulder. Wouldn't be the first crease he'd ever earned.

He figured there'd be more, at least until the one that killed him. He'd bandage it later. Until then, aspirin would have to do. He swallowed two bitter pills on the way to the truck.

Jessie had already strapped herself in. She stared into the rearview mirror, prodding at the thin, crusted scabbed wounds at her neck. Seeing the raw, red lines crisscrossing her smooth skin was like a slap to his control. "Leave it alone," he said, raw vehemence a low growl in his voice. He slammed the door, emphatic punctuation to all the gentler, frightening things he couldn't say.

Like how bone-achingly empty he'd be if she had died.

She rolled her eyes at him. "Don't yell at me."

Silas jammed the key into the ignition, turned it hard. The engine sputtered, hitched, before turning over, and he gritted his teeth. "Leave it alone," he repeated tightly, "*please*. And don't touch my mirrors." Grimacing, he twisted the rearview mirror back into place and knew it wasn't the mirror riding his ass.

He hated this. Hated her being there, in danger again.

Jessie dropped her hands. "Sorry." She didn't sound it. "Distract me, then. Where are we going?"

Silas guided the truck out of the ruined parking lot. He left the nav system off as he worked his way down old blocks, past knots of street punks, bums, loiterers. There were more than he expected.

Or maybe just more than he remembered.

When he'd gone too long without answering, Jessie turned in her seat to frown questioningly at him. Her thin eyebrows knotted. "Is there," she asked slowly, "I don't know, a plan?"

"I'm working on it," Silas muttered, and was relieved when she fell silent. This wasn't going to be easy. Naomi was right. Damn it. The Coven of the Unbinding wanted Jessie, apparently for a ritual. There were a dozen offhand that came to his mind, but without more information, Silas didn't have shit to go on.

Any number of rituals spiked in power when the blood of a relative got added to the mix. It had to be a big one. The witch bitch had said they'd been hunting for her. Specifically.

Silas glanced at Jessie, relieved to see color creeping back into her skin. Her drying hair waved gently around her face, strands of gold that made him remember how it looked spread over his chest. Clutched in his hands.

Shit.

"Okay," he said. Jessie turned an expectant gaze to him. He had to ease into it. "All right, let's go over our questions. See what stands out. What does the Coven of the Unbinding want?"

She shook her head, her expression wry. "Me, apparently. But why?"

He turned his attention fully to the road. The rain drizzled, a faint mist of water over the windshield, and he flicked on the wipers. "A ritual," he replied. Too grim. Too damned anxious. "According to her. So what kind?"

Jessie spread her hands. "You got me. That's your specialty." She shifted. "Who's the leader?"

"Caleb?"

A beat. Jessie spoke slowly, thoughtfully, "I'm not sure. That woman didn't say he was. I—" She blew out a hard breath. "I still don't think so, but I know he'll tell us who is."

Silas didn't voice his skepticism. Instead he reached under the seat and hauled the duffel to the space between them. "Front side pocket," he said. "There's an extra comm there. My number's keyed into it. Keep this on you from now on. We can track the frequencies, a kind of beacon to find each other when teams get separated."

"Are you planning on leaving me?"

Silas frowned at her. *Yes.* "When I have to."

"Have to?" She retrieved the unit, checked it over with quick, sure fingers before sliding it into her jacket pocket. She zipped it closed and slanted him a look designed to piss him off. "Good luck with that."

"Come on, Jess," he growled, too tired, suddenly too stretched to bother with nice. "Think smart for a second. You're a civilian, these are killers we're talking about here, and we don't have the first clue of what they want or where to find them. I can't drag you all over the city and hope God sends a neon sign, and I can't protect you by myself."

She twisted in her seat, slammed one foot up on the dash in a way guaranteed to make him cringe. "I'm not stupid," she said, icily pointed. "Didn't you listen to her? I'll bet you they're holed up in the ruins."

"Well, that's great," he replied flatly, shifting up to

a higher gear as they turned onto the carousel. The highway gleamed in the barrage of headlights, rain-washed and misted. "It's only several dozen miles of ruins in any direction, complete with fifty-year-old death traps and canyons that drop to the center of the fucking earth. Where should we start?"

"I'm just saying—"

"Stop," he snapped. "I can't just drag you down there on a hook and wait for them to come biting!" He glanced at her, ignored how anger turned her eyes to molten gold.

Pretended to ignore it.

Damn it, she was hell on his concentration. "There's too many factors at play here, and no one expected the coven to want you. So we need to know why."

"I told you, my brother—"

He cut her off, slashing his hand in the air between them. "That witch almost killed you, Jessie. Doesn't leave me feeling secure about Caleb's intentions."

She jerked her chin up. "You had a gun on her, what was she supposed to do? Ask nice?"

"Fuck!" Silas set his jaw, staring back at the road winding in front of them. "Look, I'm not going to just hand you to them. We're partners. That means my number one priority is your safety. That's it."

She sucked in a breath hard enough, sharp enough, that he knew he'd struck something. A nerve? A soft spot?

And could he play on it again?

"Okay." She straightened, slowly. Raised one hand to her neck, caught herself and deliberately lowered it again to her lap. "So you're going to, what? Dump me somewhere? On some poor sap's front porch? I appreciate the sentiment, Silas, but that's bullshit."

"It's not someone's front porch, Jessie, it's topside and surrounded by more security than anywhere else in this city. You'll be safe there, trust me."

"You, I trust." The thought warmed him in places he didn't want to think about. "But what about your people?" Desperation crept into her voice. "What about the fire at your safe house?"

"It's you."

Her eyes widened. "What?"

"They're dialed into you somehow," Silas explained, watching the road closely. Traffic slowed, a sea of red brake lights as a flurry of police sirens suddenly split through the muted cacophony of rain and car horns. "Shit," he muttered. "Look, maybe they're using your brother's blood, maybe it's some kind of tail I can't shake. Witches can do a hell of a lot, and you're not protected by St. Andrew's Seal like we are."

"But leaving me alone with strangers—"

"If it keeps you safe," he began, only to grip the wheel tighter when she cut him off with a barbed laugh.

"Christ, listen to you. You're like some sort of martyr, wandering in to save the girl and wander right back out again to die."

"I'm not going to die."

"You don't know that," she retorted. "You're the one who says witches are so nasty—"

"Says?" He reached out, caught a fistful of her hair in a grip designed to make her gasp. To force her to look at him. "Were you there when that bitch cut your throat?"

Jessie wrenched at his grip. Winced when it pulled at the fresh scabs just under her jaw. "You're hurting me."

"No, I'm not," he said flatly, every word an angry, even tone. She had to understand. She had to get it. "But *they* will hurt you, Jess. They'll kill you. When they want something, witches will stop at nothing. Do you need to be reminded?"

Because she wouldn't be Jessie if she didn't, she slammed her elbow into his arm. He let her go, cursing.

Proud, despite himself.

Annoyed as hell.

"I get it. I do, I see what you're saying." She rubbed at her elbow. "Some witches are bad. Fine. You want to abandon me to other people for my own protection, great, that's very noble of you. But they want me, Silas. I could bring them to you, end this sooner that way."

"The bitch said leverage." Silas's fingers tightened on the wheel. Cramped. "I'm not willing to lose you to whatever politics are eating that coven from the inside out."

"But I could—"

"No, and that's final." Silas raised a hand, cut her off again. "I don't care if I have to tie you up and drag your tattooed back screaming up the carousel, you're topside and that's the end of it."

The downward curve of her mouth tightened. Without another word, she scooted as far away from him as she could on the seat. Every bone in her body telegraphed the fuck-off Silas knew he'd just earned.

Grimacing, he took his annoyance out on the road, jerked the truck neatly in between two cars and sped up to slide into the far right lane.

He glanced at Jessie's face, found it drawn beneath a taut mask. She gripped her thighs, her skin clean and pale against the dirt and blood streaking her worn jeans, and stared grimly at the skyline spread out beside her. Strove for indifference.

Failed. A watery sheen of tears shimmered in her too-wide eyes. Whiskey and water. God*damned* son of a bitch.

When he got his hands on Caleb Leigh, Silas was going to make him pay for every tear Jessie had ever cried.

He clenched his teeth. "Look," he began, only to bite his own tongue as her shoulders wrenched back in a violent, angry shrug.

"I don't care." She didn't even look at him.

Damn it. What was he supposed to say? To do? Drag her along with him as he crawled the lower streets? Paint a neon sign on her back, wave her around like some sort of living bait? Make her watch while he executed the brother she was so stuck on?

Fuck, no.

She'd deal. He knew she was going be angry, but at least she'd be alive to have that luxury.

CHAPTER FIFTEEN

The engine thrummed as Silas pressed down on the gas. Cars around them roared and honked, a steady rumble of engines, tires on worn pavement, the rattle of old metal, old construction. Old city, all the way down.

The rusted guardrail sliding by the passenger window protected a drop that never failed to impress him.

Beside him, saying nothing, Jessie raised her fingertips to the glass and stared up at the ambient light brightening with every passing minute. The city thrust up proudly to the sky, a woven, tangled, layered maze of rock and metal, glass and the dull, ugly spread of humanity.

Too many humans. Too many grand ideas. He'd

spent fourteen years staying away from the big cities for that very reason. The press of people on all sides made him antsy.

Naomi had found him on the sunny end of a Florida cooperative, investigating rumors of a small coven. He'd enjoyed the sun, surf, the good food grown by the community.

Maybe, when this was all over, he'd find a way to send Jessie there. Without him.

Under her fingers, on the other side of the rusted guardrail, the Old Sea-Trench yawned into view. "It's so clear and bright up here. Down below, it's easy to forget that the trench splits out from either side of the city. We just . . . get used to the dark."

He glanced out her window, grimacing. What could he say? Half the city spent every day in the shadows of the looming towers above. They were only three-fourths of the way up, two levels below the first security checks, and the sunlight was already brighter. Warmer. The top levels sparkled, a crystal-clear beacon.

"Caleb was fifteen when he came up with this wild plan to fly." Jessie's voice seemed taut, strained as she stared out the window.

Silas opened his mouth, tasted the acid reply building on his tongue. Shut it again.

"He drew this thing." A small laugh crept out of her throat, fragile and weary. "This . . . contraption, with wings. Feathers and everything. He said he planned to jump off the carousel and glide down to the heart of the Old Sea-Trench."

Silas shook his head, firming his grip on the wheel

as a double-trailer truck roared by. "Sounds like a hell of a fantasy."

She nodded, but still didn't look at him. He didn't like that he wished she would. "He said there was something amazing down there, something full of adventure and treasure. He wanted to find it."

"I guess if you like lava," he said dryly.

Now, finally, she glanced at him, mouth curved into a smile. "Anything can be treasure when you're fifteen years old."

"Did you ever find treasure, Jessie?"

Silas could have bit off his own tongue when the light glimmering behind her features faded. Her smile died. "I didn't have to look. I had Caleb."

The brother who turned out to be a witch. Silas wished, for one wild moment, that he could have met that girl she tucked away so neatly into the past. Found her before the shadows had crept into her eyes, before the guilt and the grief. He shook his head. "Sunshine, I—"

Her eyes widened. A sudden sweep of urgency, tawny mirrors of alarm filled her face a nanosecond before the seal of St. Andrew sparked. Ignited.

Pain slashed through his wrist, crackled up his arm. Jessie reached for him, said something he couldn't hear as every muscle in his body went rigid. Gray clouded his vision, muffled everything, but he didn't need to see clearly to know that his arms had locked, that his hands clenched the wheel.

He struggled. *No.* Screamed it. *No!* Muscles bulging under his skin, he strained to reclaim control of the body that moved without him, but all he could do was watch the truck shudder, veer.

Listen to the denial in his own head as his mindless body yanked the wheel hard and rammed them into the guardrail.

Jessie lurched. She scrabbled at the steering wheel and choked as the seat belt locked against the impact, pinning her tight.

Sparks shot out over nothing as the truck slammed into the railing. Metal shrieked against metal, twisted and bent. The truck skidded around, planed hard across wet asphalt and listed violently to one side. The bottomless well of the Old Sea-Trench yawned below his window, pitch black where the light didn't drip far enough. It ate at the city foundations, endless and empty under the south side carousel.

The bottom dropped out of his stomach.

"Fuck!" Suddenly Silas's muscles unlocked. He exploded into action, grabbed the wheel and wrenched it back, but it was too late.

The guardrail bent, snapped hard and sheared through the door. His leg. Pain shattered shock, momentum thrust him against the wheel, slammed him face first into the twisted leather. Horns blared, tires squealed around them, but all he could hear was the blood in his own ears.

The fury of his own pulse.

And Jessie.

She would have given anything for Caleb's wings now.

Jessie clung to the strap lashed tight across her

chest, held on for dear life as the truck yawed back and forth like a seesaw. Metal bent until it shrieked with the effort, razor edges twanging back as it scraped through the truck's thin siding. She screamed again as the whole damn thing lurched.

"Don't move!" Silas flattened one hand against her chest, shoving her back against the seat. She froze, every muscle vibrating in terror.

Oh, God. Oh. God. What the hell was this? What the hell had happened? One minute, they'd been talking and the next—what?

The next, she'd watched power crawl over him like an inky, oily cloud. Watched magic roil over Silas's skin, drown the protective flare of the tattoo, and sink in. Seize control.

Drive them into the guardrail.

And it had felt, tasted like Caleb.

Panic clawed at her throat. She locked her jaw.

Cars swirled behind them, horns blasted. All she could do was stare helplessly into Silas's fog green eyes as the truck listed forward.

Her heart jumped into her throat, pounded wildly. "Silas," she whispered. "What do we do?"

He removed his hand from her chest, moved it as if through molasses to control the steering wheel with a white-knuckled grip. "Slowly," he said. "Very slowly, unlock the door."

Jessie nodded, a fraction of a jerky inch, and gradually, so carefully her arm shook with the effort of smothering the screaming urge to bolt, she reached for the lock.

White-faced, every angle a sharp edge of fury and

grim resolve, Silas kept both hands clenched on the straining wheel. "Good," he breathed. "Brake is solid. Keep goi— Shit, easy, sunshine." Rain splattered over the windshield, and the truck shuddered.

Outside, framed in the passenger side mirror, Jessie saw cars circled around them. Others slowed. A knot of shocked people stood on the shoulder of the road, some talking into their comm units. Holding up cameras. Shouting. In the distance, the first sirens wailed.

Jessie heard none of it. As the lock pulled up, as she reached shakily for the latch, the spectacular view of New Seattle pitched. Jessie screamed as metal groaned, tore, and ripped free.

The spires slid out of sight, replaced by endless black.

Swearing, Silas jerked the wheel around but it wasn't enough. Jagged claws of metal ripped at the underside as the truck tumbled off the byway and slid nose-first into nothing. Gravity slammed them both back against the rough seats, ground like a fist.

Jessie ran out of breath, thrashed wildly for purchase, and as the daylight gave out to nothing, as they fell too deep for the city lights to follow, her searching hands found warm skin, solid muscle.

Silas's forearm locked hard against her chest, pushing her against the seat, and she clung to it. Wrapped both hands around it and thought that if she had to die now, here, she'd be holding on to a man she could have loved.

Could have?

Now that she was going to die?

Oh, no.

Fury hammered at panic. Pounded through her veins. Resolve and fiery anger shredded the restraints locking down her magic, and Jessie closed her eyes. She would not go out this way. Not now. Not when so much counted on her, waited on her.

Not when she had so much left to do.

So much left to *say*.

"Hold on!" Silas roared, and she held tightly to his corded muscles as the power surged free. She let it, let herself go, snapped to that place where the threads tangled.

Saw the present, saw them plummet end over end in the veiled dark. She saw the bottom of the descent.

Deep water. Impact.

A chance.

For the second time, Silas's seal sizzled blue as her magic slipped around him, around them both. She pumped it full of everything she had, every iota of fear and determination, of the fragile thread of a feeling too uncertain to label as anything but a flimsy wish.

A tenuous cushion, but maybe it'd be enough.

She clenched her teeth. "Brace—!"

The truck hit icy water, the windshield shattered, and the muted shadows filling Jessie's vision went bright white. Painful red.

And then endless, empty black.

CHAPTER SIXTEEN

Time stopped.

Everything froze, still and quiet in a sudden silence that swallowed the world.

Silas shook, buried in ice. Bitterly, bone-achingly cold. Was he alive?

Was he dead?

It didn't feel easy. Hardly peaceful. But a lot less bloody than he'd ever imagined it.

Cold. Wet. But not alone. *Jessie.*

Silas jerked to consciousness, already choking on a breath full of icy water. His lungs burned, throat achingly raw as he expelled it. Hacking, struggling, he fought the frigid waves pouring over the dashboard.

The cab filled steadily, listing to one side. Already up to his aching ribs, the waterline rose by persistent increments. No time. He flailed in the dark, searched for her.

"Jessie?"

He couldn't see anything. Couldn't hear anything but the terrible roar of water and the blood rushing in his ears. He needed to see. Needed to know that Jessie was okay. "Hang on," he rasped, hoping like hell he wasn't talking to dead air.

He felt along the crumpled steering wheel, teeth chattering with cold. It took him three tries, but he finally found the lever for the interior lights and seized it in desperate relief.

A watery glow illuminated the dark, spilling incandescent light into the cab.

It highlighted Jessie's body, pale and luminous in the dark. She hugged the dashboard, her face a crimson mask shining in the filtered light. She didn't move. Didn't open her eyes. Silas's heart twisted, panicked.

"Jessie!" Heedless of the pain, he wrenched himself free of the tangled wreck of the steering wheel and seat belt. The rising water sloshed over them both as he placed shaking fingers against her neck. "Come on, sunshine," he coaxed hoarsely. "Come on—there. Yes, God, please." A flutter against his fingers. Or did he imagine it against his numb skin?

Shit. Shit!

Though it tore every curse he knew from his frozen lips, Silas managed to reach across the cab and pull the latch on his door. Busted ribs. His knee throbbed like he'd jammed it in the fall. Hypothermia was on the horizon.

It didn't matter. None of it mattered, he'd push through the pain. She had to get out. He had to get her to dry land, get her warmed up. Bandaged.

Bracing himself against the seat, he jammed both feet against the driver-side door and kicked out. It stuck, pushed back as the water forced it shut. Gritting his teeth, he kicked once, twice. Three times, harder, and his knee screamed in fury and pain. More water sloshed over the shattered window.

The truck jarred, tilted further. "Fuck, no, fuck me swimming, God, *come on*." Out of options, he turned toward the only exit. Grabbing the edge of the windshield frame, holding on as tight as his numb fingers could manage, Silas leveraged his body through the narrow gap. He knelt on the hood, shoved his head and shoulders back through to gather Jessie's listless, unresponsive body in his arms.

She was bone white in the fading light. Her lips edged blue. Silas cradled her close, guided her gently through the rapidly narrowing fissure. Head, shoulders, waist. Legs.

When she was free, bobbing awkwardly against him, he pushed away from the truck that had carried him through fourteen years of missions.

The old girl deserved better than a watery grave.

But then, so did Jessie.

One arm wrapped tightly around her chest, her face supported above the waterline as best as he could, Silas turned slowly in a circle and gauged his chances.

Slim to astronomically bad.

Freezing water. Darkness too thick to penetrate

even with the faint headlights sinking beneath them. No sky to guide him this deep under, and no wind.

Closing his eyes, Silas cast a fervent, mental prayer.

Let her be okay.

Let her be alive.

If she wasn't okay, then damn it, Silas would make her be okay, just let her be alive.

Shivering, he buried his lips in her wet hair.

They'd come too far to end it like this, hadn't they?

Silas took a deep breath and struck out for what he desperately hoped was shore. Any shore would do.

But it didn't take long before his muscles started to burn. He scissored powerfully through the water, diagonal to the current shoving him deeper into the trench, and thought burn was good. Burn was motion. Heat. He just had to hang in there.

The Old Sea-Trench had two sides. He'd hit one.

He just hoped there was a way out when he did.

Silas didn't know how long he swam, or at what point his extremities lost all sensation. He pushed on, pushed harder, desperately conscious of Jessie's terrifyingly still body cradled in one arm. Unconscious. Dying?

Dead?

Christ. *No.* He wasn't going to play that game. Not while the strength leached from his muscles. Frozen water curled deep inside his bones, eroded his willpower, his energy, but he'd be damned if he gave up now. Gave in to the cold. The deep.

The fear.

A bulky silhouette loomed out of the dark. The interminable rush of the fast-moving water broke with a splash, and something hit the water beside him.

Silas jerked back, lost his rhythm, and sank like a rock. The freezing river closed over his head, Jessie's head.

Drowning.

He struggled, stroked back through the current. His ears full of water, locked under pressure, he twisted with his precious burden. A flurry of bubbles swirled around him, eddies around a dark current, and he knew he was too slow.

From the black, icy currents, hands grabbed at him, hooked in his jacket. He tried to fight back. Couldn't get his brain to send the command as pale skin flashed in front of him. Dark eyes.

Red hair?

Or blood.

Jessie bled. He had to get to Jessie. Protect her.

The surface of the water split above him. Droplets rained down, fat and thick, and he suddenly found himself hanging ass-out over the side of a metal, flat-bottomed boat.

Sweet, cold air burned in his chest. Gasping, choking, he tried to push himself back out over the edge. Back into the water. "Nng!" A croak of sound. He tried again. "Jessie," he managed. Where was she?

Something caught his waistband, hauled him fully into the boat. It rocked wildly, side to side, and Silas fell awkwardly onto his wounded shoulder. The pain lanced his brain into blistering gibberish.

"Good gracious." A woman's voice. Strong hands

grabbed him by the hip, pulled him flat. "Don't move. Your lady's fine, she's right next to you."

Silas wiped water from his burning eyes. "Jess," he rasped. "Jessie, Christ." She lay splayed beside him, shades of white and blue. Her lashes spiked over her cheeks and blood oozed sluggishly from a gash at her temple.

Trembling, shaken to the core, he gathered her into his arms as the boat rocked. "This isn't fine," he growled over her head. "This isn't— Jesus, sunshine, hang on."

If the woman at the back of the boat was at all intimidated by him, she didn't so much as flick him a gesture to show it. She stood shrouded in the shadows of the trench, expertly using a long oar as she guided them along the current. What he could see was little more than a silhouette.

Her voice, Silas realized, was weathered. Firm. "She's had a nasty knock, but she'll live if we can get her to warmth," she said. "Tuck yourself around her. Keep her warm."

Warm? Christ, he couldn't even remember how to spell the word. Still, he tried. Pulling her fully into his lap, guiding her thighs around his waist, he wrapped both arms around her and held on fiercely. He rubbed her back, her arms, trying to process any friction through her wet clothes. Any heat.

"Think warm thoughts," he murmured into her cold hair. "Heat, desert sands, tropical beaches. Sun. Fuck, sunshine, you're warmth all by yourself. The way you walk, the way you smile."

Water splashed against the side of the boat. Shuddering with cold, Silas tore open his jacket, wrapped it snugly around them both. "The first time I saw you," he muttered against her temple, rubbing his hands up and down her back. Long, fast, hard strokes. "I thought you reminded me of sex and whiskey. Hundred proof, all the way."

Sex in five-inch heels. Silas let out a hard breath. He hadn't been wrong.

"Damn it, sunshine, I can't think of anything warmer." He rested his chin on the top of her head, closed his eyes. Listened to the splash and dip of the oar and the rough whisper of his palms on her back.

Slowly, subtly enough that Silas thought he imagined it, the darkness faded. It slipped under his eyelids, delicate light that blossomed as the current picked up speed. Gathered intensity. The boat rocked, and as he raised his head, looked around, the woman braced herself. "Hold on," she warned.

He did. He held on to Jessie, still as death in his arms, and jammed his knees against the edges of the canoe. He glanced over the edge, saw the eddies of white capping the suddenly angry current. Took in the solid rock hemming them in on both sides, a jagged, fractured cliff border.

And the woman, their savior, who smiled at him. Actually smiled, with her oar held out of the water and dripping across her narrow shoulders. "It'll get rocky in a minute."

Silas stared. "Who are you?" he demanded.

"Later." Tall and thin, she moved easily with the current, swaying in practiced rhythm as the boat picked up velocity. Her thick mass of red hair cascaded in a half-dry tangle over her shoulders, liberally streaked with gray.

She might have been seventy. Maybe fifty. It was a hell of a range, but Silas couldn't pin her down on either. The structure of her face had been thinned by time, elegant still, with deep lines pinching into crow's feet as she squinted against the brightening light. Brackets edged her mouth when she smiled at him.

Maybe her smile was supposed to be reassuring. But as he stared at her, at her rain slicker and too-large jeans, he felt anything but reassured.

Who was she? Where were they going?

Where the fuck were they now?

Silas's arms tightened around Jessie. "Tell me who you are," he demanded. And because he couldn't help it, added, "Please."

The brackets at each side of her mouth deepened in amusement. "Oh, have it your way. My name is Matilda." The woman pitched her voice to carry over the water. "You're safe with me. I have warm fire and food, and most of what you'll need to patch up."

His tongue felt too thick for words. Clumsy. He swallowed, tried anyway. "I—" What? What did he have? *Nothing.* He gripped the edge of the boat in one hand as it rocked violently. "Silas," he replied. "This is Jessie. Thank you."

Matilda grinned, and her face crinkled like worn parchment. "Don't thank me yet. It's not a hotel."

Silas grimaced. "We don't have any money," he began, only to grunt in mingled pain and surprise as the boat lurched hard, slamming his knee into the metal edge.

Matilda bent with the flow, shrugged off the oar and lanced it neatly, expertly into the water again. "Don't you worry about that," she said as she threw her weight into steering. "I'll take what I can get, and you've got more than you think. There we go." The canoe shook, groaning as she forced it out of the current's rapid flow.

He held Jessie close, frowning as the cliff wall loomed closer. Jagged edges, serrated rock slammed by them too fucking close. "The boat—"

"Shush." Matilda didn't look away from the wall she watched. She lifted the oar, slid it into the water on the other side, and hauled back on its long handle.

Too goddamned close. Silas prepared to kiss the water again as the right side of the boat scraped against the wall. Rock shrieked against metal. The sound gathered, a crescendo scream, and Silas clenched his teeth, his muscles.

Only to slam back against the rim as the pressure suddenly vanished. A hole in the cliff opened up in front of his eyes, a spot in the wall he'd never have seen if they'd just followed the current.

They slid over a rocky lip, dipped nose-first, and flopped into the calmest, greenest water Silas had ever seen.

Ripples splashed out around them as Matilda used the oar to push away from the rock face. "There," she said again, smugly this time.

He got the impression of color, of brighter light and a strange kind of warmth in the air.

Jessie stirred. His gut clenched. "She's waking up."

"No, she's not." Matilda quickened her pace,

rowing them across the water with surprising, tensile speed. "She'll stir and moan for a while yet. Almost there."

Silas bracketed Jessie's face in both hands, searched it for signs of awareness. Of consciousness. Her wide mouth was slack, lips slightly parted. To his annoyance, his anger and fear, he noticed that his fingers shook as he traced her cheek.

"Come along." The boat bumped to a jarring halt. Matilda clambered onto a small dock, coiled a rope around a post, and beckoned. "Hurry up, now. Too late for second thoughts."

She was right. He knew it. Everything had already slammed out of control. Way, *way* out of control.

Cradling Jessie's too-slight weight in his arms, he followed. The strange bay existed in a crescent of green water surrounded by cliff walls. He stepped off the dock, his boots crunching against a strange mix of black sand and tiny pebbles of smooth rock.

Silas stared at the house nestled in the far point of the half moon, its mix-and-match window frames a lopsided beacon set a hundred feet from the smooth, glassy green water. A sea of purple flowers curled in over the roof, and he could smell the pungent, spicy aroma of tropical blossoms, though he couldn't find them in the lush fronds that grew like privacy screens to the right of the house.

The air was humid, shockingly warm, and beyond anything he'd expected. Where was this place? Why hadn't anybody reported it? The stretch of clouded gray sky far overhead told him that the canyon was wide enough to be seen by air, but he would have remembered reports of this.

"Dawdling isn't going to help her," Matilda said as she beckoned imperiously from the porch.

Frowning, he lengthened his stride to catch up, cradling Jessie's still body to his chest. She had stopped shivering, but she didn't open her eyes. "Can you help her?" he demanded, ducking through the door Matilda held open. "Can you wake her up?"

"I think so." She eyed him, and in the daylight streaming through the windows, he saw her eyes were dark, dark brown. Steady and sure. Older than he'd thought.

Old in a strange, knowing sense.

Silas looked away, frowning as he took in the wooden bed frame, the odds and ends that filled every square inch of every surface. Pictures, old and worn toys. Wooden carvings and vases, some with flowers in them. He saw scarves arrayed over one wall, a riot of colors and patterns, and the windows glowed with variations of glass in each pane.

Only the smooth wooden floor had space to move in, and even this gave way to ancient rocking horses, antique chairs, and stools that hadn't seen a revival since before the earthquake.

A collector? A survivor?

"Who *are* you?"

"On the bed, please." Matilda bent over the mattress and pulled down the blankets, patting it. "Let me see to your lady."

"She's—" Not his lady? Silas frowned, shook his

head. He lowered Jessie to the mattress. "What can I do?"

"Get her undressed and tucked in. I'll be back with water and gauze."

Silas nodded, but she was already leaving the cottage. Hurriedly, gently as he knew how, he unzipped Jessie's jacket and tried to be as objective as he could as he slid it down her cold arms. Her gray camisole fell over her shoulder, its broken strap dangling, and he peeled it over her head with a muffled curse.

He'd buy her another one. Hell, he'd buy her a hundred, all in different colors. She barely stirred as he tackled her jeans, her boots.

When a glint of silver fell out of one black boot and clattered to the floor, he barely registered the sound. His mouth dry, he tucked Jessie's long, cold limbs under the covers. Let his fingers smooth over her skin, thumb her bottom lip at the small scab there.

She was alive. Thank God, thank Matilda, thank whomever, she was alive.

Silas edged away. Grunting, he jerked his foot up when something hard and raised wedged into the sole of his wet shoe.

The silver leaf embedded into the tread didn't look like anything he'd seen before. Had he ever seen Jessie wear it? He didn't think so, but he hadn't spent a lot of time admiring her taste in jewelry.

As he ran the cold metal through his fingers, the door creaked open behind him. "Out of my way," Matilda ordered, and set a steaming bowl of water down by the mattress. He obeyed, suddenly feeling overly large, overly clumsy. Overly in the way.

The older woman touched Jessie's wounded neck, her chest. Her stomach. Picking up her wrist, Matilda tilted her head, and then slid a shrewd glance toward him. "How are you feeling?"

Like he'd fallen thousands of feet through nothing and slammed into a steering wheel on impact. Silas grimaced, thumb running over the thin metal between his fingers. "I'm fine."

Her eyes gleamed. "Really."

"Look, is Jessie—"

"Yes." She pointed at him. "Listen here, young man. One thing I don't tolerate in this house is falsehoods." She turned her back, unfolded a towel, and dipped it into the steaming water. "So when I ask, 'How are you feeling?' you would do well to say . . . ?"

His fingers stilled over the warmed silver trinket. A dull, throbbing burn crept up his chest. His face. His ears. Feeling a hell of a lot like a kid caught smuggling candy in class, Silas very gently put the pendant on the table beside him and reluctantly admitted, "Ribs took a beating, left knee's going to lock up. My head hurts, face feels like it was hit with a brick, but all due respect, ma'am"—he nodded at the bed—"I just want her okay."

"Mm-hmm." A noncommittal sound, if he'd ever heard one. Then she smiled. "She'll be all right. You get out of my hair, now. There's a hot pool out behind the house you should soak in. Does wonders for an aching body."

So that was the smell. The odd mix of sulfur and something sweet and cinnamon, something humid and warm. Silas watched her peel back the blankets and lay the hot towel over Jessie's chest.

Should he be reassured that she didn't sound concerned? Should he leave her?

Did he have a choice?

Maybe. The seed began to germinate, unfurl slowly. Maybe this was as safe as she'd get. Maybe this was where he could convince her to stay until he came back.

"Matilda."

"Mmm?"

He hesitated. What the hell could he say that would matter? There weren't enough words. "Thank you," he managed. He'd never meant it so much in his life.

Dark eyes flicked to him. Sparkled. "Out," she commanded, imperiousness and impatience shoved into one royal syllable. "Come back in an hour and we'll dress those wounds."

Wounds? Right. The cuts, the bullet graze. Everything else he didn't want to, couldn't deal with right now. Silas thumbed the bridge of his nose.

And he went. Because what the hell else was he going to do?

CHAPTER SEVENTEEN

The rain drummed a musical beat against the thin metal sheet protecting the refurbished office from the elements. Each note shimmered like a tiny gong, sweet and oddly cheerful, but it didn't take the edge out of the air.

Didn't take the sting out of Alicia's catlike smile.

Caleb stood casually in front of the scavenged desk, his blond hair shadowing one eye. It was too long these days. In his way. He jerked it out of his face as he ignored the raven-haired witch beside him. Instead he focused on the man who stood behind the polished desk, hands clasped almost military-style at the small of his back as he studied a large, old-fashioned map pinned to the reinforced wall.

Curio, they called him. Not much of a name. A

witch didn't need much of a name, Caleb reflected grimly, when he had that much power and skill.

And a stern finger in every pie.

The man didn't suit this half-exposed office with its two standing walls and rigged ceiling. Curio's hair had once been brown, but silver now dominated most of it. His chiseled features suggested an iron disposition etched into his genes, and though lines softened the planes of his face now, Caleb had never made the mistake of thinking him soft.

The coven master was many things—genial, intelligent, manipulative, thorough—but *soft* had never been on that list.

Caleb cleared his throat. He had no doubt the man knew he and Alicia stood there. Had been there for a full five minutes already, and that after being summoned to his chosen headquarters.

Games. Always the games.

Power, the kind that really suckered people, didn't just come through magic. The man was savvy as hell.

Curio didn't turn around. He didn't take his eyes off the out-of-date map as he finally drew in a long, audible breath. "I'm afraid," he said by way of greeting, "that we have good news and bad news to contend with."

Alicia stirred. "What would you have of us, master?"

Caleb's lip curled. Greedy, suck-up of a woman.

"First, the good news." Curio turned, and his elegantly martial features were pleasant. Never a true indication, Caleb knew.

He didn't relax. Not inwardly. Outwardly he gave

every appearance of being at ease, of being comfortable. But only the dead really got comfortable in Old Seattle.

He'd buried more than a few after all.

Curio stared at him, his pale, pale blue eyes sharp as the edge of a knife. "Caleb," he said, and smiled. Not the pointed, eat-you smile Alicia favored, but something warmer. Friendlier. "Caleb, I'm pleased to say that your sister has been found."

It took every last iota of willpower Caleb had to return his gaze calmly, to raise his eyebrows and project interest. Curiosity, instead of sudden dread. "Oh?" It was a poor substitute for leaping across the desk and shoving the knife he kept in his sleeve into the man's throat.

This was not in the plan.

"That's great news," Alicia all but purred. She nudged Caleb with an elbow. "When can we get her?"

Curio's eyes didn't shift from Caleb, even as he directed his words to Alicia. "Your enthusiasm pleases me, my dear, but that segues us nicely into the bad news."

Around his thudding heart, a tiny sliver of hope had Caleb mentally crossing his fingers. In witchcraft, everything counted. "What would that be, sir?" he asked, deliberately putting concern into his tone. Into his eyes.

Lying had never taken too much effort. Jessie'd taught him everything he knew.

He used it well.

"What," Alicia chuckled, slanting him a look laced with menace. "You can't see the future?"

He ignored her.

So did the coven master. Caleb could all but feel anger rising from her in clawed waves as her barbs failed to find the soft target she aimed for. Control wasn't her specialty.

Her knife would lance out of the dark one day. But not yet.

Curio leaned down, bracing both palms against the desk in a pose typical for him. Frustration, maybe. Annoyance.

Suspicion.

The man was flexing muscle. Why?

Caleb caught himself chewing on the inside of his lip. "Sir?" he prompted.

"Caleb." Curio took a deep breath. Let it out in a long, low hum. "I appreciate everything you do for us, I've said this before."

Caleb's brow furrowed. "Yes, sir." Shit. What had he done wrong?

"I look forward to a future with you at my side. This I have also said."

Caleb nodded. Once. Beside him, Alicia's teeth audibly ground together.

"Therefore," the older man continued, pushing himself upright, "I find myself in a position where I regret the words coming from my mouth today."

Get to it, Caleb thought grimly. The man was prevaricating. What the *hell* had Caleb done that would piss off Curio? He'd been entirely too careful with everything, *everything*. There was no way—

"Caleb, did you attack a witch hunter today?"

Caleb stilled. Every muscle in his body tensed. Lie?

No. He stared into Curio's knowing, patient eyes and knew the man already had his answer.

Well. Truth, then. Caleb nodded. "I did."

"What?" Alicia rounded on him. "Who? When?"

Curio raised a hand, silencing her as effectively as a gag. But he didn't look at her. Didn't see the fury that stamped itself on her fine features. "I respect your initiative. That hunter killed four of our own, and I know John was a friend."

Caleb's mouth tightened.

"I can understand and sympathize with your anger," Curio continued quietly. Almost gently, damn him. "But you should have been more careful."

"With all due respect," Caleb said, leashing back a rising tide of anger, of impatience, "I don't understand what the problem is. He's dead, isn't he?"

Curio came out from around the desk, his broad frame clad in casual slacks and a neat sweater. He looked like someone's distinguished father, or some kind of nautical gentleman. Not the leader of a witch's coven, and certainly not like a man the city would one day learn to fear.

Caleb knew better. It took effort not to clench his fists.

"That hunter," Curio said as he stopped in front of both witches, "was not alone. One of our search parties located Jessica and tracked her to an apartment in mid-city."

Caleb stiffened. "Wasn't alone?" Hell! Was he too late, after all? Had the bastard found his sister and— Now his fists clenched. "Did he kill her? Did we lose our chance?"

It couldn't be possible. He'd *know* if his sister was dead.

Wouldn't he?

The coven master stared at him for a long, silent moment. Searched his face. His voice was somber as he replied, "That hunter killed two more, and Brian barely escaped. But at last report, she was alive. And *with* that missionary at the time of your attack."

It took a moment, longer than it should have, but when it sank in, it did with claws. He reeled. Tried to keep it off his face, and knew he'd failed.

He'd been too late. Jessie was in the truck when he'd sent the damned thing over the railing. She'd been with the hunter already, maybe even tied up and unable to help herself when Smith's body had turned the wheel against his will.

Hundreds of feet. Thousands of feet.

Did Caleb just kill his sister? Expend all of that hoarded power to overcome the damned Mission seal for *nothing*?

"No," he said hoarsely. He scraped both hands over his face. "I thought it was just him. I didn't think—Damn it. I messed up. I'm sorry, sir, I—"

Warm, callused hands settled on his shoulders and gave him a small shake. "Caleb, my friend." Curio's voice was strong. Bolstering, even warm. "You acted rashly, but in good faith. And, perhaps to fate's credit, Jessica Leigh is not dead."

Relief cut deep, a double-edged sword. "Where?" he demanded. He gripped Curio's sweater in one fist, intensity burning through him. "Where is she?"

Alicia wrapped one hand around his shoulder as

she said, "We'll retrieve her together, won't we?"

Very gently Curio disengaged Caleb's hand from his collar. "I'm afraid not," he said. Too softly. All apology. "Caleb, I know you meant well, but you cost me time and considerable effort. I've sent out teams already. We don't know where she landed, but we know her soul hasn't fled." The implication was clear.

They'd find her. Not him. He'd be removed from this task, from his sister's trail, leaving him blind and dependent on the reports of others. Damn it.

Caleb straightened, shrugging off Alicia's hand, and rapidly recalculated everything he knew. Time. Effort. Words. *Plans*.

He had one shot, one sliver of an opportunity, at doing this right. The knowledge caused a cold sweat to gather between his shoulder blades.

"All right," he said. Nodding, brow furrowed, he met Curio's pale blue eyes. "I'll gather the items for the ritual and begin prep. We should begin the purification of the site, at least, in case they find her quickly. That'll take a day, less if it's as untouched as claimed."

Curio's smile warmed as he stepped back. "Good. I'm glad you understand. Begin immediately and requisition anything you need. And, Mr. Leigh?"

Caleb paused mid-turn, glancing over his shoulder. Already half gone on preparation, it took him a moment to realize that Curio waited for him. For his full, undivided attention.

He turned back around, faced the desk. "Yes, sir?"

Curio placed the very tips of his fingers together.

Pointed them subtly at him. "If you ever act without my permission again," he said in his deep, quiet voice, "I will personally peel the skin from your bones. Is that clear?"

Caleb's hands ached from the strain of keeping them from curling into fists. His jaw shifted, teeth gritted, but he bent his head. "Yes, sir," he said tightly. "I'm sorry."

"Apologies, while appreciated, will not bring Jessica Leigh to us. If she had died, we would have to begin all over again. That is not time easily regained."

"Yes, sir," Caleb repeated. God damn it. He knew this.

Curio inclined his head. "I trust you appreciate the gravity of the situation. Do not fail me again. We need your sister."

"I know, sir."

"Dismissed."

Caleb turned, ignoring Alicia as she loitered behind him. Fear, worry, anxiety all clamored at the back of his mind. Knowing that time was running out, he fled the office.

CHAPTER EIGHTEEN

Uncertainty replaced the sweet oblivion of sleep. Jessie woke slowly, gently surfacing from the dark to a warm, soft bed, a cocoon of cozy blankets, and the comforting smell of sage and cinnamon. It wrapped around her, so reminiscent of one of many fading, flighty memories of years past.

Of a childhood almost forgotten.

Of a mother whose face blurred around the edges.

A warm hand touched her cheek, her forehead. Smoothed over her hair. Jerked and went still when Jessie snapped her fingers around it.

Her eyes flicked open.

The blankets didn't go away. The scent of dried herbs and cooking food didn't fade into nothing. And the woman looking down at her didn't look anything less than pleased to have her veined, thin wrist locked in Jessie's shaking grip.

"Well, it's about time, young lady."

Jessie blinked hard. "I'm sorry, did you just admonish me for being unconscious?" Her voice rasped out of her too-dry throat, but it didn't hurt. Surprised, she let go of the woman's wrist to touch her own neck. Soft cloth ruffled under her fingertips.

The woman chuckled, swatting her hand away. "Don't undo all my hard work. You're safe, or as safe as you're going to be for a long time. Careful," she hurried to add as Jessie struggled to elbow herself up.

Jessie groaned. "I feel like I've been hit by a truck."

"In a manner of speaking, a truck was certainly involved." The woman slid strong hands under Jessie's shoulders, supported her upright. She tucked more pillows in around her, fussed and smoothed out her blankets with effortless care.

To her horror, Jessie felt a prickle of sudden, embarrassed tears burning at her lashes. "Christ. I mean—" She winced. "Thank you, but—Look, I'm sorry, where am I? Where's Silas?"

The woman's eyes gleamed. "Your young man?" She grinned as she rose from the edge of the bed. "Not to worry, my dear. He's been in and out of here for the past few hours, making sure I hadn't cut out your heart and roasted it in the fireplace."

Jessie snorted. "Was that a concern?"

"For him? It seems likely."

She couldn't help the way her lips edged upward into a rueful smile. "I guess so," she admitted. She relaxed back into the pillows, a full-body sigh of relief. "I'm sorry."

"Don't be," the woman replied briskly. "He's a fine watchman, and a finer figure of a man. My name is Matilda." As she turned away, gray-streaked braid swinging, Jessie took the opportunity to study her.

Matilda moved gracefully, thin as a whip but elegant in her wraparound linen pants and timeless tunic-style shirt. Elegant and timeless. Good words, and they described everything else in the room with her.

Jessie's gaze skimmed over knickknacks, bric-a-brac, shelves and hooks of ornaments. Cluttered, messy, both artful and artless, they hung, stood, or rested against one another. Next to a ceramic bowl of large purple flowers, she spied an old, worn baseball with the faded ink of some long-forgotten signature on it.

Beside a bronze statue of a seminude woman, hair and garments flowing, a carved wooden box shone cherry red in the light. Its lid supported an aged wooden tray inlaid with something polished and colorful. Dried herbs bundled neatly with colored string lay on top.

Slowly, thoughtfully, Jessie took in all the signs. Old, faded hints that winked deep in her subconscious. Feathers arrayed by the windows, inks and crystals, herbs drying. Her gaze flicked back to Matilda.

The woman watched her closely, a patient half smile shaping her thin mouth. "No harm will come to you in this, my home," she said softly. And yet, firmly. Something faint, something elusive and incandescent tugged at her memory. Her awareness.

When it clicked, too slow, she gasped. "You're a witch!"

"Mmm." Matilda wiped her hands on the hem of her tunic. "Says the young witch herself." Her chocolate brown eyes crinkled as Jessie threw back the covers. Lit with laughter when Jessie realized her state of undress and jerked the blankets right back over her chest. "And a naked one, at that."

Embarrassment burned Jessie's cheeks. What the hell was the matter with her? She'd worn things that were as good as nudity to work.

But Matilda's eyes, as if she could slice to the very bone of Jessie's secrets, unnerved her. "Excuse me," she managed, a bare thread of dignity, "but where are my clothes?"

Her smile widening, Matilda crossed to an old chest of drawers. The wood gleamed in dark mahogany, beautifully maintained. The drawers barely made a sound as the woman withdrew an array of colorful fabric from inside. "Relax, my dear. These should suit," she added as she brought them over. She laid out a long patchwork skirt in shades of blue and green, a thin cream tank top.

Jessie's fingers itched to touch the material. "I can't possibly—"

"They were my daughter's, once." Matilda ran her fingers over the fabric. "They will keep you comfortable in the warm air. I insist you wear them."

How could she refuse? She bit her lip. Looking into Matilda's quiet brown eyes, she knew she couldn't.

"Thank you," she said, but she frowned. "Matilda, I swear I don't knowingly bring harm, but there may be people hunting me."

"No eyes can see past the cliff walls," Matilda assured her. If she was concerned, Jessie couldn't read it in her serene smile. "No beacon will mark you here. Get dressed, now. Your young man is waiting." She turned, disappearing back through a small doorway. A soft curtain in woven rainbow colors drifted back into place behind her.

Jessie eased out of bed, wincing as her body cataloged the aches and bruises. There were too many. Hurriedly she slipped into the plain cotton panties Matilda supplied, shimmied into the skirt. It flowed around her ankles, swirled in folds of patchwork silk, linen, velvet. The tank top was soft to the touch, and she smoothed her hands over her sides as it settled.

She felt . . . frilly. Absurdly feminine.

As she admired the ocean colors of the skirt, Matilda returned carrying a brush. "You look beautiful, dear. Here, brush out your hair."

Jessie did just that, wincing as she worked the tangles.

Matilda's smile warmed. "There, now, aren't you pretty as a picture?" Jessie flushed, dropping her gaze, then jumped when Matilda caught her chin in stern, dry fingers and raised it again. "None of *that*, either," she chastised. "You say thank you and accept it as your due. As I told your man, there's no falsehoods in this house."

"Thank you," Jessie replied automatically.

"There. Supper will be ready in an hour or so."

She gestured to a wall of light tucked into the far side of the room where a low island counter separated the living area from what looked like a simple, rudimentary kitchen. Mismatched glass windows gleamed in the streaming light.

Jessie nodded, but her mind rolled the warning around like marbles through her fingers. "No falsehoods?" she inquired. "No lies, you mean?"

The witch walked across the room. Sailed across it, Jessie thought, like a queen through her palace. "None," Matilda said over her shoulder. "So you mind what you tell that witch hunter of yours."

Witch hunter? Shit.

Jessie sucked in a breath, mentally panicked when Matilda turned, both hands braced on the island counter. "Don't do it," the older witch warned, a hard glint in her eye. "Don't test me by lying. I know what he is, probably more than you. So you mind what you say and what he tells you. Lies out themselves here."

No lies. No falsehoods. Since she'd done nothing but lie to Silas from the beginning . . . The thought trailed to an icy pit of anxiety deep in her belly.

"Find," Matilda said sternly, "something else to say to each other."

Like what? The weather? Jessie wasn't sure she knew how. "I'll try," she finally said, too aware that the older witch watched her expectantly.

"Good girl." She waved Jessie off. "Now go on. Show yourself to that handsome man before he wears another hole in himself fretting so hard." She withdrew a large butcher's knife from a wooden block, set it to a bunch of greens. Something savory perfumed the already fragrant air as she made the first slice.

Jessie hesitated. Was this ward against lies a ritual? A power? A circle?

What if Silas found the signs of witchcraft?

Did it include half truths? Omissions?

Did it matter, knowing what she knew?

Matilda cocked a faded red eyebrow, but didn't look up. "Something on your mind?"

"Yes." She paused. "No. Sort of," Jessie sighed. Her bare feet warm on the polished wood floor, she picked her way across the small room.

"Out with it." Matilda's deft fingers peeled and sliced, wielding the knife with an expert hand.

"I'm fairly sure I'm going to die."

Matilda's hands stilled briefly. "It'll happen to us all, sooner or later," she replied mildly. "You certainly labor under a destiny bright enough to scald the eyes."

Jessie's mouth curved up into a wan, wry smile. "Not reassuring."

"Sorry, baby girl, it's the best I have." Matilda scraped the leafy greens off the knife blade. "What makes you suspect your death is so close?"

"A prophecy." Jessie folded her arms over her stomach. It did nothing to quell the anxiety there. "Well, a handful of them, actually."

"Prophecies are dangerous business. More often self-fulfilled than true foresight." Dark brown eyes flicked up, gleamed. "What did this prophet of yours say, then?"

"Well, there was the tattoo of the leering jester."

She held up a finger. Then another. "And the stopped clock in the Old Seattle ruins, the tomb that time forgot. Those happened."

"Happened. You saw them?"

Jessie nodded. "Fairly literal. Last is the green house under the violet sky."

Matilda's knife thudded into the scarred cutting board, a sharp staccato that broke the easy rhythm of chopping. She fixed the angle of the blade, repositioned the pungent herbs, and only then spoke. "Where does it all lead?"

"My death," Jessie replied quietly. "Burned alive, I think."

"Ah." With a ghost of a smile, the older witch pushed the small pile of fragrant leaves aside and said sadly, "Most of us have that particular hell inscribed upon our souls. Racial memory is a terrible thing."

Just a common fear? Did she dare hope? "So, does it mean—?"

"That it's not going to happen?" Matilda shook her graying head. "While the future isn't my gift, I've been around, you know. I survived two children and the destruction of my home, and you don't come away from that without knowing a thing or two."

Jessie winced. "I'm sorry."

Dark eyes flicked to her. Narrowed. "Don't be. We all have graves inside us, Jessie. We all have coffins we carry around. You, me, your missionary. It shapes us." Matilda flicked green-flecked fingers. "My point is that I have a few tricks left up my sleeve, and you'll want to hear me when I say what I'm going to say next. So, are you ready?"

"I'm ready." She hoped. Jessie wasn't sure she could stand any more prophecy.

Matilda put down her knife, very gently. "Then listen to me, daughter," she said, and suddenly the air closed hot and thick around them both. Jessie gasped, grabbed the edge of the tiled counter.

Matilda didn't bat an eyelash.

"Nothing in this world is black and white." Her words dropped like jewels in the sunlight, practically sparkling in crystal tones. "One is merely the absence of color, which is boring, staid and without life. It is stagnancy. The other is every color, which is chaotic. Untrustworthy, unpredictable, and unstable. Neither will bear life."

Jessie sucked in a breath of air riddled with power. "I thought you said you couldn't tell the future," she managed.

"I don't tell the future." Matilda's voice didn't change, neither tone nor volume, but impatience snapped like a whip. Lashed at Jessie the way a school mistress's ruler snapped at unruly fingers. She jumped. "Listen to me, Jessica Leigh, and listen well: you cling to two beliefs. One leads to death. The other to pain and suffering. Two difficult choices. You *must* choose one, and soon, or the choice will be made without you."

"But I—"

"You do not want to be a passive player in your own destiny," the witch said sharply. And then, as suddenly as it came, the air lightened. Sweetened once more with the fragrance of freshly chopped herbs and the vivid scent of hothouse flowers.

Jessie blew out a hard sigh, swiping at a trickle of sweat rolling down her temple. "Wow," she managed shakily. "That was some kind of . . . something."

Matilda swayed, her skin ashen, but she threw up a hand when Jessie moved. "I do not read the future," she repeated, and this time her voice was just a voice. Resigned, but her own. "I read the scripture of the soul, and yours is most definitely conflicted."

Death? Pain and suffering? *Conflicted* couldn't possibly do it justice. It seemed as if death stayed hard at her heels, drawing blood with every nip. But whose death? Whose suffering?

The questions jumbled around in her head, a hopeless tangle of what-ifs and uncertainties. Jessie rubbed at her temples, hissed when her fingers pressed on bruised skin. "No kidding," she finally said. "I guess I knew that much."

"Well. That's that, I suppose." The knife blade picked up its rhythmic *thunk, thunk* as the older witch returned to her task. "Off you go, then. Supper in an hour."

Knowing that for the dismissal it was, Jessie turned for the door. She was halfway out when Matilda called out, "The hot pools are to the left. Check there first."

Jessie shut the door behind her.

Two choices, she thought. One was death, and the other pain and suffering. She shook her head, smoothing her damp palms along her thighs, and turned to step off the porch.

Her bare feet sank into oddly smooth sand. She

gasped, surprise and pleasure, as her mind focused on the scenic vista laid out in front of her.

Had she gone to heaven while she'd slept?

A miniature valley in itself, the bay was a jewel nestled in the maw of the Old Sea-Trench. An old wooden dock jutted out into wildly green water, while a low, clinging haze rolled over the polished surface.

It was warm, much warmer than she expected. Sunlight filtered down from the hazy sky far above. She tipped her face up, closed her eyes, and inhaled deeply. The thick underscoring of sulfur merged with something warmer in her nose. Something hotter, smoky, like wood charred to a black finish. It seemed, despite the conflicting fragrances, fresh somehow. Refreshing.

So serene. So . . .

Quiet. It was quiet, with none of the hum and chaos of the city to break its solitude. No police sirens, no screaming, no violent, wild music. No hum of constant electricity.

Jessie bit her lip as she stepped off the porch, awe sliding once more through her. She followed a pretty collection of smooth stepping-stones, noted the deep carvings etched into each surface. Protection. Peace. Christ, even the ritual symbols for *home*.

That emblem had once marked the first of the flag-stones in her mother's parlor. They'd lived there for only a month when she'd been killed.

Tears welling hot and sweet in her eyes, she paused halfway to a wall of rock and oddly lush fronds and struggled to collect herself. Everything had officially been upended. She needed to find a balance, and she needed to do it before she found Silas.

Jessie turned, shading her eyes against the light.

And felt it, *saw* it, click into place.

There's a green house under a violet sky.

Oh, God. There it was. Jessie wrapped her arms over her chest, cupped her elbows, and held herself as icy shivers ran down her spine.

She smiles inside that house, Jessie, but her eyes are diamonds and her bones are clay. If you let her, she'll show you how to die.

Caleb's voice rose sharply in her mind, edgy and impatient. In her memory, in her mind's eye, he gestured wildly at her. Argued with her.

We can stop this one, he'd insisted. Paced their rathole motel room in shades of fury and fear. His lanky hands splayed in the air; he'd fought so hard to convince her. *Run when you see the joker. Don't go into the tomb. And for God's sake, Jessie, don't go near a green house and don't accept her help.*

She swayed in a sea of mist. Of memory.

You follow the path she points to, and then you're standing in a broken bowl, in an ocean of red. The sky ignites, and you're burned to death, Jessie. Burned alive. Screaming my name.

But she'd dismissed him. Flung her scorn and disbelief at him, so angry with it all. Frustrated with the years of running and hiding and arguing. He'd gone silent. So silent.

As she had lain awake that night, Jessie thought to

apologize. To puzzle it out with him, do whatever she could to remove the shadows from his eyes.

But Caleb was gone in the morning.

Jessie stared at the charming cottage. Its somewhat slanted beams were rough, its patchwork details evidence of how tough a woman Matilda really was. The coat of dark green paint lent a charming elegance to a house cobbled together at the seams.

And it lent an eye-catching contrast to the sea of violet flowers that climbed the cliff wall behind it, a floral bower that swayed like an awning of sweetly scented purple silk.

The green house under a purple sky. That was three for three.

And she wasn't surprised. Not now, as the world settled around her. She'd already known it was coming, knew it from the night she'd met Silas.

Was it only two days ago?

It seemed like forever. An eternity of being hunted, of running, of lying and omitting and—*Shit*. In Silas's arms, Jessie found at least a moment of respite. Of peace. The same feeling that touched her here, in this strange valley.

She scraped stiff fingers through her hair, wincing again when it pulled the wide scab at her hairline.

Caleb's prophecies never lied. Jessie took a deep breath. Set her jaw. Death was coming.

Coming fast, it seemed, and Silas was there for every sign. He'd been the one to fight the man with the leering jester tattoo. He'd been the one to find her in the abandoned church under the frozen clock, to fill her body and her mind at her most vulnerable.

He'd been the one to bring her here.

Integral to every sign.

Would she die at the hands of the man she knew she was growing to love? Is that what this all meant? Burned alive by the witch hunter who seduced the beating heart from her chest?

Because that, Jessie figured as she turned away from the neat house and floral sky, would be sadly hysterical. Fittingly ironic. Death, just another word for peace.

And she wanted peace. God, she wanted peace.

Every cell in her body quivered with anxiety, with exhaustion. Raw nerves. Reluctantly squaring her shoulders, she followed the path to the left.

CHAPTER NINETEEN

She saw Silas before he saw her. The trail of sand twined through the leafy foliage hugging the rock, fanned out from the path. Its smooth surface touched the lip of water that gleamed in shades of green both vivid and surreal.

The water rippled, lapping against the sandy shore, and in the middle of it, Silas's body gleamed in strong, lean lines.

The man was wildly, intoxicatingly appealing.

As Jessie stepped off the path, his dark head turned, arrowed in on her as if he'd been waiting. Watching. She saw the worry, the relief, wash over his features even from where she stood. He raised a long, tanned arm and headed for her.

Richly defined muscle flexed and rippled as he cut

powerful strokes through the shimmering water. It took moments for him to reach the shallows, and as he strode up the sloping ground, she couldn't help but be deeply aware that he was naked. Completely, unabashedly naked.

A slow, wicked heat unfurled low in Jessie's belly. She couldn't, didn't want to stop her eyes from feasting on every inch of his rugged body.

For this moment in time, Silas Smith was hers to admire.

Broad shoulders tapered to lean hips, muscles cut sharply from arms to chest to the ridged beauty of his abdomen. Strong thighs flexed with every step. Scars and healing wounds peppered his skin, marred the etched perfection of his physique. She swallowed hard, forcing back the sympathy, the tide of heartache for the pain each must have caused him.

This was his job. The scars that had healed, pale against his tanned skin, and the bruises and wounds that mottled his chest in thin lines, in sweeping contusions or ragged furrows from stray bullets; all of it was his job. A job she despised.

But knowing it, reminding herself, didn't ease the wicked curl of lust, of passion, that spread languidly under her skin.

Water rolled off him in rivulets, dripped from his dark hair. As he came closer, she allowed her gaze to lazily sweep back up his body, meet his eyes head-on and without embarrassment.

She wanted him.

Those gray-green eyes darkened. Without a word, with nothing more than a low, rough sound, Silas grabbed the hem of her borrowed shirt and drew it over her head. Before it had even cleared her arms, he brought his mouth to hers. Claimed her lips, her wanton, encouraging moan.

He tasted clean and wild and masculine, all aggressive power and leashed need.

Jessie helped shed her skirt, using her feet to peel the fabric down over her legs. The soft cotton of her underwear followed, and Silas locked a forearm around her back. She stumbled into him. Let him catch her.

Hold her.

Magic writhed beneath her skin. Hungry. Desperate.

No falsehoods.

Wrenching his mouth from hers, he pressed hot, wet kisses to her cheek, the sensitive spot under her ear. Feathered them across her collarbone as he lifted her off her feet.

Where his lips touched, her skin burned. Where his hands held her, she felt weightless. Secure. *Safe.* She wrapped her legs around his waist, thrust her fingers through his wet hair, and covered his lips with her own. But he wasn't a man who let anyone have that control, and Jessie reveled when he nipped her lower lip hard enough to make her gasp.

His chuckle rumbled from his chest, vibrated against her breasts. Against her mouth.

Dimly she heard splashing. She opened her eyes to find he'd carried them back into the green water, and then gasped in mingled surprise and pleasure when he sank into it. Warmth spread through her limbs as the water climbed over her legs, her thighs, her waist. Heat soothed her ribs, jolted her as it pooled between her legs, and then sent her arching with delight when he found that hot, wet core of her and slipped in one finger.

She locked her arms around the back of his neck as he stroked her. He slid a second finger into her damp flesh and crooked both. Almost rocketing out of her skin, battered by waves of warmth and need and joy, Jessie twined her fingers through his hair and welcomed the sudden rise of pressure and tight, roiling release building inside. Welcomed it with unabashed relish, practically preening as he watched her ride his fingers. Felt her slide herself along his body, skin to hot skin.

He wanted her, too. It darkened his eyes, as shrouded as the mist that swirled around them. He spoke, low, tight words of approval, encouragement, coaxing more from her.

Her climax rippled from toes to forehead, burned inside of her as she cried out in the calm and quiet. Silas palmed the back of her head with his free hand, brought her lips to his and swallowed her wild gasps, her long, wicked moan. Hungry, demanding, he withdrew his fingers and replaced them with himself, with the hard muscle of his erection.

Before the shockwaves ebbed, before her brain could regroup, he entered her body. Claimed her, her mouth, her soul.

Claimed the witch he didn't know she was.

Practically floating in the heated water, drifting in the spectacular bloom of a second, sinuous climax,

Jessie clung tight to Silas's shoulders, his waist. Rode him as he thrust inside her, withdrew, thrust again. The water rippled, lapped at her skin, and she felt the rising flush of liquid heat in her chest. In her cheeks, roiling under her flesh.

Saying nothing at all, his eyes heavy-lidded and half lost in her, Silas spanned her waist with both hands, tilted her hips just so, and her world fragmented in a pool of glassy green.

It wasn't until she remembered to breathe that she realized he'd held her the whole time. Kept her safe in his arms, above the water.

She turned her head, pressed her lips to his shoulder. *Thank you.* Closing her eyes, she hid the veil of tears that clung behind a thin veneer of control.

It wasn't enough. It would never be enough.

They floated lazily in the water, naked and warm. Silas watched her when she wasn't looking, and every glossy inch of her sent his heart thumping erratically in his chest.

She was so beautiful. Wild and slippery as a fish when she glided past him, splashing.

He wiped water from his eyes, smiling despite the crushing fear that weighed him down. It wouldn't last. This peace, this tranquil spot in time, was going to fracture.

She was going to fracture.

How could she not?

"So what's the deal with the water?"

He glanced over his shoulder. "Volcanic," he explained. At her inquiring eyebrow, he grinned, kicking his feet to push himself farther to the middle of the pool. "We're somewhere in the Old Sea-Trench. It goes deep, far enough down to crack open a few vents into the earth's crust."

Jessie treaded water awkwardly, expending more energy than she needed. Maybe he'd teach her, later. Take her to that beautiful Florida beach and show her how to swim with minimal—

What the hell was he thinking about? Later? After she finished cradling the body he was going to put in her arms? Fuck. Silas palmed his face. Viciously stomped on his own thoughts before his mind could paint any more pretty, unreachable pictures.

"So it's all heated by lava?" She ducked under the surface, came up again with a sound of uniquely feminine delight. "It's like a tropical slice of heaven."

"Lava or steam." Silas wrenched his brain to the subject at hand. It was an easy subject, lava and heated mineral pools. A harmless, innocent subject.

Which Jessie was swimming in, every inch of her body naked and wet and warm and—

"Damn it." He ducked under the surface, let the water close over his head for a long count of ten. The world was murky green, barely visible past the reach of his arms. It was quieter, calm. Somehow soothing.

When his lungs clamored for air, he bobbed back up. Water splashed over the back of his head.

"Show-off."

Silas turned, feigned menace in his expression. "Okay, that's it," he growled, and lunged through the green water. Jessie shrieked, tried to back away, but he caught one slender foot in his fingers and jerked her back. The water closed over her golden head, and he used the opportunity to fold his arms around her.

She came up sputtering, her water-darkened hair plastered and dripping over her face. "Cheater!" she accused, laughing. Undaunted, she twined her arms around his shoulders, fingertips grazing through the hair curling on the back of his neck.

Their legs bumped, and Silas curled his hand around her thigh, guided her knees around his waist. He couldn't get enough of her mile-long legs, especially when they locked around him. "So," he murmured, tracing the wet line of her back. "I didn't take you for a tattoo enthusiast."

Her eyes crinkled. "I'm not." When his hand splayed over the bar code on her back, she moved a pale, feminine shoulder in a half shrug. "I've always had it, ever since I could remember."

And how strange was that? "Your parents didn't tell you?"

"No." She sighed, twining her fingers around the back of his neck. "We only ever knew our mother," she added, with such honesty in her summer eyes that he couldn't keep himself from leaning in to tongue the full curve of her lower lip. Kiss away the matter-of-fact way she spoke about a history that made his chest twist in answering sympathy.

She hummed something sweet, throaty, and he knew he was a sucker. Seduced by honey and whiskey; what the hell was he doing?

And why didn't he stop it?

Because he'd almost lost her. The thought didn't hover too far away. Ever circling. He'd almost lost her, and to magic. God, if only the seal had been stronger. If only he'd been able to stop the spell from overwhelming him.

To block it, somehow.

Jessie smiled into his eyes, smoothed one finger back over his whiskered jaw. "Matilda said dinner was in an hour."

"Was this"—he eased out a breath as her pelvis nudged him in the current of their bodies—"before you got here?" he managed.

"Yup." Her eyes gleamed in the light, reflecting back the shimmering depths of the green water.

"I don't suppose you're hungry?" Silas tilted his head to find that sensitive spot at the base of her ear, the one that made her body vibrate in his hands. On cue, she let her head fall back. Hitched a breath.

He was starving. Silas imagined she'd be famished, too, but the feel of her body was too good, too solid and real and goddamned *good* against him to lose it now.

"We should eat," she said, her body shuddering as he tongued that sweet, silken spot. "Silas, stop, I can't think."

"Good." But she was right. Reluctantly Silas raised his head. He tilted her chin up with a finger and covered her mouth with his, poured every ounce of hunger, of need, into that kiss.

Knew he'd hit home when her arms and legs tightened around him.

But she only laughed shakily when he kicked toward shore. She uncurled from his waist, eyes gleaming, and held his hand as they made for land.

"You are going to regret that," she promised as they climbed the sandy slope.

Silas turned, trapped her hand in the small of her back, and kissed again. Hard and fast. God, she even tasted like sunshine. How the hell did a woman taste like sunshine?

Half drunk on her, half gone already, he stepped back and shook his head hard. He noted the same dizzy lust in her expression and knew he was in deep, deep trouble.

"Let's go eat," he said.

They wriggled into their clothes. Silas kept a surreptitious eye on her as she bent to retrieve hers. His gaze swept over the long sweep of her back, her long legs. He liked the view a hell of a lot more without those tiny gold shorts she'd worn before.

A lot had happened between then and now. He'd almost lost her, almost killed them both under a witch's spell, and he knew it could happen again. He'd have to leave her.

Damn it, she'd never understand.

No, he corrected himself. He gave her more credit than that. She'd understand. But she'd never agree. The argument in the truck had made that perfectly clear.

How could he make her see how much every bruise, every cut and ache and scar that ripped at her tore at him, too?

And when the *fuck* did he end up over his head?

Except Silas already knew the answer to that one. The instant he'd laid eyes on a bare-legged, red-lipped brunette with honey in her eyes, he'd sunk.

The moment he'd kissed her in a dark, rainy alley, felt her body arch into his.

"Should I dance?"

Silas jerked his attention back to the present to find Jessie eyeing him, a slow smile curving her wide lips. He could have her again, if he wanted. He knew it.

She did, too.

Way, *way* over his head. "Food," he said roughly, firmly, and headed for the cottage.

She chuckled. When she caught his hand, twined her fingers with his, something in his chest went supernova. Silas stared straight ahead, swore viciously and silently while his traitor hand held hers.

CHAPTER TWENTY

By some sort of silently mutual consent, they didn't speak about the circumstances that had brought them to the trench. Silas had gone quiet as they walked back to the cottage, and Jessie didn't pry.

If she pried, then he'd feel obliged to ask questions. If he asked questions, she'd have to lie.

Which meant he'd know she lied.

Which meant more questions, and more answers he wouldn't like. Wouldn't, actually, tolerate.

So she'd let it be, and silence had turned into gasps of wonder and delight as Matilda led them around to the back of the small house. There, surrounding cobbles made of smooth, glassy rock, a riot of wild, rainbow color spilled from every available nook and cranny.

"I don't know what they are," Matilda said in her no-nonsense tone, "but they grow easily here and don't require too much to keep them." Despite her careless ease, her eyes sparkled with pride as Jessie moved from bucket to basin to wooden crate, touching and smelling each colorful bloom.

Silas fingered one with the edge of one finger. "It looks," he said thoughtfully, "like a hibiscus. Sort of." He glanced at Matilda. "I wonder if the environment brought some sort of progressive evolution."

Jessie eyed him, planting one hand on her hips. "Why, Agent Smith," she drawled, amusement welling up in a laughing lilt. "If I didn't know better, I'd say you sounded just like a fancy educated boy."

Color rose in his cheeks, stained his hard features red, and Jessie had to turn away before the emotion squeezing her throat spilled out. "Your garden is beautiful," she told Matilda, proud of herself for managing to sound casual. To keep the sensation, that dark, unstoppable sensation of falling down a deep, dark hole, at bay. "You must work so hard."

"Thank you, dear." The woman waved a hand at the table arranged in the middle of the glassy porch. "Everything we're eating comes from it, and the fish is fresh."

Silas was the last to sit, and he studied the fare laid out with what Jessie thought looked like approval. "You catch fish from the trench?" he asked.

Matilda grinned. "What else do you think I'd be

doing out there? Waiting for folks to fall into my river?"

"We're glad you were there," Jessie said earnestly. "It was such good timing, I can't—Oh." She reached for the first plate as her stomach growled in alarming desperation. "It smells incredible."

And it was, although both Silas and Jessie looked askance at some of the vegetables Matilda served them. Still, Silas apparently could eat anything, and the first bite of what looked like purple radishes and tasted like something entirely different had Jessie's eyebrows winging up in surprise.

Matilda laughed, shoulders shaking, when Silas crunched down on something soft and caught the hard pip squarely between his teeth. Juice spurted everywhere, spattering over the table and the front of his shirt. Jessie helped mop it up between fits of giggles.

But like everything else, it couldn't last.

Before long, dinner was over, and Jessie helped Matilda clear the table while Silas remained outside. Matilda scraped seed pits and peels into a bin of organic compost, but her eyes leveled on Jessie. "It's time you come up with a plan, baby girl."

Jessie's good mood deflated. It left her tired. More than a little reluctant. "I know," she murmured. "I wish we could stay forever."

"I wish you could, too," Matilda said, "but the world will go on spinning without you if you stayed. That's not a good thing," she added, reading the spark of inane hope Jessie knew lit her eyes.

She sighed. "I guess."

"I *know*," Matilda corrected, and nodded back toward the garden that blossomed behind the back wall. "That man wouldn't do well here. Not now. If you asked, he'd stay, and it'd eat him up inside. Choke everything right out of him like kudzu wrapped around an old oak."

"I know," Jessie said. She touched the thin scabs at her throat, tracing the light seam of raised, healing skin, and closed her eyes. "Damn it. I do know that. Silas eats, sleeps, dreams about his job. What he sees as his responsibility. But it's going to kill him one day."

Matilda set the plates on the counter. They clinked delicately.

"I think," Jessie said, pitching her voice low, "that he's hoping it will."

"It's a choice." The older witch turned, taking Jessie's hands in her own. She placed them palm to palm, folded her hands around both, and looked down into her eyes. "There's a lot of lies between you. Any fool can see it. You can't shape anything but failure on lies."

Jessie cringed. "If I tell him anything—"

"He'll do his duty," Matilda agreed. "That man will always choose responsibility. Blessing and curse. You'll have to act soon." She squeezed Jessie's hands, let her go. "So let's go make plans, then."

Silas waited in the garden, standing on the edge of the cobbled patio. He watched the sky darken in increments, frowning. "I know it's cold topside," he mused thoughtfully. "But it's as warm as a Florida beach here. It's damned surreal."

Jessie nodded, folding her legs into the chair and tucking the long, soft skirt in around her feet. "It's heavenly."

"Thank you both," Matilda said, pleasure and amusement in her tone. "I gather it's damned surreal in heaven, too."

A smile touched Silas's lips, and Jessie watched it slide into his foggy eyes as he came back to the table. But he didn't sit. "Matilda, we owe you one."

The witch smiled. "You do," she said. "And I'll tell you what you can do to repay me."

Jessie tilted her head. She said nothing, watching witch and witch hunter.

"Don't," Matilda said firmly, raising both thin hands, "tell a soul about this place. Ever." Her eyes intently bored into Silas's, level and unwavering. More than a match for the warrior's soul in him.

Hell, Jessie was pretty sure the witch would be a match for any god who crossed the boundary of her cliffs.

Silas nodded slowly. "Done," he promised. "You've carved out an amazing home for yourself. And alone. That's something."

Matilda smiled. It softened the regal lines of her face, gentled her gaze. "Good. Now, when did you plan to leave?"

Jessie opened her mouth, but Silas cut her off. "Immediately," he said, and flicked her an apologetic glance. She shut her mouth again.

That was that, wasn't it? Hell, she half expected the answer. There went her man, she thought in bitter humor. The call of duty.

Matilda nodded, as if she, too, expected the time-table. "Good. Jessie, I'm terribly sorry to say you'll have to wear your own clothes when you leave."

Jessie smoothed her hands over the beautiful colors, unable to help a sudden wash of longing. "I understand," she said softly.

Silas came around the table, stood behind her. His warm, callused hands settled at her shoulders, and Jessie's eyes closed.

"Silas, will your people be looking for you?"

Behind her, Silas's voice rumbled an affirmative.

"Good," Matilda said. "I'll take you downriver, about a mile from here. That should be far enough, and it's not too hard to say you rode the current all the way down."

"We appreciate everything." Silas rubbed Jessie's shoulders in small, soothing circles. Her heart in her throat, she opened her eyes and found Matilda watching her.

Jessie smiled. Knew it for the grim little line it was, but hell, she tried.

The older witch nodded, as if reading the answer she needed in Jessie's face. "Then let me get my boat shoes," she said, rising. "Silas, we'll meet you at the dock."

Jessie unfolded from the chair. She turned under Silas's fingers, pressed the palm of her right hand over the warm expanse of his chest. His heart beat solidly against it. Hers kicked. "Before we go," she said softly.

Something swam behind his eyes, something fluid

and wary. But he touched a finger to her lips. Let it slide, gently, to her bottom lip. Quickly, before she could think around the sudden surge of heat, of fractured awareness, he replaced his finger with his lips.

Warm, firm, oh, so gentle, Silas kissed her like he knew what she'd meant to say. Like he didn't want to hear it.

Didn't know how.

Jessie's fingers curled into his shirt as she mentally kicked herself. Of course it wasn't good-bye. Of course he didn't know anything more than what she'd shared.

Of course, she thought as she poured every bit of herself into that kiss. Into him. She drew back. Forced an easy smile to her sweetly seduced lips. "Idiot," she said lightly. Only she knew that it came on the heels of a declaration she'd never make.

Silas tucked her hair behind her ear with a finger. "I'll be sorry to see that skirt go."

She tried to say something, anything. Tried to respond with the same lighthearted, flirty ease, but it caught on her throat. Before he could see the tears in her eyes, ask her about it, she stepped out of his reach and turned away.

Hot tears slid over her cheeks before she managed to get inside.

Silently Matilda helped her dress in her worn, ratty clothes. She braided Jessie's hair, wrapped it with a long strip of ribbon, and Jessie let her.

Let her take over while her tears burned a path out from her heart. Her soul.

In the end, Matilda slid a long leather cord around Jessie's neck, and pressed a kiss to her forehead. "You're strong, my dear. When you're ready to make your choice, you'll follow through."

Jessie hefted the smoky obsidian hanging from the cord. Swirls of gold-tinged black hovered under its raw surface, facets within facets. Shadows within glass.

It warmed under her touch.

"Keep it safe." Matilda took the rock from her fingers, slid it neatly under Jessie's camisole, and zipped up the battered neoprene jacket. Jessie felt it heavy against her breasts, warm and solid. "There now," the other witch said. "No one the wiser."

On impulse, Jessie threw her arms around the woman. "Thank you," she said. "Just being here, just this long—"

Matilda flattened one hand against Jessie's back, wrapped the other around the back of her head. "You alone," she said in Jessie's ear, "may speak of this sanctuary. Use it well."

Jessie's eyes widened, but the woman withdrew, said nothing more as she led the way to the dock. Silas waited by the boat. Jessie took his outstretched hand, let him help her into the metal canoe.

As he settled in behind her, her back to his chest, his strong thighs bracketing her hips, the stone at her breast warmed to burning over her heart.

Yeah, she thought, resting her head against Silas's shoulder. The fading light turned to night. *Yeah, I know.*

* * *

The boat was silent as it glided through the current.

Silas did nothing to break the quiet, simply held Jessie against his chest, his chin on the top of her head, and watched the cliff walls fade into the inky gloom of the trench.

When it came time to drop them off, Matilda briefly cupped his face in both hands, pressed a kiss to both cheeks. Her mouth was dry, firm, against his whiskered jaw.

Then he slid into icy water and all thought, all breath, sucked out of his lungs. Waiting until Jessie was in beside him, he took her hand, held it firmly as he swam through the current that sucked them relentlessly downriver.

After what seemed like an eternity, Silas's feet scraped on rock. He found the edge of the cliff shelf with relief. Shifting his hold on Jessie's icy hand, he hauled her closer to the ledge. "Up," he shouted.

He couldn't see her well enough to know if she heard, but slowly, every motion shaking with cold and effort, she dug her booted feet into his hip, his shoulder. Nudged his ribs, which made him lock his jaw against the pained words he didn't want her to hear.

She didn't have to know how badly he hurt.

Finally her weight was gone. Within the space of seconds, he felt her fingers clasp tight around his wrist and pull. It took more effort than he liked, but with her help and pure force of stubborn pride, Silas managed to get out of the water.

Shivering, teeth chattering, he got to his feet and thrust his hands blindly in front of him. Darkness filled his vision, so thick he couldn't see anything more than the vaguest outline of Jessie's body as she wrapped her arms tightly around herself.

"J-Jes-sus," she chattered.

Silas caught her by the shoulders. "Come on," he said, hoarse from effort and cold. It seemed a lifetime away that he'd made love to her in a heated pool. Now, freezing in the cold and damp, he guided her farther back from the lip.

She fumbled in her pocket as she staggered beside him. "Here." With effort, she managed to get the zipper of her pocket open, retrieved the comm unit he'd given her before they'd gone over the edge.

In that moment, Silas could have happily kissed her mouth, her feet, and the cold, rocky ground she sprawled on. He sank to his haunches beside her. "You're amazing," he said. Rough, tender, he pressed his mouth to her temple. "Amazing."

"Ha." But her voice, breathy with cold, warmed. "You say that *now*." Jessie huddled against the trench wall, her eyes bottomless in the faint light of the comm's small screen.

Silas checked over it quickly. "I was hoping that jacket was more than just show. Everything's working." And, he noticed, plenty of calls, but no messages. Ignoring the alerts, he jimmied out the small earphone and, with monumental focus, managed to clip it to his ear.

"Wake me," Jessie said wearily, resting her chin on her huddled knees, "when the rescue party gets here. I want to kiss one of them."

He jammed half-numb fingers against the keypad. "No kissing anyone," he said, but his attention was already on the call. "Come on," he muttered. "Answer the goddamned—"

"How long's it been since your last confession?"

The voice on the line finished the work the goddamned frozen river started. Silas stilled. Closed his eyes. "Jonas," he said quietly. Suddenly too many words clambered for purchase in his throat, too damned tight with tension, but he clenched his teeth on all of them.

What could he say to the man he'd ruined for life?

Beside him, Jessie raised her head. He didn't have to see to know her eyes were fixed on him. Her ears on him. He lurched to his feet, staggered a few paces away.

"Silas!" Jonas's voice had always been a fine tenor, easy to distinguish on the electronic feeds. Now, with concern etching every word, he said, "Where the hell are you? We've had teams combing the trench for hours."

Every damn syllable kicked him in the chest. Silas closed his eyes. "Naomi reached you, then."

"Come on, Silas." His voice edged. "Don't pull that same crap on me—"

He wasn't going to deal with it now. Later, Silas promised himself, and cut in sharply, "Has Naomi filled you in?"

A pause. "Yeah," Jonas said, and laughed. "Christ, it's great to hear your voice, man. Now, where are you?"

Great to hear his voice? To work on his so-called

team? The guy was out of his goddamned mind. "I'm on my backup," Silas replied. "Track it. Papa seven delta delta one."

"On it. How much juice on that thing?"

Silas checked the screen. "Half a bar left. Send a ladder, we're still in the trench."

"Right, we'll be there in an hour."

He checked the sky, saw nothing but black, and rubbed his lips with icy fingers as he said grimly, "You better shorten that. We're on borrowed time out here."

"You got it." In his ear, Jonas called out orders to a crew Silas didn't hear, before focusing back on the mic. "We'll be there in— Cripes, Naomi! Okay, hang on—"

Silas flinched as the earpiece rattled, obviously changing hands. "You still with the Leigh girl?" Naomi's voice filled the line, clipped down to the quick.

He frowned. "Yeah, she—"

"Sit on her," Naomi ordered. "We got the blood back from the lab. Your piece of ass is a witch."

His blood froze, sharp as glass in his veins. His fingers tightened on the comm as he said, very softly, "Explain."

"One sample tested positive at the scene we cleaned up," Naomi said, sounding as if she skimmed the salient points from a report in front of her. "We got a hit off the bandage you put around Jessica Leigh's skinny neck."

Everything inside him struggled to deny the claim, to toss the goddamned comm into the icy river and drown Naomi's matter-of-fact smugness. He didn't.

Because it all made sense. Like a piece of the puzzle, it clicked. *Snick*. Brother and sister witches weren't uncommon. Her running from job to job, home to home, her easy lies. The witches that kept finding them. Trying to kill him.

To take her. A front.

He didn't turn, didn't look at the woman who'd lied to him, played him from the start.

Stiffening his shoulders, Silas's voice flattened as something bitter and frigid seeped into his chest. Around his heart. "How strong?"

"No way to tell from a fleck of DNA, but I'd guess about on par with her brother."

Shit. Shit, fuck, shit, *shit*.

Had she been watching him the whole time? Laughing at him as she led him on a merry goddamned chase? As she let him into her body? Thinking with his dick. Fuck. He'd done just that.

"Silas."

He cut Naomi off. "I'll be ready." He cut the connection, slid the comm closed with careful, precise fingers. No longer cold, hell, barely even aware of the chill as rage ate at him from the inside, Silas turned and slowly made his way across the rock ledge.

Jessie huddled where he'd left her, her cheek pillowed on one knee. In the shadows, he saw the mottled outline of the bruised gash at her temple. Saw her mouth curve.

Heard the concern, her damned fake concern, as she asked, "You all right? That sounded terse."

"Fine."

She lifted her head at his icy tone. Her eyes narrowed. "Hey," she began, only to uncoil as he stepped closer. Menace, fury, duty all roiled inside him. Conspired to hide the hurt. The denial.

The fear.

"Get up," he said, and grabbed her by the collar when she didn't obey fast enough.

"Silas?" Fear made her voice shake, but he ignored it. She should be scared.

Goddamned murderous witches should be scared of the Mission.

She struggled, but she was numb, too cold, and he was stronger in his rage. She cried out sharply when he spun her around, shoved her face first against the rock wall. "Everything," he gritted out, planting an elbow squarely between her shoulder blades to keep her still. "Everything you told me was a lie."

She sobbed in a terrified breath, but she didn't struggle now. She pressed her palms against the broken rock, fingers splayed. "Silas, I—"

"No." He didn't care. He didn't want to hear more. Roughly he stripped the ribbon from the end of her braid and pulled the tight bow loose with his teeth. She gasped when he yanked her hands behind her back.

And only hung her head as he looped the ribbon around her wrists and knotted it tightly. "You're hurting me," she said, so softly he almost missed it under the constant rush of the trench river.

He bared his teeth. Ruthlessly stomped on the pity, the guilt, that tore jaggedly through his anger. "Witch," he growled, and spun her around. Her shoulders hit the wall, bracketed by his arms as he braced both hands on either side of her head. "I should have known it when you called Naomi by her last name. I'd never told you that."

Her eyes met his, glittered defiantly.

Tears. Christ. Of course, tears.

Silas clenched his fingers into the stone, muscles rigid with strain. "Don't try it," he snarled, inches from the face he thought he'd known. And to think he'd been so suckered. She'd used him, lied to him. "What was the plan?" he demanded. "Lead me right into the coven and let them kill me?"

Her eyes widened. "No!" A tear spilled over her lashes, a trail of silver in the dim light. "Silas, please—"

"You're the reason those goddamned witches found us every time, isn't it?"

"No, I wouldn't—"

"Save it, Jessica." He curled his lips into a sneer. "You used me."

Jessie flinched.

And it was all the answer he needed.

He pushed away from the wall, turned his back so suddenly, so furiously that she staggered.

But he didn't help her this time.

She straightened. "You're so fucking hypocritical. Don't tell me you weren't using *me*," she shot back, and he said nothing. Knew it was true, and said nothing. Fists clenched, he counted to ten. To twenty.

Counted to fifty before the blinding rage lessened. Before he could look at her again without wanting to draw back his fist and—

"I wanted to tell you." Her voice, pitched low in

the dark, trembled. Silas closed his eyes. "You made it clear you'd kill every witch you met. Anyone who had that blood type. Me, you, a baby."

He shuddered at her words, thrown back like a knife between his shoulders. He turned, angry curses thick on his tongue, and couldn't do it. Couldn't stand to hear her. Couldn't fucking listen.

She sat huddled against the wall, head tilted back, eyes open, staring at the black void above them. "If you just—"

"Enough," he snarled. He knelt in front of her, jerked her forward so he could ensure the makeshift rope remained tight, that she hadn't found a rock and sawed through it. Knowing her, she probably planned to jump into the water.

"The nearest city is at least a week away, on foot," he said tightly. "I don't suggest risking the river." Her face jerked away from him, her loosened hair falling like a golden curtain over her face. "You'll be back in Seattle soon, and you can talk all you want to people who care. I don't. I've had enough of your lies."

"They weren't all lies," she said wearily. She tipped her face back up toward his. It was too dark to see, but he knew exactly how close her mouth was.

What it would taste like.

"Silas, I wasn't lying when I realized I love—"

"*Don't*." The word ripped out of him, tearing loose on a guttural roar. It echoed the pain radiating from his fist as he punched it into the wall by her head.

She froze. Her eyes enormous pools in her too-pale face, she barely breathed. Bone-deep wariness shaped her expression, and damn it, it twisted in his gut. Ruptured every weakened link of control he had left.

With a soul-wrenching groan, Silas caught her head in his bloodied, aching hand and crushed his mouth to hers.

She didn't struggle. She should have struggled, should have thrashed and shoved and tried to say no.

Instead, her breath hiccupping on a sob, Jessie's mouth opened under his, cool and sweet and demonstrative in ways no words could say. She met his thrusting tongue, matched his anger with her own. Pushed back, but not to get free. To get more.

Silas staggered away, left her to find her own balance as she fell back against the rock wall and stared at him. Her face was pale in the shadows, intent. "You tell me," she panted, "if that felt like a lie to you."

Pride, anger, uncertainty. Silas wiped at his mouth with the back of his hand. "Felt a hell of a lot like every stripper I've ever met."

Her mouth opened. Closed.

Flattened into a thin line.

The betrayal he read in her eyes told him he'd scored a direct hit. He spun around, stared at the black water, and choked back the rage that threatened to overwhelm him. She'd lied to him. From the get-go, she'd looked him in the eye and promised to help him find her brother.

Brother and sister witches. The whole goddamned branch was rotten.

Why hadn't he seen it?

Because, he thought viciously, he jumped the gun. Again. Trusted what he saw. Easy in, easy out.

Fuck. Silas waited for the Mission rescue crew, his impatience barely leashed. He watched the dark lengthen, deepen. And pretended not to hear her muffled tears.

CHAPTER TWENTY-ONE

God damn him.

God damn them all.

Caleb crouched in a tattered ring of books and paper, most pinned by broken stones he'd found in reach. He rested his elbows on his knees, fingertips pressed lightly together, and stared at the jumbled array of letters. Of pictures.

Of the last vestiges of a fading hope.

He'd been cocky. Damn it, he'd been arrogant.

Caleb had been so sure, so *fucking* certain that he'd finish the ritual in time. That he'd find a way to break Curio's hold on the coven before it came to this.

He was so close. Even now, Caleb could taste the last, sweetest current of power he hoarded. The heart's blood magic he'd stolen from the bodies of his chosen made him stronger, and he'd managed to harvest it without the coven suspecting. So far.

He'd used too much to overcome the missionary's protective seal, but time was too short. He couldn't risk hunting again.

So fucking close.

Jessie had gotten in the way, and as Caleb flicked his eyes from one worn page to the next, he knew he'd lost the opportunity. He couldn't make a move first. Had no ability to make a move now. He was going to have to wait until Curio was too invested to hesitate.

It would cost Caleb everything.

He raised his head, pushed back his too-long hair from his forehead. The scene around him was one of untold chaos. Destruction. Forgotten ghosts and crippled dreams. Torchlight danced in a circle of orange flame, raked unforgiving fingers of light over the twisted husk of a park entombed beneath layers of neglect.

Jessie had pushed it all too fast. Forced him to anticipate her, deal with her meddling when she should have stayed away.

He'd *told* her to stay away.

"Soothsayer?"

They'd come up behind him, slowly crossed the broken terrain of the ruined park while he stared at the faded words spread at his feet. Now they stood at the edge of the mottled pool of stagnant water, probably unwilling to test its murky depths. He turned his head, just enough to give them his profile.

The hard slant of his mouth.

"Sir," the girl said. Maybe fifteen. She tucked her hands under her armpits to keep her dirty, raw fingers as warm as she could. "We have an order from the master. For you," she added quickly. "If that's okay?"

An order. Fuck. From Curio. *Fuck.*

"I'm not going to hurry preparations," Caleb said flatly. "If it's anything to do with speed, even the master can be patient." Although he was sure both witches were too young, too unskilled to know more than a few parlor tricks, he used the toe of his boot to nose the book closed. Nudged it over the sheaf of dirty papers.

Just in case.

"Oh." The girl's eyes rounded, huge as boulders in her too-thin face. "Oh, no, it's not that."

The boy beside her, gangly and awkward, muffled a snort behind hands equally as dirty as hers. It was a rough life, living in the lower city. Scavenging the catacombs and hoping to find something to trade for food, for a bed.

It had always been a rough life, living as a witch.

Caleb's jaw tightened. "Spit it out."

"I-it's just that—" The girl gestured. "They have a lock on your—um, on the—um."

He wasn't going to help her. No pity. No fucking weakness. In his peripheral, she gave the younger boy a wild, pleading look.

Which he was too busy snickering into his hands to see.

Caleb unfolded. Slowly, knowing they watched his

every motion, he turned in place to levy a flat, patient stare at them both.

The boy dropped every trace of humor. It practically drained out of the soles of his worn sneakers. Young, but his instincts were sharp enough to spot a threat from a dead pool away. Caleb's fingers twitched.

"I'm sorry," she said hastily.

"Speak your piece, then go."

She blanched. "The master sent word that your sister's been found. He needs to know how your preparations go," she said, so fast the words ran together. Her freckles stood out in stark contrast to her bloodless skin.

But she didn't look away.

Caleb gave her credit. She didn't run.

Maybe she'd make something of herself. Someday.

If she didn't die in the Church's fire, or kneel to slit some human child's throat in a greedy bid for power. Caleb's hands tightened into slow, tight fists. "Time frame?"

"He said that depends on you, sir." She swallowed, her throat working noticeably. "He—he said to tell you that if it took too long, he'd come personally to . . . to find out why."

And showing up personally, seeing the progress Caleb hadn't made in the few hours he'd had to sweat and study and pray, meant the end of everything.

So which achieved more?

The sister who'd dragged him from shithole to shithole, taught him to lie, to feast on scraps? To survive in a city that feared him?

Or the coven? The coven whose power steadily climbed, whose fingers twisted through every current of the abandoned city. Whose control could one day thrust upward to the sparkling peak of the City of Glass.

"Sir?"

The city of magicians and fools.

Caleb studied his hands, the dirt crusted under his ragged nails and the calluses this city had whipped into him. Studied the twine wrapped around his wrists, gray, yellow, and black. All dulled by grime, by time.

They matched cords he wore around his neck, hung with raw flakes of amber and gray labradorite to keep him shielded. Jade to keep her blind.

And the worst. Flint, white flint to sever the bond.

"Caleb?"

He snapped his gaze up, narrowed his eyes. "Fine. Bring me Jessica Leigh."

They turned, ran before the last syllable could fade in the tomblike stillness of the old park. Caleb heard the boy's fearful, muffled voice as they faded into the dark.

He made a mental note to ensure neither was at the ritual as he unfolded his old pocketknife. They weren't faces he recognized, which meant there was hope for them.

If they survived the night.

He set the serrated edge to the cords at his wrist. One twist, a jerk of sharp edges and muscle, and the choice was made. While there was no visible sign, the magical wards twined into the string unraveled.

Grimy cords fell to the warped cement. Another slice, and unshaped beads clattered to his feet among them. It was as imperceptible as a sigh, a release of power and protection. He wrapped his fingers around the jagged, chipped edge of white flint around his neck and closed his eyes.

No spell, no magic or healing chant, would make this hurt less. He'd always been close to his sister. They'd shared laughter and tears, the pain of their mother's loss and the fear of the hunts together. She had always had the uncanny knack to find him. She knew when he hurt, and he'd known when she cried. She'd cried so much the first days of his absence.

But the flint had kept her safe. Kept him from going steadily crazy in the vortex of her emotions.

A man like him didn't deserve the choice. If he was going to go through with this, he was going to deal with every last moment. He'd know what she felt.

Remember it forever.

Grip tight, he pulled on the cord until it snapped in the strained quiet. Just as deliberately, mechanically, he dropped it amid the small pile of what had been, until this very moment, the only protection he'd ever had against his sister's senses.

For a long moment, Caleb scowled at the frayed cords and worn beads. This was the choice. A sister's life was fleeting, wasn't it?

But a coven could stand forever—*this* coven could stand forever. He couldn't let that happen. No matter what.

Swearing violently in the slant of light, Caleb drew back his foot, viciously kicked the pile with everything he had. Everything he didn't dare show the others.

Everything he wished he didn't feel.

Beads scattered over the standing water, sent ripples stretching, reaching. The thin threads touched the surface, clung for a brief moment, and darkened.

He moved to gather the papers before the last thread sank from view. There was a ritual to begin.

A witch to sacrifice.

And time was too fucking short to hesitate now.

CHAPTER TWENTY-TWO

It seemed an eternity before the first distant rumble of an approaching helicopter cut through the mind-numbing monotony of water and silence. Silas looked up, saw only the dark cliff face.

Black, twisted, empty shadow. Like his head. His hollow thoughts.

Silas turned, picked his way back across the ledge toward Jessie's huddled, silent silhouette. She hadn't said a word the whole time. No begging, no questions. No lies.

But she hadn't slept, either. Jessie opened her eyes as he loomed over her, the fragile skin around them bruised with exhaustion and her pathetic attempt at gaining his sympathy through her tears. "Get up," he ordered.

He wasn't going to touch her.

She wasn't going to make it easy.

Jessie braced her bound arms against the trench wall. The noise of the chopper gained volume. She tried to push herself up, flinched and collapsed back to the rocky floor as her strained knees gave out.

Silas's hands curled into tight, angry fists. Leashed the urge to reach for her. To help.

Lying witch.

"Get up," he said again, sharper.

"I'm trying," she snapped back, and clenched her teeth when the first lights crested the trench walls. High-powered beams split the shadows like columns of fire, blindingly real after too long in the dark.

She flinched when a spotlight skimmed over them. It swayed, swung back to highlight their perch in a brilliant beam.

Her skin gleamed bone white. Fear pinched the skin around her eyes. Good. Silas reached down, hauled her to her feet by her jacket collar.

Lingered too fucking long with his raw, bloody fingers under her chin. With her gaze wide and dark, staring up at him.

Her mouth compressed. "Let me go."

"Not on your goddamned life," he growled, and shifted his grip to her upper arm. She staggered as he pulled her along the ledge; his hold on her arm kept her upright, but barely.

Instead of looking up, he shielded his eyes with his free hand and waited for the crew to land.

They came on nylon cables, each strapped into a harness lit by small safety lights. When the first set of feet hit his peripheral, Silas spun Jessie around and hooked his fingers in the ribbon binding her hands. "Cuffs," he barked.

Wordlessly a black-masked figure tossed metal cuffs at him, then unsnapped the harness and laced out its lead. Silas snagged the handcuffs from the air, silver glinting. He flicked them open with practiced ease.

This shit he knew. This didn't ever change. Grab a witch. Bind her.

Kill her later.

The second figure tore off the goggled mask. Purple hair shone electric in the blinding lights, silver facial piercings sparkling as Naomi tipped her eyes toward the hovering chopper. "Ready?"

"In a minute."

Jessie turned her head. "I'm not going to run," she said quietly, all but muted under the heavy whirr of the helicopter's rotating blades. "Those aren't—"

Silas snapped them around her wrist. "Shut up." She stumbled when he pushed her into the first, masked missionary's arms.

The missionary spun her around, wrapped the harness tightly around her waist. Through her legs.

Silas watched her stand stiffly, staring at him as the missionary passed the lead under her bound arms, around her chest. Her eyes burned molten in the unforgiving spotlight.

Silas looked away first. "Where's everyone?"

Naomi unfolded a second harness and tossed it at him. "We're dropping off midway and the bird's headed topside," she said, and for once, there wasn't anything but cool professionalism in her clipped words. Hell of a hunter, Silas remembered as he strapped in.

Hell of an executioner.

Every movement was tight, economical as Naomi hooked solid metal rings together and tightened straps. Then she signaled the missionary wrapped around Jessie.

Probably using the comm frequency Silas didn't have, the missionary sent a command. Both man and witch swung out over the water. Silas went through the motions of double-checking the harness, but he couldn't look away from her face.

Jessie's eyes were closed, and she couldn't hide her fear as the duo rose toward the lights. The Mission.

And her inevitable death.

His heart thumped.

"Ready?" Naomi said in his ear.

"How come I have to be the bitch?" Silas asked, struggling to sound as normal, as effortless in the job as he knew he wasn't. He gave the tandem harness one last tug, signaled a thumbs-up. "Ready."

She raised the mask to her mouth, angled for the mic tucked into the reinforced fabric. "Haul us in," she ordered, then, with a smirk, "Because you're the bitch that got dumped in the trench."

The line snapped taut overhead. Within moments, Silas felt his feet leave the ground. They swung wide, a living pendulum, and Naomi swore as they hit the wall on the return swing. "Jesus, you're heavy," she grunted.

Silas said nothing, his gaze fixed on the chopper that reeled them in.

It didn't take long before all four were aboard. Deliberately Silas ignored what they did with Jessie. Ignored how they hauled her in, shackled her ankles with larger cuffs.

Pretended to ignore how Naomi kicked out her knees from under her and forced her to sit in the corner of the transport chopper, her face gone paler, almost green at the edges.

Knew he lied to himself every moment as Naomi wrapped a gag tight around her mouth and latched her to a pole strung across the hull.

It killed him.

But then, she was a witch. She'd played him from the start, and he had fallen right into it. *Sucker.*

He leaned against the pilot's chair, snagged a headset from the dash. "Let's go," he said sharply into the mic. The pilot nodded, gave a thumbs-up. The chopper climbed higher.

The ride was tersely silent.

Silas inhaled the storm-tinged wind as it blew through the open sides of the chopper. It cleared his head, drowned the memory of hothouse flowers and sulfur. Cold, rain, wind, darkness, those were the things he knew.

Below, rain drifted like a mist over the wrecked remains of what had once been outlying sub-cities of Seattle. Across the cabin, Naomi perched at the other door-less side, one leg dangling over the skids. He watched the surreal maw of the Old Sea-Trench pass beneath him, and he knew she watched him.

He ignored her, too.

His eyes raked over the landscape, strained to see

deeper into the fault. It blurred in shadows beneath him. As they ate up ground, covering the incredible distance Silas hadn't realized they'd traveled, he saw no sign of Matilda's cove. Her sanctuary.

The hot springs where he'd made love with a witch. He set his jaw.

Once they reached the city proper, the helicopter circled around the mid-lows until they approached from the east. No spotlights outlined their progress. The Mission had a standing arrangement in the New Seattle flight ordinances.

"Drop-off imminent," the pilot said, his voice tinny in the speakers. "Two minutes."

Silas took off his headset. "Link up," he ordered.

Naomi rose. "What are you doing?"

He ignored her, bypassed the other missionaries, and gripped the bar over Jessie's head for balance. "Get up," he yelled over the roar of the props. He hooked a finger in the gag around her mouth and pulled it down to hang loosely at her neck.

Jessie looked up at him. Flatly, purely terrified. "I can't," she whispered through too-dry lips. He read the shape more than heard it.

Gritting his teeth, he unhooked her tether and jerked her up by her arms. She stumbled, and for a split second, his brain shorted to white heat as she fell against him. As her body slid against his.

He knew this body. Thought he'd known the woman.

Silas thrust her back to arm's length. "By the sanctions of the Holy Order of St. Dominic," he grated out, "you are hereby accused and proven to be a witch." The old words felt thick on his tongue, too stiff. Too damned formal. Her skin deadened, went ashen, as he stared into her eyes.

They swam with glittering, unshed tears.

"For this crime," he continued, forcing himself to swallow the fury, the raw emotion filling his throat, "you will be executed. If you cede to the Mission the names and location of your heretic brethren, your death will be quick."

But never painless.

The first of her tears spilled a silver river down her cheek as she shook her head.

Silas's fingers tightened on her arms. "Jessie, do you know what happens to witches?" His voice shook under the *whup, whup, whup* of the main rotor. "Do you hear me?"

She bit her lip. Shook her head harder. Her hair rippled like gold, brushing over his hands, and he took a breath, realizing he was about to plead. To fucking *beg* her to reconsider.

Beg her not to die the torturous, gruesome death that awaited all witches within the Church.

His brain shaped the words his mouth couldn't say.

When her eyes flicked to his shoulder, Silas knew Naomi stood behind him. He jerked Jessie into his arms, spun her around and began to hook the harnesses together. "I'll take her down," he said curtly.

"Silas—"

"I said I'll fucking do it."

Naomi frowned, a deep curve of her lower lip. When he didn't show any sign, even a hint of interest in what she thought, she shrugged and gestured the other missionary to buckle in. "All right, we'll be swinging low. Everyone, prep your gear and get ready to jump. Once we hit the ground, the bird's headed topside, so kiss your captain now and thanks for flying Mission Air."

On cue, the pilot raised a hand, index finger up. One minute.

Jessie trembled in Silas's arms as he maneuvered them both to the cabin access. "Just for the record," she said tightly as he grasped the rung over her head. "I know exactly what you do to witches." She turned her face, slid him a look that made him want to shake her for being so damned stubborn and kiss her for being so fucking brave.

All at once.

Her mouth curved. Silas watched a tear slide along that curve. Clenched his jaw so tightly, his temple throbbed. "When I'm finally dead," she said as the helicopter dipped, "and you can bet your ass I'll die fast just to spite you, *Agent* Smith, you can laugh about the stupid witch who loved you."

"Go!"

Naomi's voice lanced through the cabin. On cue, she and the other missionary dropped out of the cabin. The helicopter swayed, held in place by the waiting pilot.

Silas closed his eyes. "Shut up," he growled. If she'd had anything else to say, it died as he launched them into thin air.

The harness caught easily, snapped taut around them both. Silas let out the lead in quick increments, muscles rigid with the effort.

Jessie's body was stiff with terror, and as he lowered them to the ruined parking lot of a half-shattered apartment building, he realized her hands clenched tightly on the hem of his shirt.

He wasn't going to be her safety this time.

They landed hard, pitched awkwardly. Silas twisted, wrenched her aside, and swore as he landed back first on sharp gravel. Her weight slammed into his chest.

With the air knocked solidly out of him and bright lights of pain dancing in front of his eyes, Silas didn't move when she struggled to free herself. Hair like tangled silk slid over his face, his mouth, and all he could smell was her.

Remnants of sulfur, spice, and that goddamned scent that was pure Jessie.

"Hey, Silas." Naomi's face edged into his vision, her trademark smirk. "Need a hand with the lady?"

"Fuck you." Silas unbuckled the harnesses without getting up. "Get her off me."

Naomi reached down, grabbed Jessie by the jacket, and hauled her neatly to her feet. Silas sucked in a breath, winced. "You have tape in there?"

"Ribs?" Naomi nodded, unlocking the shackles clamped around Jessie's ankles. "Yeah, bandages, tape, and then some. Come on, old man, we'll get you patched before I go topside for briefing. Jesus, I don't even get a drink between ops," she muttered. "Total waste of a win."

Silas's grin bared teeth. But it didn't last.

Jessie's expression when she turned was empty. Silently, her eyes flat and, Christ, devoid of anything resembling that spark so uniquely hers, she walked in front of the woman who marched her across the lot.

Silas rolled to his feet and followed. He'd made it four steps before the seal of St. Andrew spit blue fire.

Pain was a breath behind.

It all happened so fast.

Naomi turned in a fluid line, swept Jessie's feet out from under her, and was already moving when Jessie hit the ground. Jessie yelped, gravel biting hard into her stomach, her cheek. Her hair fell across her face.

"Miles, catch your six!" Naomi's voice rang from somewhere behind her. Too far for her to worry about Jessie.

She hoped.

"Christ, fuck." Silas's voice. His anger. "Man down! Where's Jes— *Fuck!*" That odd, sickly blue light seamed through her blinding mass of hair.

Jessie wriggled around, struggled to get her knees under her. The first spray of bullets splattered the cement walls over her head, ricocheted splinters of rock and careened wildly back through the dark. Jessie flinched, rolled to the side, as more voices shouted orders, warnings, around her.

It was too damned easy to recognize Silas's voice. The depth of his tone, the surge of adrenaline and aggression leashed tightly under hard orders. Naomi's voice, cursing. Pained.

Other voices she didn't recognize. Grim voices.

Jessie braced herself against the crumbling apartment wall, managing to get her knees to her chest. She pulled her cuffed hands underneath her and around her legs.

Gunfire rattled the night, more blue light spilled. With her arms functional and in front of her, she could get to her feet and shake back her tangled hair. She sidled along the wall, one eye fixed on the battle that surged in front of her.

Witches. Witch hunters. Magic scorched the air like ozone during a lightning storm, bullets rained metal fury. She saw Silas circling a man twice his size, his gun a dark blot on the ground. Too far out of his reach.

She saw Naomi, a long, lean shadow braced against a fallen slat of broken wall and sighting down the barrel of a large gun. She raised one hand briefly, fingers splayed, and Jessie lurched around the corner as three more armed figures darted across the street.

More witch hunters. Jesus God, how many were there in New Seattle?

Fists clenched, Jessie rapidly cataloged her choices. Stay here, get killed by the hunters. Stay here, hunters lose, get captured by the coven. Probably killed.

Run, find Caleb, extract him from his mess—with a rock to the back of his head, if she had to—and get the hell out of this death trap of a city.

Option three sounded like a hell of a bargain.

She'd learn to live with the heartache.

Jessie raised her cuffed hands and wiped at her mouth. Told her feet to move. To run, damn it.

Leave him.

But her gaze stayed on Silas. On the big man he fought back with fists and raw strength. On the seam of light spilling from his jacket cuff and the taut lines of pain carved into his face. He yelled something, she didn't know what.

Lost cause, she told herself firmly. Big mistake. She'd known it going in. Live and learn.

Emphasis on *live*.

Jessie turned and promptly kissed the ground when her feet caught on something heavy, something clumsy in the way. Tears of pain sprang to her eyes as her knees skidded on gravel and her elbows took the impact.

Jessie cursed at the ground, rolled over.

Looked into the masked face of a hunter propped against the wall.

She stifled a scream.

Dead. The man was dead. "Christ," she gasped as her brain slid into a full picture. Blood seamed the wall behind him, gleamed wet and black on his chest. His feet splayed, hands lifeless at his sides. One of those sleek black guns lay discarded beside him. A comm unit was clutched in one hand, as if he'd tried to radio for help.

Maybe he'd succeeded. Maybe that was why three more had arrived.

The sharp, staccato beat of gunfire let up for a moment. A girl screamed, shrill. Frightened.

Jessie snatched the comm from the dead man's hands, grabbed the gun, and ran like hell. Half hunched, the back of her neck prickling, she prayed no one saw her. That no one right now had a line on her in the dark, staring down the barrel of one of those guns.

Finger on the trigger.

Blood surged to her head, made her dizzy with adrenaline and anxiety. She ran for her life, knowing she did, swearing every word she knew and some she'd learned from Silas as she fled into the dark.

She rounded the street corner, out of line of sight of anyone at that broken lot, and for a brief second, relief swamped her.

Only to kick over to pure, stark fear as two men rose from a patient crouch. She skidded to a stop. For a moment, both were as surprised as Jessie was.

Witches? Hunters?

"It's her!" the younger one said.

Jessie whirled, took three running steps before something wild, something magical lashed at the back of her knees. She stumbled, went down tangled in magic. When she hit the pavement on her knees for the second time that night, she cried out, pain and shock and vivid anger.

"Holy shit." The voice behind her sounded too damned chipper. The young one. "Don't move, Miss Leigh. We don't want to hurt you."

She sucked in a breath. Let it out on a shaking sound. "I have a gun," she warned loudly. "It's pointed at my heart."

She heard the footsteps behind her still. Quickly, hunched over the comm, she cracked it open with trembling fingers and jabbed in the number she'd memorized.

"Now don't do anything rash." The second voice was also male. Older. Soothing, even. Jessie tilted her head to the left, just a touch. Just enough to see their shapes in her peripheral.

Connect, damn it. "Where's my brother?" she demanded.

They exchanged a glance. "I'm not—"

"Did I mention I have a gun?" she cut in. She fought the desire to shift, to relieve the pressure from her knees. "Cut the bullshit, guys. I know you need me, so I want to know where Caleb is. If you don't tell me right now, I'll kill myself and you can deal with the consequences. I'll be beyond caring."

The unit was silent in her hands. Jessie tucked it under her jacket, into her waistband, and prayed its built-in mic was as good as it needed to be.

This had to work. One way or another, she had to let Silas know. Let him get his bloody coven, just as long as she got her brother. That was fair, wasn't it?

And if she died in the attempt, murdered for some ritual, well. He'd know why.

The young witch circled around her. "Tell you what," he said. "Why don't we take you to Caleb?" He tried to sound cheerful. Unconcerned. Failed, but it wasn't because he wasn't good.

Jessie *knew* lies. Anger snapped around her like a cloak. A very solid, bolstering cloak. She seized it. Banked it.

Anger was real. It could protect her. Should have protected her from Silas, except she'd forgotten to be angry about his vocation. Forgotten he was a killer as he stroked her in the dark.

"What do you say?" the kid asked, hands spread at his side.

The other man circled the other way.

Shit, shit, shit.

Jessie was trapped. She jerked her eyes back down the road, back to where the gunfire had stopped. Thinking quickly, she asked, "Caleb will be there?"

"Oh, yeah," the older man said quietly.

Lightning-fast, Jessie threw the gun to the side. Both men jumped, startled, but they watched the gun. *Yes.* She raised her cuffed hands above her head. "I just escaped from the hunters. They'll be after me, so let's go."

A beat. A moment of wordless glances. Jessie waited, screamed at them to hurry in her head. To grab her and go. Take her to Caleb.

Take them all to Caleb.

The older man reached her first. He was tall, not overly wide, balding with a ragged scar hooked over his cheek. He helped her to her feet and tugged ineffectually at the metal cuffs. "We can't—"

"I'll deal," she said sharply. "Let's go."

He nodded, exchanged another look with the younger, sandy-haired witch whose freckles threatened to monopolize his face. The boy gestured.

"Ladies first. After Dawson, I mean."

Jessie summoned a grin. Teasing. Relieved. *Lie.* "So he's a real lady, huh?" she asked lightly.

The older man frowned. "Move."

They did, Jessie hemmed in between the men as they ran down the street. Away from the chaos, the hunters.

From Silas.

Her heart thudded painfully in her chest, in rhythm with her steps as the run eased into a jog. And then a hurried walk off the streets and through back alleys she'd never been through before.

Finally, as the man in front of her slowed, she asked, "How far are we going? My knees are killing me."

He glanced at her, said nothing.

Ass.

"The catacombs," the kid said behind her, and caught her as she stumbled over the leaden exhaustion of her own feet. His fingers tightened. "Are you okay?"

Jessie managed a wan smile. "I think I scraped myself up pretty bad."

"Hang in there." He let her go, but stayed close. It would have been cute, if Jessie hadn't already known his motives. Death. Pain. Ritual.

"Old Seattle's huge," she said as she tromped across broken, pitted asphalt. She'd already lost track of the alleys they'd trekked through. The streets they'd crossed, carefully, wary for signs of pursuit.

She hoped to hell that comm still worked.

The man in front of her said nothing still, but he occasionally looked back. Checked her progress, her pace. Scowled.

The freckled witch patted her on the shoulder as he moved up to match her hampered stride.

She wanted to kick him.

"There's a place about two miles in. It's an old park, or used to be. You can still see signs of trees and stuff, but only weird plants grow in the dark. Mushrooms and slimy stuff."

"Michael," the older man warned.

"What?" The kid smiled at her. "It's not like she won't see it. There's this old, faded sign. I guess they called it the Waterline. Used to be real nice."

Jessie wracked her memory. "I've never heard of it. Is that where all of you live?"

"You'll see it," the young witch named Michael said cheerfully. Too cheerfully. Too vaguely. "Soon enough."

"That's enough," the older man snapped over his shoulder. "We have to be quiet now."

Michael put a finger to his lips, rolling his eyes at Jessie, and for a brief, muddled second, she found herself charmed. Truly, delightfully charmed.

His magic clung like cobwebs, and she knew.

He was deliberately trying to put her at her ease. To charm her in all the ways possible.

Clever. Young, and mostly unpracticed, but clever. His focus had to be hidden somewhere on him.

She smiled back, willing to let him think it worked. That his magic had her. Bent her.

They worked their way quietly through the nighttime city, avoiding the carousel. They slid down ladders she'd never realized existed, bolted to the sides of cement foundations. Layer by layer, they left New Seattle behind.

And she prayed the comm stayed on.

CHAPTER TWENTY-THREE

Who is your coven leader?"

The young witch in Silas's grip spit in his face. Warm, thick spittle slapped against his cheek, wet and disgusting.

Silas returned the gesture with a fist to her face, hard enough to snap her head around. To draw blood gushing from her wide nose. "Where is your coven located?" he snarled.

The blond laughed, but it wobbled. The gunshot wound to her abdomen wasn't going to give him enough time. "Good luck with that," she managed, and spit again.

This time, blood dotted his cheek. His shoulder.

Swearing, he dropped her. Ignored her scream of pain as she hit the gravel at his feet, crumpled over herself. Naomi rose from her crouch, dirty, tousled, a field bandage wrapped tightly over her upper arm and the bullet she'd managed to acquire in the hail of gunfire.

On the ground beside her, the missionary she'd called Miles cupped his thigh, his uncovered face a mask of sweat and blood. "Bad news, boss," he said. Pain thickened his voice.

His goddamned youthful voice.

Silas strode past both of them without a word.

"Silas," Naomi said. Snagged him by the arm when he would have kept walking. "Smith! She probably just ran off in the fighting."

His heart thundered in his chest. In his ears. Every nerve slammed against his skin. "Maybe," he said, but shook her off. "Maybe not."

Naomi sidestepped around him. Heedless of the threat he projected, she got so close to his face that he could see the individual violet starbursts in her eyes. They glinted, sharp as hell. "You going after her, or after them?"

Hell of a missionary.

Hell of a time to push him. Jaw clenched, Silas thrust his face right back into hers. "I don't have time for your bitch factor to warm up, so back. The fuck. Off."

Naomi's eyes flickered. Narrowed. "Fine," she said, every syllable neatly clipped. "What do you plan to do? How do you plan to find her?"

"Fuck." Silas turned, scanned the missionaries who helped the wounded. The dead witches whose blood gleamed black and wet in the dim shine of the streetlights. "Fuck!" he snarled again, explosive. Violent. His fists clenched.

Naomi touched his shoulder. "We'll—"

"Christ!" Silas jumped as his comm thrummed against his heart, a muted buzz. He jerked at his jacket and withdrew the unit. A message. Fear, fury, a goddamned slice of hope made his hands shake as he slid it open. Jammed in the code.

"Silas?"

"Shut up," he muttered as the unit connected.

Naomi moved around him, gesturing at the two missionaries who strode by to pick up Miles. The man cursed as his leg wound jostled, but Silas didn't spare him the concern Naomi did.

Instead, eyebrows furrowing, he sucked in a hiss of breath as Jessie's voice filtered, muffled, through the electronic system. He clenched his fingers on it. "It's her. I can't hear it," he said tightly. "I can't fucking hear what they're saying."

"I know who can." Naomi strode away, one hand gesturing. "Come on. Let's go nail your witch."

His witch.

Silas's jaw popped as he clenched his teeth and followed.

She led the way across the street, to the safe house complex the Mission must have set up as a launching point. Silas passed a bare handful of other missionaries, men and women he didn't recognize.

Didn't bother to meet.

Naomi strode past the complex, past the stretchers carrying dead witches to tag and bag later for ID and toward the large truck parked just by the side.

She ignored the cab, but rapped sharply on the trailer wall as she walked beside it.

Silas limped behind her, his throat already closing over the words his brain lodged there.

He knew. Without waiting for the back door of the trailer to open, he fucking knew.

Naomi popped the door and gestured him inside. "Jonas!"

"Hey, sweetcheeks," floated from the brightly lit interior. Easy, but not cheerful. Welcoming. "I thought you'd be upstairs by now."

All too goddamned familiar.

Ignoring the tension that gripped him, that raked bitter claws of memory over his mind, Silas grabbed the latch and swung himself inside.

It was like walking into a computer lab on wheels. Electronics lined every wall, crammed into every available space and wired up in ways he'd never been able to understand. Lights blinked, glowed, flickered, wires tangled and connected.

Jonas's lean form rolled out on a chair designed to fit easily among it all. His eyes widened. Brightened. "Silas!"

Jonas Stone. Missionary. Technical prodigy.

The man who had barely survived when his tech truck exploded around him.

On Silas's mission.

Jonas grabbed a shelf with the fluid familiarity only time spent on the job gave a man, rolled forward on the padded chair. He was lanky, skinny enough to fit between the shelves and get to anything he needed. His dark brown hair hung too long around his face, and a matching, scraggly goatee shaped his mouth as he smiled. Thin, rimless glasses perched on his nose. His eyes gleamed a muddy green behind them.

The pain Silas read there, the age that reached far beyond the man's years, clutched at Silas's throat. Guilt rose like a goddamned smothering tide.

That was his fault.

And here Jonas was, holding out a scarred hand like some long-lost brother. "Hey," Jonas said happily. "Long time, no see."

Somehow, with his chest too tight to breathe, Silas managed to say, "Yeah." His fingers clenched on the comm. "Yeah. A long time."

Naomi pushed past him. "No time for reunions," she said briskly. "Jonas, we have a message from a runaway witch, too damned muted to hear. Can you work your magic?"

Jonas shifted his gaze to Naomi, rotated his outstretched hand to a cup, palm up. "For you, beautiful, anything. Let's have it."

Silas placed it in his hand. "Jonas."

"Nope." The man flashed him a grin, teeth white against his sparse goatee. "Not interested in hearing it, buddy. But if you want to look over my shoulder while I crack this baby, you're more than welcome."

Naomi raked her hands through her hair, purple tendrils escaping from her fingers. "Be quick," she said. "Time's—"

"Always of the essence," Jonas said wryly, and put the comm in his lap. He grabbed the shelves on either side, two racks of electronic crap Silas didn't recognize, and pulled himself back along the row. The tracked chair zipped easily back to the small computer with its mass of bundled wires. He clipped the comm to the computer.

After a long, tense moment, Silas followed.

"Okay, here's how this works," Jonas was saying as his long, thin fingers flew over the keyboard. A visual sound wave blossomed on the screen. "There's a hell of a lot of noise, so if I mute that, frame the main voices . . ."

Silas watched, already lost as the wavelength shifted in length and consistency. Jonas glanced at him, sidelong behind his glasses. "You look like hell."

He grunted.

"And still your charming self," Jonas continued lightly, even as his fingers continued their frenetic pace. "Still, it's good to see you, man. You kicked yourself out for way too long. Ah!" He straightened.

Silas didn't miss the grimace of pain that shaped the tech's face as he did.

"Okay, be ready to fall to your knees in awe and worship." Jonas tapped a key. The message played. Almost crystal clear.

Silas's hands tightened into slow, angry fists.

Behind him, Naomi muttered, "The Waterline."

Jonas didn't look up from the screen as he reached over and switched on a second panel. "All right, searching the databases for any historical references to the place." The second screen shimmered to life, suddenly filled with miles of scrolling text.

But Silas wasn't watching it. He wasn't seeing the computer, or the missionaries around him.

He pictured Jessie's face. *You'll take me to Caleb?*

Of course. She knew they wanted her for some kind of ritual. If she'd meant to go after Caleb, she could have found any number of ways around it, but no, she let them escort her right into the nest of snakes below the city.

That was the point. That's what the message was for. To share. To tell him.

He was sure of it. In an instant, he was certain. She was smart.

We can track the frequencies.

His own words to her before they'd gone into the trench. His skin went cold. "Whose comm does she have?"

Naomi shifted. "Hell, could be anyone's."

"Fuck." He bent over Jonas's chair, one hand braced on the back of it. He tapped the screen where the wavelength all but flattened. It was a pose so familiar, as easy as breathing, that he didn't think anything when Jonas jerked his gaze up to Silas's profile in wide-eyed surprise. "What's this?" he demanded.

After a brief, blinking moment, Jonas shook his head. "The comm stayed on, but they weren't talking. There wasn't enough pitch in the frequency to be helpful as to location, but—" The second screen froze, and Jonas grinned. "And that's why I am a god, ladies and gentlemen."

Naomi snorted, leaned in behind Silas. "What'd you find?"

As the ambient noise of the comm's message played on, Jonas highlighted the file and tapped in a few easy commands. A map filled the screen.

"Old-time plans," Jonas said slowly. Silas peered

at it, but it made no sense to his tired eyes. His roiling brain. "Prequake, post—turn of the century. Public works property, means it's in the ruins and—ha!"

Silas watched the man zoom out, rotate the map, then bring up a second to overlay in lightning-quick succession. "That's deep," Silas said grimly. "If they're going by foot—"

"They could have been picked up," Naomi cut in. She reached for the comm on her belt.

"Hang on." Jonas paused the message, then scrolled along the sound wave until it spiked, rippled one more time. He highlighted the visual hump, tapped a key.

"I really hope you're hearing this." Jessie's voice, a whisper so loud that the speakers almost reverberated with it. "We're headed deeper into the ruins. There's a lot of tunnels they use, but I can't figure out—"

"Hey." A man's voice, sudden and sharp. "She's got a comm!"

"Shit," Jessie hissed. The speakers thudded, crackled.

Silas gripped the back of Jonas's chair in both hands as Jessie's muted sound of pain cut off.

The tech tapped some keys, the *click-click* of his fingers all that filled the tense, oppressive silence for a long moment. Then his voice, apologetic. "That's it. I can't get anything else out of it."

Silas straightened so fast, he slammed his head against an outstretched shelving unit. "Fuck," he hissed. Naomi flattened herself against the shelves as he shoved past her.

"Smith," she called. "Where are you going?"

He glanced back, saw Naomi already starting after him. Saw Jonas, who very studiously watched the monitor, elbows planted firmly on the bolted desk.

"Silas!" Naomi said sharply.

He jumped from the trailer. "I'm going after her."

"After her?" Hard on his heels, she grabbed the back of his shirt and jerked him to a stop. "Or after the coven?"

Silas turned on her. Every muscle tensed as she lifted a finger under his nose.

"You walk real careful, Smith," she said quietly. "You've been out of touch for a long time. Now you're back in New Seattle and don't you think for a goddamned second anyone's forgotten."

Silas's fists clenched.

"All the successful missions in the world won't undo that." A second finger joined the first. "You consorted with a witch long enough to raise eyebrows all over the place. That alone is enough to get you sent back for processing. Give 'em an excuse and see what happens." Her eyes blazed, blue and purple fire.

The worry in her voice told him she was telling the truth. Protocol stated that a compromised hunter got sent back to the Church for processing. *Processing*, in every case, meant reconditioning. Retraining.

Maybe worse.

It was a highly classified procedure that never allowed a missionary to return to his old Mission.

He met her eyes. "Are you going to turn me in?"

"Don't make me have to choose," Naomi replied fiercely, her fists clenched.

You, me, a baby's . . . No. They couldn't *all* be guilty.

Silas wasn't going to take any more of the Church's bullshit jammed down his throat.

"I'm going after Jessie," he said quietly.

Naomi's mouth tightened. "To kill her." It wasn't a suggestion.

"No." Silas laughed, but there was nothing amused about it. Bitter, resigned, even angry, he admitted, "To save her. She isn't the enemy."

"Thou shalt not suffer—"

"*No.*"

She reached for the gun holstered under her shoulder, "You stupid—" she began, and the hard set to her mouth told him she wasn't going to give him the chance.

Silas grabbed her by the injured arm, dug his thumb into the bullet hole. Her voice twisted to a gasp, face turned shock-white. He didn't have to read her mind to know that her vision probably went the same color as the gun clattered to the pavement. A bullet hole hurt.

It hurt more when a man had his thumb in it.

"I'm sorry," he said roughly.

Her foot lashed, caught him square in the knee. Swearing, he spun her around, cupped the back of her head and slammed it hard against the trailer. The metal walls gonged.

Naomi went limp in his grasp.

"I'm sorry," he said again. "You always were too good at this job." He lowered her to the sidewalk, as gently as he could, and checked her pulse. She'd have one hell of a bruise tomorrow, but for now, she'd be safe. And out of his goddamned hair.

He grabbed her comm, spun around.

"Silas."

He hesitated. Then, because he knew he owed the man that much, he turned again. Jonas hung out of the back of the trailer, one arm wrapped on something inside.

"Don't," Silas warned flatly. "Don't get involved."

Jonas raised a comm unit in his free hand. His eyes were steady as they flicked to Naomi at his feet. Back to him. "Use mine, buddy."

Silas stared at him. Was he serious? Was it a trick?

But as he met the man's eyes, read the ongoing battle with the pain of his twisted legs, of the mess Silas himself had caused—

He caught the comm as it spun toward him.

"For the record," Jonas said, a smile twitching inside his goatee, "you're a shitty martyr. Quit it."

Silas glanced at the comm. Pocketed it. "Jonas, I—"

"Fuck off," Jonas said neatly, easily, and waved him on. "Go rescue her. Leave Nai her comm, though, she's going to need it."

"Right." Silas dropped Naomi's comm, ignored Jonas's wince as it bounced on the pavement. "Jonas? Shut up," he added tightly as the man's mouth opened. "For one second. Just hear me out."

Jonas closed his mouth again.

"I was stupid back then." Silas raised a hand when the man's eyes darkened behind his glasses. "We all were, but I was the one who made the call. So . . ." He mentally flailed. "So, just don't let me be in charge here, all right? "

A smile quirked at the side of the tech's mouth. "Loud and clear, sir."

"I mean it," Silas growled. "Don't let me set any sort of example here. Don't get any crazy ideas. Stick with the Mission. Just—" Silas frowned down at Naomi's still body. "Christ, Jonas, just be smart about it."

Jonas's smile deepened. "Silas?"

"What?"

"Go save your girlfriend."

For a moment, he met dark green eyes. Studied them. When the man raised his eyebrows, Silas shook his head, resigned, and awkwardly jogged away.

He'd find a car to steal. They weren't hard to hot-wire, especially down in lower New Seattle. As he scanned the streets, Jonas's comm hummed. Silas cracked it open.

Saw the map.

"Thank you, Jonas," he murmured in gratitude. "You idiot."

CHAPTER TWENTY-FOUR

Jessie couldn't see or hear anything past the hood they'd draped over her head, unable to tell if she was coming or going. If she was surrounded or just escorted by the same two bastards. The grip at her upper arm throbbed painfully; she knew there'd be bruises if she survived to complain about them.

What the hell possessed her to talk into the damn comm? To say anything, do anything that gave herself away?

Except. . .

Except that she was an idiot, and knew exactly what. Why.

Silas. He was supposed to have been her death, wasn't he? All signs pointed to him. Caleb's prophecies, Silas's own duty as a witch hunter.

And she'd fallen in love with him.

Just so he could kill her.

Now it looked as if he wouldn't even be the one to do that. Jessie stumbled as her feet caught on something rough and uneven. The hand at her arm jerked her upright, practically lifted her over whatever the obstacle was.

They hadn't said a word since they'd jumped her, thrown the comm aside, and hooded her in the dark. Her breath turned the air in the confined space to something too thick and smothering.

If she didn't get this thing off, she was going to keel over from lack of oxygen. Then wouldn't they be sorry?

She'd be dead, but at least they'd be sorry.

Unless they only needed her corpse.

She sucked in a breath, trying hard to ignore the pressure squeezing in at her lungs. Her brain fought her. She needed air. She needed more air, fresh air.

She stumbled as they jerked her to a halt. There was muted conversation, a rustle of movement, and fingers pulled roughly at her wrists. Metal clanged, clicked. The handcuffs fell away.

She had no time to react. The hand yanked her forward again, guided her to the destination she couldn't see. She nearly screamed from the fearful apprehension of it. The lack of conversation, of real direction.

Of air.

When her feet splashed into something thick and wet, she jumped. The hand tightened, shoved her forward. She splashed, water seeping into her boots, her jeans. Then another obstacle, this one jarring her as she barked her shins on it. Hands grabbed her by the waist, and before she could get enough air to protest, her feet landed on cement.

The hands at her hips let go only long enough to grab her shoulders and push. She hit the ground on her abused knees and swore. "Stop it," she snarled, impatience and pain.

Only to blink in the sudden light tearing through her eye sockets as the hood whipped off her head.

She saw nothing but vague outlines at first, flickering light and silhouettes. She sucked in a breath, another, gulping down sweet, welcome oxygen.

And smelled incense. Something lush and green. That creeping, tomblike mustiness of Old Seattle.

Slowly her vision cleared. Coalesced into a full, colorful picture. The light was dim, she realized now, mostly coming from patches of torchlight scattered throughout the ruin. It picked out bits of the ruined park, the dried, twisted husks of dead trees. It glinted on the occasional flash of metal, traced the pale, hollow faces of the witches around her.

Jessie's mouth tightened. Thirty of them, she figured, maybe as many as fifty. Some stood, some sat, but they all ringed the dark pond surrounding her.

Surrounding the island she knelt on.

Her gaze swung to a single stone pillar, its surface smudged with smoke and carved with symbols. She squinted, trying to read them, to read what the hell they intended, but they . . . moved. Like something oily in the dark, they refused to be read by her.

Her stomach turned, roiled uncomfortably.

This was bad magic.

She scanned the crowd again as she slowly got to her feet. The island, some sort of ruined patch of cement, was empty of everything but her.

The back of her neck prickled. Hell, her skin was doing its best to razor itself off her bones and crawl away. Her heart pounding, Jessie spun around and saw witches all around her.

Staring at her.

Her hands fisted at her sides. "Come on, then!" Her voice cracked in the odd, breathless silence. Some of them stirred, some looked at each other.

Some looked away.

Jessie turned, crossed the island in a few long, angry steps. Shaking her hair out of her eyes, she braced her hands against the pillar.

Then yelped as the stone heated beneath her fingers. She snatched her hands back so fast, her elbows popped. The stone flared, sizzled as red spots that matched her fingertips, her palms, completely faded back to rock.

"Holy shit," she muttered. Seriously nasty magic.

She looked over her shoulder as the crowd stirred, as whispered words rustled through them like a growing wind. Tucking her stinging hands at her hips, she braced herself as a knot of people parted.

A tall, broad man approached the pond. His hair was graying, neatly combed, his build solid despite his noticeably older age. He walked with confidence, ignored the witches who clustered in behind him. Ignored the hands that reached out to touch his arms, his shoulders.

Ignored the tall, blond witch who walked at his left.

Underneath a tide of grief, of bone-deep anger, Jessie closed her eyes. "Caleb." When she heard the water splash, she snapped them open again.

She couldn't fall apart now.

Bracing herself, fists at her hips, she glared at them both with every ounce of fury, of disgust, she could muster.

Topside and bathed in sunlight, the Missionary director had all but pulsed with a palpable authority. Now, thousands of feet below those sunny skylights, the superior named Peterson surrounded himself with the witches he was supposed to hunt and all but glowed like some kind of god amid his flock.

Jessie whirled, searching wildly for something to use as a weapon, anything. The pedestal beside her was solid rock, too heavy to shift. The focus pillar behind her was drilled into the cement island. Fists clenched, she turned and sucked in a shaking breath.

Peterson's feet pressed into the water, but they didn't sink beneath it. He walked on the surface, his neat shoes and pressed slacks tidy and clean, and despite knowing that magic kept him afloat, goose bumps prickled to life over her skin.

Caleb trudged in the muck beside him, his face impassive. Not nearly as showy, and his gaze centered on the ground at her feet.

"I hate you," she said tightly.

His blue eyes flicked to hers, narrowed, but he said nothing.

Ignoring her bitter greeting, Peterson stepped up

on the island, his smile warm in his craggy features. His eyes were both welcoming and razor sharp. "Miss Leigh," he intoned in a baritone so deep, it rumbled her chest.

She twisted her lips into a grim parody of a smile. "Gee. You must be the boss."

Caleb circled the island.

The leader inclined his head, a courteous half bow. "Curio," he said.

"Is that what you're calling yourself down here?"

His eyes sharpened, razor intelligence. "Indeed," he said slowly. "And you are my young friend's eldest sister. It is a pleasure to make your acquaintance."

"I'm sure." Jessie stepped to the side, knowing full well she had nowhere to run. She was trapped, surrounded by water and witches. With her heart in her throat, she squared her shoulders. "Let's cut the crap," she said crisply. The man's thick eyebrows winged upward. "Why don't you just tell me what you're doing and why you need me so much?"

"Ah." The man sighed. "Youth."

"Yeah," Jessie said tightly. "I'm sure you say that every time you recruit a new missio—" He struck like a snake, taking one step forward and backhanding her hard enough that she saw stars. Pain lanced through her cheek as she spun with it, blood welling on her tongue.

It wasn't anything compared to the pain lodged in her chest. Sneering, Jessie spat on the island between them. Red droplets of her blood splattered on the hem of his neat pants. "I know who you are, *Peterson*." She watched his eyes narrow. A flicker in ice blue depths. "And it's only a matter of time before they do, too."

But he didn't respond with fear. Or surprise.

Peterson's smile deepened the lines around his mouth. At his eyes. He looked up from the blood she'd left on his hem and took one step closer. Taking her face in his worn hands, he pressed a kiss to her temple and said gently, "In a matter of moments, my dear Miss Leigh, no one will care."

Revulsion shot down her spine. She wrenched herself away, whirled and collided with Caleb.

He caught her by the arms, steadied her. For a split second, relief filled her with a terrible kind of hope. A hope that twisted deeply, sliced to the bone as she saw his face.

Controlled. Empty. His blue eyes, their mother's eyes, looked into hers with nothing kind or gentle in them. No apology. No guilt.

Her lip quivered under the strain of biting back her tears. "Caleb," she whispered. "Why?"

He pulled her toward the pillar. She dug her heels in, but he was stronger than she remembered. Determined.

To use her.

"I'm sorry," he said. "I wish things could've been different." She staggered as he wrenched her around, gasped when the pillar hit the small of her back. Stiffening, she bit back a cry as it prickled a line of heat down her back. She wouldn't give them the benefit of seeing her flinch.

Over his shoulder, the man who masqueraded as a missionary beckoned two witches forward. Two women slogged through the water, faces set in reverent lines. Each carried something in hand. A candle, a book wrapped in a long sweep of black cloth. Her heart stuttered in fear.

A knife.

Jessie's eyes wrenched back to Caleb's. Her brother. "You realize your glorious leader is a witch hunter don't you?"

"Of course. How else were we to gain the information we needed?"

His voice was so empty, so matter-of-fact that she flinched. Set her jaw. "Nervy," she admitted, but her tone cracked with anger. "You're in bed with the Church, you know."

"No," he corrected, one hand firmly on her shoulder as he moved around her. He grabbed one arm, looped a cord around her wrist and pulled it tight. She jerked it back, but the cord bit into her flesh. Burned. "Curio has made sure that the Church is ignorant of our deception."

Deception. As if it were as simple as a few lies. She shook her head. "Why?" she demanded, shuddering. "Was it me? Did I do something wrong? To drive you away?"

"No."

She fought back her tears, craning to watch his face over her shoulder. "Then tell me. What's worth this?"

His deep ocean eyes met hers. Stabbed deep. "Power," he said flatly. "Control. To shake off the chains the Church has put on us. Walk free the way we used to and dismantle the Order from the top down."

Her mouth fell open. For a moment, no words would form in her mind as she struggled to put it together. To reconcile the brother she raised with the man who stood in front of her now.

They didn't match. Nothing, his voice, his stance, his eyes, nothing matched.

Jessie bit back a surge of anger, of grief and denial. Through her teeth, she hissed, "You're lying."

Caleb's hands jerked, pulled tight on the cord, but he said nothing. Behind him, Curio set the candle on a tall, smooth wooden pedestal. He raised one hand, and if Jessie thought the park was quiet before, it became deathly still now. Deathly silent.

The man put his fingers together, and with a quiet flare of magic, a flame gathered between them.

Parlor tricks. Any witch could do it.

Jessie looked past Caleb's shoulder. Saw the sheer rapture on the faces that surrounded them. She wasn't sure they knew it.

Slowly Curio lowered the flame to the single candle wick. There was a pop, a *whoosh* of heat and power, and suddenly Jessie's mouth went dry in terror.

Flames sprang throughout the park. Bonfires kicked off in an explosion of orange flame, blue heat. The witches cheered, raucous and wild, while Curio clasped his hands in prayer. He'd put the robe on, she realized. Draped himself in black velvet and glitter.

All the trappings of an obvious ritual. It wasn't necessary.

The leader, Jessie realized grimly, wrapped his coven up in lies.

"Caleb," she said, her voice trembling. She bent

her head, tried to see past the resolve. The iron will. The—goddamn it—the brainwash. "Caleb, listen to me."

Wordlessly he pulled a black velvet cloth from his pocket and wrapped it around her head. She struggled, but he tied it tightly around her mouth. Gagged her.

When he turned away, she stared helplessly at his back.

She used to rub that back when they were younger. Stretch out beside him on whatever bed they'd managed to claim for the night and rub his back until the nightmares receded. As he'd gotten older, too proud to let her baby him, she'd only kept him company. Played cards, talked for hours.

Wasn't it enough?

Hot tears slid down her cheeks as her heart shattered into jagged pieces at her feet.

"Bind the seer!"

Curio's voice boomed over the crowd. The same two witches circled the island, two women with eyes like dolls in their thin heads. Sisters, Jessie thought. Blood was always thicker than water.

Skeletal hands gripped her hair, jerked her face to the flame-lit sky. Smoke drifted into her eyes, making her choke on the raw heat.

Making her gag on her own screams as the first knife cut a line over one cheek. Over the other. Pain ripped through her, waves of agony as another blade dug into her forearms. She struggled, lashed out, but the sisters worked in silence. Pulled up her shirt, drew a thin line over her waist. Her thighs. Razor sharp and shallow, one over each energy point.

When they finally each carved into her calves, Jessie sobbed, hysterical with pain and fear. With the knowledge that power flowed with the blood they used to leash her, keeping her from using any magic she had. Bound by her own blood.

They tore off the gag. She clenched her teeth, gasping, trying to breathe through the pain, to ride it. Her vision swimming, she saw Caleb standing beside the leader. Arms folded. Watching.

Watching them cut her. Bleed her.

The sisters moved away, knives gleaming crimson in the wash of firelight.

Curio raised his arms as they flanked him. Flanked Caleb.

"Bind the soothsayer!" he intoned, and Caleb's face erupted into shock and anger. He whirled when the sisters laid hands on him. Furious, struggling, he managed to fling one from the cement island. She screamed as she flailed, hit the water and skidded into it.

Jessie sucked in a breath. What the hell was going on? Fighting back the nebulous cloud of her fading mind, struggling to stay focused, to ignore the lull of waiting oblivion, she watched Caleb thrust out a hand.

Power, sweet, oddly strong, lashed out. It whipped at Curio's stalwart figure, at his ornate robes. Blood gleamed in the golden glow of the candle. The witches gasped.

Curio touched his throat. His fingers came away dark, gleaming red, and he chuckled. Rich, rolling. He flicked his crimson fingers, and Caleb staggered to his knees, face ashen. He hunched over his chest, clutching at his heart.

Jessie's own seized. "No!"

The girl forged back through the water, joined her sister in wrestling Caleb to the pillar.

Jessie dropped her head as they wrenched him behind her. They tied him tightly, his hands at the small of her back and hers at his. When he cursed, when he thrashed against the bonds, Jessie knew they did to him what they'd done to her.

Bound. Bound in blood.

A witch was his own worst enemy.

"Now." Curio's voice, smooth and elegant. As if blood didn't smear her skin, or Caleb's. As if he hadn't just swatted Caleb away like he was an inconsequential fly. Jessie whipped her gaze to him.

"You're going to pay, you bastard," she seethed. "I swear to God, if I have to haunt your every living day, I will see you in hell."

He smiled. "Perhaps." Then he ignored her to round the pillar. Jessie wrenched at her bonds, tried to see over her shoulder.

Froze when Caleb's hands closed on the back of her shirt.

"I never expected you to betray me," Caleb said. His voice sounded strained, but it was strong. "What did it?"

"My dear friend," Curio said, and Jessie saw his fingers curl over Caleb's shoulder. Squeeze gently. "I know you planned to kill me tonight."

Jessie jerked. Caleb's grip tightened.

"Oh?" Noncommittal. Smooth. Despite the pain

leaching at her, her lips twitched. Wry, wan humor.

Yeah. She'd taught him well.

There was the sharp sound, flesh on flesh, and she bared her teeth as Curio said quietly, "Don't ever mistake me for a fool, Caleb Leigh. This coven is *mine*. Every man and woman, every child, is mine. How dare you think otherwise?" Another crack. "I clothed you." Again. "I fed you." Another. Jessie flinched. "I took you in from your miserable existence."

Caleb's hands remained tight on her jacket, but tension vibrated through him. "You lie like a little girl, Curio," he spat. "You've had this plan since the beginning."

Jessie could almost hear Curio's smile. "You are entirely too clever, Mr. Leigh. You always were. Yes."

"You lying son of a bitch."

"Pot," Curio said lightly. "Kettle. Your mistake, my friend, was in assuming that I didn't know about your little harvesting game. That you were safe in stealing the lifeblood of latent witchcraft. You," he said in smug disapproval, "were wrong. And that kind of arrogance will never serve in a soothsayer.

"And so!" The expansive tone accompanied his stride as Curio returned to the candle. "Tonight, my brothers and sisters, you will all witness the transition of power from two witches! Traitors, both of them, but their powers can be used to help our cause."

Jessie's shoulders tensed as Caleb's voice said softly, "Jessie?"

The witches cheered, drowning out the roar of fire and Jessie's own sob. "Don't you lie to me."

"God, I'm sorry." His fingers at her back shook. Vibrated with tension, fear. "It wasn't supposed to happen like this. I was supposed to kill the leader. End the problem before it happened." Despair thick in his voice, Caleb added bitterly, "I was supposed to stop the things I saw in my visions."

Jessie's head snapped up. Slammed the pillar. She laughed at herself, but the edge of hysteria to it only served to sober her. "Fuck," she bit out. "Fuck me. Caleb, Jesus Christ, listen to you."

"Fire and death," Caleb said softly. "Look at where we are. What's happening around us."

Jessie shook her head. "Why should I believe anything you say?"

"Brothers and sisters!" Curio raised his arms. Jessie glanced at him, stiffened. The man towered. Tricks of fire and shadow, witchy parlor tricks, but her heart suddenly pounded in her throat as supernatural terror worked to infect her thoughts. "Let us begin!"

Caleb rested his head against the pillar. It hissed. "Everything I did was for the best," he said wearily. "Every bargain, every soul, every ritual. Every lie." He turned his head, and in her peripheral, Jessie saw his strong, angled cheek. The outline of his profile. "You taught me that."

She closed her eyes. "I taught you to make good choices," she replied, but even as she said it, she sagged.

She'd taught him to lie. That the ends justified the means when they had to steal to eat. Lie to survive.

Her cheeks stung as salty tears slid into the shallow cuts. "Christ," she managed on a sob. "I'm sorry, Cale. I'm so sorry. Momma would be so disappointed."

"No." Firmly, angrily, Caleb struggled against his bonds. Managed to touch his shoulder to hers. "No. You're amazing, Jessie. And that stupid bastard of a witch hunter never should have let you go. If he hadn't, you'd never be here. You'd still be safe, and I wouldn't have had to— Damn it, Jessie, I told you to stay away."

Jessie opened her mouth to argue. To ask how her baby brother knew about that. To defend Silas. And then shut it. Cold chills swept her body.

"You tried to kill him."

Caleb was silent for a heartbeat. Then, quietly, "Yes. And no, I'm not sorry," he added flatly. "But I didn't know you were with him then."

Her mouth twisted. "That doesn't make it better."

"Jesus, Jessie." His tone roughened. "I swear to you, it was for a good cause. To stop him. *This*."

"What is this?"

"Harvesting," Caleb said flatly. "Remember when Momma died? Remember how I inherited her power? That's what he wants. He wants our magic, he wants my prophecies and your ability to see. This is the start of a force that will bring this city to its knees, and in only a few years' time, the Coven of the Unbinding will change *everything*."

"Freedom," she shot back. "It's what you wanted, right?"

"It won't be freedom, Jess," he said wearily. "It's just trading one tyrant for another. That book he's got has more power bound in its pages than this entire coven combined. It's . . . infected him. Infected all of them."

Jessie's mouth worked. She took in a deep breath, fought down the pain that muddied her head. "Would you have let me die here?"

"Don't ask me that, Jessie."

"Would you? To stop them?" She twisted, hissed when the magic in the pillar seared her arms. "God damn it, Caleb, was that your plan?"

"No!" Caleb closed his eyes. "Not at first. I tried everything to keep you away, I never wanted you in this. You should have left me alone. I told you to leave me alone."

"Really?" The word tore out of her on a sob. "Really, Cale? Did you think I would? When you were killing people?"

"I had no choice! Without the extra power I was no match for Curio."

"Peterson," she corrected on a growl. "And congratulations. You just handed the combined power of present and future to the Church."

"I didn't intend— Christ," he hissed. "It's starting." He jerked at her shirt, and Jessie realized that the witches spoke. All of them. The words rose like a howl, demons and devils.

Jessie closed her eyes as Curio's deep, resonant voice led them all.

A wind, a sour, angry wind made of knives and skeletal fingers plucked at her. Swept through her hair. It made her feel ill. Wildly, wretchedly ill.

"What are they saying?" she asked tightly.

Caleb's voice was grim. "You don't want to know." There was a pause, and then, quietly, "Jess?"

"If you're going to pull out some bullshit sappy—" Jessie blinked as his fingers twisted at her back. She sucked in a breath of that foul wind. Gagged.

"Whatever happens, get the hell out."

"Caleb—"

"Promise me," he demanded. "Things are going to get crazy in about a minute, and I need you to promise me that you're going to run."

"What did you do?"

"Jessie. Please."

She grimaced. "I promise," she said, "for all the fat lot of good that does either of us. And if you die before me, I swear to God I'll kick your ass in hell, you murderer."

Caleb was silent as the wind swirled around them. And then, to her surprise, he chuckled. Strained, taut with pain, but there. "It'll do, big sister. It'll do fine."

When the pillar sparked between them, Caleb and Jessie clung to each other. Even through the wild anger, the deep hurt of betrayal, she held his shirt in her hands. Felt his arms tightly bound around hers, and took some small comfort in it.

Even as the stone burned red hot. Even as the wind, that howling, demonic wind, wrenched cold fingers over her skin. Over her wounds. Wanting in.

Wanting out.

Feeding.

Jessie screamed first.

CHAPTER TWENTY-FIVE

Hand over hand. Pipe over pipe. Silas clung to the twisted wreck of the foundation piping and tried not to think about the jump he'd be making in a few, short moments.

It was going to hurt.

But he'd go through worse if it meant saving the woman he loved.

And he would save her. God damn it, he'd save her from whatever godforsaken magic the man in the long robe was conjuring up.

The wind battered at him, plucking at his straining fingers as if it had a life of its own. Malicious. Cruel. Silas gritted his teeth, swung to another twisted pipe. Sharp edges tore at his palm, but he was long past feeling that pain.

She was screaming. He concentrated on that. Let it push him. Enrage him. His woman was screaming.

The blood trickling down his arms made his grip slippery as hell. Grunting with effort, he reached for the next pipe. The next. Below him, fires crackled. Witches, damn them all, chanted.

Muscles aching, shrieking in pain, he pushed his body harder. Faster. His heart pounded as he saw the little pond beneath his feet.

This was it.

He wouldn't get another chance.

Silas twisted his shoulders. Slowly, achingly slowly, he rotated his wrists. Changed his grip on the pipe and eyed the distance between his feet and the frothing, murky water. It'd drop him right in front of the stone column Jessie sagged against.

Right in front of Caleb Leigh.

He didn't have the luxury of a weapon.

If nothing fucking else in this nonplan worked, he needed to hit the ground in one piece. He'd figure out the rest when he landed. Sucking in a slow, steadying breath, Silas forced his fingers to unclamp. Forced himself to let go. His stomach rolled smartly into his throat as he dropped like a stone.

It hurt like a son of a bitch. His knees detonated on a shock of pain, the water sucked at him, kept him from rolling right, and he barked an elbow, a shoulder on the shallow ground.

He expected that. Silas forced himself to his feet, already prepared to fight back the witches who saw him tumble to the ground.

What he didn't expect was the thunder.

Fire burst through the air, a blast that rolled over the crowd in a discharge of heat and furious force. Screams rang shrilly in the pounding echoes. The stench of burning flesh and chemical roiled through the shrouded park on a cloud of oily black smoke.

The blast pressure swept him off his feet. Silas slammed into the cement, hissed as the sharp edges of the makeshift island bit into his back. His ribs.

Christ on a stick, his ribs.

Another explosion, a blast of fire at another corner. More screams. But the witches who weren't displaced, who weren't scared, kept chanting. It rose. Shrill. Sharper.

"Silas!"

Jessie's voice, high and scared. Raw.

Silas rolled over, painfully aware of every shred of bruised muscle, every abrasion and cut. Sodden, slimy with algae and God only knew what else, he dragged himself onto the island. Rolled onto his back and cleared stinging sweat from his eyes.

He found himself meeting dark blue eyes framed in a mask of blood.

"Silas Smith." Caleb Leigh sounded tired. More than tired. Exhausted, drained.

Silas's lip curled.

"There's a knife in my left boot," Caleb said, cutting him off. He jutted out one leg. "Spare the pathos and get Jessie out of here. Curio won't be distracted for long."

"Caleb, no—"

Silas grabbed the man's foot, wrenched his pant leg up and left bloody smears as he found a silver dagger. It was too damned pretty to be called just a knife.

Witch's athame. How many people had he killed with this? Carved up like so much meat?

Silas wrenched it free, surged to his feet. The silver blade glinted dully as he pressed it against Caleb's throat. "Give me one goddamned reason," he growled.

Caleb met his eyes, held them. Level, steady, they were so much like Jessie's, aside from the color. So sure. "I'll give you over forty," he said quietly, nodding to the coven that screamed, ran in terror around them. Curio had vanished, lost somewhere in the sea of chaos and fire. "But only one should matter."

Jessie stretched against the rope that held her. "Silas! Silas, don't. Caleb, damn it, stop it."

"*Shit.*" Silas lowered the blade.

"Get her out." Caleb leaned away, baring her hands. The rope that bound her. Silas slashed at it until it gave, snapping loose. "I don't know where they set all the bombs, but—"

This time, the explosion rocked the cement island. Water lashed over its surface and witches screamed in terror and pain.

Jessie staggered, battered to the ground. She wrapped her arms over her head, screamed Silas's name, but the blast swept him off his feet. Sent him sprawling back into the water.

He surged back out of it, somehow managing to swipe the scum from his face and get back onto the ledge.

"Look out!"

Silas twisted, unable to see what, where, and rocked back into the water as a booted foot slammed into his wounded shoulder. He cursed, swallowed tepid water. The roar of the fires scattered over the ruined park, of stampeding people; the cacophony muted in and out as he thrashed to regain his footing.

When he came up, his hands were empty.

Silas whirled, only to slam into stillness, every muscle rigid with strain. The Seal of St. Andrew burned icy hot in the oppressive heat of the infernos separately ravaging the park around them.

David Peterson drew back his hood, revealed his graying hair. His flat, pale blue eyes. He said something Silas couldn't hear.

Silas's lips peeled back with effort. "You . . . son of . . ."

Peterson's raised hand splayed wide. Silas grunted, heaved out an explosive breath as every muscle tried to rip itself off his bones. The seal sizzled around his wrist. "Silas Smith. Didn't I tell you I'd be watching you?"

Silas's gaze flicked to the man's right. Jessie clung to the island, struggled to stand. Ash and blood smeared her skin, a gory mask, but her teeth were bared as she reached for the knife gleaming just out of reach.

His woman.

Fury whipped through him. Lashed at the unfocused restraints of magic. He moved. An inch, but he did it. "Fuck you," he snarled. "You played—"

"Every single one of you," Peterson said, self-satisfaction in every word. He moved closer, stepping off the island. Heedless of the fiery carnage around him.

Every step left Jessie behind.

Come on, sunshine.

Peterson smiled. "You surprise me," he said. A witch ran toward them, a glimmer of motion in Silas's fixed peripheral, but Peterson flicked his free hand. The tiny gesture sent the man screaming back into the fire.

Chaos had a smell, Silas realized, and it smelled like charred flesh. He strained against the bonds, felt them loosen. Then he collided into the opposite shore as Peterson slammed that magical force into him.

The world flickered violently.

A booted foot came down next to her reaching fingers. Jessie jerked, collided with a man who jammed a raw, sooty palm over her mouth. "Shut up," he hissed, seizing her collar with his free hand. His eyes, pale green in the wicked firelight, were ice cold. "Shut up, don't move."

Jessie nodded, frantic. Her gaze flicked left to right, struggled to find Silas in the smoke and chaos.

Over the man's shoulder, a woman collected Caleb's athame. Jessie saw nothing of her but a generously curved silhouette topped by a knit hat. The woman didn't stop to look at Caleb, to speak to him. Didn't stop to speak to the man who pinned Jessie, or to Jessie herself. She simply pressed the knife into Jessie's hands.

From the pillar, Caleb jerked at his bonds. "The book—" he began.

"Done. Consider us even." Another woman, a

strong-featured brunette, hugged Curio's heavy book to her chest. She spared Jessie a keen, dismissive glance. "Move!" She shouted. "Go!"

The man grinned down at her, despite the ice in his lime green eyes. "Maybe another time, sweet," he said, patting her on the cheek. "Get out while you can." He surged to his feet, following the two women into the water.

Jessie rolled over, shoved herself upright, but they were gone by the time she found her balance. Swallowed by flailing limbs, screaming witches. People.

Humans.

Jessie clutched at her throat. "Oh, my God," she whispered. Holy shit. This was it. This was the prophecy. This was where she died.

No, this is where *somebody* died.

The premonition sent shivers racing down her spine. "Caleb?" She whirled, ran to his side and hacked at the rope tying him in place. "Caleb, what's happening?"

"Easy." Caleb slung a hard arm around her waist as the rope fell away. "You need to get out of here." He plucked the knife from her nerveless fingers, shook her when she swayed. "Pull it together, Jessie!"

She shook her head hard, throat tightening. "I'm not—" A torrent of flame rose like an orange pillar mere yards away from them, and screams erupted as rubble spewed into the air. Caleb's arm tensed around her as she pushed at his chest, struggling to turn. "Silas!" she gasped, choking on a current of smoke.

"Shit, no, Jessica, *go!*" He shoved her away from

that fiery column, pushed her so hard that she stumbled over the edge of the island and hit the water. She staggered, found her balance, and turned, already knowing what she'd find.

Caleb shifted his grip on the knife and launched himself over the other side. He forged through the pond, through the water stained red by fire and blood. His jaw set, eyes fixed firmly on the mortal struggle between the coven leader and the witch hunter.

Caleb threw out a hand, barked something harsh and unforgiving. Peterson skidded, whirled as if he'd been pushed and fell into the slime. Wild rage contorted his features as he struggled to get back to his feet, wet robes tangling at his legs.

Silas's face was taut with strain and coated with blood, with mud and the ash that rained from the suffocating cloud of smoke. He hesitated when Caleb seized him by the collar, glanced between Caleb and the leader. Caleb said something; she couldn't hear anything but screams and the resonating echoes of wholesale destruction.

Silas turned his head, saw her. His mouth thinned. And then he nodded.

"No," Jessie whispered as Silas staggered back. Her fists clenched, throbbed painfully as the two men she loved in the world traded places. Traded her.

She knew it.

The leader's smile gleamed devil-bright in the flame-wrecked air. "Come then," he bellowed, barely a thread of sound under the rampant fury of hungry fire and the wailing voices of the dying.

Silas stumbled through the pond. His face was

grim, stiff, as he forced his way through the water. He grabbed her as he passed, his fingers biting roughly into her arm.

She struggled. "No," she repeated.

"Damn it, Jessie—"

"*No!* I'm not leaving him again!" Jessie swore as he bypassed her denial completely, looped an arm around her waist, and hauled her off her feet. Her shoulder rammed into his stomach, but he didn't stop. She clawed at his shoulder, his arm.

Watched her baby brother leap through the smoke and fire and clash, blade to blade, with the witch called Curio. Watched his power flare like a damned comet as he unleashed it all. Wrapped them both in it.

Burned himself with it.

The water gleamed red. Overhead, the twisted, tangled pipes glittered back in reflected flame. Jessie reached desperately for the power bound inside her, struggled to summon it through the binding magic.

But all she could feel was fury. Soul-shattering grief.

And Caleb's quiet strength.

"Caleb!" she sobbed. Silas's arm tightened, bodily forced her across the standing moat and to the other side. Her feet dragged, slick with slime. "Let me go!"

Silent, grim as the death that surrounded them, Silas held on tight. "I'm not losing you again," he yelled. "Damn it, Jessie, *move!*"

The fight left her. Exhaustion slapped over her like a shroud as she clutched Silas's filthy shirt in both hands and let him guide her. As if through a fog, she followed as he found footing on the park floor and sprinted through the maze of flames and twisted ruins.

There was another blast, another flurry of heat and pressure and seismic shudders. The ground rolled beneath them. Silas staggered, flailed, and Jessie sprawled to the ground, jarred all the way to her bones. Pain licked at her, swamped her, but all she knew was the black emptiness that suddenly ate at her chest. "Caleb!" she screamed, half a ragged howl torn from her raw throat as she struggled to roll over, push herself up to her feet.

The carnage faded to a dull roar, and just like that, Caleb was gone.

Warm hands seized her shoulders. Smoothed over her arms, her waist. Strong arms lifted her bodily from the ground. She sobbed, clung to Silas's broad strength, buried her face in his shoulder as he carried her out to safety.

As icy realization slid through her veins, as grief tore her resolve to shreds, the obsidian stone warmed against her heart.

"Come on, sunshine," Silas murmured unsteadily into her hair. His arms tightened around her back, one long-fingered hand splayed in her hair as he cradled her weight. "Let's get out of here."

CHAPTER TWENTY-SIX

Heat wrapped him in a velvet blanket. It seeped into his bones. Into his abused muscles, his battered body. It was heaven, pure heaven, and he wondered what he'd done to get him there.

A nice, gentle change from the hell he remembered last.

Silas's eyes fluttered open. Slowly focused. Color coalesced into lush foliage. Brilliant green water.

And the shining gold of Jessie's honey eyes filled with tears. One spilled over even as her wide, sweetly kissable mouth split into a smile.

His heart jerked hard in his chest. "Don't," he rasped roughly. He reached out, freed his arm from the hot, sulfurous water, and skimmed the tear away with a wet thumb.

More followed it. "Thank God," Jessie breathed. "Oh, Silas, I thought— Christ. *Shit*," she managed through laughter and tears. She caught his hand, raised his bruised knuckles to her lips. "Matilda!"

Silas shifted, found himself laid out on a sandbar built into the hot pool. The currents rippled over his wounded, naked body, soothing his wounds.

He struggled to sit up.

Jessie grabbed his elbows, slid through the water to help him. Her shades of ocean skirt swirled around her like a lush flower, clinging to his skin. When she would have let him go, he grabbed her waist, dragged her over his lap, and into his arms so he could bury his nose in the soft curve of her neck.

She laughed, hiccupping, but she didn't pull away. Instead she twined her arms around his shoulders. "I'm so glad you're awake," she said fervently. "So, so glad."

"I'll never leave you," Silas said roughly. "Fuck me, Jessie, I'll never leave you again."

"I can come back if you'd like to make good on that," said a dry, familiar voice.

Silas raised his head to grin wickedly at the red-haired woman standing on the shore. "Would you mind?"

"Silas!" Jessie palmed her face, reddening even as she gazed imploringly at Matilda. "Ignore him."

The woman's eyes crinkled, sparkled merrily as she set down a basket draped in an old-fashioned checkered cloth. "Among other things, I bring food. Silas, my dear, how are you?"

Silas opened his mouth, hesitated. He looked from

woman to witch—witch to witch, and it was so fucking clear now—and smiled. Slow. "I feel good," he said simply.

Matilda cleared her throat in quiet amusement. "Good. You gave us all a turn, but you seem healthy enough for a few tomorrows, at least."

Jessie cupped his face in her hands. "I was scared. You got us out, and then—"

And then nothing. Silas shook his head. "What happened?"

When Jessie's mouth pursed, he cupped her hand over his cheek. It was Matilda who answered, filling in the blanks Silas's mind couldn't. "You managed to get as far as you could before you collapsed. Jessie brought you to the trench. And," she added crisply, "to me."

"I thought that was it when we got to the edge of the water," Jessie admitted, flinching at the memory. "Matilda came along in her boat just in time."

The older woman put her hands on her hips, surveying them both from head to water-logged toe. "You, my dear boy, are too stubborn."

Jessie chuckled. Watery, but warm. "She picked us up. Took us back to the valley. I—" Her eyes clouded. "I don't know what happened with Caleb. I think— He just . . . stopped. Stopped being there." With one shaking hand, she touched her heart. In the valley between her breasts, obsidian stone gleamed beside a silver leaf pendant.

Silas bit his tongue before he said anything, bit down hard enough to make himself flinch.

"Things are rarely so clear when prophecy is involved," Matilda warned, and withdrew the cloth from the basket it covered. "You need to eat, the both of you. I didn't go to all that trouble just to lose you to starvation, now, did I?"

"No," Silas said quietly, but it was Jessie's face he watched. The downward curve of her mouth, the sadness shimmering in her eyes. He'd helped put that there.

Knowing he'd meant to all along didn't make it any easier. The fist of regret in his throat ached.

In his peripheral vision, he saw Matilda turn and quietly retrace her steps along the path.

Jessie laid one hand over his heart. It thudded in answer. "I know you . . . think he's terrible," she whispered. "And maybe he did terrible things, Silas, but I—"

Silas touched a finger to her lips. "He's your brother, sunshine. I know." It was the best he could do, under the circumstances. Knowing Caleb had planned to kill her, or didn't stop it. Knowing he'd killed others, it was all he could say.

"Yeah." Jessie sucked in a deep, shaking breath. Kissed his finger.

He didn't want her to think of her own brother as a murderer. She needed Caleb to be the man who had traded his life for hers, in the end. He wanted her to remember that.

"No falsehoods, right?" he said softly. He pushed his hands through her tousled hair. "So, I feel like I've jumped from a high ceiling, went fist to magic with an insane witch, been beaten, bloodied, shot at, and dropped into a boat to be ferried to heaven." He searched her eyes. Studied them.

Praying he didn't ruin it all. That somewhere, despite his anger and his stupidity, his violent denial, she still felt what she claimed.

"Silas," she whispered. "There's so much between us. So much *around* us."

"There always will be," he said, and shook his head slowly without breaking eye contact. Wanting her, *willing* her, to read the words in his soul. "It's new ground for us both, but we're as good as dead to the outside world. We can start over."

Her lashes flared. "As good as dead," she repeated, and something raw slid behind her eyes. She captured his face in both hands, leaned in to press her lips gently, move them softly over his. And shimmering in a molten sea of whiskey, shining in her eyes, he read her grief. Her uncertainty.

And a love so fragile, it took his breath away.

He could work with that, he thought, and fit her mouth more firmly to his.

Later, much later, when he'd thoroughly explored every inch of warm, wet skin beneath the easy access of her voluminous skirt, when they'd sat stiffly, achingly, on the sandy beach and shared a meal of nameless vegetables and cold fish, they returned to the cottage hand in hand.

Matilda rocked gently on the porch, a wooden pipe held loosely in her fingers. Her smile warmed as she saw them.

Silas helped Jessie ascend the steps, grinning at her groans of pain. They were so different from the moans of pleasure he'd coaxed from her earlier.

"I'm glad those fit," Matilda said, critically eyeing the jeans resting low on Silas's hips.

"Thank you." Silas gestured at the lake. At the cliffs. "For everything."

"Ah, well." The woman smiled. "Sit yourself down before you undo all the work I put into you."

Silas sat, feeling somehow warm inside. Aglow. Christ, was this what happiness was?

Was this what normal felt like? What it could be for him?

Jessie scooted into his arms, and he rested his chin on top of her soft golden hair. "So, what now?" she asked. She twined her fingers with his, squeezed. "What does a former witch hunter do?"

Matilda's chair creaked as she set it rocking. A thin trail of smoke wound from her old pipe. It smelled, to Silas, like herbs and something . . . faded. Nostalgic. He rubbed his chin gently against Jessie's hair and said, thoughtfully, "I guess I *am* retired."

Matilda's rich dark eyes flicked between them. "Retirement," she said slowly, a long, drawn-out sigh, "has its advantages. And its disadvantages." She raised the pipe to her mouth and added around it, "It's damned boring, if you ask me."

Jessie's laughter thrummed against his chest. "Matilda, if you're looking for excitement—"

Her eyes flashed. "I've had more than my share of excitement," Matilda said evenly. "I think I'll leave the rest to you children."

Silas pursed his mouth. A seed, a faint idea, bloomed inside his head. "Matilda."

"Mmm?"

He studied her. "Knowing what we know, what you've said about lies, I'm going to ask you a question."

The older woman's eyebrows knitted. "Ask, you impertinent ex-hunter, but I reserve the right to say nothing at all."

Jessie squirmed, wriggled around so she could study his face. "Are you sure you want to ask?" Her eyes searched his. They were lighter, but she would need time to heal. Time to grieve.

He touched her cheek. Slid his gaze to Matilda's lined face. "You didn't just stumble on us, did you?" Silas asked. "Both times, you were in the right place. How?"

In the lengthening dark, Matilda's eyes took on a mysterious sheen. Almost animal, they gleamed at him now, a brilliant reflection of her smile. "I have an interest in Jessie," she said, her tone matter-of-fact.

In his arms, Jessie stiffened. "An interest?" she asked slowly. "What do you mean?"

Matilda tapped the sweeping curve of the pipe's bowl against her palm. "It's nothing personal, baby girl," she said with a quiet chuckle. "Don't get your back up. Young witches like yourself are a rare thing. I know a good soul when I see it."

Jessie covered the strange obsidian pendant with one hand, and Matilda's smile deepened.

"I'm looking at two good souls here," Matilda said. "A fine start for redemption, don't you think?"

Silas frowned. "Redemption for what?"

"Oh," Matilda replied with a long sigh, and jammed the pipe stem once more between her teeth.

Around it, she added, "That's a long story, and not one I'm telling now. Go on inside, now. You're tired, and I like my evenings to myself."

When it became clear she was done talking, Silas nudged Jessie to her feet. Despite himself, he accepted her help to stand as his muscles throbbed and twanged.

Jessie slipped inside the front door, eased it gently closed behind him. "I have no idea what that was," she whispered, shaking her head, "but I like her."

Silas caught the front of her soft, cream tank top. Yanked her to him, soft to hard. Her warmth to his need. "I don't care what that was," he said against her lips. "I love you." He said it again at her throat, willing her to hear him. To understand. She gasped, clutching his shoulders.

Somehow, they managed to make it to the bed. Their borrowed clothes scattered over the floor, and Jessie arched breathlessly into his hands. His mouth.

His heart.

Later, wrapped around her, her legs tangled with his, her heart beating strongly against his own, Silas stroked the smooth line of her back and murmured, "We'll figure it out, sunshine."

She stirred, sleepy. Soft as silk as she rested her chin on his chest and blinked at him. "Hmm?"

"Don't worry about anything." He skimmed his fingers over her bottom lip. Her cheek, and the thin, scabbed line there. It was healing quickly, but still there. His chest tightened. "We'll be okay."

Jessie tilted her head, speculative. But she yawned. Shook her head, and stretched to touch her mouth to his. "I know. I . . . I love you, Silas. I don't think I should," she added with a crooked smile, "but I do."

"I'll never doubt it again," he promised with such intensity that it rumbled through his chest.

Jessie braced herself on an elbow. "I've been thinking."

"Oh, no."

"So funny," she drawled, tweaking his nipple in reproach.

He hissed, caught her hand with his. "You'll get yourself in trouble," he warned, flattening it against his chest. Against his heart. "Go on."

Amusement faded. "I don't know if Caleb is dead." The words slipped from her softly, husky with emotion. With things that twisted him up inside. Her eyes were luminous in the semidark. "I just don't know. But I'm going to hope he isn't."

Silas frowned. "Jess—"

"I know." Her fingers tightened over his chest. "I know. He did— It's just that I think there's good there still. I hope so. And if—"

"Enough." Silas twined his free hand in her hair, drew her head down for his kiss. Her lips trembled over his. Parted on a soft exhale, a whimper of a sound. His heart aching inside his chest, battling with the fury that pressed hard when he thought of how close he'd come to losing her, he drew her closer to him. "I have a lot to learn, I know. I hope to God that I can undo what a lifetime of Church teaching has turned me into."

"You'll never have to figure it out alone," she murmured, her fingers warm as they stroked over his chest.

"It won't be easy. I've spent my life believing that all witches deserved to die. Some do, we saw proof of that, but—" He cut himself off, tried hard to moderate himself, his anger at the man who had betrayed his own sister. Finally, unable to get enough, he touched her cheek. Her lip, soft and warm. "We'll keep an eye out," he said. "If he shows up, we'll . . . talk." It was all he could promise.

All he could force himself to promise.

"Thank you." She sighed. "It isn't over. I know it isn't."

He nodded. "We'll be okay, sunshine. Whatever you need, we'll do it together."

She murmured something wordless, sensual, and uniquely feminine, completely Jessie. She curled up against him in the narrow bed, and Silas couldn't stop himself from touching her. Gliding his palms over her back. Her shoulders. Her hair.

He'd almost lost her. Christ, it had been so fucking close.

And as Jessie drifted off to sleep, her healing cheek pillowed on his shoulder, Silas stared into the dark. Stroked her warm, silken skin, and ran it all back through his head. The fire that ate at the Mission safe house, the magic that had sent them over the trench and her blood, an obscenely bright smear on her skin and still so terrifying that his grip tightened protectively at her waist.

Peterson's face, his power-hungry eyes as he'd stared at Silas across the Mission table, then again as Curio in the depths of the ruined city.

How did a witch get to be a missionary? How the

hell did the leader of the Coven of the Unbinding become the Mission director?

And would the Mission team think Silas was dead, too? Would Naomi try to find them?

He didn't know. There were no answers in the dark to guide him.

He tangled one hand in Jessie's silken hair and closed his eyes, breathing in the aroma of her scent. Sunshine and woman mingled with the spicy haze of the bay's treated water, and somehow, he was content.

He had no desk job, and there was no Mission team to lead. He had a safe haven to rest and recover, and a strange ally in the mysterious witch that owned it. Though he had no answers to give, no direction to take them as they began this new life, he had something stronger. Something that would bolster him through the darkest nights.

Jessie stirred, splayed one long-fingered hand over his chest and sighed. In that whisper-soft sound, Silas heard relief. Hope. Comfort. His name.

They were alive. They were alive and she loved him.

It was more than enough.

Turn the page for a sneak peek at
the second book in

KARINA
COOPER's

Dark Mission series
LURE OF THE WICKED

Coming July 2011

Naomi West was a damned good missionary. Her Mission file lauded her as one of the best witch hunters in New Seattle.

Nice to know that the Holy Order of St. Dominic had faith in her. At least her fellow Mission operatives thought she was hot shit.

If they only knew what crawled under her skin and sent her heart pounding hysterically within the cage of her ribs, they'd yank her off the streets faster than a bullet to the head.

The voice in her ear faded and she tucked a finger against the tiny comm speaker. Alan Eckhart's voice sharpened into crystal clarity as he continued to outline the operation specs. The team briefing after the Mission briefing. Blah, blah, fucking blah.

Naomi's muscles vibrated, taut with strain as she listened to the team lead drone while studying the panoramic view from the top floor of her lavish hotel suite.

She touched the surface of the floor-to-ceiling windows, her fingers silhouetted to shadow by October's dying sun. It turned the thick smog blanketing the lower levels to burnished fire, seeped into the rat-infested shithole that was New Seattle's barely civilized foundation, and vanished in the ever-present miasma. Most of the metropolis was too far below her to see, but Naomi didn't have to see it to recall the acrid stink of rotting garbage.

Anxiety, thick and vicious, curled in her throat as she turned away.

"Look, I don't care what the Mission says," she said into the tiny mic inset into her ear. "I am not going to be stuck up here forever. This is bullshit."

"A week, tops." Eckhart's voice aimed for soothing. It scraped over Naomi's raw nerves like a serrated knife. "If I'm lucky," she muttered.

"You don't have to be lucky, Nai, you're good."

Good, nothing. She was trapped. Stripped of her piercings, scrubbed and buffed, wrapped in designer clothing, and locked behind the walls of a gilded fucking cage.

"I'm better than good," she told him flatly. Not ego. Fact.

"Exactly. Which is why you were chosen."

Give me a fucking break. "Aside from the security check coming in, I'm not seeing much by way of surveillance. I told you, *anyone* could do this job."

Eckhart chuckled. Or choked, she wasn't sure.

"Of course there isn't major surveillance, Nai. It's a spa," he replied dryly. In the background, she heard the familiar white noise of the mid-low Mission offices. Where she should be right now.

Where she desperately wanted to be. She took a deep breath, held it for a long moment before easing it out on a carefully modulated sigh. "I still don't see why Parker couldn't get someone else to play dress up."

"No one with your credentials." It came out a sigh. No matter how many times they'd had this argument, she wasn't going to eat it any easier. She grimaced, opening her mouth, but he cut her off. Wheedling, for fuck's sake. "Come on, Naomi. It's not exactly a maximum security prison."

It may as well have been. She turned, saw sumptuous furnishings and bold color, and closed her eyes against the insistent pressure in her head.

It was as if she'd gone back in time. Only she wasn't a child. And her name hadn't been Naomi Ishikawa for almost twenty-five years.

Except now it *was* again. Because the Mission said so.

She flinched. "Shitfuck."

"You're so pretty when you go blue." Eckhart sighed again. "All right, give me the rundown on the place."

Naomi's fist clenched over the hard metal of the comm. "The city to grounds elevator takes eight minutes to get to the top. Surveillance is minimal and discreet, but hard to hide with all the glass. One camera at the lobby doors, one camera in the main elevator inside the resort, and that's it. The lobby's full of money and empty of people. Eckhart, I need those goddamned blueprints."

The man whistled a distinctive three-note tune. "Jonas is still working on it. Says the blueprints are locked up tight."

"Why?"

"Dunno, but smells like money or politics to me. Probably both."

"Great," she snarled. She shoved her free hand through the glossy strands of her black hair, took the three steps to the divan, and turned. "What you're saying is that the Church doesn't have a legitimate in, which is why they whored me up and sent me up here." It lashed out, a vicious whip of anger too sharp even to her own ears. She jammed a thumb and forefinger into her eye sockets, squeezed them shut until the pressure ate away at the light searing the inside of her skull.

Politics. Goddamned politics.

"What I'm saying is—" Eckhart began sharply, only to cut himself off. She knew why. It was another old argument, one that they circled like wary dogs. He lowered his voice; his version of soothing. "Look, not everything can be handled with a gun and an attitude."

Except Naomi *knew* he was wrong. Almost anything could be handled by just that, and right now, she was missing one half of the fucking equation.

Naomi paced to the window again, already knowing what she'd see as the setting sun sank toward the smudged horizon. A shimmering pool of polluted air ate at the dark spaces long since gathered between the towering skyscrapers. It hid the filth, the desperation, the shoulder-to-shoulder chaos that lived—no, that *existed* miles below her.

She was anonymous down there. Unknown, a damned good witch hunter in a team of them.

But up here, she was just a tool of the Church who had run the show since the earthquake had eaten the old city. Fifty years of guidance, of planning, had raised New Seattle from the ashes of the old ruins. Fifty years of powerful Church support had installed the Mission to a place of prominence; each operative was trained from childhood to protect humanity from the murderous practitioners of the witchcraft that had killed hundreds of thousands of innocent people in one devastating sweep.

Naomi had been a missionary for over twenty years, and she still didn't play the political game. That was why she was just an agent, and not a team lead. Or a desk jockey, like the director.

She was an operative.

A killer.

And Naomi liked it better when she could pull out her gun—which she didn't fucking *have*—and get to work the way she worked best.

"Whatever," she said tautly as she whipped around and stalked back to the fancy sofa, "can we just get to the part where you get me a gun?"

He whistled again. The three-note tune that said he was working it out. That it was complicated. "Nai," he said slowly, "what's going on?"

"It's a rich bitch haven—"

"No," he cut in. The sound of voices faded in the

background. His voice lowered. "I don't mean right this second, I know you hate topside. I mean, what's going on with *you*? You were in jail when we went looking for you."

She snorted. Trading one jail cell for another didn't warrant any kind of gratitude. Pitted cement walls or sleek wallpapered hallways, it was all the same to her.

Naomi dropped her hand, stared at the sectioned, gilt-framed mirror hanging over the polished snowy marble fireplace and didn't recognize the naked face staring back at her. Lavish mouth, high cheekbones sharp enough to cut, straight black hair without a trace of the electric blue streaks she'd worn until yesterday. No piercings.

God, she missed her piercings.

Aside from the crusted scab slashing diagonally over her nose, she looked rich. Pampered. Soft.

She looked like her mother.

It was enough to send her pacing again. Windows to sofa, sliding bedroom door, and back to the sofa.

Damn the Mission. Damn the new Mission director who'd decided that locking her up behind the polished doors of New Seattle's premier resort and spa was the only answer to a problem they'd all decided was going to be hers.

And damn the panic riding her so hard, it hummed like an electrical current inside her chest.

Abruptly Naomi sank to the arm of the sofa. "Alan," she said wearily, "why the fuck am I here? Joe Carson isn't a witch, he's a missionary. Why do I have to execute him?"

"Joe Carson isn't your average missionary, Nai. You remember that mess with Smith? Imagine if he'd survived long enough to go rogue."

Ice pooled at the base of her spine.

It had been only three months. Three goddamned months since the missionary she'd first known as a boy in a godforsaken orphanage had turned on them.

Turned on her.

Missionary Silas Smith and his witch lover had gone up in smoke, caught in an inferno set by a coven of witches deep in the ruins of Old Seattle. There hadn't been anything more than rubble and charred, unrecognizable flesh by the time the Mission had gotten through the chaos.

The new Mission director had some serious questions to answer, and another rogue agent on her turf wasn't going to help her do it.

Naomi pressed her fingers to the front of her designer jeans, to the spot low on her abdomen where the seal of St. Andrew lay dormant. Protective.

An early warning signal that arced with blue flame when witchcraft was used on her, calling on the holy energies of St. Andrew to combat whatever malicious intent a witch's magic would cause. Which came in handy when she was on a mission to kill *witches*.

There were no witches here to kill.

She rose again, strode past the decorative awning that separated the bedroom from the parlor, and surveyed the too-large bed with its lavender and gold silk bedspread. Her nose wrinkled. "The sooner I do this, the sooner I'm out, right?"

Relief tinged his voice as he replied, "Right."

·

"And little Miss Parker isn't planning some sort of bullshit extended operation?"

"*Director Adams* knows how much you don't like this op, Nai," Eckhart said, correcting her with a sigh. "You made that extremely clear. Just get the job done, and you're out."

"Okay, lay it on me."

"Joe Carson is a murderer."

"So am I."

He hesitated, just a fraction of a second. It was enough. Her mouth twisted in edged, cutting humor. "It's different," he finally said. "Carson's wanted for the murder of two Church officials and four civilians, and he's a suspect in the disappearance of Mission evidence."

She frowned. "Wait a damned minute, this wasn't in the briefing. Mission evidence? Was our vault compromised?"

"No, thank God, not ours. We don't keep anything really dangerous there, anyway," he said. "The director's headquarters got hit sometime last week and they only just found the breach. Be glad you weren't there yesterday. Adams damn near froze the place out."

"Nothing pulling the stick out won't fix," Naomi muttered. She rolled her eyes when he cleared his throat in pointed reprimand.

She didn't have to like Director Parker Adams, but she did have to work with her. *For* her.

"Sorry," she added. "What was taken?"

"Let's see. Some old newspaper clippings and a

pot full of odds and ends. Pre-quake junk, as far as we could tell."

"Helpful. I still think instead of hunting him, we should just bring him in for processing."

"Not our call."

"But if his team had done *their* job—"

"Again, Nai, his local missionaries tried. As soon as the flag landed on his file, he vanished."

And they couldn't process what they couldn't find.

Naomi grimaced. No one knew what processing really meant, but the rumors persisted. Everything from chemical lobotomy to brainwashing; torture disguised as cleansing to simple disposal.

Dangerous, heretical rumors. The Church didn't like rumors. Or questions it couldn't answer.

"This has been going on awhile. A missionary doesn't just wake up one day and decide to murder six people."

"Doesn't matter. Get your attitude together and do what needs to be done. They're watching you, Nai."

"Fuck off."

"I'm serious." Eckhart hesitated. "Naomi, you've been flagged by the Church for surveillance."

Flagged. Like Joe Carson.

Anger wrapped itself into a tangle, a knot of fury and sudden fear. Naomi blew out a hard, laughing breath. "Well, that's great. Guess I'll run off and murder for them some more."

"Jesus, Nai, don't say that. That's the kind of stuff you're always getting in trouble for. The only thing saving your ass right now is your success record.

You're a damned good missionary, but you've been pushing it and you know it."

Translated, if she didn't toe the line this time, she'd be out on her ass, no matter how fucking good she was at what she did.

Same old song and dance. "Whatever," she said not bothering to try for sincere. She turned away from the pile of luggage that stored a fortune in exclusive clothing and stalked back out of the bedroom. "What I meant was, I should go tend to this mission that the Holy Order of St. Dominic has found to be necessary and just."

Eckhart paused. She could practically hear him grinding his teeth. "Naomi. You're cracking at the seams. Get it together, or you're going to get us *all* flagged."

"I'll be in touch soon as I've got something worthwhile to report."

"Naomi—"

"Understand this." Naomi tucked her index finger against the tiny black mic at her ear, pushed it in closer so that he couldn't possibly miss a single note. "One way or another, I'm going to put a bullet in this shitfucker's brain. When I get out of here, I'm going to get my piercings back and get laid." She smiled at his snort. "You are welcome to come along for either."

"You need help, West."

"Yeah. Get me a Beretta."

"I'll see what we can arrange," he said, and didn't waste his time saying good-bye.

As the line clicked off in her ear, she gave in to the

fury licking at her every breath. She tossed the palm-sized unit savagely across the room. It rebounded off the brocade settee, thudded to the carpet.

It didn't make her feel better.

Watched. She was being watched by her own fucking team.

Flagged.

Fine.

Smoothing her hair back over her shoulders, she yanked her crumbling concentration firmly back into focus. It didn't matter what Carson was. Missionary, witch, or other.

The Church said kill.

She'd get right on it.

She took one step toward the bedroom and froze as the oiled metal doors of the suite elevator hissed open behind her. Sudden, visceral awareness lifted every hair on the back of her neck.

Nerves prickled; a circle of fire searing through the tattooed seal low on her belly. *Witchcraft*.

Instinct took control of her body, launched her to the side as pain and power converged inside her skull. Sheer adrenaline ate away at the last vestiges of confusion, and she hit the ground rolling.

She collided with a polished end table, saw boots and a sage green uniform in the corner of her eye, and swore as a lamp crashed to the floor by her head. Pain made her slow, sticky under the hammering of magic and the protective burn of the Mission tattoo. The edges of her vision wavered in black and excruciating red.

"What the fuck," she gritted out as she struggled

to get to her feet. Her knees wobbled, shredded by the witchcraft drilling through her skull.

"Jesus, she wasn't kidding." A masculine voice, gritty. Focused. "You're tougher than I thought."

Sucking in air, her lips peeled back from her teeth and she came up swinging.

His curse fractured as her fist found his ribs; she cursed hard enough for both of them as her knuckles collided with bone. He bent double with the impact and she stepped in, grabbed his wrist and slammed him viciously against the back wall. Naomi locked her forearm against his throat, panting with the effort.

A painting swayed, crashed to the ground in the sudden silence of his constricted airway. The pain receded.

He was old, she realized. Older than she'd thought, underneath stocky muscle and hands made of calluses. The fingers he locked around her arm in desperation were work-scarred, nails clipped to the quick. His hair was cut in severe military lines, liberally peppered with gray. A full bar mustache covered his upper lip, but it couldn't hide the scar puckering the skin just by the side of his mouth. His bulbous nose and bushy gray eyebrows should have conspired to give him a harmless, kindly demeanor.

The wild glint in his deep blue eyes betrayed the truth.

Even as one part of her brain cataloged his description, the rest of her battled back the too-fast surge of her own heartbeat. Too much adrenaline. Too damned fast. Pins and needles prickled at her face.

Not now. Scraping her attention together, she bared her teeth and gritted out, "Who are you?"

"Fuck y—" He choked as she flexed her shoulder, driving the edge of her forearm harder against his throat.

The fragile bones in his neck grated together as he turned purple. She thrust her face into his. "You have about thirty seconds before— Shit!"

Harder, stronger than she expected, the witch seized her sweater and shoved. Seams stretched, popped. Her feet tangled in the one he locked behind hers. She flailed, hit the floor on her ass. He stepped in immediately, cocked a leg, and rammed one booted foot into her ribs. Again. She rolled with the momentum as pain screamed through her chest, but she couldn't see past the colors swimming through her head. Vibrant reds and bruised purples.

A rough hand closed over the back of her neck, shook hard and sent her sprawling. Pain rocketed through her body as she collided into the settee. Ass over skull, her knees buckled over the low cushions and sent her flailing over the back of it.

The back of her head slammed into one unyielding corner of the small end table beside it and the scene flickered, a synaptic overload of pain and magic.

Naomi shook her head hard; her chest squeezed, labored to inhale the oxygen that wasn't making it to her brain. She tensed, teeth clenched as she forced her muscles to move. He didn't come at her again. When the onslaught of magic ceased, it ended so completely that it left her reeling.

She clung to the back of the elegant couch, gasping for breath as her lungs constricted. Hysteria. It wrapped around her chest and made it too damned hard to breathe.

Her peripheral vision flickered. Naomi launched herself out of the way, hit the table again, and clutched it for support as the room whirled.

Nothing came at her.

Forcing air into her struggling lungs, she dragged herself to her feet as the suite elevator doors closed. Leaving her with the impression of sharp blue eyes and the lingering snap of killing magic.

"Son of a *bitch*," she snarled, and lunged for the control button. Her palm slapped down too damned late. She sucked in a breath, held it. Let it out. Another. Calm.

Controlled.

Fuck. Naomi kicked the steel doors until the suite echoed with it. Her toes throbbed in protest.

She watched the light buttons as the elevator descended with the powerful witch inside. Seventeen. Sixteen. Fifteen . . .

Should she try to outrun it and take the stairs? Hell, he could get off at any floor before he reached ground level. She'd never catch him.

By the time the elevator made it all the way back to her suite on the top floor, she'd scuffed the hell out of her knee-high leather boot and knew her assailant would be long gone.

The doors slid open with an expensive *whoosh*. She limped into the elegantly mirrored box and barely kept herself from putting her fist through the reflective glass.

No gun, no bullets. She'd thought this bullshit operation was going to be as witch-free as Sunday Mass, but the lingering prickle around the skin of her abdomen proved her wrong.

Dead fucking wrong.

The woman who shot out of the residential elevator and into his arms rang every bell in Phinneas Clarke's head, and then some.

Most were alarms.

Trouble. Capital T kind of trouble, with long, long legs and a taut, trim body that fit against him like a custom suit. Plastered to the wall by her surprised momentum, the back of his head rebounded from the wallpapered panel and knocked a peal of thunder through his skull as he found his hands suddenly full of warm wool and soft curve.

She buckled, slid against the front of his body until his brain shorted out and she caught herself against his chest. One knee jammed between his legs—mercifully shy of wracking Phin's vulnerable flesh—and her fingers twisted into the lapels of his suit jacket, providing an awkward angle of support.

Warm, denim-clad curves filled his palms, and he realized he'd caught her by the definitely taut muscles of her ass. For a long moment, only the whispered lilt of the created spring behind them filled the shocked silence.

His lips twitched.

Naomi Ishikawa. According to the dossier he'd compiled from her people, his newest guest was an heiress who couldn't stay out of the kind of trouble that got rich girls put on a very short list.

Phin could see what her handlers meant.

Her hair was sleek and black, reminiscent of the Japanese heritage that defined her cheekbones and shaped the almond tilt of her eyes. She was fine-boned, slender, but tensile; clearly a woman who enjoyed a good workout. The easy strength he felt in her slim body was proof enough of that.

The rest of her was pure American supermodel, right down to the wildly long legs that tucked her at just about his eye level.

His gaze centered on her flushed face, and the raw-looking scab slashed diagonally across the bridge of her fine, straight nose. Miss Ishikawa looked as if she'd stepped into the ring with a prizefighter and lost.

The elevator doors eased shut beside them. Her eyes narrowed. "Are you all right?"

He wasn't sure. Were his fingers still curved around her rear? Did having a beautiful woman plastered against his chest count as all right?

He shook his head. Hard.

"Shit," she said, a husky snort. Sharp eyes searched his face as one warm, long-fingered hand slid around the back of his neck. "What's your name?"

"Phin," he managed, and shifted. Just enough. "And I don't mean to be rude, but could you remove your knee?"

The hand at the back of his neck stilled. Desperately he tried not to smile as she looked down at his chest. At the locked press of her hips against his and the sleek, denim-clad leg she'd braced between his knees in the confusion.

He hoped to God she couldn't feel his pulse against the curve of her thigh.

Her gaze flicked back up to his. Crinkled just enough to let him know she did. "Sorry," she said lightly. "Tell you what. You move your hands from my ass and I'll move my leg from your—"

"Got it," Phin said hastily before the heat uncurling through his veins could get any hotter than the pressure at his crotch. Carefully Phin pulled his all-too-eager hands away from her body. She eased from the tangle of balance and limbs, and as the warm weight of her withdrew, Phin was absurdly grateful that he could breathe again without inhaling the raw, clean scent of her skin.

"Sorry about that," she said, readjusting the loose neck of her sweater. She frowned down at the fraying threads at the collar. "I should come with a warning."

And how.

He straightened, prodding gingerly at the back of his bruised skull. "I can think of worse ways to make your acquaintance, Miss Ishikawa."

Her shoulders stiffened, subtly enough that he would have missed it if he wasn't watching her. Her gaze slammed to his in sudden, razor-edged acuity. In that split second, Phin felt as if those strange blue-purple eyes had taken him in, cataloged every inch from his expensive shoes and newly rumpled suit to his brown, curly hair, and shelved him neatly under a label he wasn't sure would be flattering.

Then her mouth curved up; an easy, blinding smile.

Phin's gut clenched, liquid quick awareness that bit deeper than it should have.

"Naomi," she corrected.

"Naomi, then." He offered a hand. "Phinneas Clarke. Welcome to Timeless. Normally we strive not to maim our guests."

Her gaze flicked to his hand. When she took it, her grip was firm, her skin cool and somewhat damp. Phin managed not to look down in surprise when his thumb brushed over the rough indication of her abraded knuckles.

Trouble. Definitely trouble.

"No harm done." She extracted her hand a shade sooner than manners strictly dictated polite. He didn't miss the way she dragged her palm against the fabric of her sweater. "Did you see anyone else go by?"

"Not until you trampled me."

"Damn." Her gaze skimmed the interior atrium courtyard behind him, dimly lit by the lampposts scattered under the cultivated trees. "Is your head okay?"

Her eyes were shadowed, too hard to read. He couldn't tell what she was thinking. Not that he was sure he'd have any better luck in full daylight, either.

Intriguing.

He smiled, crooked with apology. "I've had worse. It's definitely one way to make introductions."

She tipped her face to the early night sky, ten floors above them and trapped behind the wide skylight. "You were headed into the elevator," she observed, tucking stray tendrils of black over her ear. "Don't let me keep you."

It had been a long time since Phin had felt so thoroughly dismissed. Challenge rose like a banner in his chest. "Actually I was on my way up to see you."

One fine black eyebrow arched. "Me?"

"To introduce myself."

The sound she made was noncommittal.

His gaze dropped to her mouth, and Phin couldn't help but realize how easy it'd be to taste that overly lush curve of her lip. She was tall enough in her boots that he'd only have to tilt his head a fraction to close the distance.

And earn himself a mean right hook, if the condition of her knuckles was any indication. No, thank you. He liked his features exactly where they were.

She watched him, sliding her fingers into the front pockets of her hip-hugging jeans.

"And now that I've successfully made an impression," he added, his voice roughened. "I'll let you get back to whatever it was you were doing. This really can't get any more awkward."

The look she slanted him glinted. A darker kind of humor. Something that bit. "I bet you say that to all the girls."

"Just the ones who throw themselves at me."

Her laughter surprised him, rich and throaty. There was an edge to it, a brush of smoke. Just wicked enough to remind him of the warmth of her skin against his hands, the texture of her soft wool sweater and the curves beneath. Just feminine

enough to make him remember it'd been too long
since he'd met with anyone for an evening out. Or
in. Phin pursed his lips and whistled soundlessly. He
made a point to keep his hands off the guests. They
weren't here to be hit on, and that kind of fraterniza-
tion was bad for business no matter how prettily it
came packaged.

But Miss Ishikawa was going to make him work
for it.

"I was exploring," she said, shrugging one shoulder. "Point me toward the nearest exits, won't you?
Briefly," she added.

"Your wish is my command. The lobby is behind
me, through the park."

"Park?"

"Well, it's not as big as the old parks, but you're
welcome to explore it at your leisure." He raised a
finger toward the wide double doors at the end of
the courtyard. "The ground floor maintains the
pools and a fully equipped gym. There are personal
trainers for your convenience, if you require assis-
tance." Then he pointed to the elevator doors behind
her. "Seventeen residential suites. Each on their own
floor."

Naomi glanced over her shoulder at the elevator.
"Is that the only way in?"

"Stairs lead to each floor, but they're for staff use
and emergencies only. Your people got you the top
floor," he continued with a smile. "Best view."

"Anything else?"

Phin jerked a thumb to his right, where a green
exit sign glowed in the distance. "That's the services

center. There are ten floors, ranging from dining to socializing to relaxation and beauty, all yours from that elevator. Did you receive your program?"

"Program?"

"Your people scheduled your services in advance," he explained, and couldn't help curiosity from leaking into his voice as her mouth twisted. "If you don't like the choices—"

"I'm sure whatever they are will be fine and dandy," she said, her expression so indifferent that he wondered if he'd misread the signs.

"The program should be in your suite." He'd make a note to check with housekeeping. "This atrium connects all three towers." As if she'd read his mind, her gaze flicked to the third set of doors. Answering her unspoken question, he added, "That's the family quarters. As much as I'd love to show you my parlor—"

"Got it, slick," she said, her lips twitching. "I'll keep that in mind."

"And that's it." It was the shortest, most precise tour he'd ever given.

Not that she cared, he realized wryly. The smile she flashed him was distracted. "Great," she said, dismissal once again clear in her tone. "Thanks."

"Of course." He stepped out of her path, easing down the few steps separating the surrounding walkway from the central garden. "Welcome to Timeless, Naomi."

The next few weeks were going to be woefully long with this particular heiress around. Phin let out his breath in a silent sigh of relief as she turned away.

"Good night, then," she said. "I'm sure we'll meet again soon."

"Do you need anything right away?"

Naomi flung a hand to the side without turning. "No. You're an interesting man, Phinneas Clarke."

He grinned at her back. "Phin, and if that's not a compliment, I'd like to take it as one."

Her shoulders lifted. "Take it however you—" she began, then froze as a muffled, ragged scream echoed through the courtyard.

At Avon Books, we know your passion for romance—once you finish one of our novels, you find yourself wanting more.

May we tempt you with . . .

- **Excerpts** from our upcoming releases.

- Entertaining **extras**, including authors' personal photo albums and book lists.

- Behind-the-scenes **scoop** on your favorite characters and series.

- **Sweepstakes** for the chance to win free books, romantic getaways, and other fun prizes.

- Writing **tips** from our authors and editors.

- **Blog** with our authors and find out why they love to write romance.

- **Exclusive content** that's not contained within the pages of our novels.

Join us at
www.avonbooks.com

An Imprint of HarperCollins*Publishers*
www.avonromance.com